VODOUN

Also by David Madsen

U.S.S.A.
Black Plume: The Suppressed Memoirs of Edgar Allan Poe

VODOUN

A Novel

DAVID MADSEN

WILLIAM MORROW AND COMPANY, INC.
New York

It is the policy of William Morrow and Company, Inc., and its imprints and affiliates, recognizing the importance of preserving what has been written, to print the books we publish on acid-free paper, and we exert our best efforts to that end.

Library of Congress Cataloging-in-Publication Data

Madsen, David.
    Vodoun : a novel / David Madsen.
        p.   cm.
    ISBN 0-688-10563-7
        1. Journalists—Washington (D.C.)—Fiction.   2. Voodooism—Haiti—Fiction.
3. Americans—Haiti—Fiction.   I. Title.
    PS3563.A344V63   1994   94-6615
    813'.54—dc20   CIP

Printed in the United States of America

First Edition

1 2 3 4 5 6 7 8 9 10

BOOK DESIGN BY SUSAN HOOD

For Christine and for my parents

ACKNOWLEDGMENTS

I would like to thank my wife, Christine, and my friend Julie Robitaille for reading this book in its various stages, and for their invaluable comments. Carine Fabius and Pascal Giacomini were always supportive and helped smooth my entrée into Haitian culture.

In Haiti, I am grateful to Mireille and Claude Fabius for their hospitality and their insights, and especially to Michael Tarr, a perceptive and witty tour guide into voodoo and the Haitian imagination.

Finally, thanks to my agent Norman Kurz, a great advocate and ally.

VODOUN

PROLOGUE
JULY 1986

THE SMOKING GROUND kept them warm through the long, moonless night. Twenty hopeful, reckless men, women, and children squatted at the edge of the charcoal pit, sipping *clairin*, singing Carnival songs, and dreaming of Miami. Their leader, known as Ti-Rasoir—"Little Razor"—because of his cutting wit and fondness for improvising weapons from a certain common household implement, thought of the charcoal pit as a symbol for disappearing Haiti. All over the country, peasants were cutting down trees, rolling them into craters like this, lighting them ablaze, then burying them to slow-cook the wood into charcoal. The jungles of his childhood, the jade-green lianas and glistening mahogany that had brought rain and cool air, had all been uprooted for cheap fuel. To Ti-Rasoir, it signified the death of life.

In Miami, he'd heard, there were still trees.

Ti-Rasoir walked to the edge of the coastal road that ran beside the charcoal pit. No headlights in either direction; no soldiers, no Macoutes. Perfect. The peaceful waters of the Windward Passage rolled onto the rocky shoreline in reassuring rhythms. Like most Haitians, Ti-Rasoir did not like to be out at night, but he had no choice. You did not flee your country illegally in the glare of the midday sun.

Baby Doc was gone at last. Ti-Rasoir had seen it himself, on television in the lottery shop—"Baskethead" Duvalier and his *putain mulatte* wife, Michelle, running from the presidential palace in a foreign car. Now a furious and vengeful political uprooting was underway: the *dechoukaj*. Long-suffering Haitians were determined to erase all vestiges of the Duvalier regime, which had ruled Haiti for twenty-nine years. Normally mild shop owners became seasoned blood hunters. Shy, inarticulate farmers learned to be cruel and unforgiving. Mistakes were made; innocent people died. Ti-Rasoir's uncle was disinterred, his body incinerated because someone had misread the name on the gravestone. It was impossible to be innocent; sooner or later, one side or the other would come for you.

Ti-Rasoir and his group of fishermen and market women from the small town of Anse-Rouge had never been political. Politics happened in Port-au-Prince—it was all just blah-blah-blah, and didn't touch them in any way that they could appreciate. So they decided to turn the dechoukaj to their advantage. Chaos weakened the state's defenses, the army was stretched thin, the Macoutes and their network of rural informers in hiding. Now was the time.

Wood creaked in the darkness of the sea, followed by a sharp whisper. A tiny black skiff angled toward the beach—decrepit, paint-peeling, probably leaky, but to Ti-Rasoir it was a glorious sight. Something snakelike coiled through the air and struck him in the face. A rope. *Tie it off you idiot, before this wonderful apparition drifts away again!* Ti-Rasoir turned to call his group, but they were already up, gathering their belongings.

"*Fè vit, fè vit!*" he snarled.

They hurried across the road as the skiff carved to a stop in the sand. Ti-Rasoir, the only one who could read, smiled at the name painted on the hull—*Pas de Problème*. But the captain looked like he could be a problem: sour, muscular, arrogant, twin machetes dangling from his belt, a Haitian version of the

Western gunslingers Ti-Rasoir had seen in Dominican *fotono-velas*. He refused to shake Ti-Rasoir's hand, and immediately demanded full payment from his passengers. Ti-Rasoir tried to negotiate for an installment deal, but the refugees threw him aside, pushing soiled gourdes into the captain's face with panicked, bony hands. Tempers rose, curses flew. Suddenly, all his plans were unraveling.

Then, distant dots of light appeared on the road, growing larger, leading the rumble of a misfiring engine. Everyone scrambled for cover; there could be no innocent excuse to be out on the road at this hour. Ti-Rasoir crouched next to the captain, watching from behind the ship's hull, as a large truck approached, then slowed down. It turned off the road, and its headlights painted the *Pas de Problème* in garish yellow. It skidded to a stop in the sand, and the driver turned off the engine. The lights went out.

Black truck, black ship, black ocean, black sky. And a prickly silence. Ti-Rasoir held his breath and waited. Who was in that truck? What did they want? Finally, the door swung open and the driver appeared. He jumped—no, he seemed to fly onto the hood. He was tall and slender, dressed in a white linen suit, a flower-patterned foulard bunched at his neck. He held a flashlight to his face, so the hidden refugees that he sensed were there could see he was flesh, not spirit. He had a mulatto's features and skin tone, a lush, precisely clipped mustache, and wavy, pomaded hair swept straight back from a high, smooth forehead.

A rich man, thought Ti-Rasoir. A *gwo neg,* for sure.

"Who's in charge of this boat?" the rich man shouted, in a voice that was used to having its questions answered. He spoke in the meticulous French of the Port-au-Prince elite, a language few peasants fully understood. The captain edged wordlessly forward.

Ti-Rasoir marched up to the rich man in a rage. "This boat is chartered, monsieur. Reserved!" The other refugees filtered out from their hiding places, sensing that their salvation was about to be bartered away.

"Well, how much have they paid you?" the rich man asked the captain.

"Fifteen hundred gourdes." He puffed out his chest. "Apiece."

The rich man made a quick head count. "Thirty thousand gourdes. I'll double it!" He pulled a gun out of his jacket pocket and waved it. The handle was rainbow-hued, like an abalone shell. "And another thousand for each of you passengers . . . provided you help me load my cargo in time to get underway by dawn."

A thousand gourdes—one hundred dollars, nearly a year's salary! The crowd broke off into knots, trading argumentative whispers. This was too good a deal to ignore. There would be other boats; they could build their own boat for that kind of money! The captain was anxious to make the deal, and he snaked among the refugees, excitedly pressing their refunds on them. Ti-Rasoir tried to rally his people to indignation, tried to show them how this rich man was buying away their freedom, and backing up the deal with a gun, just as the rich bought everything in Haiti.

Eventually, Ti-Rasoir became hoarse and disgusted. He sat down on a rock and decided to get better acquainted with the jug of clairin he'd been saving for the voyage to Miami. He watched the money change hands, and took one sip of the murderous, unfiltered rum for each dream that was sold.

After the financial transactions were completed, there was a moment of pure theater as the rich man threw open the rear doors of the truck, revealing his precious cargo to amazed gasps. He organized the peasants into a brigade, and they passed his belongings one by one, hand over hand on to the boat. It was as if an entire museum had been packaged for transport: there were antique, gilded chairs; oil paintings swaddled in blankets; delicate crystal and a silver tea service; a giant mahogany desk, inlaid with copper and tortoiseshell. Ti-Rasoir, his head buzz-sawing from the rum, watched the treasures pass through his neighbors' hands like water. Some, he knew, were worth more than he would earn in his lifetime. If he could just flake off a bit of gold leaf with his fingernail . . . Finally, the rich man himself carried a large clay urn wrapped in faded red velvet onto the boat, handling it with care and reverence. Ti-Rasoir recognized the urn as a *canari,* a mystical artifact he had often seen in the voodoo peristyles of his village. A canari could contain powerful magic, its contents used to heal, or to kill. Now Ti-Rasoir saw the rich man with different eyes—he was not just another vain, Europeanized city dweller.

Before his thoughts could wander farther, Ti-Rasoir realized everyone was shouting at him. He was squatting on the rock to which the boat was tied. He backed away, and watched as his shortsighted, greedy neighbors shouldered the rich man's skiff through the sand. The captain ruddered the *Pas de Problème* out beyond the lee of the rock, where he raised a patched sail to catch a pallid breeze. Ti-Rasoir finished his bottle of rum and watched freedom fade into the horizon.

———

THEY barely spoke the entire first day. The captain plugged leaks and watched for the American Coast Guard cutters that plied the Windward Passage between Cuba and Haiti. The rich man, secretive and distant but polite, sat on one of his gilded chairs, made notes in his diary, and brewed spiced tea, which he served from the sterling-silver teapot. He generously shared his provisions: sour oranges, mangoes, and breadfruit, dried conch marinated in lime juice, and hibiscus-flavored Barbancourt rum. The wind was brisk, the seas gentle, and even the sharks kept their distance. The captain had never traveled in such effortless elegance; it was as though his passenger's wealth had leapt ahead to bribe and placate the elements. The captain, being a true Haitian, knew his good fortune would not last.

An hour after sunup on the second day, a shape appeared in the northeast, mingling with the dark bumps of the Bahamas. The captain peered through his scarred binoculars and spotted a trading sloop slicing towad them. Concern flashed in his eyes.

"Pirates!" He took a quick inventory of the wealth collected on his deck and panicked. "They expect to find cigarettes, women, maybe a few gourdes at most. One look at this treasure trove . . ." He shuddered, leaving the threat unspoken. He began to take down the sail. The rich man jumped up, grabbed the captain's muscular wrist.

"What the hell are you doing? Turn into the wind!"

"We can't outrun them. Our only hope is to bluff our way out. I hope you can speak as well as you write. Now, let's get everything covered." The two worked feverishly, draping the sail over the museum pieces, hiding every last glint of gilt and burnished wood, as the pirate ship bore relentlessly down on them.

Within minutes, the trading sloop had cut them off at the bow and was circling to pull even with the port side. For the first time, the rich man glimpsed the so-called "pirates." Much too literate a description, he thought. It carried connotations of high adventure, and ship-to-ship sword fights, as in the Errol Flynn movies he'd picked up on the satellite dish. These men looked like boat people themselves, with their stained T-shirts and torn jeans, hand-rolled cigarettes, and rusted machetes.

They vaulted aboard, shouting a crude mix of back-country Creole and Dominican slang. Their leader, lanky and goateed, wore sunglasses and an "I Love New York" T-shirt with cutout arms. The captain immediately offered him a tribute of rum— the raw clairin, not the luxuriant Barbancourt—but the pirate slashed it out of his hand. He was already drunk. The pirates prodded at the canvas sailcloth with their machetes, while the captain protested that he was just a poor boatman blown off course, running a load of rice to Port-au-Prince. But the pirates could easily read the panic in his voice. The leader grinned and pulled a tiny machine gun from a sports bag. For the first time he seemed to notice the man in the white suit, standing there rigid and unperturbed, his eyes fixed on the bright red heart on the leader's T-shirt.

"You like my clothes, huh? I like yours, too. You want to trade?" asked the pirate.

No answer from the rich man. Just a constant stare, the whites of his eyes matching the brilliant glare of his suit.

"I bet you got a lot a good things to trade here." The leader cocked the machine gun and dragged the barrel across the blanketed treasures.

"Nothing to tempt a virile man such as yourself," spouted the captain, stooping to shameless flattery. "No guns, no money . . . just rice, cooking oil. Women's implements. A humiliating cargo, I admit. That's what we are, really, seafaring market women." The captain grabbed the leader by the T-shirt. Spit formed on his lips, his tongue stumbled over the words. "Listen, friend. An hour ago, thirty, forty degrees off port, we passed a magnificent yacht. Filled with *blancs,* dancing, throwing champagne bottles overboard. You could smell the money on the wind. You can still catch them, if you sail at once. Why waste your time with us? We're just poor Haitians, after all."

But the pirate wasn't listening. Something brilliant flashed on the deck, and he bent down to pick it up.

An engraved silver teaspoon.

At that moment, the captain knew he was going to die. *Tonnère,* he'd brought this on himself, this was his reward for his ill-considered greed! He should never have succumbed to this rich man's bribery; he should have done the charitable, the Haitian thing, and transported those pitiful refugees. He gazed up at the sky, at the ocean, back toward Haiti. Where *did* one look for God?

The pirate leader loosed a spray of machine-gun fire into the air, then took aim at the shrouded belongings.

Suddenly, the rich man's head jerked forward, as though he'd been shot in the back of the neck. His chin dropped to his chest. A tremor ran the length of his right arm, rippling the muscles beneath the white linen sleeve. He grabbed the mast with his right hand, and it shook, too, transferring its energy to the deck, which began to vibrate.

With a movement so quick it was nearly invisible, he snatched the captain's machete and wedged its handle into a split in the deck. The pirates begged their leader to shoot, but he'd gone numb, his finger frozen on the trigger. The rich man raised his arms to the sky, then bent over the tip of the machete. He

17

pushed off the deck, and spread-eagled in mid-air, his body balanced on the razor-sharp point of the blade.

The pirates backed away from the miraculous sight. Their leader managed a single, awestruck word: "Ogoun!" The captain collapsed to his knees in worshipful hysteria, splashing rum on the machete—the Barbancourt this time. When the rich man looked up at his audience, his face was transformed: the fine-boned, upper-class features had become the carved anger lines of Ogoun, the spirit of fire and thunder, of war and revolution.

Terrified, two of the pirates jumped back into their boat. Their leader could only stare at the machete where it pierced the pristine white suit without drawing a drop of blood. The captain flicked a match onto the deck. The puddle of rum caught fire, a trail of flame rushed up the machete's blade.

Once the pirate leader knew what he was dealing with, he responded instantly, like a scolded child. He fired his machine gun into the sea, emptying the magazine, little geysers of water erupting beneath each bullet. Reverently, he laid the defanged weapon into the flaming rum.

But he could see by the venom in Ogoun's eyes that he had not done enough. He glanced about the boat in panic. There was no longer any question of robbing these people. But what offering could he make, what act of devotion could he perform here in the middle of the ocean?

Then he had it, the idea he would later call genius, the gesture he just knew would buy him a lifetime of spiritual goodwill. He took out a pocketknife and hacked at his T-shirt with clumsy, jagged strokes. He tore off the cotton heart in the middle of "I Love New York" and held it up for Ogoun's approval. He threw the heart onto the deck next to the machine gun. The flames had died out, and the heart seemed unnaturally vivid in the low morning sun. How perfect that red was Ogoun's color.

Drained and ecstatic, the pirate leader stumbled back into his sloop. He would let this mysterious boat and its protected passenger sail to the ends of the earth. He gave orders to cast off immediately, to set a direct course back to Haiti. If other, more unsuspecting prey crossed their bow, fine. If not, then Ogoun's message was quite clear—the world would be better off with one less pirate.

The captain knew he'd witnessed a miracle. He tried to memorize every detail, already imagining himself the center of attention as he embellished the story in his favorite bar. He stared at Ogoun, precariously perched on the machete's point, and was seized with an irreverent urge to push the body, spin it like a human compass. Then, Ogoun's stiff limbs went limp, and he wilted to the deck. The captain knelt by his side, ready to offer tobacco and more rum, but Ogoun was already gone. The reserved, imperious rich man was back.

He took a moment to focus his vision, then bolted to his feet. He zigzagged across the deck, tearing the blankets back from his museum pieces, inspecting them with a critical eye. He unpacked every suitcase, ran his hands lovingly over every piece of porcelain, every stick of silver.

Reassured that all was as it should be, he turned a careless gaze on the captain and calmly asked, "Well, are we going to America or not?"

1

I JUST KILLED someone but I'm not a murderer. I used a stolen gun, but I'm not a thief.

The revolver rests on my thigh, feather-light. Shouldn't I wipe off my fingerprints? My victim's lying out there in the moonlight, faceup. Shouldn't I try to bury the body, cover up the evidence? Beeline to the airport and book the first flight out? The problem is, I don't feel anything. No panic, no remorse. I can see myself in the mirror; my eyes are glassy, but there's no life in there. The radio's up full blast, but I can't hear it. If I press the glowing coil of the cigarette lighter to my wrist, I barely feel a quiver of pain, even as the skin smokes and the hair burns. This isn't me, that's the only way to explain it: my personality, my morals, my willpower are all gone. The police are already suspicious of me. They'll never believe the truth, that someone else invaded my hands and pulled the trigger.

Just because I don't understand it doesn't mean the act was random or unmotivated. Quite the opposite. Tonight was the premeditated climax to a story that began . . . when? It's impossible to pinpoint the precise moment when I fell off the edge of my world and into another. But we journalists like things to have a beginning, middle, and end, so the police siren on that sticky August evening will be my lead.

I had been free for a year. An ex-reporter, hiding from Washington, D.C., my ex-beat. I'd collected thousands of bylines, won most of the major journalism prizes except the Pulitzer, done the Sunday-morning news shows and *Nightline,* been quoted in Congress and vilified by a half-dozen presidential press secretaries. But I had dumped it all, run away to the Virginia countryside, moved into a two-hundred-year-old Georgian house, which I was restoring brick by brick. A little progress each day, the goal always in sight. No pundits or spin doctors telling me that a screwdriver's really a hammer, that the ceiling's really the floor. If the house turned out great, I took all the credit; if it fell down around me there would be no one I could shift the blame on to. And that was about as far from Washington as you could get. It seemed impossible that anything worldly could pierce my cocoon.

At first, the siren was just another sound that belonged to the night, as unremarkable as the trilling of crickets. But it didn't wind down, and I realized that my neighbors' dogs weren't wailing along in their usual chorus.

I armed myself with a crowbar and went outside. The moon had gone down, and the lawn was a black, forbidding ocean. The untamed boxwoods looked angry as they clawed at the air; the driveway led out to the county road like a narrow corridor of escape. The air was stifling, the siren still echoing musically. But no cherry-red dome lights blazed in the woods, no ambulance or fire truck hurtled past my driveway. Beyond the tree-line I could see the dark bulk of the nearest house: no lights were on, no bathrobed neighbors clustered curiously on the lawn.

I began to worry: Jesus, am I the only one who can hear this siren? This is happening inside my head! I'm having the aural equivalent of a hallucination!

A wave of dizziness swept over me; the lawn seemed to tilt, like the listing deck of a sinking ship. The ground burned beneath my feet, and I felt a needling heat rush through my body. I'd had two of these attacks before, a sudden fever mingled with disorientation, but had attributed them to the varnishes and strippers I'd been inhaling for months. I splashed my face with water from the garden hose. The dizziness abated, but the siren kept up its chant.

I became convinced that the siren was meant for me, its Doppler shriek an urgent summons in a mechanical language that I should have known. It was a siren in the mythical, personified sense, alluring, almost feminine. It extended its arms and grabbed me.

I left the front door open and the hose running. I felt myself pulled into my car. I tore down the driveway in a storm of burning tires, pumping the gas into my 1965 T-Bird's giant engine, gasoline matching the furious flow of my adrenaline.

I drove north toward the city, guided by a force that held me prisoner. I was dewy with sweat; my blood was screaming. I gave myself a quick, panicked study in the mirror: my gray, deep-set eyes were dilated with fear, the thick, melancholy brows drooped with perspiration. My hair was a wind-torn tangle that seemed black and rotten as old seaweed. I looked like an escapee from a sickroom, a patient who has torn off his IV and is on his last, wobbling legs.

The sight of the Washington skyline triggered a tremor of nausea in me. When I fled D.C., exhaling with relief at my escape, laughing with a mixture of pity and contempt at those still trapped in its liar's air, I hadn't expected anything would have the power to call me back.

As I skirted through southeast Washington, I rolled down the window and heard the physical siren for the first time, its lonely wail blending perfectly with the scream in my imagination. Though I never actually sighted its source, I followed the siren down Pennsylvania Avenue, across the Sousa Bridge. South of the Anacostia River is Ward 8, a Washington, D.C., without tourists or monuments, a neighborhood of decayed public housing that will never be the pet project of any preservation committee. The siren died as I rolled down a street of pockmarked brownstones. The sidewalks were empty, no blood-happy gawkers marked the crime scene, yet I knew right where to go—the abandoned housing project that squatted bleakly at the end of the street. An empty project is today's haunted house: rats, trash and rusty nails, rumors of unspeakable basement rites. A place you hurry past, a place you don't want to be trapped in after dark.

So why did I feel an irrational need to explore it? Fight it off, wait until your reason returns, I told myself. I locked the car doors, cinched my seat belt. But the compulsion had all the magnetic power of the siren now, and it yanked me out of the car, down the sidewalk toward the housing project. I could feel my heels digging into the ground in protest, even as I was jerked forward.

I stepped cautiously over trampled chain-link into the dim courtyard. Ten stories of water-stained concrete blotted out the stars; the building seemed to list, a plywood-patched Tower of Pisa. The breeze that tickled the rest of the city didn't blow here—it was a meteorological dead zone. As I felt my way around the building, my footsteps seemed muffled, like steps on the moon.

Suddenly, a hand shot out of the darkness and vise-gripped my shoulder. Though built like a bulldozer, Detective Walter Paisley was furtive and light-footed. Once he recognized me, he froze in shock.

"Ray Falco! That you?"

"Afraid so."

"Where the hell'd you come from?" He looked over my shoulder. "Any more of you out there? Any TV? Jesus Christ, this is all I need."

"Just me and my notebook."

"You always did have a hell of a nose. And after a month of blue moons, you show up on *my* handle." Paisley gestured around him, and I realized the night bristled with cops, charcoal figures betrayed only by the white lines of their T-shirts. V-8 engines rumbled out on the street as more police arrived on the scene. I saw vague movements on the steps that led to the project's boarded-up lobby. "I mean, you've been out of the picture for what, a year?" he asked. "I heard you retired to the Bahamas to raise jellyfish . . . all kinds of weird rumors."

"Well . . . I've sort of been in semi-retirement."

"Retirement! You're what, forty, forty-one? Jeez, some guys chomp down on the silver spoon and just never have to spit it out."

"You look like you're doing OK yourself. Last time I saw you, you were in uniform. When did you start dressing like a Southern gentleman?"

"Since I made detective, Ray." Paisley was black, yet now he dressed like a caricature of a Richmond tobacco baron—baby-blue seersucker suit, white shirt, red suspenders, Orville Redenbacher bow tie. "These are my 'fuck you' clothes, as in 'I know I'm black and we're not supposed to dress like this, but fuck you, I'll wear what I want.' "

"The confidence that comes with success," I said.

"And when I make deputy chief of homicide, maybe I'll try slipping my bones into a little Armani." Paisley lowered his chin and whispered into his headset. "Shit!" he hissed. "I got a top-dog medical examiner coming in from Bethesda, and he blows a tire. Second deputy assistant to the underassistant to the president's alternate doctor. Figured I'd bring in the best."

"What are we looking at here, Walter?"

He glanced at the steps, where a uniformed officer was setting up a halogen flood. "You telling me you're back on the job?"

I didn't know how to answer. An hour ago I was a gentleman carpenter retired from the wars, and now I was back on the front lines. I just wanted to freeze the action for a minute, draw a little blood so I could see who was real and who was imaginary.

Walter shone his Maglite in my face. "Ray, you in there? You don't look so good. Retirement seems like it's been pretty tough on you."

The next words out of my mouth came as a complete surprise: "Look, Walter, I don't know how to explain this, maybe it's a compulsion, maybe I'm insane. Whatever, I need this story."

"You don't even know what it is yet."

The floodlights sizzled like lightning, then held, freezing the front steps in a frosty white glare. Something human-looking was draped there. Paisley and the other cops crowded around it in a hushed, businesslike group. He gestured down at the steps in a wide, sweeping arc. "I don't think we'll need a stretcher—a coat hanger should do the trick."

It lay twisted sideways at the waist, right arm thrown over left, the legs splayed in an unnatural arc that usually signified broken bones. It looked brittle, like it would flake away if you touched it. It was the color of burned parchment, slightly translucent, the dirty concrete dimly visible beneath it.

"You're the wordsmith," Paisley said. "You tell me what we got here."

I felt my throat constrict. Words seemed the most inappropriate tools in the world to describe this grisly discovery. "It would appear to be a human skin," I gasped. It was a black male, handless, headless, the ankles and wrists frayed and fringed with dried brown blood. I knew it had to be a patchwork (the headline MADMAN'S QUILT sprang to mind) and that closer inspection would show it to be crosshatched with Frankenstein-like sutures. But the first adjective to worm its way through my horror was "casual," as though a human being had slipped out of his skin as naturally as he would throw off a blanket on a hot night.

I switched into journalism mode, slipping into the role of the questioning but detached observer. I realized it had been lingering near the surface, twenty years of nosy ambition refusing to be discarded.

"How'd this come in, Walter? Lost and found, disturbing the peace?"

"Anonymous phone tip. Potential homicide victim in an area of known drug activity. The mayor's on an image kick—she'd like our murder stats to drop out of the number-one spot before the next election. So now, when a coke dealer gets blown away, it's political nitro."

"Her honor should be relieved," I said. "This doesn't look

like any drug murder I've ever seen. I mean, Christ, how would you even physically manage something like this . . . provided you had the stomach for it?"

We bent closer to the skin. It had a reddish tint to it, perhaps the aftermath of massive internal bleeding. It gave off an odor, a rough mix of chemistry and decay. I fought off an urge to touch it, and tried to chase away sicker thoughts: would they take it away on a stretcher, or would they fold it up like a shirt and pants, taking care to preserve the creases and the pleats?

"We're going in," Paisley said. "Still no sign of the goddamn coroner, so we'll have to wait to find out who . . . or what this is." Paisley gave a hand signal to his men. Leather creaked, gun safeties clicked off. As he slipped out of his headset, he shot me a stern, inquisitive stare. "Something's nagging at me, Ray: you want to tell me how you managed to end up here in the middle of the night?"

I hesitated; a plausible lie just didn't come fast enough.

"I mean, out of all the reporters, all the TV crews in Washington, you're the only one to show up."

"I was monitoring the scanner," I hedged.

"Dispatch sent this call out on a secure channel. No way you could've picked it up. Goddamn it, you know something about this case, Ray Falco!" He'd always called me by both names when he was annoyed, a Southern custom, true, but also a psychological nudge to make me feel like a child in need of a scolding.

"Reporter's luck, pure and simple. I was just driving by, heard the sirens—"

"Just driving by . . . in this neighborhood. For a world-class reporter you sure tell a bush-league lie."

You can lie effectively only when you have a believable truth to conceal, I thought. Walter tightened his hand around my upper arm. I noticed the bulletproof vest bulging beneath the seersucker. "If you had an inside track on this thing . . ." he squeezed my arm harder, right up to the edge of pain, ". . . you'd tell me, wouldn't you?" He let it sting for another moment, then snatched his hand away, message delivered.

One of the cops crowbarred the plywood back, and we squeezed into the lobby. It was like an underground parking garage, concrete-bound, trellised with pipes and heating ducts. A stairwell led to dingy heights; the battered elevator reminded me of a shark cage. The project had been condemned for months, but it still seemed ripe and wet with the fluids of closely packed humanity.

The cops divided into three teams of two, leaving me odd-man-out. "Your waiver's still good, isn't it?" Paisley asked.

I nodded. As a journalist who had often patrolled with the police, I had a waiver on file, absolving the department of any financial liability if I died while covering them. That night, facing a ten-story search-and-destroy mission, where every dark flight of stairs and derelict corridor reeked of ambush, I thought, If I am doomed to die on duty, it will be here.

"Good," he smirked. " 'Cause this looks kinda dicey, and I don't want you to cost the department so much as a nickel."

We started up the stairs, backs pressed against the wall. At the second-floor landing, hallways veered off to left and right, narrow, impossibly long—APTS. 100–112. Ten floors of this? We left one team behind, and continued up to the third floor. It seemed darker, the ceilings lower. Two more cops split off here. Paisley led us to the fourth floor, while a cop named Mike, a bit casual and undernourished, I thought, brought up the rear.

We stopped at the intersection of the two corridors and listened. Slowly, the building began to reveal itself: "Let the scene come to you"—Journalism 101. Somewhere in the distance, muffled by layers of concrete, water dripped. Cables gently clanged in the hollow of the elevator shaft. From deep in the basement, at the lowest threshold of hearing, came a steady mechanical rumble. Out of all the boilers, air conditioners, and water heaters that had once served this building, a single, un-identified machine refused to die. But there was no human sound.

We took the right corridor first, Mike's Maglite pointing the way. The door locks had been removed, destined for recycling in other public buildings. Our breath seemed enough to push open the first apartment door. We sent Mike in ahead: let the rookie take the bullet. The unit was functional and lonely, like a recently vacated prison cell. There was no furniture, the bathroom fixtures had been stripped, and in the kitchen, stubbed lengths of plumbing and gas pipe protruded from the walls like amputated limbs.

Every apartment was identical, and after two hours of hand signals, of tense entrances and exits, I began to feel dizzy: the place was immense, maybe even growing as we explored it. I was alone in the ninth-floor hallway when I heard the voices. I smelled gasoline, too. I should have alerted Walter and Mike, who were searching an apartment two doors down; that would have been the rational move. But I was greedy, I wanted the discovery, the danger, for myself.

I crept into the other corridor, which yawned like a long, black throat. The voices were deceptive, seeming to come from left, right, above, below, but they finally focused at the vanishing point, straight ahead. I was proud of my predatory creep, my gloom-adapted eyes operating on the dimmest of light. Then my foot hit something solid!

I recoiled instantly, every inch of my skin tickled with fear. I looked around wildly, expecting a hammer blow to the back of the neck, or a glassy-eyed corpse at my feet. It was just a length of fire hose, coiling along the corridor like a pale, dead anaconda. But my stumbling had extinguished the voices. No surprise attack now. I glanced over my shoulder. No sign of Mike or Walter. Ghosts or gangbangers, I'd have to rout them out myself.

I padded from door to door, stopping to listen for a telltale exhale or a rustle of clothing. A bright red sheet of paper peeked out beneath the last door on the left. I slid it out. It was a homemade, photocopied flier of some kind, a photograph of a scholarly-looking black man with glasses and luxurious gray hair, beneath a rub-on-letter headline in French—JEAN-MARS BAPTISTE: "POUR UN HAITI LIBÉRÉ."

I edged open the door. What I found was more unnerving than the shooting gallery I'd expected: it was an office, equipped with a typewriter, a filing cabinet, a copy machine. Neat, organized. It didn't make sense; how could anyone do business in such a wasting, dangerous environment?

Then I saw them, two figures crouched like light-stunned cats on the concrete balcony: a black teenage boy wearing a Bullets sweatshirt, lanky, all arms and legs, and a woman of about fifty, stocky, conservatively dressed, her face deeply lined and angled. Gold earrings nearly as big as Hula Hoops dangled from her ears; her wrists and fingers glittered with costume jewelry.

"Look, I'm not a cop, OK? You don't need to be afraid of me," I said.

"Who are you, then?" asked the woman.

"My name's Ray Falco. I'm a reporter."

"*Journaliste*? Hah!" Her "hah" was a verbal spit. "We not interesting for you. Not rich, not Colombians, sell no drugs. This just *politique,* you know," she said in a melodic, Caribbean accent.

I shut the door behind me and walked closer. "I'm very interested in politics."

"Not Haiti politics," she said. Her voice, even when annoyed, was sweet and thick like oversugared coffee. "No one interested in Haiti politics. Not even Haitians."

"Tell me about the skin downstairs. Is that what you're frightened of?" The woman and boy traded wary looks, which told me they knew all about the horror on the front stairs. "Or is it the police? Listen, they're all over the building. If there's something you don't want to tell them, don't want them to see . . ."

"What's in this for you, man?" asked the teenager. No accent there. Hundred percent American, hundred ten percent "fuck you."

Why was I befriending these people? I cast a cold reporter's eye on my motives, and saw nothing that made sense.

"Believe me, I'll think of something. In the meantime, I just want to help you." The offer just spilled out of me. Even the power to control my own thoughts seemed to be trickling away.

"Yeah? And what do the cops want?"

"They think they've got a murder downstairs, and they're searching the building for suspects."

The woman's face ratcheted from fear to panic to indignation. She stepped into the apartment, across the jagged glass teeth that jutted from the frame of the balcony door.

"That not a crime down there, you listening? No murder, no robbery. Nothing for the police, you understand?" She sipped from a paper cup, swirled the liquid around in her mouth, then spat onto the balcony. Gasoline. She refilled the cup from a mayonnaise jar and handed it to the teenager.

"Etienne, bois!"

He gave me a look that halfheartedly appealed for pity, but was ultimately resigned. "Hey, man, it's not so bad: it's unleaded."

"Petrol protect the blood. My blood, my nephew's blood. Not protect your blood, sir, you don't need it. They completely not interested in you. Unless you really interested in Haitian politics . . ." She gave me a smile that curled into a sneer, as though I had become the punch line to her private joke. "Then they get *very* interested in you."

"Who're *they*?" No answer. Etienne gingerly tasted the gasoline, the woman's face went blank. "Come on," I prodded. "An hour ago I was safe at home with an ice-cold drink. I didn't plan to be here, yet here I am. Call it destiny, fate, whatever, but I need to talk to you. And you need to trust me!"

The woman's eyes dimmed with indecision. If you emigrated from a world where the police were little more than the government's Department of Terrorism, where the press was a pipeline of lies, would you ever trust the same institutions in your adopted country? I was forcing her to trust, forcing her to choose.

"For fifteen years, I'm *marchande* in Port-au-Prince. I learn to read the most sharp-eyed customers. This is not an offer from you, this some kind of sharp deal, right?"

"If the cops find you here I guarantee they'll arrest you for murder. But I know them; I can delay them. In return, all I ask is that you save the truth for me."

Her market woman's eyes came alive, flickering like an abacus as she calculated the cost of the deal.

"So, if it's not a murder down there . . . what is it?"

One last pause, one last sigh, bazaar flattery designed to fool the customer into thinking he's gotten the best of the deal. *"Loup-garou,"* she hissed, her voice taut with fear. To my look of ignorance, Etienne reluctantly translated, "Werewolf."

It was such a horror-movie word that at first I had no reaction. I realized that disbelief or laughter would be wrong, that she was waiting for my indignation or solemn understanding.

I focused on Etienne. "You really believe that?"

"It's not like on TV, you can't kill 'em with a silver bullet or anything," Etienne said.

"But how do they . . ." I stumbled over my thoughts, not just tongue-tied but tongue-bound-and-gagged. "How do they separate the skin from the body like that?"

"They don't."

I looked confused. The woman gave me an irked smile: apparently the simplest concepts of werewolfdom were beyond me. "The skin, that *is* the loup-garou. They leave their skin behind them, *comme un serpent,* then travel through the night, always at night, to do their trouble, their mischief. To punish, to warn."

"To warn you?" I waved the political flyer. "Or to warn *him?* Is he your husband, this Jean-Mars Baptiste?"

She nodded.

"And whoever did this, they're out to frighten him . . . or worse?" Her silence was a yes. It was also a sign that I had pressed her as far as I could. Etienne quickly gathered the paperwork. I opened the door, verified that Paisley and his men weren't in sight, then pushed them to the fire exit.

"I don't get you, man, but thanks," Etienne said. "Not that I'm coppin' to anything illegal . . ."

"I'll need a way to get in touch with you. We're not finished."

The woman was still suspicious. Out in the corridor, footsteps drew closer.

"Come on, give it to him," Etienne said to his aunt. "I don't feel like waiting around to mix it up with no white cops."

She scrawled an address on a scrap of paper. "Helene Baptiste," she whispered, introducing herself as she said good-bye. As they descended into the vacuum of the stairwell, I figured miracles weren't beyond them, they'd manage to slip through the police cordon, as soundless and weightless as smoke.

I saw an ambulance roll into the driveway below. I pictured the skin lying on a stretcher as a team of doctors probed it with scalpels and electronics. "Diagnosis, Doctor?"

"Looks like we're dealing with another Haitian werewolf, wouldn't you agree, Doctor?"

"Given the absence of pulse, blood pressure, and neural activity, and considering the total lack of body material, I must concur. A classic case."

———

On the drive home, I tumbled into a dream. It enveloped me suddenly, like a mask of anesthesia held over my face. At first, it was similar to my previous attacks, a scalding fever that shot straight to my forehead. But then my vision blurred, sounds and colors stopped making sense. I gripped the wheel, trying to focus on the strobing white centerline. My feet got tangled; I mixed up the brake and the gas. I finally decided to coast, letting the car drift to the shoulder. I lost my fix on time and place. The pale glow of the instrument panel faded to darkness. There was a moment of dead, black limbo, then suddenly my vision was bursting, a mental slide show saturated with color. I was in the middle of an undulating sea of green, and above me was an azure sky, blackened on the horizon by bulging thunderheads. I felt a lazy, soothing breeze, and the sea defined itself as a million swaying strands of sugarcane. I tried to reach for a stalk of cane, vaguely aware of the sweet, sticky nourishment it held, but I couldn't move. It was comforting and unspoiled there, a nice place to park a daydream. But then the cane began to ripple violently as something large thrashed through the fields toward me. I just stood there, rooted dumbly like one is in dreams, and waited to be ambushed. I heard a scream, a wolfish howl directly in front of me. The green curtain parted, revealing my attacker. I didn't notice if the body was young or old, man or woman, or indeed if there even was a body. It was the face that compelled: fierce, metallic, eyes like black wells, a wicked leer . . . and no mouth!

The vision, the déjà vu, whatever it was, did not last longer than a few seconds. I hadn't even turned off the engine. I drove home at fifteen miles an hour. Focus on the familiar, I told myself. Look for the road signs you know, the curves in the road you've memorized.

I staggered through my open front door, double-locked it behind me. Whatever's wrong with me, it's *out there,* I told myself. If I could just hang on until morning, there would be sunlight and strong coffee; the lulling routine of life would save me.

Now it's impossible to imagine how naive I was. My journalistic toughness had deserted me—nothing would ever be routine again. I would not be saved and, within a week, I would be driven to murder.

2

Sleep couldn't erase the truth—the night's events had been unearthly but real, and I was being sucked into a news story against my will.

On paper, I was the wrong man for the job, a reformed reformer. I hated the press so violently because I had once believed in it so religiously. My life had been a straight line from childhood. I wrote, edited, published, and hawked my own newspaper at the age of eight. I uncovered the first scandal on my block (a neighbor's bomb shelter wasn't up to code) and gave it plenty of play in a special late edition. I fled California at eighteen to study journalism at New York University, left college and its cloistered, hands-off environment after three quarters, and embarked on a fifteen-year career/apprenticeship at assorted *Bees, Bugles, Clarions,* and *Bulletins* in small towns around America. I finally graduated to Washington, D.C., ground zero for political reporters. I worked Metro, blazed through beats at Congress, the State Department, and the Pentagon. No sleep, no doubts, no time for anything other than work. At night I would drive back and forth over the Potomac with the country's most revered landmarks—the Lincoln Memorial, the Jefferson Memorial, the Washington Monument—

as a dazzling backdrop, and think, This is where my entire career has been leading, this is why I became a reporter. The wonderful arrogance of knowing what others did not, the thrill of cutting into a secret that is dark and remote to everyday eyes. In a city where the stakes were high, where a journalist could even bring down a president.

I was everywhere at once; if I wasn't there, I had sources that were. If Sam Nunn shared a tête-à-tête with Larry King over crab cakes at Duke Zeibert's, I was at the next table. If there was a back to be stabbed at an embassy cocktail party, I brought the knife; if there was an ass to be kissed at a Kennedy Center gala, I puckered up. I lived in the bars and restaurants on Capitol Hill and Dupont Circle, where the political press backbite and gossip over imported beer and mineral water. I was one of them, I wore their khaki slacks and pressed white shirts, my tie loosened to suggest the perfect note of newsroom grind. So convinced of the power of the pen. Sadly, hilariously, I thought I mattered.

By the time I met Livia Holcomb in the congressional press gallery, I was just going through the motions of a journalism career. Livia was a financial reporter, a rising star at National Public Radio. She had started out dryly intoning the dollar's advances and declines on foreign markets, but had recently begun doing full-fledged economic reports. Her career ascent left her little time for a social life, but intellectually and biologically she knew she needed one, so we began a typical Type A romance, blocking out hours and occasional weekends on our Day Runners and Filofaxes. Somehow, despite our best efforts, genuine affection developed. Her clothes and jewelry began to trickle into my Adams-Morgan town house, at first purely as professional backup outfits to save her a trip home after she spent the night. A notebook computer followed, then a second phone line. One evening, Livia crossed the yuppie Rubicon and moved in her fax machine.

Poor Livia picked the wrong end of my life to share. Instead of bolstering my ambition, her professional enthusiasm for my work made me see myself more clearly. I was hollow; there

35

was no journalist's heart in there anymore . . . you could stick an arm right through me.

She would lie on her side of the bed, transmitting faxes from her night table and reading my old clips. She would express her admiration in varying degrees, and I would trash it.

"What about this one, Ray?"

"Story backfired on me. Got sued for libel."

"This one?"

"Bastard got out after four years on good behavior. Currently pursuing new, highly successful career as serial rapist."

"This here?"

"Congressman in question cleaned toilets and played racquetball for two years in federal custody; criminal lapses forgotten by constituents, reelected to a ninth term."

She would get mad, leap out of bed—her golden Midwest hair and long, freckled legs beaming health and heartland—run to the wall, and point out the awards.

"This plaque from the American Newspaper Editors . . ."

"Given to a species of writer endangered at the time, and now extinct."

She would scream, "You act like an alcoholic, and you don't even drink. You act like a washed-up hack, and you're at the top of your game."

"True, I'm disgusting. I just don't appreciate the tremendous power I wield. Why, if column inches were influence . . ."

It ended on what should have been the proudest night of my life. I had written a series detailing an alliance between renegade Drug Enforcement Agency advisors and Peruvian growers that would cut out the middlemen who soaked up the drug industry's profits; they would process, smuggle, and sell the coke in the United States themselves, even hire moonlighting cops as security. It was a story that brushed individuals and institutions with a nasty coat of guilt; it was syndicated across the country, quoted in Congress. It led to indictments up and down the drug ring's chain of command. It was the high point of my career, gave my reputation a scratch-proof gloss.

The day I was to receive the award for international reporting from the Society of Professional Journalists, I began to hear rumors: the indictments stepped on the Peruvian government's sensitive feelings of national sovereignty, and it was going to back out of an economic treaty that had taken years to negotiate (something about tuna-fishing rights, believe it or not) unless the case was dropped. I stayed on the phone all day, worked the car phone on the way to the awards dinner at the Willard. By the time I walked to the podium, the case was dead: the high-ranking Peruvians were on their way to the airport under government escort, and the DEA officials were cleared. But a single indictment held: a rookie cop linked to the ring was found with a quarter-gram of cocaine in his duty locker. I had gone after the men at the top, and had ruined the career of a tiny player at the bottom.

I never drank much as a reporter, but that night I bought a bottle of Stolichnaya pepper vodka on my way home and had finished most of it by the time Livia and I climbed the stairs.

"Thank you, thank you!" I shouted. "Hold your applause, please. Really, you're too kind. You don't know what this means to me, getting recognition from one's peers . . ."

"Go to bed, Ray," Livia said.

"You coming?"

"It's what a girl dreams about: waking up in a puddle of vodka puke."

I wandered into the bedroom, Stoli in one hand, chrome-and-glass trophy in the other.

"You see now, don't you, what a shit career it is?"

"Speaking for yourself, of course."

"No, speaking about journalism, period. As an endeavor to devote one's life, one's soul to. No matter what we write, nothing ever changes. Got that? Nobody benefits . . . kill that, you know who benefits? All the goddamn C-SPANers . . . those asshole pols who build their reputations investigating the conspiracies we stir up, all those Water/Contra/who-gives-a-fuck-gates . . . it's shit."

"Thanks, Ray. My career is shit, I am my career, therefore I'm shit by association."

"Welcome to the club," I snapped. "Didn't know they gave

awards for it, did you?" I hurled the trophy at the window. It pierced the glass like an artillery shell. With delight, I watched the trophy spiral to the sidewalk and shatter; what kid doesn't love to drop stuff off tall buildings? But Livia nearly dove after it; she winced, and shut her eyes as it broke apart, and shivered in the cold night air seeping through the broken window. After a while she said, "I didn't even get to hold it."

Sometimes I still wake up to her voice. Disoriented, I reach for her on the bed, then realize it's just the clock radio. She's on in the morning now; it's where she belongs, it's her time of day. I'm not particularly nostalgic, and I could easily wake up to another channel. But I don't.

———

HERE, in the darkness, with blood on my hands and the gift of hindsight, I know that I was targeted. My house in the Virginia countryside was no refuge; the Baptiste story could pass through walls, it would have found me anywhere. It began like all the great ones, with a hook so sharp and shiny it glowed in the dark. My protests and struggles were self-deceiving—I see now that it was a story I genuinely, desperately wanted! It led me into another world, where the rules of love and war are not only unfair, they're nonexistent. Where time and history and character are frustratingly fluid.

The world has a name. I found it on the first page of the first book I opened when I began to research Jean-Mars Baptiste and Haiti, the country he had fled. Possessor of a gallant, colorful, almost Shakespearean past, Haiti had been plundered by a fool's parade of dictators so monstrously that new statistical devices had to be developed to measure its misery: three-fourths of Haitians lived below the poverty line; 1 percent of the population earned 48 percent of the income; 90 percent illiteracy; 60 percent unemployment; average annual income, $120; average life expectancy, fifty. And coursing through its history, both a salve for the country's wounds and a knife in its throat, providing a reason to live and just as often a better one to die, was the religion, in its French-Creole spelling . . . *vodoun.*

3

THE NEIGHBORHOOD WAS a map of the Third World: Addis Ababa Cleaners, Deli Yerevan, Botanica Cubana, Café Port-au-Prince. Amid the Spanish, Armenian, and Thai I saw one or two signs in Creole, with its spiky juxtapositions of *K*'s and *Y*'s. The Baptistes lived in a clapboard row house, and their anti-crime precautions were spectacular: double-barred windows, iron-mesh security door, triple dead bolts. Razor ribbon ran along the eaves like a deadly stretch of Christmas lights.

My knocks produced no response. The curtains were drawn, candle stubs lined the windowsills. Passersby were no help— they either didn't know the Baptistes or didn't care to acknowledge that they did to a stranger. I cut through a dead yard to the alley. Wooden balconies hung listlessly from the row houses, dressed up by an occasional flower box or herb garden. But the Baptistes' back door and windows were frighteningly secure. Jean–Mars Baptiste had brought the Haitian politician's natural paranoia with him to America.

I had assembled a rough picture of Baptiste. He was a candidate without an election. Educated at the University of Port-au-Prince and the London School of Economics, Baptiste was an economist turned perpetual presidential hopeful. He was a self-designated "rational centrist," a "national healer" who'd run in each of the bloody pseudo-elections held soon after the overthrow of Baby Doc. But Haiti hadn't wanted healing, or rationality—his neutrality had aroused the murderous attentions of both the right and the left, and he had fled the country four years earlier. Now he traveled the Haitian exile circuit—Miami, New York, Montreal—kindling outrage against the Port-au-Prince regime and soliciting donations for his political "comeback." His home base was Washington, where he could consult regularly with the American government officials he claimed supported his candidacy in the election that was never to be.

I prowled the streets, hoping for a glimpse of Helene Baptiste or her nephew in one of the neighborhood's tiny businesses, the video stores, doughnut shops, and fast-food franchises that are the new immigrants' toeholds. I asked about her in the Creole market, a dark, fragrant stall hung with gnarled roots and gourds, and was met with smiling shrugs.

As darkness fell and people hurried home from work, radios were turned up a notch and placed in open windows, crowds congregated on front stoops, drinking beer and gossiping. But the Baptistes never returned. I waited across the street in my car, watching; their house seemed to watch back.

A light rain on my hood woke me around eleven-thirty. I rolled down the window. The sidewalks were empty, and the streetlight in the middle of the block had burned out, turning the Baptiste house into a maze of shadows. I peered through the rain, hoping for a patch of light behind the curtains, but there was nothing.

Then I spotted a slight change in the texture of the shadows. I squinted. There it was again . . . movement. There was someone on the front steps!

I waited to see if it was one of the Baptistes. At this hour who else could it be? A burglar, desperate enough to attempt a front-door entrance? I could distinguish the outline of a figure now, cloaked in a billowing raincoat, moving slowly, vaguely.

I immediately pictured the night before, and another set of front steps, another figure bent over its precise, grotesque work. I could imagine the twinkling scalpel, the thin jets of blood.

I squeezed open the car door. The figure seemed unconcerned. It lingered a second longer, then whirled around and seemed to float down the steps. I started across the street, calling out in high school French: "Excuse me . . . *excuse moi, je suis un ami de Helene Baptiste.*" I ran, but the heels ran too, heels that could have belonged to a man or a woman, carrying the figure away. The raincoat was black and shiny, like brilliantined hair. If I could just get close enough, I could see my reflection. I pursued the raincoat to the corner, where it vanished, slipping into the kettledrum purr of an expensive, expertly tuned car.

I returned to the Baptistes' doorstep. The locks had not been tampered with. I looked under the mat, ran my hand along the ledge of the crime door. I felt that familiar, childish exhilaration, the thrill I used to get when investigative reporting would become part burglary, part detective work. I spotted a mail slot in the bricks, camouflaged with rust. I reached in, fearing a dog bite, a boot heel, or worse, and found a square of paper taped to the inside of the wall. It was a business card: "Galerie Creole—Haitian and Caribbean Fine Art." A wealthy visitor descends furtively on the poor, terrified house, literally under cover of darkness . . . and leaves a business card?

———

I phoned the Galerie Creole the next day. The next afternoon to be precise—not only was it an art gallery, it was a Georgetown art gallery, which qualified it for double-snobbery privileges, including the absolute shortest of opening hours. The woman who answered the phone sounded bored and superior until I mentioned Jean-Mars Baptiste. There was a meaningful silence, followed by urgent whispers.

"Who's calling, please?"

"I'm a friend of Mr. Baptiste's. I'm trying to get in touch with him and I was led to believe that he was connected to your gallery."

Another pause, more whispered promptings.

"Who told you that?"

"What is this? Is your receiver wired up to a lie detector or something?"

"Sir, there's no need to get hostile."

"Look, I'm sorry; it's just that Helene and Etienne assured me I could find him through you, and now it appears they were wrong."

I heard a startled inhale. A hand was pressed over the receiver. When the voice returned, it was soft and congenial. "Were you aware that we're holding an art sale tonight to benefit various Haitian charities? Drop by . . . you might find it interesting."

Before I could reply, she hung up. I had been screened, and had dropped the proper names. I was curious now about the Galerie Creole; it promised more than the typical Third World fund-raiser, swarming with anthropological do-gooders nibbling carrot cake and banana bread.

The last, pale threads of a daylight-savings sunset were fading as I parked semi-legally on M Street. I wore my retirement version of formal: jeans, button-down white shirt (a holdover from my newsroom days, when white shirts were dress code), and jacket. Washington is a conservative city where suits rule. But my power suits were out of service now; I had painted in them, taking a sloppy delight in their symbolic destruction.

The Galerie Creole was wedged between a Benetton and a price-tag-free antiques store that specialized in farm equipment of Colonial Virginia. (If you have to ask how much that ox-harness costs, you can't afford it.) The gallery filled all three floors of a bay-windowed Federal-style building; it was seductively lit, and the musical mix of Caribbean languages and laughter gently vibrated the windows.

The phone voice met me at the door. She was in her mid-fifties, cold and shiny—a style of Washington woman, usually married to a mid-level government figure, who finds solace working for museums and historical societies. She plucked the twenty-dollar donation out of my wallet with pearl-colored fingernails.

"Will you be requiring a receipt? Your donation is tax-deductible."

"What isn't in this town?" I lowered my voice, to abide by the gallery's suspicious protocol. "Is he here yet?"

She smiled blandly and said, "I'm afraid I don't know who you mean."

I had been away from the muted etiquette of cocktail parties for so long, I felt like a backwoods hick with a plug of tobacco bulging in his cheek let loose in the big city. There's a routine here, I reminded myself. Settle the nerves with a drink and the stomach with an hors d'oeuvre and look for someone you know.

This was a shimmering, tightly creased group. The men wore cream-colored slacks and black jackets; or the perfect reverse, they were plumed with scarlet pocket handkerchiefs and yellow foulards. The women wore frothy red salsa dresses and taut black miniskirts. Waiters circulated with rum and mineral water; there wasn't a piece of carrot cake in sight.

The interior had been opened up into a three-story atrium. The second and third floors were crowded, people bunched against the balconies in loud, flamboyant groups. I hunted for Helene and Etienne, and listened, picking through the Creole and Caribbean-accented English. The name "Baptiste" was mentioned several times, usually quietly and with respect, and I eventually pieced together the truth behind the evening's vague mystique. Jean-Mars Baptiste, political firebrand and exile extraordinaire, was an elusive figure whose speeches were never publicly scheduled. He would decide on a time and a place, then issue rumors to the grapevine. He might show up, or he might not; it seemed he often deliberately canceled appearances just to keep his followers, and presumably his enemies, on their toes.

I first saw her on the third floor, her head thrown back in laughter as she pressed a business card on a flirtatious admirer. I picked her out, at first, because she was also underdressed, but underdressed to kill: tight black jeans and a copper-colored sleeveless V-neck blouse. Her hair was a wild, black spray, gathered into two ponytails, one above the other. She had a beauty from another era: her face was fuller, plusher than the collapsed-cheekbone look that dominates today, and her eyebrows were charcoal-colored, Marlene Dietrichesque sketches. Somehow people looked different fifty years ago—their expressions were more open and easier to read—and I've often wondered if our constant, obsessional photographing and videotaping haven't altered the geography of the human face, made it angular and suspicious. Her skin—I'm desperate to avoid the cliché of café au lait here, but determined to keep it tropical—was the caramel color of a Cuba Libre after the sun has melted the ice.

As she scanned the party, I convinced myself that her eyes lingered on me for an interested moment. I'm no love predator: duty has taken me to a thousand cocktail parties in Washington, D.C., and I never used them as a dating springboard. It would have felt too much like an office romance. But that night my professional defenses wilted.

I made it up to the second floor. Armed with a glass of rum, I watched her descend the stairs, simultaneously conversing with two men behind her and a prosperous-looking older couple in front of her. She handed them each a business card, and there were cordial handshakes all around. Left alone, she turned furtive. She glanced around the room to make certain she was unobserved, then extracted a fresh stack of business cards from her purse and transferred them to her blouse pocket. She entered a few quick sentences on an electronic agenda, jotted something in a notepad, then realigned herself into party mode.

When our eyes met she realized I'd witnessed her performance.

"You give new meaning to the phrase 'working the room,' " I said.

She gave me an embarrassed smile. "I guess we Haitians are just born hustlers."

"Hey, it's nothing to be ashamed of. I'm actually here to work it myself." I pushed over to her and we shook hands.

"I'm Raymond Falco. Hi."

"Hi. Lucy. Lucy Marcelin."

"Is that all?"

"Is what all?"

"I'm waiting for your sales pitch."

She began to sway slightly to the rhythm of the music pulsing from the first-floor speakers, music I could barely hear. "I'll spare you; I think I've earned a little break."

"I'm surprised that you're Haitian. I don't hear an accent."

"There are schools that help you lose it, you know."

"That sounds ambitious. Are you a painter, too?"

"God, no, I'm a lawyer."

"And proud of it," I cracked.

"Why shouldn't I be?" She raised her chin, her penetrating brown eyes an advertisement for her professional competence.

"I'm sorry. It's been so long, especially in this city, since anyone's introduced themselves as a lawyer and not apologized for it or undercut it with a self-deprecating remark . . ."

"I specialize in immigration and business law. Helping Haitians navigate through the INS sharks, getting them small-business loans, government assistance grants . . . And what is it that you do, Raymond?"

"Oh, boy." My eyes dropped to my feet, and I began to count the scales on my snakeskin boots. There was no point in fudging it. If these people were secretive, they would be just as secretive with a journalist as with anyone. On the other hand, if they were inclined to talk, a journalist could offer them a public forum.

"I'm a reporter," I said.

"Not enough of those in town."

"Not enough good ones."

"And you're good?"

"Read me and find out."

I think she liked the note of arrogance; she was not going to waste her time on a man who wouldn't rise to defend his profession.

"Come on," she said. "Help me find something to buy." We toured the paintings: they were primitive, naive, abstract, and religious, both polished and raw, but all blazed flagrantly with color, as though the artists had dipped their brushes in a palette of melted tropical fruit.

"So, what are you reporting on tonight?"

"Does the expression 'loup-garou' mean anything to you?"

I detected a trace of alarm in her eyes, but she immediately masked it with a delighted laugh. "I haven't heard that since I was a child. I thought they were everywhere back then."

"You must've had a more exciting childhood than I did."

"I'm sure you had your own monster in the closet or hobgoblin under the bed. That's what a loup-garou was for me. I had an aunt who often visited. Hysterical, fussy like unmarried aunts are. She told me how a loup-garou could shed its skin and fly through the night, its path marked by a luminous trail in the sky. She always tucked me into bed with a warning: if I didn't behave like a good little girl, a loup-garou would slither under my door while I slept and suck out my blood."

"Wow. Grimms' fairy tales, Caribbean style."

"My first night away from home, staying with a girlfriend, I couldn't sleep. I stuffed my pillow case into the crack beneath the door and kept a terrified, all-night vigil. Then, right before dawn, I saw it, a bright trail in the sky. God, did I go nuts. I ran through the house screaming, knocking over vases, lamps. Finally, as I was heading toward a shelf of family heirlooms, my friend's mother was able to grab me and tell me what it really was." She snagged a fresh glass of rum from a waiter and downed it in a single gulp. "Eastern Airlines, heading for Miami. It was the first time I'd ever seen a plane."

"What would it mean if a loup-garou were to turn up on your front door today? Here in D.C.?"

"It'd mean I had too much rum."

"That's all?"

"I don't plug the cracks underneath the door anymore. Those are old fears; they belong to another place, another time."

We had stopped in front of a painting of tall, limber figures dancing around a crucifix. The picture was adorned with intricate symbols that reminded me of iron latticework on a New Orleans balcony. As I stared at the picture, the figures seemed to come alive, animated by the *soca* music that had been cranked up to compete with the rising conversation. I loosened my collar and rolled up my sleeves. This was sensual overload—the music was too loud, the paint was too bright, the crowd was pressing in on me. I blinked furiously. Sweat clouded my eyes, wet and stinging.

"Ray, you OK?" Lucy clasped my shoulder, but her touch felt remote, as though the surface of my skin were ten feet away from my body. These were the same ripped-from-reality symptoms I'd felt in the car; it was another attack! Horrific images burst onto my vision, but I could make out only bits and pieces: a red-hot branding iron burning into a human shoulder . . . a sugarcane field crackling in a wall of fire . . . black hands brandishing bloody machetes, white hands reaching for knives and pistols . . . bodies tumbling into a boiling blue sea . . .

"Here, take this." Lucy handed me a cup of mineral water. I drank it, then greedily downed three more cups, the cool liquid easing me back to reality. This attack had been shorter but more visceral than the first; I felt like I'd been kicked in the stomach.

"I'm fine now," I gasped. Lucy's curious stare demanded an explanation. How could I communicate my fear to a stranger, how could I possibly do justice to the mysterious embroidery of my symptoms? Keep it simple. I held a cup of ice against my neck. "It was probably just the heat."

"The air-conditioning's going full blast. You ought to get to a doctor. I've never seen anyone look so sick so fast. It was pretty frightening, actually."

"I guess it must be the art," I only half-joked, nodding at the painting. "Guy really knows how to communicate with a brush; I mean, talk about having a gut reaction . . ."

"*Vèvès*. Symbols of the *loa,* the spirits of vodoun. They *do* tend to affect people in dramatic ways." The voice was as airy and as insinuating as the man to whom it belonged. He had somehow materialized next to us without jostling a shoulder in that tightly packed crowd. "Even if they never touch you, they never let you go." He was tall, as sleek as a jade carving.

He was a light-skinned mulatto, more au lait than café, with delicate features. His thick, wavy hair was moussed and gleaming, his mustache was meticulous. He looked cool and imperious in a white linen suit over a cornflower-blue shirt. He nodded at the painting: "Stivinson Magloire—I think of him as the Haitian Picasso. At four thousand dollars, somewhat underpriced, I think." The Caribbean lilt had been totally planed away from his accent, which was French, probably Parisian, very likely traceable to a specific arrondissement.

He held out both hands in a priestly gesture. Lucy and I each took one. His skin was smooth and young, his nails professionally manicured, and his grip steely. "Faustin Gabriel. Welcome to my little gallery."

"The loas let go of me a long time ago, Mr. Gabriel. The day I left Haiti, to be exact." Lucy introduced herself, groping for a business card.

"And now, just like that, you are one hundred percent agnostic, one hundred percent American."

"As red-white-and-blue as my green card allows."

"And yet you are here tonight," Gabriel pointed out.

"No contradiction. I'm a Haitian-American lawyer, I go where the Haitian-American business is."

Gabriel wiggled a patronizing finger in Lucy's face. "Not completely assimilated, I see, thank God. Otherwise you would have referred to yourself as an *African*-American."

Gabriel turned to me. "No introductions required from you, Mr. Falco. I've seen you on the Sunday news shows. Mr. Falco is a very influential journalist," he said to Lucy. "Now that we speak of it, Mr. Falco, I haven't seen your name in a good while. On sabbatical, I presume. Or will you be favoring us with a book in the near future?" He gestured around the gallery. "On Haitian painting, perhaps?"

Still shaky, I struggled to get back into conversational gear. "I'm more of a social critic than an art critic, Mr. Gabriel."

"Yes. Sadly, society offers much to criticize. I imagine you are kept very busy."

He smiled arrogantly and led us to a more private corner.

Lucy looked at me devilishly. "Influential, huh? How much did you pay him?"

"I've had my successes."

Amazing: one caustic quip from a beautiful woman, and I rushed to defend the career I despised.

Gabriel took a bottle of rum from a mini-refrigerator and poured the three of us a glass. "My private stock: Haitian Barbancourt Five Star. Pure, without the diluting spices so beloved by the cruise-ship tourists . . . once upon a time, when Haiti had tourists. So much that is wonderful is subject to dilution these days, don't you find?"

"I blame it on two little letters: TV."

"But the press has also played a role in the cheapening of our world, Mr. Falco. Maybe you intend to write about vodoun—you'll permit me to be phonetically accurate—but I must caution you that loup-garous, zombiism, these are only the most colorful, extreme aspects of the religion. Vodoun was not created in Hollywood; it was born in history, when the slaves of Dahomey, Yoruba, Mandingo, Ashanti were brought to the New World; in order to keep their religions alive, they secretly grafted their African gods onto the pantheon of Catholic saints the French slave owners forced them to accept. It is not a cult; it is a complex worldview which articulates the relationships between man, nature, and God. In my country, it is often the final arbiter of social and spiritual life. As we say, Haiti is eighty percent Catholic and one hundred percent vodoun."

"I'm a professional, Mr. Gabriel. I don't cheapen and I don't sensationalize."

"Did I imply that?" Gabriel asked.

"I came here hoping for an interview with Jean-Mars Baptiste. He's my story, and if I were one of his followers I'd be grateful for the publicity. If that leads me to vodoun I'll do my best to respect your sensitivities."

"Sensitive reporting for sensitive times. That's all we ask."

Lucy tapped her watch. "Speaking of Mr. Baptiste, shouldn't he be here by now?"

"I was just about to make a disappointing announcement

concerning our esteemed guest speaker. Sadly, recent . . . developments have compelled Mr. Baptiste to conclude that an appearance here tonight could severely compromise his personal safety. Will you excuse me?"

"Wait a minute . . . you just talked to him? Where was he?"

"My answering machine talked to him. And I have not the vaguest idea." Gabriel knifed toward the balcony, the crowd peeling away in front of him.

"Lucy, how many Haitians can there be in Washington? It's a small, confined world, right? You must have heard something. What's going on? Tonight's part of a bigger picture, isn't it?"

"I don't know."

"No guesses? I'm beginning to wonder if this Baptiste guy even exists."

"Maybe nothing's going on. Haitians love theatrics, they love to be the center of attention. This dramatic, last-minute no-show will probably stir up more interest in Baptiste's cause than a hundred speeches."

"Come on, Baptiste is so frightened, he runs his office out of an abandoned housing project, his own home is as impregnable as a bank vault, and no politician, I don't care whether he's Haitian, American, or Martian, turns down an invitation to make a speech unless he absolutely has to."

"I'm just a businesswoman, Raymond. The devious schemes of these exiles, their endless plotting, their armchair coups, it's all kind of pathetic. I really can't help you."

"Just a little background. I'll buy you dinner. I don't have an expense account, so that's an honest invitation."

"You want me for a source?" she asked, sounding insulted. "Informed, anonymous, whatever you call it?"

"Hang on, I didn't mean to push any buttons. We're talking about your own culture here."

"Of course it's my culture! Well, so what? Is that what I am, my culture? Because I'm from a foreign country I'm here to be exotic and mysterious for you? I'll bet you see us all in costume." She ran her long, delicate hands from her neck down to her thighs. "Look at me: jeans—Levi's; blouse—Blooming-dale's. I'm a lawyer, not a voodoo priestess."

I'm pretty good at cocktail party thrust-and-parry. The ability to fling sarcasm at receptions and fund-raisers is a precious professional weapon. But I decided not to press Lucy; from her perspective I'd crossed a line, so I figured I should just wait until that line moved a little closer to me.

We said it both at once: "Well, nice meeting you, there's some other people here I really should say hello to," and moved apart, the party-goer's retreat. Of course I had no one else to say hello to, but I watched jealously as she kept her end of the bargain, laughing, flirting, handing out business cards with a sensual flourish of her smooth, brown arms. She was nearly six feet tall, and when she stood on her toes to pass a card to someone on the second floor, she was a panther on its hind legs, stretching for prey hidden in the treetops.

I was still watching her when the lights dimmed and Faustin Gabriel appeared operatically at the balcony. He seemed to love crowds, loved pleasing them, and loved disappointing them too. "Ladies and gentlemen, I share your desolation at tonight's unlucky events, and join you in anticipating a day when Monsieur Baptiste can speak to us freely and without fear. However, we must not allow disappointment to dampen our charitable impulses, and so may I present to you a brief film detailing the recent activities of a worthy organization with which I'm sure you're all acquainted, Zanfan d'Ayiti. I know this reminder of the grave conditions afflicting so many young Haitians will stir your hearts . . . and your generosity." There were televisions bolted to the walls on every floor, and the same image bounced onto the screens simultaneously: a smoky Port-au-Prince slum, shot in the fading colors of outdated film. The picture then cut to a striking, statuesque black woman with ebony skin and African features, standing against a wall of children's photographs. As she spoke to the camera in a husky, voluptuous voice, I felt a guilty, sexual thrill; I found her magnetic and enthralling, a black Garbo who seemed to be speaking directly to me.

"I'm about to take you to the poorest corner of the poorest slum in Port-au-Prince, capital of the poorest country in the western hemisphere. By the time you see this film, one third of these children will be dead."

Television, with its violent immediacy and technical gloss, has cheapened misery. We're so close, and everything's so well lit, we're right there as that fly crawls into the starving African baby's eye. Agony has production value now, dying people look prompted and stagestruck.

But the promo for Zanfan d'Ayiti, with its shaky camera work, made the familiar images of poverty seem freshly appalling; the sheer amateurishness was honest. Dozens of children stared into the camera in desperation; women walked for miles in search of potable water, rusting buckets balanced on their heads; men slept standing up to relieve the crowding in their cardboard shacks. The camera captured telling fragments of a Port-au-Prince childhood: a young boy's hair, orange from malnutrition; babies writhing with gastroenteritis; a school soccer game, the goalie up to his knees in sewage, trolling through the muck for a vanished ball; a dog licking the open wounds of a crippled teenager. Every few minutes, a heavy shadow passed across the screen, darkening the slums: departing airliners, flying so low it was like a deliberate taunt, so close you could hit them with a rock.

"For a modest donation of twenty-five dollars a month, you can help give a Haitian child a fighting chance. You'll receive regular letters, and a personal videotaped greeting . . ."

I glanced around the room to gauge the audience response. Some were contemptuous, unmoved; others dabbed at their tears and fanned through their wallets and purses. I spotted Faustin Gabriel seated at a Louis XIV desk in the rear of the gallery, well out of TV viewing range. His posture was arched and catlike, and he swept his right hand across the desk in a series of fluid gestures. He held up the sketch pad he'd been working on, studied it critically, then focused a hard stare in my direction.

I realized he was drawing me.

4

THE NEXT DAY, I followed the scent of Walter Paisley's tobacco through the maze of the police evidence room. I wonder now: did I give anything away? Good cops can read criminal intent, they can hear the ticking before the bomb goes off. Did Walter see the premeditated murder in my eyes? Did he know I was stalking my victim even before I knew it myself?

Paisley sat at a folding metal table working a laptop computer, the pipe smoke clouding above his head in the glow of a fluorescent light; he reminded me of a small-time mafioso, counting the night's take from an illegal craps game. He was surrounded by dusty cardboard filing boxes, each housing the violent and mundane artifacts of a crime. I recognized a few names, people whose stories I'd told in terse Metro style: who, when, where, why, and what with.

I hoped that Paisley's newfound ambition would make him eager for press coverage, and that he would share his progress on the loup-garou case with me. But he had other ideas.

"Look, I'm not gonna play favorites with you, Ray. When I call a press conference, you'll be informed."

"Just one quote, Walter. Not for attribution."

"I'm sorry, I haven't heard anything."

"We're talking about a human skin, here! The department must be buzzing with rumor and speculation. If I know your lab guys, they're stabbing each other in the back to get at this thing. Plus, I thought we had a gentlemen's agreement. I *was* the first reporter on the scene."

"Which you still haven't explained."

"Walter, it's me! Not some ax-grinder from the ACLU newsletter."

Paisley kept his back to me, focusing on his computer. I rose onto my toes, trying to absorb the information on the screen without any giveaway eye movements. It was a list of evidence impounded from the Baptistes' housing-project office: a Smith-Corona manual typewriter, two boxes FaberCastell felt pens, five reams xerographic paper, a copier, four rolls of exposed, thirty-six-shot print film. Amid the jumble of paperwork on the table I spotted four buff-colored envelopes from the crime lab. They'd already developed the pictures: four rolls of photos, 144 potential leads!

"Come on, this could be a real break for me," I said, trying to cover my involuntary shiver of excitement. "You sent cell samples to the FBI lab for DNA testing yet?"

Cold silence. Walter hit the screen blanker, cutting short my spying.

"At least give me the name of your bureau contact. For the sake of . . . I won't call it a friendship . . . for the sake of the good, solid working relationship we used to have."

"That's where you're making a mistake, Ray. Trying to stir up a nostalgia you know damn well that neither of us feels." Then, in a hostile tone he added: "You didn't just wander into that housing project. I think you knew about the crime already. Or you were going there to meet someone, a source, maybe. The last thing you expected to run into was a wall of cops."

Walter swore—his pipe was out. He scanned the desk for an ashtray, then stalked irritably across the room to the wall of evidence boxes and began to pick through them. With his back turned, I furtively slid the middle photo envelope out of the pile and slipped it into my jacket pocket. Walter plucked a chipped Hay Adams Hotel ashtray out of a plastic evidence bag and brought it back to the worktable. "Secretary from Toledo brained her boss with this when he tried to rape her during a business trip to our fair city. Fucking lobbyist, got what he deserved." Walter knocked the strings of dead tobacco out of his pipe. "Ordinarily, Ray, I don't mind it when a reporter tells a few tall ones—can't ask a leopard to change his spots, can we?—but this is no ordinary story. That wasn't just your friendly neighborhood crack house operating up in that project. We didn't find so much as a gram. No cash, no weapons. Fingerprints that don't appear on any database in the country. We're either dealing with a psychomaniac who's extremely skilled with a scalpel, or we've got a gang that skins their enemies, which would make the Dominicans and Colombians *combined* look like pussycats. I'm assuming that the office and the skin are connected, so then the question becomes, who ran that office?"

"Yeah?" I didn't like where he was headed.

Walter lit his pipe, then reached slyly into his jacket and pulled out the familiar black-and-white picture of Jean-Mars Baptiste; it was probably the original photograph that had been composited with text to make the political flyers. The slogan and the name were missing.

"You recognize him?" Walter asked.

"He doesn't look familiar," I said calmly. "Of course, that may not mean anything. My job's a little like yours—I must've interviewed a couple thousand people over the years, can't remember them all."

"I'm not talking about 'over the years.' I'm talking about that night. A hot night, the kind of weather that makes you want to drag your mattress up on the roof to get a good night's sleep. Which one very observant couple in the building across the park did. They said they saw two, maybe three people up in that office."

"Must've been cops. Your men were all over the place."

Walter didn't fully appreciate that journalists are interroga-

tors, too. We've seen so many people attempt to squirm out of
our questions that we've learned to do it ourselves. I knew I
hadn't given away anything; I felt like I could've beaten a lie
detector. I backed confidently toward the door, the "borrowed"
pictures secure in my pocket.

"Must've been," Walter said flatly. "*But* . . . if it turns out
to be something else, if I catch you holding back information
or witnesses, that's a guaranteed indictment. No First Amend-
ment fallbacks. And no more *Washington Post* to pay your legal
bills. Welcome to life as a freelancer, Ray."

———

I tore into the pictures while I was still in the parking lot. At
first glance, they seemed to be random street scenes, often out
of focus, several shot through the rear windshield of a moving
car. But as I shuffled through the photos a second time, a vague
fear collected in my shoulders, then crawled up the back of my
neck. The shots were all of the same two, boxy American cars,
as though the photographer were being followed. They were
flat black, mid-seventies sedans. They had no license plates, and
the passengers were invisible behind smoked glass. I fanned the
pictures out across the seat, and as I drove home, my eyes were
drawn to them at every stoplight. Haunted, I glanced in my
rearview mirror, as though I expected the mysterious cars to
glide out of the pictures into real life.

Then, caught in the shiny slipstream of traffic, I realized what
disturbed me about the pictures: the cars had been stripped of
their chrome. They had no bumpers or hubcaps, no gleaming
headlight shrouds. In one shot taken at night, in a mirror dripping with rain, the photographer had caught the pursuing car
in a close-up: its headlights were a deep, mysterious blue. The
cars seemed transformed; these all-American cruisemobiles,
with their V-8's and whitewalls, prowled through the pictures
like unearthly predators.

———

I spent the rest of the afternoon on the phone, conference-calling with former colleagues in New York and Miami. Some were glad to hear that I was back at work, others were unaware I'd even left. I had questions, they had complaints. My Miami contacts were fed up with shopping-center sprawl, 99.9 percent humidity, and twenty-four-hour salsa stations; they longed for the theater, the European compactness of New York. The New Yorkers, battered by slush, sleet, rust, and neglect, yearned for the tropical brilliance of Miami's Art Deco District, dreamed of its warm waters, its daiquiri-and-ceviche afternoons. Between the crankiness and gossip, I managed to gather the pieces I needed for my story.

Over the last six months, there had been a number of attacks on Haitian exile groups, beginning with the attempted murders of two disc jockeys at a Creole-language radio station in Miami. The violence was seeping northward: a firebomb had destroyed a Bronx domino parlor that doubled as a political club; the publisher of an opposition newspaper in Boston had been mugged by two men he identified as Haitian intelligence officers. Jean-Mars Baptiste had good reason to be afraid.

I needed official comment, a power-corridor reaction. When a tragedy occurs, or when a vein of fresh, frightening knowledge is unexpectedly cut open, the first question people ask is, What is the government doing about it? It's the question that employs all of us in Washington.

Tony Randolph met me in his office, feet on desk, sleeves rolled up, Orioles game on low in the background. It was his downtime at the State Department, the breath-catching hour between the afternoon's last press briefing and the evening's first embassy cocktail party.

"This is how you hit the comeback trail? With this Haiti thing?"

"It's not a full-fledged comeback. I'm just testing the waters."

"Look, Ray, when you called I was genuinely excited. At last, the man is ready to give up this hammer-and-nail charade and get back to work. I actually miss our public jousting matches."

Tony Randolph was an official State Department spokesman, one of those functionaries whose doleful duty it is to stand at a podium in front of a world map and field pushy questions from the media. With his homespun features and just-plain-folks delivery, Tony was a PR fantasy figure, government as the boy next door. He was a traditional enemy who had evolved into my closest friend; of all the spokesmen the government scatters in front of reporters like nails on a highway, he was the least comfortable with lies.

"I just don't want you to stumble down any blind alleys," he continued. "Man's on the D.L. for a year, he's got to work his way back carefully."

"I'm the grizzled veteran here. I should be dishing out advice to *you*."

"Yeah? I'm not the one who threw a Hall of Fame career away. So forgive me if I don't fall on my knees and beg for *your* advice."

There it was, the Washington code of behavior, neatly summed up. If you leave their insular world, you're not moving on, or exploring career alternatives; you're "throwing your career away." You become a traitor, or worse, a civilian. Tony softened, sensing that the last barb he threw was a bit too sharp. "Look, I'm sorry. You don't return our calls, don't invite us out to the house—maybe you had your reasons. You got a name for it yet?"

"The house?"

"Sure. I thought all your Virginia plantations were named. Something like Sunnymead, Falconia . . ."

My throat felt parched, my lips dry, unable to form words. I reached for a pitcher that bore the State Department seal.

"Drink up," Tony said. "That pitcher of ice water—I heard it was gin in Dean Acheson's day—has gotten me through many a press conference."

"God, I'm actually nervous," I squeaked, downing two

glasses of water. "Just get me jump-started. You want to be an 'unnamed source,' you got it."

Tony smiled and sighed heavily. "All right. What the hell, Watergate started with a piece of tape on a door. Jean-Mars Baptiste, sure, I've heard of him, seen him at a couple diplomatic functions. The Harold Stassen of Haiti."

"He was supposed to speak at a fund-raiser a couple nights ago, but didn't show," I said. "People are worried. You think he's prominent enough to take out?"

"Prominent as Haitians go, sure. It'd be nervy as hell, though, whacking a well-known exile in this town. Especially since I know the Secretary likes him, sees him as solid, middle of the road."

"What about organizations, groups with violent tendencies? Duvalierist thugs accidentally getting protected status from the INS, for example? Any stray Tontons Macoutes showing up on your radar screen?"

I glanced at the world map that filled the wall where there should have been a window, and thought about the geography of anti-Communism. In 1957, a lower-middle-class doctor named François Duvalier came to power in Haiti, and to protect himself from the violent capriciousness of his country's politics (and the violently abbreviated terms of his predecessors), he created a private militia, the Volunteers for National Security, or, in Creole slang, the "Tontons Macoutes," named after a bloodthirsty nursery-rhyme bogeyman who prowls the night to punish naughty children. They quickly evolved into a Haitian gestapo, and Papa Doc just as quickly became the self-designated "President for Life." In 1959, Fidel Castro took over in Cuba, sixty miles across the Windward Passage from Haiti. Papa Doc was mercurial, paranoid, and kleptomaniacal, a melodramatic terrorist who dumped his opponent's bodies beneath the WELCOME TO HAITI signs that line the airport road, a pseudomystic who rewrote the Lord's Prayer to read, "Our Doc, who art in the National Palace for Life, hallowed be Thy name by present and future generations. Thy will be done in Port-au-Prince as it is in the provinces" . . . but he was no Communist. His "redmail" worked; we forked over the foreign aid and he became our breakwater, holding back the Caribbean's Marxist tide.

"Ancient history, Ray. Papa Doc's gone, Baby Doc's gone. The Macoutes were scattered to the winds."

"And some of them were blown here."

"Let me save you the Freedom of Information Act paperwork. Over the years, we funneled money to some pretty bad guys down there. That's public record, we don't deny it. Some of 'em may have thought that meant the welcome mat would always be out; a few may have slipped into the country without wiping their shoes, OK? But we have no knowledge—none— of any organized group of ex-, current, or future Tontons Macoutes operating in this country."

"So, is that a yes?"

He shook his head in disgust. "Let's throw strikes here. Does Haiti produce oil, rare alloys the Pentagon can stick into an F-15? Cars, VCRs, some gourmet fucking delicacy that your Georgetown yuppie'll pay a hundred bucks an ounce for? No. What Haiti does produce with assembly-line efficiency is more poor Haitians."

"But we would prefer it if they wouldn't export them."

Tony sighed. "Look, it's a new season down there, new management. As always, the army installs the president, but the guy they've got in there now, Rene Isidor, he's different, a rookie. An ex-schoolteacher from the slums, meek little guy with Coke-bottle glasses, seems like he couldn't scare a fly. I seriously doubt he's behind these attacks."

"But he's no democrat, either," I said.

"He wasn't elected, if that's what you mean. But the poor people love him because he talks a good game—wealth redistribution, anti-Americanism, you know the drill. Officially, we've called on him to restore civil liberties, unmuzzle the press, and schedule fair and open elections."

"Think it'll happen?"

"Think the Dodgers'll move back to Brooklyn?" He dropped

his feet loudly to the floor. "Look, Ray, there's nothing there. Voodoo death squads are not advancing up the eastern seaboard with orders to kill Haitian refugees." He propped up a picture that had fallen facedown on his desk: Livia Holcomb, standing on the porch of Tony's Chesapeake Bay weekend house, blond hair flying in a stiff wind, squinting hopefully into the horizon. We stared at the picture, as though we hoped Livia would say something to break the uncomfortable silence.

"I told her you'd called; that you were on a story again. Obviously, she was thrilled."

"Obviously."

"Why can't you accept it, Ray? There are people who care about you."

Tony had always had a crush on Livia, but with a diplomat's finesse, he had waited until we broke up to act. They lived together in Georgetown now, and they were much more compatible than Livia and I had ever been. They weren't professional competitors, and they were both equal parts jaded and gung ho.

"Want to try dinner at our place again?" Tony asked. "Really make it happen this time? Better yet, what about a weekend on the bay? Celebrate your return to the majors. I know she'd like it."

Following our breakup, Livia had allowed a decent mourning period to elapse, then had begun issuing dinner invitations, insisting that we maintain a civilized friendship. I had always found an excuse to cancel, not out of jealousy or the fear that old wounds would be reopened, but because she and Tony were such perfect icons of the life I had fled. But strangely, they did care about me more than most; even though I'd frequently hounded Tony into a corner on national TV, and I'd hurt Livia.

"I'll think about it."

"Good. I'll tell her you're leaning toward it." He slapped me on the back. "Welcome back to the game, Ray. Yours is a voice that was missed. And Haiti, seriously—it's a nonstory."

Tony could lie flawlessly on camera; I'd seen him squirm unwounded out of a Sam Donaldson-Mike Wallace pincer movement. But off camera, he was often transparent. He was definitely hiding something.

I made my way to the exit, along pale corridors swarming with ID-badged drones. A tour group crossed my path, bustling out of the diplomatic reception rooms. A familiar-looking woman dodged out of the group and pursued two bureaucrats toward the elevator bank, gesturing at them aggressively. They spun around and looked at her with startled recognition. The three of them immediately plunged into conversation, the woman slashing irately with her index finger, the men cowed into defensive shrugs.

It was the woman who had narrated the documentary at the Galerie Creole! The State Department officials seemed to know her well. As I watched, they managed to calm her down. The three bowed their heads in an argumentative huddle, just out of my earshot. She was in her late forties, hair pulled back and tied in a ribbon, and her skin was a deep, exotic black. She stood out among the drab government workers with her discreet flashes of silver jewelry and expensive charcoal suit, all of it so precisely chosen, it was as if she had copied a page from a fashion magazine. She had an assertive, sensual femininity, and her sharp, prominent eyebrows were frozen in an arch of contempt. I'd seen it before, the hostile, bottom-line gaze of the crusader—but on her, moral urgency seemed exciting. I could imagine those scolding hands caressing the back of my neck, that confined hair cascading onto naked shoulders, those striding, delicately muscled legs racing me to the bedroom.

I ran after her. The elevator door opened. It was crowded; the woman and her two escorts entered and immediately broke off their discussion. Just before the elevator door nipped shut in my face, she looked up. She gave me a smile that was both erotic and dismissive. A smile that made me feel like a teenager reaching out of my sexual league. She knew me, I was certain. But I had only seen her on film.

———

I still didn't know what kind of story I would sit down to write—murder mystery, missing person, political intrigue, supernatural? But Jean-Mars Baptiste, dead or alive, was at its center. I stopped by the Galerie Creole that evening, hoping the owner, Faustin Gabriel, might have news about Baptiste. Though the gallery was closed, someone was playing opera inside, loud enough to vibrate the paintings off the walls. When Placido Domingo finally paused for breath, I rang the bell. The door swung open.

She was there. For the first time I saw that her eyes were a deep lustrous blue, striking and incongruous on her African face, like jewels set on a bed of black velvet.

I introduced myself and explained that I was developing background for a story on Jean-Mars Baptiste. "I'm Carmen Mondesir," she said, inviting me in. "Director of Zanfan d'Ayiti. You have found me counting the receipts from our recent benefit. Look around if you like."

I followed her to Gabriel's Louis XIV desk. A cigarette burned aromatically from an ivory holder; she picked it up and inhaled picturesquely, head thrown back, eyes closed.

"I saw you at the State Department," I said.

"Me?"

"Yeah, just a couple hours ago. Going into a fifth floor elevator."

"Maybe. I am obliged to beg for donations at so many of your government's *bureaux,* they all seem alike."

"The way you looked at me . . ."

"Yes?" she said, pinning me with her dramatic blue eyes.

For some reason, I censored myself. Instead of saying, "You looked at me like I was the teenage lover you once spent a careless afternoon with," I just stammered, "It was like you recognized me."

"So many men tell me that. It is the eyes, I think. They take people by surprise; people feel they are being watched. But perhaps I should be grateful that I am a curiosity. Now, what can I tell you about Monsieur Baptiste?"

I didn't trust her. There was some furtive and deeper connection between us, but in the interests of a professional interview, I tried to ignore it.

She couldn't add much to my knowledge of Baptiste. In her frank opinion, he attracted followers because he was neither dangerous nor realistic. He was a well-meaning man who placated the exiles with speeches, when what Haiti really needed was a devious crusader.

"From your perspective, would the Isidor regime have an interest in silencing Baptiste?"

"Perhaps. If you blow out the match, you make sure a real fire never starts." Her smile became frightening, marked by sharp, vertical creases at the edges of her lips. She waved a copy of *Haïti en Marche,* an exile newspaper published in Miami. On the cover was a portrait of a gaunt, almost malnourished-looking man with thick glasses and a goatee, dressed in a guayabera open at the neck. "This man, this President Rene Isidor, this *voix du peuple,* as he calls himself, he would cut off his left arm if it meant his right arm would stay in power."

Her assessment seemed to contradict Tony's description of Isidor as a timid intellectual who'd stumbled into the Presidential Palace. "If he wanted a political opponent in Washington, D.C., to vanish, do you think he could pull it off?" I asked.

She flashed me a cunning smile. Of course, the Haitian grapevine had already told her Jean-Mars Baptiste was missing.

"Isidor is a demagogue. He imagines himself to be the Creole Castro. You see, he doesn't wear suits, because he feels it brings him closer to the average peasant. He trades in cheap symbols, but the result is the same: Stalinism. No free press, no respect for law, no political opposition. He has nationalized everything—capital has fled the country. For Miami, for Switzerland, the Cayman Islands. Haiti is dying. If the starving children do not plague his conscience, would the death of an enemy?"

Carmen Mondesir's political hatred seemed to suck the air out of the room; it drew the light to her outraged face. Her hands were restless with excess energy; they were deeply carved and seemed much older than the rest of her. She took a bottle of lotion from her purse, and rubbed the lotion vigorously into her hands.

She agreed to let me quote her. I collected brief biographical background: she was from the northwest coast, from a small village near Gonaïves, where she grew up speaking Creole, unable to understand a word of French. "Poverty you will not imagine, dead land, no trees, no hope." She had been married, "not married, really, but I had a man who lived with me, played the lottery, lost our land, and emigrated to the Dominican Republic." Musical as a girl, she had gone to Port-au-Prince, hoping to become a dancer in the National Folklore Troupe, but soon learned that the tourists liked their "natives" lighter skinned.

"Skin color is the central fact of Haitian life," she said. "The mulattos have the money, you see. Light skin blesses you," she ran her hands across her cheeks, "but dark skin condemns you."

She learned French and English in an attempt to re-create herself, to make inroads into the mulatto elite. She managed to make some money "the way most Haitians make money, out of the air," and bought a house, which burned. Eventually, even the air itself seemed to die, and she fled Haiti in 1987, on an overcrowded open skiff. It was a stormy, nightmarish voyage, and she was forced to take charge, resorting to survival tactics that she hinted were brutal but necessary. Thanks to her ability to make money out of air, she ended up in the charity business, raiding the pockets of exiled Haitians and conscience-stricken Americans.

"I was a beggar on the streets of Gonaïves at the age of six; now I'm a beggar on the streets of Washington at forty-six," she said. The music stopped. She rushed to reload the CD player: Jessye Norman, performing her namesake, *Carmen*. "I adore opera. Perhaps because my life has been so operatic. I was poor, I had money, I was poor again. I had a house, I lost a house; I had a country, I lost a country." She seemed drunk on the music. Her voice dropped an octave: it was seductive and scratchy, the brandy-drenched voice of a French chanteuse on her last set of the night. I closed my notebook. Carmen

Mondesir held the stage. Cigarette in hand, she swayed through the gallery, nodding her head to the music, her body weaving beneath the charcoal suit.

"Have you ever seen a loup-garou?" I asked.

She laughed. "All Americans love voodoo. My town, Gonaïves, is the heart of Haitian voodoo. When I grew up, everyone was poor and everyone served the loa. Well, everyone is still poor. Let me tell you, a loup-garou is just a ghost out of vodoun. And vodoun is really nothing more than the poor people's opera."

———

I thought it would be harder to ease my way into my first story in a year. But I wasn't driving this story, it was driving me. Under the heading "Prominent Political Figure Vanishes," I described the disappearance of Jean-Mars Baptiste and his family, delving into his political background, tying in the upsurge of violence directed at Haitian opposition figures in the United States. I quoted a "Haitian exile" who blamed the regime of President Rene Isidor for the attacks. Because I had struck a gentlemen's agreement with Walter Paisley to hold the loup-garou skin as our ace, I mentioned it only as the "ominous warning" that prompted the Baptiste family to go into hiding.

I needed a reaction, instant judgment. I needed someone's approval. I dialed the number on Lucy Marcelin's business card just as I glanced at the alarm clock. . . . I let it ring anyway.

Answering machine. Message in Creole and English. Why was I so jealous that she was out at five-thirty in the morning, when I had the audacity to call her at that hour? I left a brief message, then faxed her my pages. Literary critique, my ass. I was flirting, but it was electronic flirting, distant, American. Far from the atavistic pull of voodoo gods and childhood myths. Maybe she'd even like it.

5

MY ARTICLE APPEARED two days later, in a dozen East Coast
papers. I wasn't after a big-bucks magazine paycheck, I wanted
coverage. Summer is a slow news period in D.C., and I landed
a front page. The response was underwhelming. There was no
official reaction from the Haitian embassy, no congressional
outrage, no phone calls, no fax from Lucy Marcelin.

Twenty-four hours later, the Baptistes' home was firebombed.

I watched the house burn on the six o'clock news—even the
Baptistes' crime bars couldn't fend off a well-aimed Molotov
cocktail. Jets of water arced onto the curling, tar-paper roof,
while a news-clone, a Pat or a Bob, speculated on the possible
body count with relish and referred to my "tragically pro-
phetic" article.

My first reaction was guilt: had my piece somehow sparked
this assault? Then confusion: who was behind it and why? Then
dread: who would be their next target?

My phone rang, at first shrill and deafening, then receding
into a tingle at the edge of my hearing. I recognized the warning
signs of another attack: my peripheral vision seemed to crack

and break off; suddenly, my house was gone! The entire scene I was looking at—the TV, the lath work, the bare wires— shattered, revealing another scene behind it. I was back in the sugarcane field. Rain battered the lush, green spears, panicked voices mingled with gunfire and thunder. The gruesome, mouthless, metallic faces were still there. I saw hands running in blood, their palms pierced by knives. A giant dog lunged toward me; he had the polished coat and sinewy legs of a hunter, shreds of human flesh were impaled on his incisors. Blood dripped onto the moist soil at my feet.

Just as suddenly I was whipsawed back to reality. The phone was still ringing, but I ignored it. I was boiling. I wobbled to the bathroom and ran a cold shower across my face. I tried to take my temperature, but it was impossible to focus, the mad- dening, silver thread of mercury slammed back and forth like a metronome. I swallowed a handful of aspirin and glanced in the mirror. I looked sunken, bleached out, wild eyed.

I drove into the city. I parked at the end of the Baptistes' street, just beyond the chaotic periphery of fire engines and curiosity seekers. I sat in the car, monitoring the two ambu- lances, their rear doors wide open and waiting, the crews yawn- ing, smoking, cigarette ash snowing onto the spotless white stretchers.

The fire died, darkness fell. The crowds dwindled and the ambulances drove off empty-handed. I felt a surge of relief— the Baptistes had gotten out in time. I stepped out of the car, intending to question the firemen and arson investigators that slogged through the damp, hissing ruins.

Then it hit me, doubling me over in pain, a hot spur between the ribs, the same spot where we feel love or fear. It commanded me to walk, so I walked. No destination in mind, no sense of time passing. Again, the terrifying loss of willpower—turn left here, turn right there, go straight! Was this a nervous break- down? A personality collapse? Premature Alzheimer's? I passed phone booths, potential lifelines. I reached for one, but my hand fell away, unable to muster the strength to call for help.

I walked across a bridge into southeast Washington. What

did I look like to passing cars? A hypnotized street bum, flesh-and-blood litter? Finally, I stopped on a deserted commercial street. It was a block of boarded-up businesses: an ex-bar, an ex-watch repair, and an ex-X-rated theater. I found myself in front of a pawnshop, its neon CASH LOANED sign a dusty orange glow.

The handguns were neatly lined up on a swath of faded felt, an arsenal of household names: Smith & Wesson, Colt, Beretta, Browning. I cased the neighborhood for cops, security guards. I was alone. I smashed in the window with my boot heel, triggering a burglar alarm that rang as harmlessly as a school bell. I grabbed the Smith & Wesson .357—with its stainless steel and wood grips, it seemed the most businesslike—and a box of ammo. I thrust it into my belt, buttoned my jacket around it, and strutted off with the composure of a pro.

Then, the realization of what I'd done slammed into me: I had become a criminal, a low-to-the-ground hustler who breaks into gun stores. Dazed, I staggered backward into a cinder-block wall. I felt the cold steel burrowing into my groin. I tugged out the gun and stuffed it into a litter bin, burying it beneath a sticky pile of fast-food refuse. I rushed away from it; let it contaminate someone else's life. I had a cartoon vision of the gun slithering out of the trash, hobbling after me on its barrel like a one-legged man. I didn't need the vision—I went only two blocks before I spun around and went back for the gun.

I slouched into a vaguely familiar bar. I watched people watching me. Did guilt give off its own distinctive glow? I ordered a double Jack Daniel's. Sweat drizzled from my forehead onto the ice. What had come over me? Why steal a gun . . . almost, by definition, an untraceable gun?

Run a few tests, I told myself. Verify that you're really back in control. I raised my arm, flexed my fingers. All bodily systems responded; I was back, but for how long? Was there anyone out there who could explain what was happening to me? I felt panic rising in me like vomit; *why isn't there a 911 for this!*

Come on, Ray, you're a journalist. Your job is to assemble the

pieces of a puzzle into a coherent, manageable whole. Connect the
dots: the visions, the fevers, the lack of willpower, the Baptiste story,
with its strangling tentacles that shot out of nowhere . . .

"Raymond Falco? Is that really you?"

The voice was a dim reminder of my surroundings. Now I
recognized the red leather, the framed headlines: this was a
reporters' bar! That was someone I knew sidling up to me:
trim, tanned, Corona and lime in hand.

"It's Doug, you son of a bitch! Doug Holloway. Don't pretend you don't know me; we only toiled next to each other in
Metro for eight months."

I gave him an uncomprehending stare. I paid my tab and
jumped off the bar stool. He spotted the black grip of the .357
in my belt, then trained his eyes on me like twin microscopes.

"Man, you do not look like a happy camper. When was the
last time you saw the sun? Or a doctor, for that matter?"

I fled for the door, Doug Holloway's words echoing off my
back. The joshing camaraderie, the tiny, hard-earned relaxa-
tions, the *normal* . . . it was a trivial, lost world to me now.

———

LOOKING back, I should have stopped myself at that moment.
Thrown the gun into the Potomac. Driven to an emergency
room, demanded an armed guard be posted outside my door.
Not to keep people out, but to keep me *in*. Instead, I kept to
trajectory, moved up the scale from thief to killer. I can see
blackness bleeding to gray beyond the treeline; it won't stay
dark forever. Will I have the courage to look as the first streaks
of sunlight angle across the body? I should search my victim
for fibers, telltale smudges, loose hairs, anything that can be
traced to me. But I feel a curious disinterest in my own self-
preservation. I keep seeing the face: painted with relief, mouth
turned up into a smile, eyes wide and trusting. A face that never
suspected a thing.

———

I remember wandering the streets, the stolen gun in my belt. Washington is not a late-night town: the row houses I passed were mostly dark. A rooftop swamp cooler rumbled, a television audience laughed at a talk show joke, but otherwise it was quiet. I heard their whispers first; then, as I approached the corner where I'd left my car, I saw them, silhouetted against the garish light of a liquor store. I stopped walking, they stopped talking. We nervously surveyed each other from a distance. There's a high-noon quality to encountering an unexpected stranger on a dark city street: who will draw, who will cross to the other side to avoid face-to-face contact?

I continued slowly up the sidewalk. The two figures left the light and came purposefully toward me. It looked like a classic big-city mugging. They were between me and the car; was it part of a deliberate plan to cut off my escape? I dodged across the street. The faster of the two broke after me; I knew he had the speed to head me off. I turned to run . . . then remembered I had a gun. *Death Wish* and its sequels flickered through my mind, jolting me with a sudden, horrifying epiphany: when you die it's not your life that flashes before your eyes, but its B-movie equivalent. Go down in a plane, the last thing you see is *Airport;* overdose on pills and it's *Valley of the Dolls.* As I reached into my belt, I recognized loose-limbed Etienne Baptiste and the bulkier form of his aunt Helene behind him.

"Jesus, Etienne," I exhaled in relief.

"Black face comin' at you out of the night. Scary stuff, man. Where you been? I've been auto-dialing you for an hour."

"Never mind that. Thank God you two got out alive. Did your uncle make it too?"

"Yeah, man, he's fine," Etienne replied. "None of us was even there. We waited till now to come down and check it out, you know, till the cops were gone and everything." He glanced over his shoulder; the streets were still puddled from the fire hydrant overflow, the air was sharp with the smell of charcoal.

I turned to his aunt: "Look, Mrs. Baptiste, somehow I feel

71

responsible for this. I know that your losses must be considerable. If there's anything I can do . . . cash, clothes. I'm sure I can pull a few strings with the local relief agencies."

"It's OK, man, we moved out of there a couple weeks ago. I mean, there was some personal shit, my CD collection, but mostly we came back for my aunt's . . . religious stuff."

"Hang on: you gave me the wrong address?"

He shrugged. "We didn't know if we could trust you." He spotted my hand, frozen on the gun grip. "Don't tell me you're strapped! What is it? A nine?"

"Etienne," said Helene, "we got no time for that kinda shameful gun talk. You tell Mr. Falco the number."

"What number? Come on, we'll go to my car. You shouldn't be out on the street like this."

"Street the safest place. They send loup-garou to the office, they send fire against our house. Better we talk out here. Easier to run."

I started to object, then stopped myself. You can't argue sensibly when nothing makes sense. "Let's at least make ourselves less conspicuous." I drew them into the shadows of an alley behind the liquor store, to the steps of a cement loading dock that seemed a safe distance from the street.

"Now, come on, tell him the number, Etienne," Helene ordered. "You see, Mr. Falco, Jean-Mars, he don't tell me the number . . . it's for my own protection, he says."

Etienne looked nervously up and down the alley, and spoke in whispers. "005-4869-6736 . . . I convinced my uncle to rent a car phone. He keeps in touch with his people that way, never stays more than one night in one place, sometimes he even sleeps in the backseat."

I excitedly reached for a pen.

"No!" Etienne snapped. "Don't write it down, man. Memorize it."

As I drilled myself on the phone number, Helene Baptiste ran her hands over the dozen heavy, rattling necklaces that ringed her neck: homemade strings of tiny plastic babies, hand-painted saints, jeweled hearts, costume pearls, even airline liquor bottles. Like a blind woman reading braille, she seemed to take knowledge, even comfort from them. "So there you have America: families separating, everyone falling apart, like strands in a piece of old rope. But my husband, he think you can help us." She pulled a wrinkled newspaper clipping out of her dress and gingerly flattened it. I was flattered that someone would treat an article of mine like a valuable piece of parchment. "Jean-Mars see this. He's a little vain, you understand? He like to read about himself. He joke, he say to me, 'How the hell come there is no picture?' But he like what you write, want to meet with you anyway. Tonight."

"What she's sayin' is, the Haitians can put up their fliers and print their little newspapers and have their dances and whatnot, but unless we got access to the white, mainstream press, we're fucked!"

"Etienne!" she scolded.

"*Screwed*, OK? How's that? That polite enough?"

"I'm not sure. It is still a vulgarity." She looked at me for guidance.

"Not sure? You've been here four years and you're not sure?" Etienne slapped his thighs in frustration. "You see what I'm dealin' with? I mean, I've been here since I was five, you know? I'm taking computer classes; I already know DOS Six. I got friends. I know about bargain matinees and how to tap into the goddamn cable, shit like that. I'm *here*, you know what I'm sayin'?" He stood on the top step of the loading dock, towering over me like a fire-and-brimstone preacher warming to his sermon's climax. "They'll never fit in"—he tapped his forehead—"where it counts. I dream in American; my aunt and uncle, they dream in Haitian."

"So why are you helping them?" I asked.

"They raised me since I was ten. If they want to waste their lives trying to fix their lousy little country . . . I guess I owe it to 'em to help."

"You may be more Haitian than you think."

"I get something out of it too, man. 'Be cool, motherfucker, my uncle's the president of Haiti.' "

"So, Mrs. Baptiste, where is Jean-Mars now? Where does he want us to meet?"

"I don't know. I never know anymore. You call him on that number, he tell you where. He don't tell me." Her face sagged with the sad realization that her husband had been reduced to a mobile-phone number, a vagabond voice in the night calling from nowhere. Reading the concern in my eyes, she plumped herself up, clapping her hands with childish excitement. "Hey, what's wrong with us? We not dead yet, are we? We serve the spirits, they serve us, right? Just now I am thinking they see all this *tristesse,* this strife, they think we no good, go somewhere else, help someone else. Come on, Etienne, we drink to our *blanc,* huh? We drink to our white writer!"

She took off the necklace holding the airline liquor bottles and uncapped them—one scotch, one rum. She read the rum label and snorted. "Bah! Puerto Rican. You will excuse me for that, Mr. Falco."

We toasted and drank; huddled in the liquor store alley with our miniature bottles, we looked like a gang of alcoholics in training. "Listen, I've got to bring this up: if you and your nephew would let yourselves be taken into protective custody—"

"The cops! No way, man!" Etienne exclaimed.

"Just until we find out who's after you."

"That just another writer's joke, I bet," Helene said. She thumped her collarbone violently. "We all bad guys to the police, all us Haitians. They got a plan for us, let me tell you. They buildin' big boat somewhere secret, just waiting for a chance to push us all out to sea, all back to Haiti. We go, sure, but only when we are ready, OK!"

She looked up at the sky, shuddered with fear. "Come on, Etienne, I think they find us."

Etienne and I scanned the sky and saw nothing but a handful of weak stars, their power bleached by city lights.

"It's there. It just take practice to see a loup-garou that far away."

Nervously fingering her necklaces, Helene Baptiste started toward the mouth of the alley.

"Look, why don't you stay at my place," I said to Etienne. "It's out of town, away from everything. Just temporarily." No answer. "At least leave me a number, some way to get in touch with you."

"Just talk to my uncle, OK? He'll tell you what to do." With his aunt's back turned, Etienne gave me a resigned shrug. "She may bitch about him, but she doesn't listen to anyone else." He followed her to the street and I followed them both.

I argued a couple more minutes, but I kept stalling against their contradictions. They wanted me, but they didn't want me; they shared astounding confidences, yet held others in reserve. They started walking to the corner.

But then Helene whipped around impetuously and ran back to me. She handed me a silver flask. "Coffee and rum, with three drops of petrol. You must drink it. I warn you already once, don't I?"

I grimaced. "I had a couple scotches earlier. You really shouldn't mix your drinks—"

She grabbed my wrist and pushed the flask roughly to my lips. "You must protect yourself, Mr. Falco. The loup-garous, they interested in you now."

Both Carmen Mondesir and Lucy Marcelin had laughingly dismissed the loup-garou as a cultural legend that didn't translate to urban America. But as I looked into Helene's angry, commanding eyes, my skepticism began to waver. Intense belief can be contagious. . . . I sipped gingerly from the flask, not really tasting the gasoline but feeling its caustic burn in my nostrils.

Helene Baptiste gave me a tiny smile of triumph. I tried to hand back the flask but she refused it.

"I make more for me and Etienne. But you keep that. I think maybe you need it more than we do tonight."

Something flashed in the corner of my eye, like a match being struck in a dark room. I looked up at the sky. Was there really something there? For a moment, I wanted desperately to confide in Helene Baptiste, to tell her all that had happened to me, to beg for her advice.

But the pragmatic journalist rose to the surface: *you're going to ask the help of a woman who makes you drink gasoline? That streak of light? The afterglow of a shooting star, a dying satellite burning up as it plunges to earth.*

I watched Helene and Etienne Baptiste disappear around the corner. They didn't vanish with the swirl of a velvet cloak, they didn't soar off on a carpet. They were probably heading for the bus stop. I felt better. Back to logic, back to the dispassionate demeanor of a reporter. I unscrewed the flask, and emptied it onto the sidewalk.

6

Jean-Mars Baptiste answered the phone on the first ring.

"Yes?"

"Mr. Baptiste, at last. It's Raymond Falco."

"Mr. Falco. Good of you to ring." He sounded unconcerned, as though I were calling to verify a casual lunch date. He had a generic English accent, probably adopted during his stay at the London School of Economics. "However, since we haven't met, you won't mind if I subject you to a quick 'vetting,' as it were?"

"Go ahead. But I don't think there are that many people who'd get a charge out of impersonating me."

"You're much too modest."

He asked a series of questions designed to verify that I had actually met his family. I described their physical appearance, their clothing, their gestures. "And my nephew, a fine boy, a computer wizard, already up to speed with DOS Five . . ."

"You mean DOS Six."

"Of course. I stand corrected." I was certain now that Etienne had dropped the DOS reference into his conversation as a code word to be checked by his uncle.

"So, where do we meet? Where are you now?" I asked.

"On a street where I do not intend to linger. Two quite unsavory characters have become intrigued by my car phone."

"OK, a bar, a restaurant, that's out. For your own safety we should avoid a public place."

"I quite agree."

"I suppose you could come here . . ."

"Absolutely not! Nowhere in Washington is safe for me at the moment."

I unfolded a map, scanning the unfamiliar suburbs for a secluded meeting spot. The only place I could come up with would not bring me greater glory. "Meet me in Rosslyn. It's just across the river; the place totally empties out at night. We'll link up in the *USA Today* parking lot and go from there."

He didn't answer for a moment. I heard his fingernails drumming against the receiver.

"That sounds acceptable. I only hope you won't lead anyone to me, Mr. Falco."

"I'll watch my rearview mirror."

"That may not suffice."

"What do you mean by that?"

"The interested parties are talented, resourceful, and quite committed. They have ways of defying one's expectations, of working around the protective measures one takes against them."

" 'Them,' 'they,' 'the interested parties.' I'm going to need specifics, OK? The meat of a story is in the details. If you're not prepared for that, we might as well just call off this little rendezvous."

The relationship between journalist and source is one of mutual parasitism, the greed for limelight balanced against the lust for bylines. A source must be reminded of this early and often, otherwise he ends up running the show.

"Oh, I'll provide specifics, Mr. Falco. That I promise. But I would just ask you to do me this one little service."

"And that is?"

"I would ask you to abandon all your preconceptions. About me, about this story."

"No problem. Most of my preconceptions went out the window the night we found the loup-garou skin on your front door."

"But I'm afraid that, too, is a preconception. Ghosts are not always ghosts, soldiers are not always soldiers. *Dans une heure,* Mr. Falco?" He hung up abruptly. I stared curiously at the phone, as though I hoped the rest of our conversation was trapped in there; if I shook it, the meaning behind Baptiste's enigmatic caginess might come tumbling out.

Rosslyn, Virginia, was a nine-to-five chrome-and-glass annex of Washington. By day, its consulting firms and government agencies formed a crowded, humming offshoot of the federal ant farm; by night, it was deserted except for the janitorial crews.

I cruised slowly through the wide, empty streets, beneath skyscrapers checkerboarded with light, adrenaline-charged now that I was finally going to meet the elusive Jean-Mars Baptiste. The giant glowing USA TODAY sign was my North Star, guiding me to the short-term parking lot at the building's main entrance. I turned off my lights so I wouldn't attract the attention of the security guard, whose face, illuminated by a tiny TV, seemed to float disembodied in the lobby's darkness.

I waited fifteen minutes, but not a single car appeared. I realized I had forgotten to ask Baptiste what he drove. I grew unsettled by the quiet, the sleek emptiness of the place. I tuned in the all-news channel, comforted by the reports of distant traffic jams and cops being dispatched to a hostage situation.

I never expected my car phone to ring. It was Jean-Mars Baptiste.

"Do you see them?" he asked. His stiff-upper-lip tone was gone, erased by undisguised fear.

"See who? Where are you?"

"I'm close."

I scanned the dark street. No prowling cars, no lurking figures.

"Look across the street," he said.

A silver catering truck was parked at the curb directly opposite me, preparing to serve the janitors on their 2 A.M. "lunch break." A brassy *cumbia* filtered out of the truck's cab. A shadow bobbed to the music inside.

"They're behind it," he whispered. "Two of them."

Infected by Baptiste's paranoia, I nudged my car forward until I reached an angle where I could look behind the catering truck. It had parked in front of the entrance to an underground garage, which sloped down into darkness. At first I couldn't see anything, just a jumble of angular shadows. But then I realized the steep grade of the driveway concealed most of their bulk; only the smoked windshields of the two black cars were visible.

"Where the hell did they come from?" I asked.

"A rhetorical question, at this point," came the answer in the night. I had to react: I felt a commitment to Jean-Mars Baptiste now; he was dependent on my guidance, my protection.

"OK, follow me. Now!"

I shot away from the curb, swerved wide into the center of the road, and lined up with the entrance to the *USA Today* employee parking lot. I hit the gas and jammed down the long curving driveway, slipping into darkness, one hand on the wheel, the other sorting furiously through my wallet. Cash, credit cards—all that purchasing power—totally useless! I skidded to a stop at the automated gate. Headlights burned behind me, I heard the screech of bald tires. I checked the mirror: Jean-Mars Baptiste drove a dented, silver Toyota, definitely not in keeping with his standing as a presidential candidate.

I couldn't find it in my wallet! I rifled the glove compartment—nothing. Baptiste honked, he pinwheeled his arms frantically.

"Bloody hell, Mr. Falco!" he screamed through a wall of static. "They're coming!"

I didn't need to look behind me. I could already see the invading blue glow of their headlights.

There it was, nearly hidden beneath the floor mat! A Gannett Newspapers parking pass, a perk I had pried out of management while attending editorial meetings to discuss an article of mine, which they eventually killed. Fuck you, McPaper, I thought. At least you can help me keep my source alive.

I fed the magnetic card into the slot, and the gate lifted. I roared into the garage, and Baptiste's Toyota slipped in behind me. I watched the gate descend, then saw the first of the mysterious black cars appear, revealing itself slowly like the lethal snout of an alligator rising out of a swamp. It stopped at the gate, unsure whether to smash through or back out and try to cut off our escape elsewhere. I didn't wait for it to decide.

I led Baptiste on a squealing slalom course, racing beneath the *USA Today* skyscraper toward an exit that I remembered from my previous visits. The garage narrowed to a dim, claustrophobic tunnel. It twisted upward in endless spirals, and when we finally burst out, into patchy city lights and the high, black dome of sky, I felt like a panicked diver breaking the surface of the ocean.

I merged onto the Jeff Davis Highway, which skirted the edge of Arlington National Cemetery. Robert E. Lee's Greek Revival house glowed white above the graves, a graceful monument to a lost cause. "I hope those are your headlights behind me, Mr. Baptiste," I said into the phone.

"I'm still here," he said, his breathing clipped. "That was quick thinking back there. Bloody marvelous, actually. A genuine American car chase!"

"How long have you been photographing them?"

My question forced a heavy silence. We continued south, passing the Pentagon with no sign of pursuing blue headlights.

"They started to appear about a month ago," Baptiste answered. "Pure intimidation. They follow me at a distance, park outside my home, circling like fighting cocks but never actually striking."

"What about the bombing of the Haitian political club in New York, the attacks on those DJ's in Miami? Are they connected to those incidents? Are they responsible?"

"When it comes to Haitian politics, Mr. Falco, it is difficult, if not impossible, to determine who is responsible for what. Consider the current situation in my country. We have a president, Rene Isidor. Not an elected president, of course, but nevertheless he reports to work at his office in the presidential palace every morning in civilian clothes, not a military uniform. Yet he is more dictator than democrat. Before that we had a general, who briefly permitted a reasonably free press and an independent judiciary. As it turned out, he was more democrat than dictator. *But,* and it's a bloody big *but,* neither of them was really in charge. They were—oh, what's the damn word?—stand-offs."

"Stand-ins?" I offered.

"Precisely. A stand-in for the elite who wish to rule without physically mucking about in politics. We Haitians call it *la politique de doublure,* a politics of masks and disguises. The key to survival is knowing where the real power lies."

"That's something you've got to learn everywhere."

"True. But in Haiti, you can't really learn it. You must *sense* it."

In my rearview mirror, all I could see of Baptiste was a silhouette, his glasses reflecting the glare of oncoming headlights.

"I think we better get off the highway," I said. I exited into the suburbs, a quiet no-man's land of lawns and neat brick houses. The streets were leafy, lush, and humid, and when I stopped at a light, I could hear sprinklers hissing.

"Where are we going?" Baptiste asked.

"A little evasive action. Just stay close."

In fact, I *didn't* know where I was going, yet I never consulted a map or hesitated at an intersection. I took shortcuts and side streets, moving farther away from the city, guided by a mysterious inner compass that had taken the decisions out of my hands.

"You know these streets well. You must've grown up here."

We passed a high school, with its late-summer aura of benign neglect: a weedy front lawn, a marquee with drooping letters wishing last June's grads good luck.

"Somewhere just like it. Three thousand miles away."

I kept going. I was on autopilot now, certain that if I took my hands off the wheel, the car would steer itself. I felt a fresh dose of fear; I didn't know where I was going, but what if our pursuers did? Would they be waiting there for us, with their blue headlights and smoked-glass windows?

"OK, I think I've indulged your digressions long enough. I need to know who's in those cars."

"I would have thought it was obvious by now. A loup-garou is a very adaptable creature."

"Sure, just another witch trading in his broomstick for a late-model car."

"I hear that you're still not a believer."

"And you are," I snapped sarcastically. "European educated, a disciple of John Kenneth Galbraith who believes in the power of werewolves."

"Spoken like a true American. And your reaction is quite understandable: in America, politics is a secular battlefield. Not in Haiti. I'll give you an example. I have a friend who's a furniture salesman. Every time there's a coup, the new regime comes to him and buys all new furniture. Why? Because they are afraid the outgoing regime has hidden a *wanga,* an evil charm, in the old furniture. You call it superstition; a Haitian would call it a security measure." Baptiste chuckled. "Politicians have always used vodoun. Papa Doc was very good at manipulating its symbols. He was always turned out in black— black suit, black tie, black bowler—the traditional garb of Baron Samedi, Lord of the Dead. His thugs, his Tontons Macoutes, liked to hide behind sunglasses; if you couldn't see their eyes, you couldn't tell if they were zombis. The simple uncertainty could terrify a true believer."

"And the true skeptic?"

"In Haiti, there are no true skeptics."

"But why go after you here?" I asked. "Why not wait until

you return to Haiti, where they can cover up the crime much easier or even make an example out of you?"

"Because I know too much about them. I've learned certain aspects of their plans. This is not about one humble politician. It is not a little skirmish between jealous exiles. It is about something much bigger."

His words hung there, a bright, spangled lure inviting me to bite. I turned onto a country road. It was overgrown: berry bushes scratched at my fenders, trees arched overhead, blotting out the stars.

"Let's just head down here a little farther," I said into the phone. "Keep your eyes on the mirror, make sure we've lost them." The road got darker, narrower. There were no mailboxes now, no porch lights twinkling in the woods. I drove another mile, to make sure we were beyond sight and sound of civilization.

I pulled onto the shoulder and stopped. Baptiste drew up behind me and shut off his engine. It sputtered, dying reluctantly. We turned off our lights and waited. The woods seemed to be advancing, like a camouflaged army cutting off our escape. The road was a thin gray ribbon, swallowed at both ends by shrubbery and darkness. I rolled down the window; just the drumming of bullfrogs and the drone of crickets. The only light came from stray fireflies and the glow of my cellular phone. We hadn't been followed.

I got out of my car, Jean-Mars Baptiste got out of his, and we edged toward each other like duelists. Even though we'd talked on the phone for almost an hour, our first face-to-face meeting was tense; we moved hesitantly, breaths held as though an invisible alarm were strung on the air between us, and a sudden exhale could set it off.

He was stockier than his picture on the photocopied fliers. He wore a conservative blue suit, white shirt, and red tie. He removed a pair of aviator glasses and slipped them into his jacket pocket as he extended his hand.

"Mr. Falco, I must say I appreciate your concern for my

safety. I think our precautions will pay off in a relationship that will be rewarding to us both."

It was the unsuspecting smile that I will remember as I shot him.

I raised the hand that he expected to shake his, the gun feeling heavy and dead. I fired twice, the muzzle flash as blinding as a lightning strike. I struck him in the chest, piercing the pocket that held his glasses, the impact catapulting him six feet backward. I felt my body vibrate from the recoil, and I knew that he was dead before he hit the ground.

Blood sprayed onto my fender, my windshield, my clothes. But I was a callous observer; I stood back and watched him fall, as though I'd simply chopped down a tree. His heels skidded on the gravel, and he tumbled into a bramble-choked culvert beside the road. No panicked birds flew from the treetops, no hound dogs brayed. The bullfrogs and crickets stopped, but started in again almost immediately—nature was unconcerned.

———

I'VE been a murderer for an hour now, according to the dashboard clock. I don't feel transformed, just tired. And though I've mentally retraced the steps that led me here, I don't feel enlightened. How many *W*'s do I know? Four: who, what, when, where. "Why" seems an impossible distance away.

———

IT was the sun, finally, that drove me away from the scene. It came up explosively like it does in the tropics, radiating at full power. I couldn't bear to watch its unsparing rays warming Jean-Mars Baptiste's body.

I came home to a murderer's house. Those were a murderer's unwashed dishes, that was a murderer's Mr. Coffee, a murderer's hair was clumped in the bathtub drain. But I wasn't the murderer. I felt like the victim of a botched personality transfusion—someone else was bumping around in my veins, but I was still in there!

I felt myself dragged into my office, where heat blazed through the plastic window coverings and houseplants panted for water. I threw my computer onto the floor, swept my desk free of floppies. I got out the fountain pen I hadn't used in years, and filled it from an antique, garage-sale inkwell. I unwrapped a ream of paper. My hand flew across the page, each word a claw scratching its way into another world, a world I had glimpsed before, in random bursts of tropical madness. My hand, my pen, my paper. But it was the murderer writing. . . .

7

PORT-AU-PRINCE, SEPTEMBER 1792

The wealth of Saint Domingue was evident from the moment our armed merchantman lowered her sails and swung to anchor in Port-au-Prince harbor. My impression was one of overwhelming lushness: green waves of sugarcane; fields of banana trees, their giant, well-nourished leaves providing shade like a thousand parasols; neat rows of coffee trees rising to meet forested mountains. It seemed one had only to drop a seed here to make one's fortune.

And truly, it was the lust for a fortune that had sustained my shipmates during our storm-tossed passage from Norfolk. There was the Boston molasses trader, the Charleston indigo merchant, the New York gunsmith, the Congregationalist minister, perhaps hoping to harvest a fortune in Negro and French Catholic souls. As we marveled at the harbor's ceaseless mercantile activity, I reflected that I, too, was a fortune-hunter to some degree. I had come to the Indies, to this prosperous pearl of France's Antillean realm, to make my political fortune. I removed the precious document from my pocket, its corners curled by long exposure to the sea air, and read it for the hundredth time.

Dear Sirs,

This is to introduce my envoy, Nicholas Whitney Townsend of Virginia. Whereas Mr. Townsend is a duly sworn and delegated representative of the United States, it is my hope that you will extend to him the courtesy of your good offices, and wherever possible, aid him freely in his inquiries.

Given under my hand at Monticello, the 9th day of August, in the year of our Lord One Thousand Seven Hundred and Ninety-Two, and of the Independence of the United States, the sixteenth.

Thomas Jefferson
Secretary of State

I carefully refolded the letter and descended into the French pilot boat. A trio of white-cockaded soldiers rowed us to shore, where I was met at the customs house by a portly official in pristine civilian dress.

"Gilles Condillac, deputy intendant. The intendant had wished to welcome you himself, but unexpected . . . affairs of state have claimed his full attention. However, I am quite capable of seeing you comfortably settled."

"Has there been more trouble?"

"No, no. The situation at present is quite peaceful. Royalists and Patriots have smoothed over their differences in the interests of the colony. There are no guillotines in our squares, poised to descend on French throats . . . or American ones, for that matter."

"That is not the trouble to which I referred."

Condillac gave me a chastising scowl. I noticed that the white Royalist cockade pinned to his lapel was of an unmistakable revolutionary red on its opposite side. Was the course of politics so easily reversible on Saint Domingue? The meticulous first impression Condillac made did not stand up to closer inspection. Tropical lassitude had done its worst: his white suit was stained with sweat and dried blood; vest buttons had popped off, under attack from his corpulence, yet he appeared malnourished. His complexion was sallow, his skin glistened with a dirty perspiration. His hair was stringy and hung limply from his scabietic, sun-blackened scalp. I wondered how long it would be before I resembled my dissipated host.

The political climate into which I had sailed was mercurial and confusing to even the most seasoned of diplomats. In metropolitan France, the revolution was in full flower, though of late the blossoming had become bloody. The Tuileries had been stormed, hundreds of the king's Swiss Guards and his royal attendants butchered by an enraged populace. Louis and Marie Antoinette were imprisoned, the monarchy abolished, their fate in the hands of the radical and bloodthirsty lawyers who had assumed prominence in the National Convention. Britain and Holland were massing their troops for war, determined to keep the fanatic anti-Royalism of revolutionary France from spreading across their borders. And in August, the infernal and efficacious *machine* of Dr. Joseph Ignace Guillotin was erected on the Place du Carrousel, where it stood waiting in steely ambush for the enemies of the revolution.

France was coming asunder, and I fully expected the chaos to be mirrored in her *outre mer* colonies. The blood that flowed down the cobblestoned byways of Paris could not be contained—the great Atlantic currents would eventually sweep it to the Americas.

"Welcome to the richest colony in the world," Condillac said as he led me aboard an official carriage. He slipped a pastille beneath his tongue, then lubricated his thirst with a drink from a pocket flask. He nodded to the driver, who cracked his whip with a shade more brutality than I felt was required, and, escorted by a detachment of soldiers with fixed bayonets, we plunged into the city.

How to describe the exuberance, the anticipation that possessed me at that moment! I, Nicholas Townsend, at twenty-three delegated to a mission of the utmost gravity on behalf of the United States! As the richest colony in the world, Saint Domingue was of great strategic interest; with a plantation economy similar to that of our American South, its future was a mirror of our own. Stories of a slave revolt had reached our shores; such a revolt, if it were to spread northward, could destroy the prosperity that fueled our young republic's growth. Essentially, I was to be the government's eyes and ears—I was to learn what the facts were concerning the revolt, and if possible determine how it could be stopped.

I began my work at once, sharpening my observational faculties on the myriad sights and sounds of this torrid seaport. I was determined to seek the truth behind the dull statistics Condillac had begun to recite with the weariness of a minister who has lost his faith.

"Our tiny island produces more than your United States, our revenue exceeds that of all the Spanish Indies combined, our foreign trade is double that of the British crown colonies. Last year alone, our exports of cotton, indigo, cocoa, tobacco, and sugar filled the holds of four thousand ships!"

The fortune of which he spoke had not created a scenic or commodious capital city. Port-au-Prince was, in the main, ramshackle and decrepit. It had rained the night before, and its streets were scarcely passable, little more than muddy thoroughfares streaming with effluent. Its citizens threw all manner of refuse, animal waste, and table leavings from their balconies onto the heads of their fellow citizens below.

"One in five French citizens owes his livelihood to our labors. Cotton for the looms of Normandy, one hundred sixty-three million pounds of sugar produced per annum, stoking the brandy manufacturers of Bordeaux, sweetening the coffee of Europe and America."

Sheep, pigs, and goats wandered untethered, adding their defecation to the general foulness; we passed the city's single public fountain, in which the population bathed, washed dirty linen, and soaked manioc for their kitchen tables. The outward manifestations of wealth appeared confined to the hillsides.

Freed from the architectural constraints of metropolitan France (and otherwise severed from the strictures of good taste), the planter barons of Saint Domingue had erected great houses of grotesque and exaggerated style, monuments to themselves and the success they had found in the colonies.

"All of it accomplished under the supervision of a mere thirty-eight thousand whites and an equal number of freed mulattoes."

The people of Port-au-Prince did not seem a happy breed. The whites were a motley group, primarily French, of course, but there were also Spaniards, Maltese, Italians, Portuguese, all of whom were suspicious, ill tempered, and appeared to be engaged in illegal pursuits. It struck me that the underworlds of Europe had been drained by the disgusted hand of God, with the unintended effect of diverting the flow of human refuse to Saint Domingue. But by far, the majority of the faces were black, their skin tones ranging from the coal-dust tint of Guinée to the perfectly proportioned mixture of black and white that was the mulatto's trademark to the *sang-mêlés,* who were so fair-skinned as to be indistinguishable from white. Though freed from plantation servitude by a complicated legal code I but dimly understood, these town Negroes also went about their daily business with a distrustful, burdened gait.

Presently we drew up in front of a substantial establishment, the Hôtel de la République. It faced a broad boulevard, whose landscaped median gave it pretensions to greatness. But the tropics cannot be denied, and the median was nothing more than a narrow strip of jungle, resisting all efforts to discipline its riotous growth.

"The finest hotel in the district," Condillac declared. "You'll be well cared for."

"But I had planned to visit the intendant straight away," I protested.

"As I said, he has been detained."

"But surely his schedule will permit us to meet at some point this afternoon."

Condillac grew irritable. "He will contact you when he is

ready, I am sure." I was about to offer further protest, but my valises were already being carried into the hotel by a quartet of ostentatiously costumed Negro porters. "You Americans and your insistence on getting down to business. You have had an arduous voyage, and you must take the proper time to refresh yourself. Do not attempt to interfere with the rhythm of the tropics, Monsieur Townsend. The patterns have been set for hundreds of years, and they are quite implacable." With those words, he deliberately shifted his bulk to afford me a view of the cane knife he carried inside his coat, then departed with a smile. He had used a diplomat's language to convey an ominous warning—there were profound and vexing forces at play here, and I was to interfere only at my own risk.

I had no time to entertain further musings, as I was immediately welcomed into the lap of Creole luxury. The hotel proprietor himself, Monsieur Fleuriot, a large, fussy man with an ornate, drooping mustache, showed me to my room. As he settled me in, I posed several questions concerning colonial life and his answer was always the same: "Paradise. It's a perfect paradise." I quickly discovered that in his version of paradise, a white man did nothing for himself, if he could secure a black man to do it for him. Fleuriot had only to stamp his boots on the floor to summon several silk-clad Negro attendants. Thus was I bathed, shaved, and groomed—one Negro to comb my hair, a second to cut it, a third to dress it. Fleuriot supervised at the point of a broadsword, and the slightest cosmetic miscalculation was met with a fierce slap across the back with the flat of the sword, and the threat of sharper reprisal should a second mistake be made. So total was Fleuriot's command, a young black was even permitted to shave me, his hands guiding the razor across my throat with a practiced delicacy that shed not a drop of blood. No sooner were my ablutions complete than a full meal was set before me by the prodigious kitchen staff—cold beef, vegetable soup, cod with browned butter, beetroot salad, fruits, and cheese—such as might have been enjoyed by a Parisian family of the lower bourgeoisie.

"A perfect paradise," Fleuriot repeated. "Back in France, I

was a miserable ploughman, perpetually in debt and drunk before noon. But here . . ." He did not need to complete the sentence, as his good fortune was quite obvious. He drew a finger across his upper lip. "The tropical climate has been unkind only to my mustache."

I had planned a quick, reviving meal and bath before setting out to present my credentials to the intendant, his schedule permitting or not. But the heavy dinner, the excellent brandy, the air, moist and smothering, and the general atmosphere of pampered indolence combined to produce a drowsiness so overpowering that I fell asleep on the bed fully clothed.

When I awoke, a night breeze was rippling the lace curtains, and I was no longer alone. Groggy with wine and sleep, I registered only impressions: the whisper of petticoats, the lush sensation of another's skin on mine, a warm breath against my face, smelling of pimiento and rum. She lay across me, permitting me generous glimpses of smooth, dark flesh, and murmuring musically in an African dialect. So deep had been my sleep that she had succeeded in opening my shirt, and her warm hands traveled my chest, following a lazy course leading ever lower. Though my Puritan brethren may find it painful to admit, the attraction of black women for white men is incontestable. I grasped her unbanded hair, a black spray that was indigo-tinted and lightly perfumed, and drew her mouth to mine. Her tongue seemed to have been dipped in red pepper. Her kisses burned, and soon kisses were not enough. In my young man's ardency, I became fevered and heedless, tearing and unlacing, abandoning all sense of delicacy, until I awoke fully and my reason abruptly returned. I sat up, propelling her backward onto the coverlet.

"Who are you?" I demanded.

Her answer was a disinterested shrug and a ripple of indecipherable Creole.

I grabbed her by her shoulders. They were hot, dewy with the perspiration that had passed between us. I lit a candle and drew it up to her face. She was quite beautiful, and though not yet out of her teens, her features conveyed an aura of unflappable worldliness. "I'm certain you were not included in the price of a room. Now, who sent you? What are you doing here? Come on, out with it."

"Je suis un cadeau," she said, without a hint of shame, in a French that was heavily accented. *I am a gift.*

"From who?"

"Monsieur L'Intendant. He would like you to meet him to-night at the opera."

"Opera! Port-au-Prince has an opera?"

Again she shrugged. "So it is said."

She slid off the bed and began matter-of-factly to relace the drawstrings my hands had undone. There was a sadness to her face in profile, her chin lowered, head tipped forward in a pose of perpetual obeisance.

I leapt to my feet, splashed myself with water from the basin. I was gravely insulted! I, a representative of the United States, that most egalitarian of nations, had been offered the bribe of a woman by a foreign official who I had yet to meet. I would confront the intendant that night, and disabuse him, in stinging terms if necessary, of the notion that an emissary of Thomas Jefferson's could be trifled with.

And what of my visitor? Though momentarily ablush with shame, my feelings of arousal had returned. I wondered if her kisses, despite their mercantile taint, had been offered with any passion at all. I cautiously approached her where she stood at the window, her skin bleached by moonlight.

"Miss, shall I call a carriage for you? Or would you prefer to share mine?"

"A mulatto? Sharing a European gentleman's coach?"

"I'm an American, if that makes any difference."

"Must you be so naive? Skin color is all that matters." She waved at the bed. "This is where the mulatto sprang from; in the eyes of the blancs, this is all we are good for."

———

As I mounted the stone staircase of the opera house, surrounded by the cream of Creole society, I reflected that the true spectacle of disguise and artifice was not the scheduled musical offering, but the theater itself. Though modeled at great expense after the majestic buildings of Paris, its rude, tropical underpinnings were everywhere evident. Water stains ran the length of its marbled walls, groundwater seeped through the floors like dirty blood oozing from a wound. The lobby's stained-glass dome had been split open by an invading vine, from which cavorted a screeching monkey, the bane of a bewigged, uniformed attendant whose sole job it was to drive the intruder back into the forest before curtain time. Tiny brown lizards gamboled everywhere, and I was startled to see several proper French ladies shake these annoying reptiles from underneath their skirts without losing a conversational breath.

But I was soon to realize that these ladies weren't proper at all, and the gentlemen scarcely merited the description. I entered the theater in search of my host, and spied Gilles Condillac in the balcony, among several well-dressed men and women. I made my way to their box via a back stairway, flinching as I passed a brilliant green snake coiled languorously in a candle sconce.

Condillac welcomed me showily, then introduced me to his superior, the colonial intendant, second only in authority to the governor of Saint Domingue himself. "Monsieur Townsend, may I present his honor Bertrand Rousellier, Duc de Caligny. Monsieur Rousellier, this is our . . . our American."

Rousellier was another species of colonist altogether. He was a man enjoying the full arrogance of his prime—tall, broad shouldered, impeccably dressed in black silk with a Royalist white cockade pinned to his lapel, his hair discreetly powdered and filigreed at the collar into taut ringlets. Powerful, sun-weathered hands extended from the effete embrasure of lace cuffs and shook mine with a threatening vigor.

"Duc de Caligny?" I said as our formal introductions concluded. "So you still employ your title?"

"As long as Louis XVI lives, I am his loyal servant."

"Which may not be much longer . . ." hissed Condillac, and I saw that he was quite drunk.

"Gilles! Please conduct yourself in the manner befitting your station. What will our young American guest think?" Rousellier said, in a tone more ironic than scolding.

". . . not much longer, not much longer." Condillac wobbled toward us and produced a gleaming straight razor from his breast pocket. "One of these fine days our 'nation's razor' will give dear little Louis Capet an expert shave . . . and your aristocratic neck will soon follow, Monsieur L'Intendant!" Before any of us in the box could react, Condillac had brought his razor to within a centimeter of his superior's throat. Rousellier was unperturbed and his eyes sparkled with mockery.

"You can see for yourself, Monsieur Townsend, the caliber of public servant which the revolution has produced, in its dedication to the advancement of the lower classes. When the dissolute and the barely educated are permitted to rule, our colony is doomed."

The rest of us in the box waited for Condillac's reply. But he had been rendered speechless. His razor hand shuddered, his eyes were red with drink and anger. Gradually, the aristocrat held sway over the commoner. Condillac's wrist fell limp, permitting Rousellier to snatch the razor from his hand. The intendant pushed his assistant away with callous disgust, as though discarding a suit of clothes that was no longer fashionable. Condillac stumbled drunkenly backward, landing literally in the lap of God—that of a priest who looked up irritably from the lascivious pamphlet he was reading, *Anandria,* a popular work detailing the alleged Sapphic liaisons of Marie Antoinette.

"So, Mr. Townsend, now that we have freed ourselves of this distraction, let us turn, in the minutes remaining before curtain, to a discussion of your little mission."

"Minutes!" Somewhat peevish, I pulled up a brocaded chair next to the intendant. "I had hoped for an interview of some depth. Not only with you, but with a broad cross-section of society. In addition, I have extensive travel plans . . ."

"Come, come. Your assignment involves a study of our political institutions, does it not? I must say, you Americans are inordinately fond of studies. As our island's preeminent politician, I am at your service. You need extend your study no further."

He turned away and exchanged sugary whispers with a trio of mulatto—I can only use the word *courtesans*—who had joined us.

"My orders are quite clear and quite comprehensive," I declared. "I am to gather intelligence on the current state of political affairs in Saint Domingue, especially as it applies to the question of slavery, assess the implication of whatever I might find on the foreign policy and well-being of the United States, develop recommendations, and deliver a report in person to my superior, Secretary of State Mr. Thomas Jefferson. The current state of affairs, as I understand it, includes a Negro revolt in the countryside. And that is where I intend to go."

"Revolt!" Rousellier exclaimed. "A word too dramatic by half. I would not use it to describe the riots of discontent which occasionally trouble us."

"Forgive me, Monsieur Rousellier, but there are half a *million* slaves under French jurisdiction. A 'riot,' as you term it, could quickly combust into insurrection."

Rousellier waved his hand dismissively. "Even were there ten million, surely you do not consider the average Negro laborer, this poor, docile soul with his diminished capacity to reason, and his even lesser affinity for discipline, capable of mounting a serious military campaign? Wars require planning, of which the Negro is incapable, and men of genius, which their race has failed to produce. Black skin and black blood do not admit the light of intellect, it's that simple."

Our discussion was interrupted by the strains of tuning violins. "Ah, our musicians have taken the stage. They may not be the equal of the orchestras of Paris and Vienna, but I have great plans for them. When the opera house is finished, I hope to persuade Master Haydn himself to appear."

"Oh, I'm sure he can be yours for the price of an ocean voyage and a mulatto whore," I snarled, but the overture drowned out my remarks. The performance, as I expected, was dreadful, without finesse or nuance. To distract myself from the music,

I studied the audience, beginning with the scandalous occupants of my own box. Rousellier followed the performance from a musical score spread in his lap, while his female companions stroked him lasciviously and strategically, all the while drinking from a crystal decanter of rum. The women possessed a ravaged beauty—their once pristine skin was blistered with insect bites, their eyes yellow from disease. Even the priest did not want for mulatto companionship. He made for a notorious picture. His genitalia were exposed, shockingly white against the black of his cassock, the object of leisurely caresses by a young courtesan who sat with her head on his shoulder, smoking an opium pipe and staring vacantly into space. Completing this scene of surreal decadence was a large iguana lizard tethered to the same courtesan's ankle. A fat and pampered pet with a diamond pinned to its throat sac, it roamed freely and energetically, occasionally eliciting squeals of delight as its nimble tongue darted into an ear.

The audience below was raucous and inebriated, drinking and eating with abandon. Though dressed in the finest silks, their purses bulging with silver, their crude origins could not be disguised. It was as though a broken mirror had been held up to the true aristocracy, and these pitiful parvenues were its fractured reflection.

Suddenly, as the orchestra was struggling through a diminuendo passage, one of these faux aristocrats bolted to his feet, screaming. His hands flew to his throat as blood spouted from his mouth. He was a large, strapping fellow, but he seemed to shrink before our eyes, doubled over in agony. *"Quelqu'un m'a empoisonné!"* he shouted. *Someone has poisoned me!* His words unleashed an uproar in the auditorium. Plates and bottles shattered on the floor as the audience cast their provisions aside, fearful they had been tainted.

Rousellier tore himself free of the women and, joined by several armed dragoons, charged down the back stairs and into the fray. My blood coursing with excitement, I was but a few paces behind. The scene was one of utter confusion, with everyone shouting and pointing in different directions. I quickly deduced that we were dealing with a deliberate attack, rather than an accidental poisoning.

"Seal the building!" Rousellier shouted to his officers. "The culprit must still be close at hand." The soldiers dispersed throughout the hall, bayonets at the ready. A young doctor arrived and bent over the unfortunate victim, who had fallen to the floor, writhing on his back in a frenzy. Though the doctor managed to administer diverse medicaments, his efforts proved fruitless. The victim soon expired with a fearsome death shudder, and a final spray of odious green bile issued from his cracked lips. A silence gripped the room, but the doctor summoned his professional detachment and immediately subjected the victim's teacup to a rigorous examination.

"An admixture we have not seen until now," he told Rousellier at length. "Sea worm, althea root, asafetida, perhaps a disguising trace of attar of roses."

"This has happened before?" I exclaimed.

Rousellier did not answer. He stroked his chin thoughtfully, well aware of the frightened faces looking to him for leadership. He removed his broadsword from its scabbard and slammed it into the floor with brutal authority. "Damn it, I want this bastard on the scaffold within the hour. The poisoning of our citizens by these . . ."

"Docile souls?" I interjected. Before he could reply, there arose a scuffle on the stage. A dozen soldiers appeared, bearing in their escort a tall Negro dressed in the breeches and brocaded waistcoat of an opera-house usher.

Rousellier stiffened with cold hatred. He marched deliberately to the stage, his sword extended in front of him, its tip on a perfect line of collision with the Negro's ebony throat.

"You are the criminal who has perpetrated this outrage?" he asked the Negro. "Mind how you answer . . . when a member of your race lies, it is readily transparent."

The black captive was silent. He was young and well muscled, with penetrating eyes and heavy, weathered features that bore the lash marks of a stern plantation overseer.

"Well?" the intendant prodded.

When still the Negro refused to answer, Rousellier bored the sword point into the swell of his Adam's apple, then drew it slowly downward, cutting through the silk fabric as though it were butter, bringing it to rest at the man's groin. The crowd pressed forward, anxiously awaiting the malefactor's confession. Instead, he threw his head back, and exposing his yellow, rotting teeth, emitted the most horrible, nerve-rattling laugh. At first the assembly was stunned, as the laughter echoed off the high-domed ceiling and coiled through the galleries, a music of defiance. But the seed of vengeance soon took root, sprouting clamorous calls for the poisoner's execution. Several men drew pistols, ready to perform the deed on the spot.

A calm descended on Rousellier's features. "No, that is too simple. We must never allow ourselves to be overcome by the narcotic of the mob, to descend to the level of the rabble over which we preside. They are not the *enemy,* they are the *property.* Why should we not profit from them, even as they misbehave?" Focusing a scornful gaze on the prisoner, he concluded with an ominous proposal: "Having forced an intermission on our entertainment, I see no reason why he should not serve as the second act. I invite all of you herewith to my home, where we will bring this interrupted evening to a memorable conclusion."

———

BERTRAND Rousellier lived, or rather I shall say *reigned,* from a hillside villa, a tropical homage to Versailles. An armada of official carriages bore us up into the cool mountains; a regiment of liveried servants met us beneath the porte cochere and escorted us into the ballroom. It was a scene of rococo splendor worthy of the Bourbons themselves, an outpost of excess far removed from the revolutionary terror that gripped metropolitan France. We guests arranged ourselves against walls lined with rare books and Gobelin tapestries, while servants circulated with trays of crayfish, partridge, and truffles imported from Périgord. My appetite was diminished by the scene just witnessed, yet the others set to with a hearty diligence. I sensed a crackling aura of anticipation; the conversation was conducted in excited whispers. Despite my questions, I, as the only American and indeed the only outsider, remained unaware of what the evening portended.

Suddenly, a hound brayed and a hush fell over the assembly. From one end of the hall, a quartet of soldiers appeared with the Negro prisoner, now stripped of everything but a loincloth. Eyes widened, and ladies gripped the arms of their gentlemen escorts with a sensuous ardor. Through the opposite doorway strode Rousellier himself, leading, or more properly, led by two of the fiercest, most formidable mastiffs I had ever seen. Their fawn-colored coats glistened in the oil lamps, saliva dribbled from between rows of deadly, artificially sharpened teeth. Their eyes I would never forget—roving hellish pits colored with a red-hot fury and a hatred of all things human.

When Rousellier spoke, his words were counterpointed by the deep growls of the hunters, anxious to be let at their prey. "You see before you two of the finest examples of the slave-dog breeder's art. They come to us from Jamaica, where the English, despite everything we may think of them, have made startling advances in canine husbandry. Over there," he continued, motioning to the prisoner, "we have Narcisse, as he tells me he is called, an African of impressive stature, well bred in his own way, twenty-five years ago in the kingdom of Dahomey. In a contest to the death, I am sure the superior breeding will show."

The crowd thrilled to this speech, and money changed hands as bets were placed on man or animal. The dogs were clearly in fine fettle, but a controversy soon arose as to the physical condition of the Negro. "Test for yourself," Rousellier offered, then added with a licentious smile, "better yet, let your ladies test for you."

As Narcisse strained ignominiously in his bonds, several women approached him. They danced their tongues across his neck, his cheeks, his ears, even pirouetted lustfully between his lips, using the slave trader's trick of verifying a man's health through the taste of his perspiration. Clearly flushed and aroused, the ladies pronounced Narcisse in the peak of condition, and retreated (rather reluctantly) to the embraces of their men. With that, Rousellier executed a grand flourish, and at the same instant, Narcisse and the dogs were unleashed.

At first it was little more than a manhunt, with Narcisse playing the runaway slave, and the Jamaican dogs assuming the roles for which they had been bred. The chaotic chase unfolded throughout the mansion, the Negro's powerful legs outpacing the mastiffs, whose claws skidded on the marble floors, depriving them of traction. The guests pursued as best they could, shouting drunken encouragement to one side or the other. The contest took a heavy toll on Rousellier's furnishings—Oriental vases toppled to the floor, entire settings of the finest Sèvres porcelain were smashed to bits, claws and teeth ripped their way through velvet upholstery. But the intendant only laughed at this wanton destruction, explaining that he would simply order replacements from France. At length, this cruel spectacle led to a small parlor from which there was no exit. Narcisse seemed doomed, his back pressed against a great limestone fireplace as the hounds closed in. It was at that moment that the nature of my mission changed, and my view of the world was forever altered.

Fear vanished from Narcisse's face, and he grew distant and stoic. A deep, rolling African chant issued from his lungs, and the whites of his eyes seemed to expand. As the first dog launched himself at Narcisse's throat, the Negro shot out his hand with the speed of a coachman's whip and snatched a candelabra from the mantel. Just as the greedy incisors were about to close down on his flesh, Narcisse thrust the flaming candles into the dog's face. Howling in agony and shock, the mastiff dropped to the floor, from where Narcisse plucked him with ease. He whipped the stunned creature above his head by its hind legs, then hurled it through the stained-glass window that gave out onto the garden. I had a brief glimpse of the dog hobbling into the night, his back ribboned with blood and studded with glass fragments. Then, the second dog sprang to assault. He fared worse than his companion, for Narcisse was able to intercept him in midair. Narcisse sunk to his knees, encircling the dog's neck with the ever-tightening force of his grip, until, not twenty seconds later, the animal expired. The Negro carried the dog to the doorway, where Rousellier waited in disbelief. As though it were no more than a sack of grain, Narcisse contemptuously dropped the prize Jamaican hound at the intendant's feet. The Negro spoke for the first time, in a pidgin Creole-French, which I shall here paraphrase: "This is why you French are doomed—you send dogs to fight the wars you are afraid to fight yourselves!"

This brazen remark drew a sharp inhale from the crowd, but Rousellier did not lower himself to respond. Instead, he summoned his soldiers and addressed them in a petulant tone. "This man has justly won his victory here tonight, and has earned the only true freedom any of us will ever know." For a moment, there was the dimmest flicker of optimism in Narcisse's eyes. "You may escort him to his prize—the scaffold, in the Place des Armes—tomorrow at noon, so our hardworking citizens may share in his reward."

If nothing else, Rousellier displayed a subtle flair for cruelty as he confounded Narcisse's nascent hope for freedom. I concluded that this was symbolic of his style of governance, the whip hand alternating with a brief promise of mercy, the codified punishment of French justice complemented by the capricious tortures of a planter class that were a law unto themselves.

But as Narcisse was led away, now wilted and drained of all rebelliousness, the true mystery of the evening's events seized me. From whence had this ordinary black servant taken such composure, such fearlessness, such inhuman strength? I had remarked it in his eyes and in his hands: he had become somehow other than he was. It was as though in his moment of supreme crisis, he was able to summon a transforming agent from the blood itself. I surveyed the other guests. Had they not seen it? Or were they simply too terrified to acknowledge it?

I walked back to town alone, desirous of the company of my own thoughts. The night gathered around me, a night heavy with secrets. Chief among them was the black secret, the African secret, the source of the awesome power that had descended on the humble frame of Narcisse, the poisoner. I realized that I had been transformed, too. I was no longer the blushing envoy who had stepped ashore that very morning. I felt possessed by a fresh and feverish ambition. I would discover the source of that power myself, no matter what the cost, and no matter what the danger.

8

It was dawn when my hand cramped and my mind went limp. I stared at the fifty pages I'd written. Where had this voice come from, this Nicholas Whitney Townsend who'd seized control of my pen to write his two-hundred-year-old diary? I now realized that the visions I'd been having had sprung directly from these memoirs, like magazine excerpts from the past. This was insane—was I turning into some sort of literary Shirley MacLaine?

But I had a larger problem than my apparent total personality collapse. I was in a potential life-ending jam, so far beyond any trouble I'd ever imagined that it didn't seem real. What do you do when you've just killed a man? Not a mugger, not an intruder who you gun down in the shadows of your bedroom, but someone who innocently befriended you, someone who even the police know you were looking for? *Don't panic, Ray, think!* You empty your bank account, change your name, and head to the nearest country that doesn't have an extradition treaty with the United States . . .

. . . or you call a lawyer.

Lucy Marcelin answered her door in a bathrobe that was so

blocky and shapeless, it seemed designed to make its wearer as unattractive as possible. But even in my derangement, I saw that it wasn't working: she was as appealing as she had been the night we'd met, maybe even more so because now she was off guard and unposed.

"Mr. Falco. First you call me at five A.M., then you fax me, now you show up in person at six. Are you sure this is really the way to a girl's heart?"

"You going to offer me a drink?"

"What?"

"Never mind. I've got one." I rooted a bottle of vodka out of my jacket pocket. "I stopped at a market on the way over and paid the kid a twenty to sell it to me. You want . . . nah, it's probably too early for you."

She tried to close the door in my face. Good for her. If she'd welcomed me with open arms, I would have been suspicious.

"Lucy, please. I've got to talk to you. I know, my mind isn't connecting the dots very well right now . . ."

"You *do* look like shit," she said.

"Just give me ten minutes. After that, if you don't want to hear anymore, I'll throw myself out. I've had plenty of practice."

She opened the door, offering a narrow fissure barely wide enough for me to slip through. Her apartment was well kept and sunny, but surprisingly unexotic. There was no trace of her Haitian heritage among the department-store furniture and Impressionist prints. Even the palm tree was plastic. Half of the living room was partitioned into a law office. It looked like it had been furnished on a single shopping spree to a discount warehouse: there were matching desk, chairs, bookshelves, and coffee machine, even a tiny waiting area complete with the requisite boring magazines.

"Coffee?"

"I'll stick with the vodka."

"You need coffee."

"How about when I've finished the bottle?"

"You're plea-bargaining already?" She saw me flinch with alarm and said, "It's a joke."

"I wish it were." Concerned, she sat across from me, and I caught a flash of brown thigh between the prudish folds of her robe. I sank into the couch, suddenly aware of my intense exhaustion, of my desire to drift into a comforting sleep in this woman's apartment: maybe I could awake to her kisses, fragrant with the tropics, and find myself in a new life, where we paraded around naked and wore hibiscus blossoms behind our ears, a life where I wasn't a murderer. Instead, I nipped at the vodka and let it do its icy damage.

"Raymond, what is this about?"

"Do you have any criminal-law experience?"

"I studied it, of course."

"I mean practical experience."

"I've defended a couple clients against shoplifting charges, that kind of thing. I got 'em off, too."

"Misdemeanors. That's better than nothing, I guess . . ."

She produced a box of Gitane cigarettes from her robe and lit one with jerky impatience. "They're French, the one youthful habit I find impossible to break. Now, come on, Raymond, lawyers are the specialists in delay and obfuscation, reporters are supposed to get to the point."

"OK, here's the point: I killed someone tonight."

Before she could react I described the death of Jean-Mars Baptiste, but then, the dam burst around me and I spilled it all—the sickness, the visions from the past, the destruction of my free will. I spit out my story violently, skipping over words and pauses, rushing without breath to the end, grateful that at last, someone else would know what I knew.

"Why come to me, Raymond?" she asked placidly.

"Weren't you listening?" I exploded. "I just killed a man for no reason! My whole life is spinning out of control, and I have to get a grip on it somehow. I need a doctor . . . shit, I probably need a lobotomy, but at the very least I need a lawyer! I mean, you're no Alan Dershowitz with millionaire clients. I'd think you'd fall over backward for a case like this!"

She sighed, and her shoulders sagged momentarily. She walked to the window and opened the Levolors, admitting a hazy light. With her back to me, she said, "There are a hundred highly qualified criminal attorneys in this city who would kill— forgive the pun—to represent a prominent journalist like you. Again, why me?"

"I need a Haitian lawyer, Lucy. This whole thing . . . it's closer to your experience than it is to mine."

She puffed thoughtfully on her cigarette, taking a lawyer's time. But when she turned around, there was something beside cold deliberation in her look; there was fear.

"Raymond, I'm sure *something* happened to you out there . . ."

"That's right. Something! Not murder, not self-defense, but some new species of crime altogether. No blue-chip D.C. lawyer is going to take that leap of faith with me. I need someone with an open mind."

She waved her fingers at me in a hocus-pocus gesture. "Someone with 'oogah-boogah' on their résumé, is that it? Someone who knows their way around a voodoo doll?"

"Am I trespassing on hallowed ground here or something? I didn't go looking for Haiti, it found me. My money's good. And I'll make a perfect client—I'm direct, I avoid unnecessary adjectives, and I always try to tell the truth. If you have a real reason for turning me down, tell me."

Her gaze bored straight through me, through the wall behind me too. "I'm sorry, Raymond. It's not you, it's not the money. But this whole thing, it takes me back. And I hadn't planned on going back there. Ever." But for several long moments she *was* there, in her past, a place where werewolves flew and America was a hopeless dream.

I realized that her cool facade was a defense against the buried emotions my case had exhumed. "I think you've seen this kind of thing before," I said. "Back in Haiti . . . this has happened to other people, hasn't it? *Tell me this has happened to other people!*"

Lucy drew the bathrobe drawstring around her so tightly, I

thought she would cut off her breath. "Maybe . . . I mean, people say it has . . . I heard stories my whole life. . . ."

"More than stories," I shouted. "The loup-garou was a story, too, but now it's here!"

"Sometimes you can't tell fact from fiction in Haiti, you can't separate myth from lies. So many people down there believe so many things. . . ." Her eyes began to water, her lips were trembling. "That's why I love the law; the finite language of a contract, it's so consoling." She peered uneasily through the blinds, then looked up at me, the invader who'd pierced her orderly exile. "But there are no laws to cover what's happening to you, Raymond."

"So we'll set a legal precedent." I finished the vodka with a grimace; it had turned strange and bitter. "There's something weird about fear, Lucy. No one wants their fears to be unique; but if you can find just one person to share it with, then you've got a shot."

Lucy started to light a fresh cigarette, then stopped; the match slowly burned itself out. She was wavering, ambition warring with doubt. "Is that supposed to describe you, or me?"

"Take your pick."

———

THE murder scene was quiet, except for the trilling of summer insects. The blacktop was already baking in the early morning sun as we got out of my car and walked across the road to the culvert. The car was gone; the body was gone!

I dropped to my knees and dug furiously through the weeds. "Are you sure this is it?" Lucy asked. "These country roads do kind of look alike."

"It's not something you forget, OK?" I snapped. "Your first corpse tends to stick in your mind." I worked my way along the culvert for a half-mile, knee-deep in brambles and beer cans, but it was useless.

"They came back for him," I declared at last. "There's no other explanation."

" 'They.' Meaning the loup-garous."

"Don't give me that look, Lucy. I know what I saw, I know what I did!"

"But why would they take the body away?"

"Maybe they want the whole idea of Jean-Mars Baptiste to simply disappear. No eleven o'clock news, no bloody pictures to stir up the emotions. No publicity, no funerals, no martyr."

"And the most important question of all," she said. "Why kill him in the first place?"

"Political rivalry, I assume. Plus, he was about to break some major story to me. He said he'd discovered what they were up to . . ."

" 'They' again."

"God, I don't know. Maybe this is just an elaborate scheme to make me seem crazy. I think it's succeeding." I shook my head, squinted into the dizzying heat. Seconds later, I threw myself back into the search for evidence, madly rooting like a bloodhound, reaching into rat holes and snake dens.

"Raymond, please, you don't need to do this."

"Oh, yes, I do. You don't believe me. And I don't blame you."

But I finally ran out of room as the culvert narrowed to a dead end against a tar and gravel driveway. I stayed there on my knees, letting the flies and gnats slap at me as the sweat ran stinging into my eyes.

Lucy came up behind me and, spreading her hands across the back of my neck, began a slow, consoling massage. "I believe that you believe, Raymond. Sometimes that's the most the defense can hope for."

"You don't think I'm a raving lunatic with an outrageous fantasy life?"

"I'm saying I'll take the case. I'll start it, at least. Eventually, we'll need a bigger gun, someone on our team with more court experience."

I couldn't pick her face out of the low sun that flared behind her, but her hold on my neck was sure, almost possessive. I had been waiting for the perfect moment to tell her about the Nicholas Townsend diary, but now I held off. I didn't know how it fit into the Baptiste case, but it definitely was not an advertisement for my sanity. Why add an additional layer of craziness now that she had agreed to represent me?

"I think you're worth saving, Raymond. One thing I've noticed about life—too often the good people drown, and the scum manage to swim to shore."

I took her hand. Her narrow brown fingers were hot, and agile as a spider's legs. I felt a pulse pass between us, a definite non-lawyer-client buzz. I had an urge to kiss her, to seal our contract. But then I saw them, tiny fragments glimmering in the shadows of a storm drain that ran underneath the driveway. I had trouble picking them up; they kept skittering away against the smooth metal of the drain. But finally I pincered a few between my fingertips and brought them out into the sunlight.

They were the slivered remains of Jean-Mars Baptiste's glasses, tinted with his blood.

———

"WOULD you like to see a psychiatrist?" was Lucy's first question on the way back to the city. I drove; she entered furious notes on her electronic agenda. "He could run a couple tests, just so we have something on the record."

"I know right from wrong, if that's what you're getting at. I can appreciate the meaning and consequences of my act, which I believe is the legal definition of sanity. I don't hear voices, and I don't feel persecuted—any more than your average member of the press does—which lets me off the hook as a paranoid schizophrenic."

"I was just asking. I know a good one if we need him."

"An insanity defense? Come on."

"The more traditional approach would be to develop a not-guilty plea, but that won't quite work in this case, will it? By the way, where's the murder weapon?"

"Back at my place."

"You better let me keep it. You have the papers on it?"

"Actually, I stole it. But that should help, shouldn't it, make it harder to trace?"

She shot me a look that wavered between disgust and admiration. "You thought this thing out quite carefully, didn't
you? That sounds like premeditation to me."

"I didn't know what I was going to use it for! Besides, there's
no way to connect me to that gun . . . unless the pawnshop
had a video camera."

"Which I intend to investigate." She touch-typed herself another note.

I merged onto the commuter gridlock of the Beltway. "Look
at them: drinking coffee, listening to talk radio, planning how
to hit the boss up for a raise. The daily grind never looked so
good." I took Lucy's hand. "And none of them knows about
me. About the potential threat I represent. What if it happens
again? Who'll I go after next?" Lucy shivered and I saw the fear
collect in her eyes.

I felt a moral duty to hand myself over to the police. But I
was also practical, and I knew that our justice system was not
flexible or creative enough to accommodate my crime and its
inexplicable motives. I pictured the trial, and the ambitious,
quotable prosecutor who would gleefully tear me to shreds in
front of a disbelieving jury. The Flip Wilson defense, he would
call it: "The devil made him do it!"

Lucy and I decided that the best move I could make would
be no move at all: I wouldn't turn myself in, but I wouldn't
run off to an isolated cabin, either. I would pester Walter Paisley
from time to time, show him I was still in hot pursuit of the
loup-garou case. Let myself be seen around town, a journalist
on the comeback trail, working a story of political intrigue.
Meanwhile, Lucy would help with the cultural translations as
we tried to decipher just what the hell was happening to me. I
dropped Lucy off, then went home. It took an hour of sanding
on my new hardwood floors until I was exhausted enough to
sleep.

———

I wasn't used to lawyers getting results so quickly. By the next
afternoon, when I picked up Lucy in front of her apartment,

she had traced the loup-garou cars to the Haitian embassy. My voice rose an octave as I sputtered in disbelief. "Incredible! And my retainer hasn't even cleared the bank yet. This seems awfully easy."

"Maybe I'm just awfully good."

Lucy looked strict and respectable in a business suit, her wild, lush hair restrained by a conservative ribbon. "I spent the morning in Baptiste's neighborhood. People are terrified: maybe they'll be the next to be burned out. But some of them want revenge, too. A guy I once did some free legal work for saw your mystery car leaving the scene the night of the fire bombing. It still had its dealer tags."

She handed me faint, carbon-copied sales contracts for two 1975 Pontiac Bonnevilles, purchased from a dealer in College Park, Maryland, by an export-import firm at 2311 Massachusetts Avenue.

"There aren't many addresses in this city I know by heart, but that's one of them—it's the Haitian embassy."

I allowed myself a dose of excitement. "If you're right, Lucy, if this connection holds up, that's 'Made in the USA' terrorism: this story just jumped to the front page!"

Lucy tilted her head at me quizzically. "A story, Raymond? That's how you see this?"

"We have an allegation, and now we look for corroboration. Journalism 101."

"This is your life, not a goddamn headline! I'm putting together a murder defense here. When we get to the embassy, I'll do the talking."

"*I'll* do the talking," I retorted.

We glared at each other in a frigid stand-off. Lucy curled her lower lip and blew the hair out of her eyes, a habit I would come to know as a warning sign of supreme, pissed-off irritation. She wasn't completely tuned in to me. She couldn't sense the battle that was raging inside me, the desire for self-preservation pitted against my compulsion to write the Jean-Mars Baptiste story.

The Haitian embassy was a haughty, nineteenth-century

mansion on Sheridan Circle, the discreet, regal heart of embassy row. The shades were drawn to conceal its occupants' obscure duties: shredding documents, denying visas? The Haitian flag, drooping in the heat on a rooftop armed with communications antennae, was the only reminder that this was the outpost of a Third World nation.

I drove right past it.

"Raymond, what are you doing?"

I headed northwest, toward the city limits. The cars around us were filled with homeward-bound bureaucrats, loosening their ties and rolling up their sleeves, dialing husbands, wives, dates on their mobile phones.

"Turn around. I had to do some serious string pulling to get us an appointment. We may never get a crack at them again!"

I realized I was following signs that led to the Beltway, the border between Washington and the rest of the world. I tightened my hands on the wheel, turned on the radio.

"Come on, what is this?"

"Is it hot in here?" I asked. I turned on the air conditioner. It acted its age, wheezing and gurgling, filling the car with gasoline-tinged room-temperature air. I merged onto the Beltway, reversing directions, southwest bound now.

"Oh, God, it's happening, isn't it? Right here, right in the middle of everything." I watched her press a hand to my forehead, hold a thumb to my pulse: *watched* her, but didn't *feel* her. "You don't have a fever, but, God, your pulse is just roaring." She looked crazily out the window: four lanes of shrieking traffic, taxis, Metrobuses, eighteen-wheelers, all driving with big-city arrogance, sixty miles per hour, bumper to bumper. "Take the next exit . . . no, we'll head for a rest area or a turnout, there's got to be one coming up . . . no, pull over now and let me drive. Pull over *now!*"

I ignored her, veered onto the Dulles Access Highway. It was rush hour in the skies too; I saw jets backed up to the horizon, silver dots in the setting sun.

"The airport?" she cried. "Come on, talk to me, tell me what we're doing!"

My voice was paralyzed. No, not the voice, the synapse, the nerve bridge, whatever it is that links thought with speech . . . it was burned out! I looked at Lucy with eyes that I knew communicated nothing. I was pleading with her to read my mind: *I don't know where this is leading, Lucy . . . I don't know how to stop it . . . it could be just a weird, harmless detour or . . . it could be something much worse; the last time this happened . . .*

Search the car, Lucy. Search the car!

Traffic was beginning to clog as we approached Dulles International Airport. Pinpricks of anxiety exploded on my skin—was something going to happen here? Surrounded by thousands of people, would I . . .

"Listen, I'm going to stay with you, Raymond. You don't need to go through this alone." Lucy tightened her grip on her purse, on the armrest; Lucy at her self-possessed, managerial best, ready for battle. *That's great, that's very reassuring . . . but search the goddamn car for a gun!*

I was on the departure level now; I cut in front of three lanes of traffic and stopped in a loading zone. I focused on my hand, mentally ordered it to move. It twitched minutely, the fingers flexed, testing themselves; then, like a paralyzed limb rediscovering the thrill of movement, it reached in front of Lucy and opened the glove compartment.

There was no gun this time.

Lucy's eyes flared with understanding. "Where's the gun, Raymond? Help me out here!" She rooted between the cushions, snaked her hands beneath the seats, peeled up the floor mats. "The trunk!" She vaulted out of the car, ran to the back, lifted the trunk lid. I heard her rummaging, thudding the jack against the fender. She slammed the trunk shut, then announced, "There's nothing there, thank God."

But I was already on the sidewalk, marching toward the terminal entrance. She caught me at the automatic doors; they hissed open like a panicked inhale and held there as she tore at my shirts, my pockets. "Is it on you, did you buy another one? This isn't some country road in the middle of the night, you can't just . . ."

Two airport cops beelined toward us, alerted by Lucy's rising voice and the loud complaints of luggage-heavy travelers who were forced to detour around us.

"Is there a problem here, ma'am?"

We stepped completely into the terminal. Lucy was breathless and frazzled; I was sure I looked ravaged, stunned, like some creature who had spent its life chained in a basement.

"Ma'am?" The cops pressed in on us; curious passengers drifted closer. It was the crossroads: here were armed men; if they heard the right words from Lucy, they would take me into custody. If I had murder in mind, she could stop me here! Like twins, the cops simultaneously stroked their regulation mustaches and switched to wider stances. Their earnest good looks invited a full confession.

"It's my husband's plane!" Lucy blurted. "If he misses it, the boss'll kill him. C'mon, honey, they're boarding!" She dragged me away from the cops, who continued to stare, knowing they hadn't heard the whole story, wondering if it was worth pursuing. I tore free from Lucy's grip and sliced through the ticket lines, stepping over suitcases, pushing loaded baggage carts to the side. I stepped onto a down escalator, following the signs to the baggage-claim area.

I counted the escalator steps in front of me as they were sucked into the floor, into mechanical, greasy darkness. I pictured the headline: REPORTER SEES LIFE DISAPPEARING ONE STEP AT A TIME.

When I ran out of stairs, I realized I'd reached my destination. It was here.

What was? If I looked carefully, maybe I would see it. I wandered through the loud, energetic hustle, paying close attention: shiny baggage carousels spitting out suitcases, hysterical, high-pitched reunions, cats crying behind the bars of their carriers, skycaps balancing towers of luggage.

"Ray, you all right?" Lucy laid a hand on my shoulder.

"It's here, Lucy. Right in this room."

She wilted in relief. "Thank God you're talking again. You

scared the hell out of me . . . I mean, you really *are* back, right?"

This attack had been sneaky, gradual, the physical symptoms less violent. I had lost, then regained control of myself with surprising ease; did that mean I was getting used to it?

I was definitely back—suddenly, Lucy's presence was immediate; fragrant, physical. Her dark, incisive eyes were moist, sweat pearled on the smooth brown skin of her neck, then began a lazy, downward trickle. I curled an arm around her waist, felt her skin flutter beneath the silk blouse, felt our thighs brush, making heat contact. "Let's get out of here," I said. "I don't know what the hell I'm looking for."

"Hold on, if there's something here, I'm going to find it!"

"How? You got a way to plug into my brain?"

"Maybe it will help if we get your impressions down while they're fresh. I've got a cassette recorder in my purse; we can go to the coffee shop . . ."

"Lucy, please . . ."

She shifted out of my embrace. "You hired a lawyer, not some go-fer you can dismiss with a wave of your hand whenever it's convenient. This is a twenty-four-hour relationship, OK? And it is a *two-way street*! These feelings, these urges, whatever the hell they are, they are the keys to your defense."

"Would you please move?"

"What?" she barked, with all the indignity she could muster. I simply planted my hands on her shoulders and moved her myself.

The steel wall gleamed behind her like a chrome monolith. Luggage lockers, wall to wall, floor to ceiling. I ran over to them in a fever of discovery: "This is it, this is what I'm supposed to find!" I raced along the rows of lockers, gliding my hand over the cool, smooth surface, reading the numbers with my fingers as if they were braille: 134, 135, 136 . . . I stopped in front of locker 140. It was on the top row, nearly beyond my reach. I stared up at it, magnetized, expectant.

"It's locked, Ray," Lucy said. I shook it, gently, then violently, but the door wouldn't budge. Lucy took my hand: "The key, don't you see? The key's gone."

"The key. Right. What was I thinking?" I reached into my pocket, an icy channel that seemed to go on forever, that threatened to swallow my hand, my wrist, even my arm . . . and pulled out the key to locker number 140.

The lock was sticky, but it yielded. I swung open the door; Lucy pushed onto her toes.

Empty.

Lucy's chin fell. Too disappointed to meet my gaze, she turned away to watch the luggage moving down the endless conveyor belt.

I reached into the locker, probing through dust and shadows. It lay flat against the back wall. I closed my fingers around it and slid it out. A manila envelope. Inside was a videocassette.

———

IT'S dark, there's no sound. But someone's there—cigarette embers glow, flitting about like fireflies.

Overhead, a light flickers stubbornly to life, casting a dim, dirty cone. Pale yellow walls, peeling paint, water stains. A calendar of Swiss alpine scenes. A workbench strewn with tools—wrenches, pliers, hammers, calipers. It looks like a garage.

Two black men pacing, smoking. Neither over twenty-five. One wears denim overalls, the other jeans and a T-shirt.

There's a desk. A stack of paperwork, ruffled by a slow moving fan. Empty beer bottles. Battered, rusting electrical devices. Jumper cables.

A metal chair. There's someone in the chair, legs, arms, and waist bound to it with thick leather straps. Face and figure obscured by shadow. But the ankles are those of a woman.

The man in the overalls lifts her face into the light: brown stringy hair, eyes purple with bruises, cheeks stippled with cigarette burns, lips split open, caked with dried blood. Cuts and lacerations, some tiny and surgical, others ragged and crude.

A single tooth has been knocked loose and lies orphaned on the woman's collar.

The man in the overalls reaches for a bottle, a soft drink. The label is barely visible—Teem. He props her head back, takes lazy aim, and swings the bottle into her fragile jaw.

A sticky green explosion. Glass sprays. Thick, sweet, syrupy liquid dribbles down the woman's neck. It glistens, it gels. Flies circle and land.

She does not react. No muscular quiver, no neuron flinch. She may already be dead.

A door opens, a tall, wiry figure fills it. He wears a khaki uniform with purple and red accents, his shoulders are heavy with gold braid. His face is gaunt, his eyes appear hollow. He issues an order, then withdraws.

The man in the overalls calmly picks glass from his clothes. Then opens the woman's blouse; aloof, businesslike, immune to the soft white skin. The man in the T-shirt fine-tunes a setting on a piece of electrical equipment. Tests the jumper cables, knocking them together with a fierce red spark.

He walks toward the chair with the jumper cables. Behind him, on the desk, the fan blows a sheet of paper aside, exposing the blue and gold cover of an American passport.

The screen goes black.

9

WE WATCHED IT over and over in Lucy's apartment, transfixed and silenced. Guilty spectators, unable to turn away from even the most brutal moments. I tried to imagine the woman's last seconds of consciousness, her final glimpse of life—had it been the torturer's bony hands closing around the bloody calipers, or had she managed to fight beyond that, casting her gaze over his shoulder to the Swiss calendar on the wall? Darkness falling on brilliant green meadows and bright snow.

The doorbell rang. I nodded at Lucy, and she answered it. Tony Randolph pushed in, wearing jeans and a sweatshirt, unshaven, serious, carrying a briefcase, a cellular phone, and a Styrofoam coffee cup.

Hurried, sober introductions: Lucy became a Haitian lawyer whom I had hired to help me in my research.

Tony sat on the couch, watched wordlessly. He rewound, and ran through it again in slow motion.

"I'll have two thousand words by noon," I said. "Accusing the Haitian government, acting with the full knowledge of President Isidor, of terrorism in the Baptiste firebombing, assault and intimidation of exile opposition figures legally resident in the United States, *and* the torture of an American citizen. It would be nice if I could also report what our government is doing about it."

He paused the tape, freezing the digital date at the bottom of the picture. "Three weeks ago. Where'd you get this, Ray?"

Lucy and I exchanged shifty looks.

"For the record," I said, "a source who insists on remaining confidential. After seeing the tape, can you blame him?"

"Any idea who she is?"

"None," I answered. "An American in Haiti, she probably registered with the embassy down there . . . that'd be a good place to start."

Lucy fast-forwarded to the moment when the uniformed figure appeared at the door. "The uniform is that of a colonel in the *garde présidentielle,* President Isidor's private security force."

"It's not the army?" I asked.

"The *garde* is there to protect the president *from* the army. Ever since Jean-Jacques Dessalines, Haitian leaders have been deposed by the military, even when they were generals themselves. Papa Doc finally understood this; he created the Macoutes as a buffer against the army. Baby Doc took it one step further and added the Leopards, basically a private paramilitary unit, like having your own Green Berets to play around with."

"Didn't help *him* much, did they?" Tony pointed out.

"Who knows how long he would have lasted *without* them?" Lucy stopped the picture at the exact second when the bottle exploded into the woman's jaw: "Here's the point: this atrocity was approved at the highest levels of the Isidor government."

Tony rubbed his assaulted eyes. He skimmed through my notes, which were neatly arrayed on the coffee table. "This kind of hot-button item, it gets on the airwaves, we've got a public outcry. You get Rather going, 'We should warn you that the following pictures are graphic,' and the whole goddamn country suddenly snaps to attention at the dinner table."

"I would hope so."

Tony's forehead furrowed suspiciously. "I hope I'm reading your signals wrong . . ."

"I paid a guy I know who works at an all-night lab to dupe it for me. The day after my story appears, the networks and CNN will have the tape."

"Damn it, Ray, this should be handled through diplomatic channels; this is extremely sensitive material!"

I nodded at the TV screen; the picture was still frozen on the unidentified woman's battered features. "*Sensitive* is not the word that springs to mind."

"I appreciate your outrage, and believe me, I share it. But life is not that clear-cut."

Lucy snorted. She lit a Gitane and blew an angry jet of smoke toward the ceiling.

Tony ignored her. "For example, what if this woman turns out to be an intelligence asset of some kind? By broadcasting this tape, you are also running a very high security risk. You may even be endangering the people around her. . . ."

"You're falling back into government-speak, Tony. Does Livia let you get away with that shit?" A taut silence. A new element had snuck into the conversation. Tony glanced at Lucy, then back at me, probing for the nature of our connection. "Haiti's a 'nonstory,' remember?" I added. "Why would we have intelligence assets down there?"

Tony began to pace. Lucy and I watched him squirm—government in action, the decision-making process up close, without makeup.

"OK, listen. I'll talk to the seventh floor, see if I can get some movement on this. Maybe we can at least call in the Haitian ambassador, see what he has to say in private before . . ." His voice trailed off, as his attention was drawn back to the torture video, morbid, compelling, accusatory. "Jesus Christ, I can think of at least five congressional-committee chairmen who are going to go ballistic. They'll call the White House, the White House'll call the Secretary, he'll call the deputy secretary, he'll order an investigation, and I'll have to go to bat against a press throwing hundred-mile-an-hour fastballs. You've really nailed me to the hot seat on this one, you know that, Raymond? But then, that's what you love about this, isn't it?"

———

By the next evening, America had seen what I had seen (albeit in an abridged version) and had read my latest story, or at least heard it quoted on their local news. I was perversely gratified to find that my reputation endured:

"Raymond Falco, a reporter with a national reputation for hard-hitting exposés . . ."

"If these shocking allegations are true—and considering they were made by a highly respected veteran newsman, we have no reason to believe they are not . . ."

I had once been a tireless tirader against the growing influence of television news. I had pontificated in bars and newsrooms against TV anchorclones and their mini-vocabularies, their Bahamas suntans and their double-breasted suits, their looks of faux sincerity (as in "troubling story, Joan, really makes you think"). And now, this same dumb-as-spit institution was paying me their respects.

But I couldn't deny the power of pictures. The tape had the mesmerizing immediacy of the Zapruder film. It was a shock to the national system: everyone knew that torture went on in Third World dungeons, but people didn't usually torture Americans, or they weren't cocky enough to photograph it. Other reporters joined the chase; the national news magazines moved in on the story. Haiti, that poor, exhausted dot on the map, was growing, it had media sex appeal now.

The next afternoon, Lucy and I attended an anti-Isidor demonstration outside the Haitian embassy. Like most Washington protests, it was a mixture of carnival, righteous indignation, and misinformed nonsense. Soca music thumped out of boom boxes erected on the fringes of the crowd, speakers chanted and harangued through megaphones, fists were raised, slogans improvised. Of course it was all for the cameras.

A Mercedes limousine wound its way through the crowd. Haitian flags fluttered on the fenders, the most symbolic flag in the world—the French tricolor with the white ripped out, replaced by an insignia of palm trees, cannons, drums. The protestors and the media surged toward the ambassador's car, pulling us along. I saw the ambassador get out, a plump, gold-decorated, double-breasted figure dazed by the TV sun guns. I forced my way to the front, my voice rising with a power and volume that stunned me; I became a magnet for lights, lenses, and tape recorders. "Mr. Ambassador, is your government doing anything to guarantee the safety of American citizens in Haiti?" I yelled. It was a nice sound bite, guaranteed coverage.

He turned to the other reporters, pointedly ignoring me. "I would like to assure you that Haiti is a civilized country, and that all visitors are treated with courtesy and respect. However, I have not had time to fully analyze the videotape in question, and thus am not prepared to comment on the matter at this time."

The smirking insincerity didn't play; angry questions went off like a string of firecrackers. Camera crews closed in hungrily, forcing the ambassador and his bodyguards into a stoop-shouldered retreat. I started after them, then felt Lucy's nails dig into my hand. Annoyed, I tried to pull away. Then a faint mental alarm went off—Lucy didn't have long nails.

I was holding someone else's hand!

Suddenly, everyone else seemed two-dimensional; Carmen Mondesir stood out from the crowd like an elegant piece of black iron sculpture, silver earrings set off against black hair like distant stars. It was the first time I'd seen her in natural light; her beauty seemed slightly damaged, there were trace lines of age beneath her eyes.

She skated her fingertips up my arm, then closed her hand roughly around the back of my neck, as though she were about to pull me into a violent kiss. Her lips hovered just above mine, her eyes were dark invitations. We seemed linked in a suspended, erotic charge. "Just to let you know that I'm watching," she said.

Before I could answer, she slipped away. I felt warmed by her afterglow, but unnerved by her cryptic warning. I became aware of the demonstrators again, saw Lucy pushing toward me.

"What the hell happened to you?" she asked.

"We got separated somehow."

"No, I mean, you look odd, like you saw something."

"It's nothing, really," I said. I scanned the crowd, which was breaking up now that the ambassador had fled indoors.

Lucy led me to the car, pecking on her electronic agenda. "Listen, maybe you can squeeze some headlines out of all this, but I'm not getting anywhere." She gave me a frank, demanding stare, hands planted on her hips. "I need five hundred dollars."

"OK . . ." I stammered.

"You're entitled to an explanation, you know."

I didn't react; I was still distracted by my encounter, trying to explain Carmen Mondesir's puzzling appearance. She was watching me—was that an expression of approval or a threat?

"Expense money," Lucy said. "I have to go up to New York for a couple of days to see a . . . specialist."

The word caught my attention, with its nebulous but alarming implications. "Medical or psychological?" I asked.

"Maybe both . . . then again, maybe neither."

––––––

I couldn't sleep. Nothing anesthetized me, not even a six-pack of beer with a vodka chaser and a Halcion nightcap.

The figures in my life were out there, moving: Lucy in New York, consulting with her "specialist"; Walter Paisley ordering a genetics report on the loup-garou skin from a lab in Cambridge; Etienne and Helene Baptiste, hiding and plotting; State Department bureaucrats and Haitian embassy officials deciding how to handle the crisis I'd brought them; and the killers who'd twisted my hand toward murder . . .

And I was here, pressing the brakes and the accelerator at the same time. There had to be something I could do.

The answer was obvious and natural: a writer writes. I walked downstairs to my office and took out the Townsend manuscript from the fireproof safe. I readied ink and paper, trimmed back the wick on an antique oil lamp I'd overpaid for at a Fredericksburg auction, and struck a match. I felt optimism in its warm, smoky glow; I could lure Nicholas Whitney Townsend's voice back to these blank pages. He would feel at home here, among these two-hundred-year-old beams and bricks. Exploring worlds that don't appear on everyday maps, forcing out answers—that's what journalists do. If I could just control this one thing—words—maybe I could begin to reclaim myself.

But it didn't happen that way. I stayed there all night, without writing a line. The oil burned down, the sun came up and rolled slowly across the sky. I didn't move from the desk, didn't eat or drink, even as the afternoon heat sucked breath out of the air, and I thought I would faint; I knew that if I got up, the words would never come.

Darkness, the second night. I refilled the lamp, threw away the sweat-stained top sheet of paper. I was miserable, cramped, my head pounding in exhaustion. Then I heard church bells. Louder than usual, they chimed in relay, ringing across the countryside. Somehow, they were a signal. My writing hand jerked to life, spastic in its eagerness to be into the ink and onto the paper.

10

Even in death were the races of mankind separate on the island of Saint Domingue. The church bells tolled in announcement of the pending executions: two white murderers awaited their appointment with the scaffold in an upholstered carriage parked under the shade of an acacia, sipping Malaga wine at royal expense and enjoying the last-minute attentions of grieving relations; while the black condemned, among them the proud Narcisse, squatted in mahogany cages, denied all refreshment, exposed to the ferocity of the meridian sun.

I saw that the regiment which guarded the slave compound had grown distracted by their dice games. I hurried across the Place des Armes and bent down to engage Narcisse in conversation. The other slaves were at their prayers, if one might call them that, murmuring tearfully in their African tongues, drawing obscure symbols upon their bodies with scraps of charcoal and reading the cowrie shells, as though attempting to divine God's intentions once they had passed into his care. But Narcisse sat apart, seemingly unafraid, his penetrating gaze focused on the scaffold.

"I believe I am addressing Mr. Narcisse?" I began in my halting French. My words provoked no response. I saw, upon closer inspection, that his brow was carved in concentration, his lips moving in a studied cadence, as though he were meditating upon some profound matter. "Lately in the employ of the Royal Opera?" I added.

At last he looked up at me, neither welcoming nor hateful. From my portmanteau I withdrew a portion of salt fish, which I passed to him through the bars.

"Your food is wasted," he said. "I shall not live to appreciate its nourishment."

"You'll live long enough to enjoy its taste. Can I at least offer you that?"

I observed a flicker of humanity in his eyes. He accepted my charity, dividing the fish among his wretched comrades. "Tell me, why does a blanc deliver food to a condemned slave for any purpose other than sport?"

"I was at the intendant's home last night. I was an eyewitness to your astounding display of courage, of resilience . . ."

He snorted with contempt. "A spectator, after all."

"A reluctant spectator, though I don't expect you to believe me." As we talked, there was a sudden slamming of doors and shutters as the merchants who plied their commerce on the Place des Armes closed their establishments. Each report elicited a corresponding shudder of fear from the captives. "The hour approaches," Narcisse observed. Executions were scheduled at noon so that slave and citizen alike might enjoy a bit of spectacle during their midday respite.

"Then I shall press my inquiries with haste. Mr. Narcisse, I am not unfamiliar with the institution of slavery, nor do I deny that the seed of rebellion does on occasion take root in the Negro heart. But the calm rage I witnessed last night, the self-possession, the strength required to dispatch those two mastiffs—these are not tools God grants to the ordinary man." I grabbed the mahogany bars with such force that the blood fled from my knuckles. "I must know the source of this transforming power! Is it alchemy? Can you summon it at will?"

Narcisse smiled. "You are a young man, with a young man's questions. Tell me, what sort of society is America?"

"Open-minded, I should say. We welcome new ideas, we embrace progress, we love mechanical things."

"And are Americans capable of heeding a warning when it is offered to them?" he asked, his voice darkening.

At that moment, a regiment of soldiers entered the square, followed by the intendant's coach—a traveling salon, to be more precise, inlaid with ivory, the decorative bronze wheels designed for the cobblestones of Paris spinning in the tropical dust. The crowd, knowing the moment of high drama was at hand, gathered in excited groups; vendors moved among them, offering demijohns of brandy and assorted confections.

"Warning?" I asked in alarm. "Please, Mr. Narcisse, if you wish to unburden yourself to me, in God's name do it now!" I arranged quill and paper so that I might preserve his final thoughts in my report.

But he was once again fixated on the scaffold, where the executioner, an amply fed official who saw no reason to conceal his identity beneath a cowl, was making final adjustments to the tools of his trade. "Nineteen and three-quarter minutes," Narcisse pronounced. To my look of perplexity, he added, "By calculating the height of the gibbet and the strength of the rope, and considering my own weight and heart rate, I have concluded that death will take me nineteen and three-quarter minutes after the trapdoor opens. Mark it on the church clock and see if I am not correct."

I was stunned by this simple slave's mathematical prowess. But before I could resume our conversation, the guards appeared. Shackled at the ankles, the Negroes were led past the laughing, bloodthirsty crowd, their iron chains stirring a wake of dust to mark their doleful progress. I trailed after them, giving Narcisse sips of rum from my pocket flask. The irony of a Christian offering sustenance to a condemned pagan on his way to the gallows was not lost on me, yet so desperate was I to comprehend Narcisse, I risked this religious transgression.

The church bells ceased their tolling. So silent was the crowd, it was as though a giant hand was pressing down on them from heaven. The intendant himself, Bertrand Rousellier, Duc de Caligny, took up a position at the head of the audience, flanked by his ministers and several ladies of exuberant voluptuousness and pampered complexion. They were dressed for the occasion *à la sauvage,* an African-influenced style that was then the rage of Paris: breasts swelled beneath diaphanous silk; thighs beckoned from beneath daringly cut skirts of gauze; bare, well-turned ankles were ringed by diamond circlets. Rousellier snapped his fingers, and his aide, Gilles Condillac, appeared at his side bearing an enameled box. From this Rousellier withdrew a scented and powdered wig, an explicit symbol of unrepentant aristocracy, which he carefully arranged on his head. He then called for the executions to begin.

The whites died first, so that the blacks might suffer in dreadful anticipation, so they might witness the agonies and better imagine the noose on their own necks.

The whites died on their own scaffold, an expertly carpentered affair of polished wood and carved balusters, trimmed with gilded crucifixes and attended by a doting priest. Their time of death was noted to the second by a trio of physicians; they were cut down immediately and transported from the scene in black-draped coffins.

By contrast, the Negroes were dispatched with a shoddy brutality. Several stumbled while mounting the steps and had to be whipped into completing their last walk. They plummeted through the trapdoor wild eyed and without benefit of blindfold, their last vision of life on earth that of a joyous, leering audience of their masters. They were allowed to hang there, flesh baking in the sun, the crowd pelting them with fruits and vegetables, wild dogs nipping at their legs. Finally, a frisky, tousle-haired youth raced beneath the scaffold and placed a live explosive charge in the mouth of one of the corpses, wedging it under the dead, blood-spattered tongue. The blast that followed was grisly beyond description: the body was not fully detonated, rather it was ripped open like a peeled banana, sending forth a fetid cloud reeking of human entrails and fluids. It was all to the delight of the crowd, and the anticipation of the carrion hunters circling above.

I had seen more than enough. I marched across the square and confronted the intendant. "As a sworn representative of the United States, and as a loyal ally of the French people, I insist that you call a halt to this cruelty!"

The ladies giggled, the ministers exchanged disapproving whispers, and Rousellier offered me an indulgent smile. Over my shoulder, I saw Narcisse mounting the scaffold, stoic and unbowed.

"And how would my young American friend propose we administer justice to a slave?" Rousellier said. "With a slap on the wrist and an appeal to his reason?"

"With a quick and merciful touch. With respect for the human body, even after the soul has departed. And without this immoral theater!"

Rousellier pushed forward in his chair. "I've read the letters of introduction that preceded your arrival, my young friend. I have acquainted myself with the details of your biography. As the heir to a Virginia fortune, modest though it may be, you are the sole owner of one hundred Negro slaves. *Your* property, over whom you exercise utter command from birth to death. And you presume to lecture *me* on morality!" Rousellier leapt to his feet, raised his hand, then dropped it to his thigh, an unmistakable signal to the executioner. "Our citizens have waited long enough. Let's kill the black bastard, and have done with him!"

As the rope was fitted around his neck, Narcisse's eyes found mine. I made my way to the gallows, Rousellier's accusations ringing in my ears. "Tell your Americans that General Xavier Charlemagne marches under the flag of the gods of Guineé," Narcisse called down to me. "I am but one of thousands of his devoted soldiers, his immortals. You blancs will never tame him, never defeat him."

"This General Charlemagne, where can I find him?"

"Follow the path of the burning cane in the Plaine du Nord."

I pressed him to amplify this enigmatic response, but Narcisse was lost to me by then, lost to this world. Behind shuttered eyelids, his vision was already wandering, back to his youth perhaps, back to the Africa of his ancestors. He began the melodic chant I'd heard at Rousellier's mansion the night before. He briefly opened his eyes, and spoke in French-Creole, addressing himself to some distant point in the sky: "The god who created the sun which gives us light, who rouses the waves and rules the storm, he watches us. He sees all the white man does. Our god who is good to us orders us to revenge ourselves. He will stoke our fires, and direct our arms . . ."

Then the trapdoor opened, and he dropped. I watched the church clock, and it was as he had predicted: nineteen and three-quarter minutes elapsed before the last breath of life escaped his body.

I lingered in the Place des Armes long after the crowd had dispersed and the torpid rhythms of the day had reestablished themselves. I stayed there even as the sun descended into the miraculous blue Golfe de la Gonâve, and the dangling form of Narcisse passed into shadow. The scavengers flocked, vultures and hawks feasting on the sweet flesh of the corpses.

Only Narcisse was untouched.

———

THE great Plaine du Nord was the agricultural heart of Saint Domingue, and was well served by commercial transport. I booked a seat on a fiacre bound for Le Cap François, a prominent harbor town on the island's north shore, and home to the governor and the Colonial Assembly. I slipped out of Port-au-Prince as quietly as possible, informing no one of my intentions—that I had vowed to find, and if possible interview, this black general Xavier Charlemagne, who seemed to inspire such selfless loyalty in his followers.

The road leading north was well established, and the traffic, pedestrian and equestrian, was as bustling as one might find on any Richmond thoroughfare. My traveling companions were a young, bespectacled Catholic priest from Angers, Father Rochefort, studious and highly polite, and a Maltese ironmonger, his sample case bristling with the deadly-looking appliances unique to the sugar refiner's trade. Quite content to exchange harmless pleasantries, they both fell silent when I introduced the subject of General Charlemagne. When I pressed the topic, the ironmonger addressed me in an exasperated tone: "By the accent I can hear that the gentleman is a foreigner, so permit me to enlighten him. This is not a name which is discussed among whites in the northern provinces. If the gentleman hopes for successful travels, above all for safe travels, I advise him to abandon this line of inquiry." With that, he wormed into his corner and dropped into sleep. Father Rochefort regarded me over his spectacles with suspicion before returning to his Breviary.

Thus, I contented myself with remarking on the passing landscape. It was a terrain of immense and diverse productivity, marked by sweeping vistas of sugarcane, lush fields of tobacco. Great plantation houses, their latticed galleries open to the tradewinds, presided like palaces above gentle acres of cotton and indigo, one man's holdings often extending a dozen leagues or more. And the mountains! Towering, verdant peaks blanketed with mahogany forests, enough wood, seemingly, to float the world's navies.

But as dusk drew on, the commerce of the road acquired a more sinister tone. Soldiers appeared, often escorting columns of slaves that extended from horizon to horizon. To our heavenly God they must have appeared as black ants, and indeed they were treated as such by their French masters. The cultivation of sugarcane required prodigious numbers of workers, and because it was more economical to work a slave to death than to provide an adequate level of sustenance, thousands of fresh recruits arrived each month. Many of the unfortunates that we now passed wore tin face muzzles to prevent them from nibbling at the raw cane during their labors; others bore knife scars in the hollows of their knees, the sign of a tendon deliberately severed to prevent escape.

By nightfall, the highway was deserted save for our group. The coachman grew more insistent with the whip, and our pace doubled; even the horses, it seemed, were keen to reach shelter. Anxiety mounted in my fellow passengers as they leaned out of the carriage, closely marking our progress. I lit a lamp, in an attempt to dispel the fear that was gathering about us, but it served only to accent the darkness of the tropical night just beyond the road, a night blacker and thicker than those of my native Virginia. We rode on in moody silence, each alone with his thoughts and dreaming of light.

Thankfully, we reached our destination within the hour. Au Savanne Rouge was a sugar plantation that also served as a travelers' inn. It lay at the crest of a fertile plain, flanked on three sides by trackless jungle. We were met by an energetic cadre of stable boys, who immediately saw to the horses and the billeting of our driver, while we passengers were led up a stone path to the main house by a valet de chambre of indeterminate age and dignified bearing.

But the warm and welcoming aura of gemütlichkeit vanished as we passed beneath the canopy of chinaberry trees that overarched the path. What a repulsive, unforgettable sight! Affixed to the tree trunks were all manner of human body parts—black ears, black feet, black hands severed at the wrists, the palms pierced by spikes, the fingers curled in an agony that seemed a grotesque mimicry of the crucifixion. Genital parts dangled from overhanging limbs. I saw a human head impaled on a pike, a beautiful and flamboyant bird perched contentedly on its decaying scalp.

The author of all this horror met us at the door. To my surprise, she was a comely young woman, not yet out of her twenties. She introduced herself as Esther LaMartiniere, recently widowed and cast, despite her tender years, in the twin roles of innkeeper and plantation seigneur. "I hope you'll forgive the decor," she said. "But there are Maroons hereabout; escaped slaves who have formed themselves into armed bands. I thought I should give them a taste of what they can expect if they ever show up for the full meal." To my look of astonishment she appended: "Well, I didn't kill them myself, sir. It was the fever that done that." She patted her cook's apron impishly. "Though when called upon, I am handy with a knife and cleaver."

Thereupon we were shown to our rooms—rude but adequate—and after a brief bath, I met my compatriots in the dining room for the evening meal. There were six at supper, we three from the coach, a married couple from the north, and Esther LaMartiniere, who joined us. She supervised her servants with a discreet but attentive hand, and, judging by the alacrity with which they performed their duties, the relationship between mistress and staff was a congenial one. The meal was superb, not the French cuisine of the capital, but an expertly prepared buffet of provincial dishes—hawksbill-turtle soup, boucanned pork in coconut milk, river pike in a sauce of black mushrooms, calves brains in spiced butter. And the wine! A more delightful display of vintages was impossible to imagine, even in the great salons of Europe.

Taking notice of my undisguised enjoyment of her table, Mrs. LaMartiniere gave me a conspiratorial wink. "Shall I share my secret with you?"

"But I've always heard a good hotelier never parts with his secrets!" I exclaimed.

"When the secret comes at the expense of those damn Continentals, I don't mind a whit," she said. She refilled her glass, then drained it at a single sip; she was certainly no stranger to the fruits of the vineyard. "There is a class of people in Paris— those damnable creatures of the *grands appartements,* with their snuff and their lavender water—who regularly send the best bottles from their cellars to Saint Domingue and back, so that the wine will age on the sea voyage. I have . . . 'contacts' down at the harbor who snatch the occasional shipment, replacing the stolen bottles with identically labeled duplicates. So tonight, while we drown our sorrows in this Haut-Brion, the Vicomte de So-and-So must settle for . . ." she took a second, identical-appearing bottle from the *chariot,* and passed it around so that we might smell it, ". . . pomegranate juice!"

As we guests lingered at table, enjoying the product of this chicanery, the ambience of the inn underwent a change. Esther LaMartiniere hurriedly supervised the clearing of dishes and the lighting of additional lanterns. She secured the front door with a staggering variety of locks, then lowered into place a massive iron bar. She and her staff repeated these precautions at each of the windows and doors. Within minutes our inn was transformed into a veritable citadel. I felt like a medieval crusader bracing for a Moorish onslaught.

The pitch of anxiety rose as brandy was served, the fire was stoked, and we drew our chairs into a circle. When Esther joined us with flintlocks and ramrod, her apron pockets heavy with powder, the picture of fear was complete.

It was then that the drumming began.

"That is the sound we heard the night we lost our plantation." It was the husband of the married couple that spoke, his voice freighted with terror. He was a coffee grower named Tessier, with a hawk's-beak nose and thin, fleecy white hair. He grabbed the brandy to fortify himself, and as I took assiduous notes, he told us his story: "It began with the poisonings, first in the cattle that withered and died, then in the coffee trees themselves, which were felled in scores by a disease which the most skilled herbalists of the region failed to diagnose. Then it spread into the house: one by one, our dogs died, and we endured a sudden plague of snakes and reptiles, all of them venomous. The poison found its way into the wine, the wells, even into the fruit which we plucked fresh from our yard. Suspecting our own slaves and servants, we banished them from our service and tried to continue the operation ourselves. Marie-Christine and I were forged in the snow-driven *cols* of the Jura Mountains; we were not so easy to dislodge." Here he caressed his wife's thigh, and drew a forlorn smile from her pale lips. "So they turned to other tactics."

As the drumming increased in volume, Tessier walked to a window and pressed his hand to the shutter. "They came on a night such as this, the drums so loud they breached the very walls of Hell. By morning, it was all gone." He swept his hand in a circle around the parlor, asking us to picture the devastation.

"Foolishness!" spat the ironmonger. He pointed toward Esther's flintlock. "Show him the barrel of a pistol, and there's not a nigger in the world who won't show *you* his backside."

Esther, with her own property to consider, felt an obvious kinship to Tessier, and appeared greatly moved by his tale. *"Et maintenant?"* she asked. "What of the future?"

"England," he sighed. "Or Switzerland. A small shop, perhaps. A simple life, as far from Saint Domingue as God and our meager savings will permit."

Esther considered this for a moment, then began to load her pistols. "All well and good for you, Monsieur Tessier. For me, an impossibility. My husband did not die so that I might surrender Au Savanne Rouge to those thieving hordes. I have always treated my blacks fairly, provided them with a living ration, left them their Sundays free, even when it was my account books that suffered, not theirs. Look at them!" she shouted. Her servants, from scullion to liveried valet, were going tirelessly about their duties, oblivious to the drumming, which had become increasingly fevered. "Do you read anything other than respect on their faces?"

"Perhaps the African's face is not for us to read," remarked Father Rochefort, who had been silent until now. He took the hand of a young servant boy, who had arrived to replenish the brandy, and drew him into the firelight. "Regard the mouth, the eyes . . . can any of you extract even a spark of commonality from his expression? He may appear bland, unaffected, but it is a disguise he adopts in our presence. He feels the drums, I assure you."

"Bah, what of it?" sneered the Maltese.

"The drums summon their gods. The African slave is a highly religious creature, and as history has taught us, a soldier with God on his side is a formidable force, indeed." Father Rochefort's words cast a spell of dread over us. I found myself contemplating the shuttered windows, intrigued by the nocturnal activity unfolding just beyond, wishing for a cat's eyes to pierce the darkness. "Indeed," he added, "many remote outposts have banned the *calenda,* the night dance at which the slaves call down their gods."

"It seems you have made a study of these issues, Father," I observed. He nodded in humble acknowledgment. "Would you deem it possible that a slave, in the presence of these gods or otherwise held in the thrall of his religion, might perform impossible feats of strength, might acquire talents far beyond our imagining?"

"A penetrating question, monsieur," he replied.

I blushed slightly with pride. But then, my blood quickened—here could be an explanation for Narcisse's behavior!

"A brief instructional might be useful. Mark this word, for you will hear it frequently the further you penetrate into the interior—*vodoun.* It is the slaves' religion. The word derives from the Fon language of Dahomey, and means 'God,' or 'spirit,' but do not think the African views God with the sublime enlightenment of we Christians. There is a Supreme Being to be sure, *le bon Dieu,* but he is a distant father figure, no more awe-inspiring or threatening than a petty French official. The true follower of vodoun serves the *loa,* the spiritual manifestations of God that are responsible for the phenomena of life: love, nature, war, power. In their ceremonies the Africans do not simply worship these gods, they strive to become them."

Father Rochefort polished his spectacles on the sleeve of his cassock, then stared into his untouched brandy glass. When he spoke again, his voice was firm, yet subdued. "Thus, the African regularly commits a sin that is beyond theft, beyond adultery, beyond even murder. By seeking to become God, the African insults God, weakens Him, even calls His very existence into question."

Father Rochefort walked to the parlor window and drew back the shutters. So violent had the drumming become that the glass vibrated in response. Pinpricks of fire were visible on the far side of the valley, their flames reflected in Father Rochefort's spectacles, lending the young cleric a wild and hellish demeanor.

"Which is why the Africans on our shores, and their religion, must be *exterminated!*"

Throughout this discourse, I had been quietly readying my dueling pistols. The table discussion, at first stimulating, had grown tiresome. In my forthright, American way, I longed for action. I had been about to propose that we form a scouting party and set out in search of the mysterious drumming, but the force of Father Rochefort's words shattered my resolve. Here was a man of God, a sober and articulate thinker, so intimidated by the Negro forces that he was proposing drastic, and dare I say, inhuman reprisals. While I intended to rely on my wits, my pistols, and my enthusiasm.

I felt small and foolish. But I did not tarry in my recriminations, for at that moment, a face appeared at the window behind Father Rochefort! It was a terrifying visage, and I briefly imagined that we were under attack by an unknown race of mankind; but then I realized it was a slave, wearing a tin face-plate as a disguise.

"They're inside the wall!" shouted Esther LaMartiniere. I ran forward, and just as the cane knife flashed toward the glass, I slammed the shutter against the would-be intruder. Footsteps coursed violently outside the house; the shutters rattled and threatened to splinter as though shaken by a driving tempest; the iron bar that secured the front door thundered. Esther handed out muskets and organizing ourselves into brigades, we ran from window to window, holding back the assault.

In response to a shattering of crockery, I led a charge into the kitchen. The china cabinet that had been used to barricade the back door had toppled. A welter of black arms tried to force their way in, ferocious tin faces gleaming in the lantern light! Taking careful aim, I fired my father's pistols in anger for the first time. The attackers withdrew, and by listening to their retreating footsteps, I judged them to be few in number.

"An advance party," I said. "They're just testing us. If they had sufficient forces, they would have broken through by now." It was the truth, but it did nothing to lessen the terror of that long night, as the enemy, unseen and therefore doubly dreadful, probed at us, played with us, raising our hackles in anticipation of a final assault that never came.

No one slept, no one dared abandon the lamp-lit refuge of the parlor. Bottle after bottle of brandy was consumed, and the drumming threatened to drive us all to the brink of lunacy. But as dawn began its weary advance, the drumming receded, and by sunrise, silence had descended on Au Savanne Rouge.

Exhausted, yet grateful to be alive, we emerged cautiously onto the grounds. The activities of nature seemed to have been suspended: birds did not cry, insects did not trill. Even the grass scarcely rippled beneath our feet. The air was thick with the smell of burning sugarcane, and smoke hung on the horizon like soiled linen. The fields on the far side of the plain, so verdant the night before, were scarred black; through her spyglass, Esther verified that two of the neighboring plantations had been put to the torch.

Just then, the servant boy who had been the subject of Father Rochefort's attentions ran up. In the Creole dialect, he breathlessly reported that a dozen slaves had deserted during the night, carrying their cane knives with them. "Twelve more damn rebels," Esther spat, "living for the day they can return to slaughter their masters."

"It was the same the night our plantation burned," observed Tessier, the coffee grower. "It is the work of the black general, Charlemagne."

"Then he exists! He is not a myth!" I shouted, grabbing Tessier by the collar. "Have you laid eyes on this Charlemagne yourself?"

"No white man has seen Charlemagne. The Negroes explain this by attributing to him the power of invisibility; I say he's simply a damn fox, as comfortable in the jungle as you or I would be on a city street. He is said to be an expert marksman, a tactical genius, so skilled with a cane knife he can behead a man without spilling a drop of blood on his collar." Tessier raised his gaze to the jungle that loomed behind Au Savanne Rouge. "Since he appeared in the Plaine du Nord during the last rains, the numbers of local Maroons have grown by thousands. Plantations, even villages have burned; atrocities have been committed against the *grands blancs* of the north. This is not the sporadic terror we have grown used to, runaway slaves settling personal debts of revenge. This is a campaign of conquest; under the command of General Charlemagne, our ignorant slaves threaten to become an army."

I had reached a perilous crossroads in my mission. If General Charlemagne was truly the figure of awesome prowess both follower and foe made him out to be, if his army was poised to sweep across the fertile landscape of the richest colony in the world, bent on destroying the institutions that were the engines of European, even American prosperity, then I was at a crossroads of history as well! Perhaps I was swollen with youthful ambition, overripe with confidence; perhaps I pictured myself returning to Virginia a conquering hero, rising to the upper echelons of government on the coattails of Thomas Jefferson, who I was certain would one day be our president; or perhaps, having missed the opportunity to distinguish myself during our War of Independence, I simply longed to be blooded: I could not divine the current that predominated in my emotions; I knew only that I must act.

I inhaled the smoke from the distant, dying cane fires, and, imagining it to be the smoke of battle, addressed the frightened assembly: "Then let us track down this General Charlemagne, and take his measure ourselves. He cannot be far. A small company, traveling light and moving expeditiously, should aprehend him by nightfall. Do I have any volunteers?"

11

I WAS RIPPED out of an exhausted sleep by the twentieth century—the demanding chirp of a cordless phone. It was late morning, the oil lamp had burned down, and the ink had dried on thirty-five new pages of my alter ego's diary. Somehow, I had fumbled into bed, mummifying myself fully clothed in the spread.

The answering machine picked up: "Ray, it's Walter. Call me on my private line as soon as possible. I think we may have a problem."

I had always hated that phrase. When "*we* may have a problem" dribbled from the lips of authority figures—editors, doctors, cops—it always meant "*you* have a problem."

I locked up the journal in the fireproof filing cabinet. I showered and coffee-ed, sharpening myself for my conversation with Paisley. He answered on the first ring.

"We got an ID on the body at the project, Ray."

"Really?"

"What, you didn't think we could do it?"

I didn't let on how relieved I was to learn that we were dealing with a flesh-and-blood corpse instead of a werewolf. "Police

142

science marches on, Walter. Nothing's beyond you guys. So who was he?"

"We don't know."

"I thought you said—"

"He's parts of a couple people, actually. About a month ago, Howard University Medical School reported the theft of two teaching cadavers. They buy them from medical suppliers, who buy them from morgues, hospitals—usually they're John Does. Our mystery man was assembled from the cadavers, stitching done with transparent fish line so it would look seamless if you stumbled across it in the dark."

I tried to piece this information into the story. Clearly, someone had gone to a great deal of grisly trouble to frighten Jean-Mars Baptiste and his followers by playing on their voodoo beliefs. But what works in the Haitian countryside hadn't worked in America—Baptiste hadn't backed off. Was that why the gun had been placed in my hand?

"Sicker than shit, isn't it, Ray? Demented, totally whacked-out stuff . . . but it's not murder."

"So then we *don't* have a problem."

"I didn't say that. Last time we met, I showed you a picture of a man we now know to be Jean-Pierre Baptiste . . ."

"Mars," I corrected. "His name is Jean-Mars."

"Well, this whole goddamn case is from Mars, so that doesn't surprise me. I don't know what his connection is to our . . . John Doe, but it appears that he's been missing since that night. Anytime a well-known politician, exile or otherwise, drops from sight, we go on full auto. Mr. Baptiste is now an official missing-persons case. Any idea where he might be?"

"Still missing, if you read my article."

"I read it with great interest. As a matter of fact, I've come across a ton of interesting reading lately. Baptiste's mobile-phone record is a real page-turner."

I stiffened, held the coffee in my mouth, felt it burn my tongue.

"The night after your first article appeared, he called you on your *car* phone, at nine forty-six P.M. That conversation lasted for fifty-three minutes and nineteen seconds. He's awfully damned communicative for a missing person, wouldn't you say?"

Dead air over the phone sounds doubly suspicious. I rushed to fill it: "How do you know it was Baptiste himself who made the call?"

"Are you denying that you talked to him, Ray?"

"I'm certainly not going to deny anything: I haven't been accused of anything."

Walter sighed. "So that's how it's gonna be, huh?"

I didn't know how much Walter knew. Was he leading up to a bombshell? He'd gotten hold of Baptiste's phone records; what else did he have?

"Look, Walter. I want this to be a civil discussion, OK? But I'm starting to think you guys are just stumbling around in the dark. You're way behind the curve on this case, and you thought by coming on so hard-ass, you could intimidate me into helping you."

The ego ploy; it works nine times out of ten.

"The day I need a reporter to do my police work is the day I hang up my doughnuts. You want it straight up, cop to citizen? Here goes: do you know where the hell Jean-Mars Baptiste is?"

"No!" I snapped. "I don't have the slightest idea." I hung up—at least it was an honest answer. I tried to relight the Coleman stove to heat the coffee, but my hand was shaking so much, I couldn't control the match. The conversation had focused my situation down to one essential point: I was guilty, Walter Paisley was smart. In a rational world, he would win.

I reminded myself that I no longer lived in a rational world.

THE voodoo doctor drove a camper.

He arrived on a wave of primary colors and overamped music. By the time I ran downstairs, he was already at the front steps, slamming the door knocker in a calypso rhythm. He was in his mid-thirties, tall, almost painfully skinny. He was flawlessly color coordinated, dressed in ultra-tight black jeans and a purple sharkskin sport coat. Purple socks, black Reeboks; purple lapel flower, black handkerchief. His hair was carved in an intricate *vèvè,* the symbol of a voodoo god.

"I'm Prosper Telemache," he barked, shaking first my right hand, then my left. "Ambassador of the gods, musical mix master to the spirits of Africa. Read this, please. Aloud."

He handed me a sheet of paper on which a prayer was written in delicate calligraphy. I stared at it, nonplussed.

"Just read it, Monsieur Falco. The gods may have eternity on their side, we don't."

I gave in, feeling foolish, like an atheist forced to impersonate a priest. "Radegonde Baron Samedi, guardian of the cemetery, you who have the power of going into purgatory, give my enemies something to do so they may leave me alone."

Prosper frowned at my delivery. "Not thinking about a career in radio, are you?" He snatched the paper away and marched us into the kitchen. "Let's see. Ideally this should be sewn into the cane-weave wall of a peasant *kay,* but we got to work with what we got." He considered a moment, then affixed the prayer to the refrigerator door with a magnet. "Now, don't fill me up with a lot of self-explaining; Lucy told me everything. I got to jam: the Lord's search party, it's runnin' late."

Then he began to ransack my house. As he tore through the kitchen cabinets, another car pulled up. Lucy. I met her at the door.

"*He's* the specialist?" I asked.

"Sorry. Marcus Welby was unavailable," she snapped. "He's a *houngan,* a voodoo priest. We're lucky to get him."

I took in the full garish splendor of Telemache's camper. Every inch of it down to the hubcaps was painted in bright, swirling colors. Stylized diamonds and stars, swords and machine guns, tigers and snakes writhed everywhere, overlaid by a black spray of musical notes. The hood was a metallic orgy of horns and mirrors; a string of flashing Christmas lights ran around the roof of the camper shell. Music boomed from speakers mounted on the fenders. Flowing across the windshield in flaming-red script was the phrase, "La Bête de la Musique."

"Art on wheels: tap-taps are the main source of public transportation in Port-au-Prince," Lucy explained. "Prosper missed them so much, he built his own."

"Jeez, how many tickets did you get on the way down here?"

She smiled impishly. "None. Before we left, Prosper made an offering to Legba, the god of roads."

"Sort of a divine Fuzzbuster," I cracked.

"Prosper can be a handful, I know. One thing you have to know about Haitians: they're world-class bluffers. Sometimes bullshitting and tall tales seem like the normal modes of conversation. Maybe it comes from the slave days, where you had to lie to survive, who knows? If you see through him, use good manners—don't call him on it, OK? He may come on strong, but he's good." She blew the hair out of her eyes. "I don't know what else to do, Raymond. Whatever's happening to you, it's not in my law books. Maybe it's in his."

There was a crash as the shutters on the second-floor bathroom window flew open. I looked up to see Prosper Telemache climbing onto my roof. I ran back inside. The interior of the house looked like it had been lifted off its foundations and dropped back from a great height.

"Don't worry," Lucy said, "he'll put it all back."

"Can he finish the tongue and groove while he's at it?"

Prosper met us at the top of the stairs. "There's nothing in the gutters," he reported. He mopped his brow with the purple handkerchief, which was stitched in black with a vèvè identical to the one in his hair. "I didn't see it, and I don't feel it, so there must not be one here."

"One what?" I asked.

Prosper looked at Lucy, astounded by my ignorance.

"A *wanga,* man. A charm, a talisman—heavy magic. Something your enemy might hide in your house. One look at it is enough to make you sick. Live with it a few weeks, and you may as well unplug your amp and pack up your ax, because the gig of life is over, man. I'm also a musician: parties, weddings, bar mitzvahs, spiritual convocations. Here: carry it in your wallet for easy reference."

He handed me a business card, purple, naturally, with the name of his band, "Kombinayson," printed in black. He brushed to the door, hissing at Lucy: "This one's tougher than I thought."

He was back a minute later, wearing a Walkman and lugging two giant suitcases. Inside the cases were bottles of herbs, spices, and plants, all neatly labeled; other bottles held unidentifiable animal parts, bristly with hair, floating in a viscous, brown broth. There were strings of beads, amulets, bottles of rum, cartons of cigarettes; scarves and party streamers, a dozen varieties of candles; rosaries, plastic Virgins pierced by daggers, crucifixes oozing blood and tears; sheet music, money, an assortment of penises—some cast in cheap wax, others carved from teak and mahogany.

"I guess a man in your line of work makes a lot of house calls," I said.

"In Brooklyn, my clients come to *me!*" he huffed. "This is just my road kit." I was slightly let down when he bypassed the penis collection and the bottled animals in favor of a series of colored lithographs, which he fanned out on the kitchen table. They were pictures of the Catholic saints, vibrant with blood and sorrowful eyes. "These are picture representations of the loa," he said. He rambled through the pantheon, matching each saint to its vodoun counterpart: "Saint Patrick stands for Damballah; that little prude the Virgin Mary is Erzulie Frèda; you got Saint Gerard for Gede, Saint Lazarus for Legba. Thinking from what Lucy told me, I suspect that one of these loa has been "bought," that means turned against you by some asshole you probably don't even know. Vodoun's a good religion—*benevolent,* you call it? It's all about keeping your act together here on earth, but when it gets twisted around like this, it can be nasty shit. I'm gonna need hammer, nails, and something to pound on."

I laid a piece of plywood between two sawhorses. Prosper arranged the lithographs with the care of a magician preparing a card trick. "Now, let's see which one of these has it in for you." He lowered his head, closed his eyes; his loud, smart-ass attitude vanished. He began to chant softly, English mixing with Creole and French. One by one, he pounded nails through the lithographed saints, adding another wound to their blood-stained martyrdom. After each blow he patted me down like a cop frisking a suspect, searching, I suspected, for sudden stigmata. He kept up the chant as he worked, head bobbing rhythmically.

"Is he communing with the loa?" I whispered to Lucy.

Prosper smiled, pointing to his headphones. "Mariah Carey," he said, as he drove a nail into Saint Patrick.

Even before the ritual was over, I could read Prosper's disappointment. He threw down the hammer, inspected me from head to toe. "This is a stubborn one. We going to have to get serious; you can handle it?"

"What do you mean by *serious*? We're not talking power tools, are we?"

"A houngan works just like a medical doctor," Prosper answered. "We start out looking for a cold, and sometime we find cancer. I'm not sayin' you got cancer, but it isn't no common cold, either."

I appealed to Lucy, but she immediately went into a Creole huddle with Prosper. "He suspects an *expédition de morts,* a sending of the dead against you," she explained to me. "It's like a spiritual virus; once it's been injected into a biological organism, it's very difficult to extract. He needs my help, he needs your total cooperation." She clapped her hands, over-enthusiastically, I thought. "So, what are you doing for the next six hours?"

First, they force-fed me a quart of salty tea. Then they laid me on the kitchen table, stripped off my shirt, bound my jaw shut with twine, stuffed my nostrils with cotton. Prosper scattered coffee grounds on the floor in a spiraling vèvè. As he worked, he talked Lucy through the preparation of some mystery broth: herbs, spices, crushed almonds, flowers retrieved from my own garden, holy water, rum, champagne (California, not French), and perfume (Opium and Shalimar).

Prosper began to pray. The minutes inflated into an hour,

and I dozed off to his hypnotic incantations. When I awoke, he was consulting a compass. North verified, he filled his mouth with the soup, and blew a fine mist to each of the four cardinal points.

Lucy bent over me, a diabolic gleam in her eyes. "Remember, you *asked* for the Haitian treatment."

Prosper and Lucy flicked the boiling broth at me with their fingertips, my bare skin erupting in pinpoints of scalding pain. I twisted, gasped, unable to scream as they doused me slowly and methodically, a torture bath that lasted until the pot was empty.

"That was the water," Prosper pronounced with satisfaction. "Now for the fire."

I groaned and shut my eyes. I felt a sudden burst of heat next to my face; violent tears forced me to open my eyes again—Prosper's hands were on fire! As he clapped my shoulders, there was an excruciating blaze of pain, then the flames flickered out. He dipped his hands in a bowl of flaming rum and repeated the treatment, slapping me from head to foot. I grew delirious; Lucy dissolved into a rippling, smoky figure obscured behind a wall of heat shimmer.

I had really had enough. I felt like an idiot: a phone call away from the high-end technology of American medicine, and I was allowing myself to be treated by this Caribbean door-to-door salesman. I tried to sit up, but Prosper forced me back down. He kicked up the tempo of his prayers, slurring the words: "By thy will, Good Lord, Saints and Dead, by the power of Monsieur Guede-nuvavu, Tou-Guede, I, houngan Prosper, ask you for the life of this man, I buy him, I pay you, I owe you nothing."

He held a TV packing case over me, tracing circles in the air. "This container will take the expedition from your body, and the dead soul will trouble you no longer." Then, he confided, "This should really be a giant calabash gourd washed seven times in the Artibonite River, but good voodoo is like jazz—you gotta know how to improvise."

Nothing happened. I didn't feel any dead souls fleeing my

body, and now Prosper seemed alarmed. He shook the box furiously, chanted even faster. Lucy brought him a glass of rum, but he rudely slapped her away. "That's not gonna do no good."

He stopped abruptly. He dropped the box, kicked it across the floor in frustration. Prosper ripped off his headphones, then untied my jaw.

"There's something you ain't told me, Monsieur Falco. Right?"

"What do you mean?"

"I mean you got something else workin' on you, other symptoms you ain't been truthful about."

I saw Lucy's eyes narrow with concern. Prosper took a medical penlight from his bag of tricks. He inspected my eyes, probing gently beneath the lids as he muttered to himself. He rooted through his suitcase and pulled out two identical black spheres, which he then placed in my hands. "Which one is heavier?" he asked.

"They're both about the same," I answered. He unclasped my hands and tossed the balls to Lucy. She caught the first one easily, but when the second ball slapped into her palm, it jerked her arm sharply down to her thigh.

"One of them is aluminum and weighs six ounces," Prosper said. "The other is solid iron and he weighs nine *pounds*."

The significance of this revelation was lost on me, but it was clear to Prosper, and seemed to hold a dim resonance for Lucy. The mood turned somber; Lucy and Prosper were crippled for words, as though they had just driven past a horrific highway accident.

"What the hell is going on here?" I vaulted off the table, sloshed cold water onto my skin. "Come on, this isn't quaint or exotic anymore."

Prosper took my arm. "Let's go into this outside, OK? Under the sun and the sky. In my experience, the realm of nature is the best medicine against shock."

———

THE trees sighed contentedly; the warm air held the magnolia and honeysuckle like a delicately scented handkerchief. A perfect Virginia afternoon.

"Bullshit!" I erupted. "You mean like the night of the fucking living dead?"

"Zombification is not a B-movie thing, Ray." Prosper held out his arms and marched stiff-legged toward me. "No monsters crawl out of their graves, with flesh dripping from their arms. Zombification really means you got no free will . . . a slave to someone else's control."

"But I can see, I can hear!" I tapped my forehead. "I can *think*."

"That's what makes it so frustrating. A zombi sees himself going through all this stuff, doing all these strange actions that he doesn't understand. But he can't control them. Tell the truth—isn't that what's been happening to you?"

My mind was like a dark, locked room. I felt the concept of zombification trying to creep in, a tickle of light under the door. "No, no, I just don't believe it, I'm sorry. It's way too . . . *Twilight Zone*."

"*Twilight Zone*! You saw it yourself, man. A zombi can't distinguish between light and heavy objects, and neither can you. Look, you believe in hypnosis, right? You believe in brainwashing, in religious hysteria—I mean, check out Jonestown. Even mass political hysteria, Hitler, Goebbels. People lose control of themselves all the time! You think you call all the shots on this earth?"

Prosper stalked angrily toward his camper. Lucy went after him, protesting in Creole, but he faced her down in English for my benefit. "Look, I been in this country seven years, OK? In Brooklyn, I got all the best clients. I'm a hero, OK? And this guy, this . . . *blanc* . . . what's he think we are, a bunch of natives dancin' around with bones in our noses?" He climbed into the cab, sulking to a soca beat.

Lucy gave me a chiding glance. "Listen, Raymond . . ."

"Zombis, Lucy? Think how that sounds to me."

"No. You think how that sounds to a Haitian. Back in the slave days, your only taste of freedom came when you died,

151

when your liberated soul could travel back to Africa. Flash forward two hundred years to the present. What's the worst thing a Haitian can imagine, the ultimate nightmare for a follower of vodoun? To die free, only to be raised up as a zombi, into a slavery that continues even after death. That's what zombiism is—a mirror held up to history. Hollywood got it all wrong: Haitians aren't that afraid of zombis; they're afraid of becoming one!"

"So how could this happen to me? No, wait, I know: I walked into a bar, bartender said, 'What'll it be?' I said, 'Make me a zombie' . . . and he did."

As a journalist, I had always refused to admit that there were worlds beyond cynicism, beyond understanding. But . . . within the vodoun cosmology, the concept of zombiism offered a sophisticated, specific explanation for everything that had happened to me.

"Just find a way to apologize to him, OK?" Lucy said. "He wants to help, but he needs to feel a certain respect. The loa can be touchy as hell; a good houngan's even worse."

"What am I paying you for, if not to negotiate?" I groused. I trudged to the camper, knocked on the glass.

Prosper's voice boomed out of a chrome speaker mounted on the hood. *"What?"* he snarled.

"Listen, I'm sorry. About that *Twilight Zone* crack."

"How you like it if I tell you Christianity just another sci-fi movie, huh? The resurrection, it was all just special effects?"

"I wouldn't be insulted. I don't take religion all that personally."

"Hah!" he spat. "That's the thing right there. Vodoun is very personal. I know the loa, they know me. They give me everything, man; they turn these fingers into magic wands when I sit down at the keyboard." He mimed a furious piano glissando on the dashboard. "And they give me the truth about you . . . even when you don't deserve it."

I glanced at Lucy. She made a nudging motion with her chin. "Prosper, I need you to help me whip this thing. I'll switch off the skeptical half of my brain, OK? Just tell me your conditions."

"That's insulting. I don't have no conditions, other than mutual respect . . . well, maybe there is one thing . . ."

He opened the cab door. From a briefcase propped on his lap he handed me a professionally printed, full-color press release, highlighted by a stylized logo of a conga drum rocketing out of a television set.

" 'The Voodoo Channel'!" I read incredulously.

"It's not really a channel, not yet. We got a half-hour of public access, once a month on a Brooklyn cable station. Lucy tells me you got big pull with the media. You help me get this in the papers, a lotta investors goin' to see it. We got maybe half a million Haitians in New York. That's powerful demographics, man!"

"Prosper, you're amazing. What's Creole for *chutzpah?*" I could only laugh, shaking my head in appreciation. "I'll see what I can do."

"It's the loa who're amazing, Ray. I'm just their PR man."

Later, we sat in the cab of La Bête de la Musique, drinking rum, Prosper and Lucy smoking like campfires, air-conditioning at full blast, Tabu Combo, Boukman Eksperyance, and Skah Shah on the tape deck.

A lesson in vodoun metaphysics, as described by Prosper Telemache: the human body is just characterless flesh without the soul, known as the *ti bon ange,* to animate it. It is the repository of an individual's personality and willpower, and can be stolen from a recently deceased corpse by a skilled sorcerer. A ti bon ange is a powerful weapon in the hands of a malevolent sorcerer, sort of a voodoo nuke.

"A real good sorcerer, he can take that ti bon ange and put it anywhere: into a lion, an insect, even a carburetor, I guess. But it works best when he puts it into a human body; maybe somebody big in politics, somebody powerful he can control. Then you got a serious zombi."

"The ti bon ange that you say was put into Raymond, whose was it?" Lucy asked.

I slumped lower in the seat. Prosper shot me an accusatory look.

"Ray, what are you holding back?" Lucy asked.

I would have to say something. The flashbacks had happened twice now; Nicholas Townsend's life was starting to feel like a prologue to my own.

"Do souls have expiration dates?" I joked. Then I told them the story of Nicholas Townsend, beginning with the random bursts of memory I'd first experienced, ending with the second diary entry. "Is this guy a well-known figure in Haitian history?" I asked. "I've never heard of him."

Lucy shrugged. "Neither have I."

"Typical," I said. "Other people get reincarnated as Egyptian kings, Roman emperors . . . I'm stuck with a bit player."

Prosper was lost in thought, running his hands over the plastic saints that lined the dashboard. "This complicates things," he said.

"Oh, really?" I snapped.

"But it helps explain things, too. This Mr. Townsend, he's the tool they used to get inside you. You got two souls fighting in there now; that's enough to kill a lot of men." Prosper slapped me on the thigh. "But you're a tough guy, right? Anyway, they don't want you dead yet. They still got plans for you."

12

THE SUMMIT CONFERENCE lasted all night. I made coffee, thick and sweet, Haitian style. When I started a spaghetti dinner, Prosper disappeared into my yard for an hour, returning with a handful of herbs that I'd never seen before. "Every good priest is a good *dokte fèy,* an herbalist. This makes an outrageous pesto, increases your sexual vitality, too!" He minced the herbs and flung them into the sauce. Then he began to hunt through the spice rack. "Got any ground lizard?" I blinked in horror. "Just kidding."

On my tenth cup of coffee, I grabbed Prosper desperately by the arm. "Have you ever actually seen a zombi yourself?"

He thoughtfully stirred his coffee. "Once. Late at night, outside the town of Jean-Rabel. I was foolish, man, rode my bicycle right through the crossroads—that's the last place a Haitian wants to be after dark, but I just had to visit my girlfriend, you know? Thinking with my *zozo* again. Then I saw him, stealing the tires from a public bus parked by the side of the road. It was a guy everybody in the village knew, a car mechanic, you know? Thing was, he died the year before! My band even played at his funeral. He just stared at me like his eyes were made of glass. Man, I got out of there fast! When I looked back over my shoulder, I saw him disappear into a cane field."

I didn't say anything. The night was dead quiet, as though even the crickets were listening. "They exist, Raymond!" he said. "The Haitian government even had to pass a law against them. Under article two-forty-six of the old penal code, you could go to prison for creating a zombi."

I rubbed the exhaustion out of my eyes. "OK, let's say for argument's sake I accept your thesis. How do we deal with it?"

"You got to find the *bokor,* the sorcerer that's thrown this thing on you. I never heard of a white victim before, so I guess that means the bokor that's yanking your chain is a major player!"

"What the hell do I do in the meantime? Just stumble through life in a trance?"

"Listen, man, there are things we can try, things that cut right into the heart of vodoun. But you ain't ready—what I got in mind is too radical. You're still too arrogant to let the loa help you. So first, I'm gonna study this Townsend diary; maybe there's some clues in there. And I'm gonna listen to the gossip, see what I can find out. Anyway, he don't pull the strings on you twenty-four hours a day. Most of the time you can lead a normal life. Eat, watch TV, make love."

"But when he says, 'Jump,' I jump!" I said. "No willpower, no self-control. Why don't I just check myself into St. Elizabeth's and get it over with? I mean, this is pure insanity!"

"And it may be the beginnings of our legal defense," Lucy said calmly. "Complete personality dissociation, no control over your own actions or emotions, total psychological sub-mission to an outside force . . .."

"And I'm sure you can find a jury to believe that . . . on Mars."

———

Music blaring, his illuminated hubcaps spinning like pinwheels, Prosper Telemache rumbled out of my driveway at dawn, with the flare and furor of a carnival leaving town. By then, I had stopped believing him.

For the next two days, while Lucy attended to her other clients, I went on a medical rampage. I got two complete check-ups, one from my doctor, another from his expensive competitor across the hall, a well-known internist whose patients included a Cabinet secretary and the speaker of the house. I consulted a nutritionist, an acupuncturist, an acupressurist, and three allergists. When I finally stumbled out of the last doctor's office, clutching computerized printouts of my physical status, Lucy was waiting.

"Well?"

"Say hello to the only man in Washington who's terrified that he's in perfect health." Before the gloom of reality could completely settle on me, I heard a familiar, sunny voice.

"Ray? It *is* you!"

It was Livia Holcomb, energetic, always running, Tony Randolph breathlessly bringing up the rear. She saw my tragic expression, matched it with the medical building.

"Nothing's wrong, is it?"

I shook my head and introduced Lucy. Livia gave her a competitive once-over; knowing Livia, she would never have tolerated seeing me with someone less attractive than herself. "So you're the miracle worker. Well, let me give you my heartiest congratulations, Lucy. I spent every last ounce of homespun, Midwestern charm I had trying to get this guy writing again, but you pulled it off." She waved toward a row of news racks. "Look at that. Black-and-white proof that the great ones never die. Tony and I are going to dinner; you'll join us, right? Somewhere nice to celebrate your comeback?"

"I don't think so, Liv . . ."

"Come on, I'm not talking about a gut-wrenching evening of group therapy. We'll just have a good time, catch up . . ."

I tried to signal my panic to Lucy—in my mental state, a night on the town sounded like a recipe for hell. But Tony had already seized her arm, just as Livia had mine. Escape without arousing suspicion was impossible. We were condemned to be sociable.

We ended up somewhere sleek and trendy, Twenty-one Federal, I think. I told myself that Lucy and I were just another couple, and this was just another evening out with fellow professionals. Reporters I knew stopped by the table, bought me drinks. "Helluva job," they all said. Two congressmen found me and dropped excited hints: they were launching an investigation into the torture tape, calling witnesses. A member of the Senate Foreign Relations Committee draped a fatherly hand across my shoulder and promised a full-scale human-rights inquiry. Livia basked in a strange pride of ownership, as though her status as ex-girlfriend allowed her some of the credit for the success of my Haiti pieces. For a moment, I was tempted to pass her a note, to tell her everything! She looked beautiful in the candlelight, her hair piled up like a golden halo, her skin pale yet alive. She and Tony were happy together; their world glistened.

But their world was full of little rituals that seemed like the customs of a foreign country: the small talk, the rose-shaped pats of butter, the scholarly sips of wine. Lucy's hand found mine; her fingertips grazed languorously along my inner thigh. I suddenly felt bound to her, united against these well-meaning strangers.

Midway through the meal, I knew I had to leave. I jerked to my feet.

"Ray, what is it?" Livia asked.

"Something's come up, something urgent . . ."

"Right, that appointment!" Lucy said, covering for me. "I'm afraid we just forgot . . . will you excuse us?"

"Ray, are you sure you're OK?" Livia asked.

"I'm fine. There's been a break in the story, that's all." I dragged Lucy up from the table and ran through the restaurant, weaving through schmoozers and lobbyists, Tony and Livia in pursuit.

"Break in the story, my ass! That's not the voice of Ray Falco in hot pursuit of a headline." She caught me by the arm. "Listen, I didn't say anything earlier, but take a good look at yourself." She held a makeup mirror up to my face. I stared into my glassy-eyed, haunted reflection.

"I'm fine, goddamn it! But don't take my word for it. Here's the scientific proof." I shoved the computer printouts into her hands.

"Whatever you're going through, Tony and I care for you, you know that," Livia said. She began to leaf through the printouts with her skeptical NPR eyes.

"I know, Liv. But I just can't be here now, OK? I don't know any other way to explain it to you."

"I'm trying to help you, Ray Falco!"

"None of you can help me, OK?" I shouted. "No one in this fucking room can help me!"

The conversation at the bar stopped. Eager faces swung toward us, their scandal antennae bristling. The only sound was the drone of the TV: CNN was reporting that the United States ambassador to Haiti had been urgently recalled to Washington.

Livia looked hurt. "I'm sorry you feel I have nothing to offer. After all we've been through." She glanced at Lucy, and managed a bland look of encouragement. "I hope your lawyer will be able to help."

Outside, the four of us stood in prickly silence, waiting for the valet to bring Tony's car. I felt like a ghost, the life of the street passing right through me.

A red light flashed on Tony's hip. He slapped his hand over a tiny electronic device that dangled from his belt.

"What's that?" I asked.

"Nothing. My car alarm." He sounded anxious, looked shifty.

"Bullshit." I grabbed Tony's wrist and twisted. The device fell into my hand. It looked like a tiny stock ticker tape: a series of mathematical symbols and linguistic gibberish paraded across a digital screen.

"What's wrong with you?" he hissed. "Someone gets hold of that, I'm in a shitload of trouble. Now, give it back."

"Just tell me what it is."

He glanced over his shoulder, like a spy about to reveal a state secret. "It automatically updates the password and ID sequence for the seventh-floor computer networks. Every two hours. Say I want to go back to the office tonight and work late. Without this, I can't log on. It's a precaution they use whenever we move to a higher alert status."

"It has to do with Haiti, doesn't it?"

"Ray, come on, you know I can't . . ."

"It was my reporting that moved Haiti off the back burner. Without me, you would've missed the whole ball game!"

The parking valet screeched around the corner on two wheels, but coasted to a safe, sober stop for Tony's benefit. "I'll tell you in the car."

"We're not riding with you. Tell me now."

Tony sighed, looking up at the full moon as though he expected the answer to his ethical dilemma to magically appear there.

"Come on, man, you owe me," I prodded.

"OK, look. Since that videotape showed up, Haiti's gotten a lot of heat. We got Langley and Pentagon brass in and out all day long; the guys on the Caribbean desk are throwing their weight around like their budget got tripled. Amnesty International and Americas Watch are pushing us to push the Haitians to schedule elections, *plus* Congress is all over us for our failure to protect American lives abroad. And word is, the Secretary's got his personal staff working round the clock on an NSAM dealing with Haiti."

NSAM's—National Security Action Memoranda—were government marching orders distributed to a select few. Terse and urgent, TO:, FROM:, RE:, they were meant to be read, shredded, and acted upon.

He waved his hands, cutting me off. "That's it. That's all I can say. And I will *never* reveal the contents of an NSAM, not for money, not for friendship . . ."

"Not even to save my life?"

"Don't get melodramatic with me. Besides, what makes you believe there aren't more lives at stake here than just yours?"

He climbed behind the wheel, leaving Livia standing with us. "Something's wrong in your life, Ray," she said. "Something bigger and more wrenching than anything that happened while we were together." She kissed me on the cheek, studiously avoiding brushing against Lucy. "If you don't think it's beneath you, you can still call me for help. You can't kill off your friends that easily."

Lucy and I walked back to my car. I started the engine, then turned it off. "I just couldn't spend another minute in that world," I said. "It's like I can't breathe when I'm around people who don't know. . . ."

"You can breathe around me?"

"Maybe *only* around you."

"I don't know if I like that," she said. "Shouldn't a woman be able to take a man's breath away?"

"Why, counselor, I think you're flirting with me," I said, taking her hand, kissing it. "Or is it voodoo . . . the loa as matchmakers?"

"That's the mysterious thing about vodoun. Some people say it creates new desires, others say it just brings to the surface the ones we already have."

"Choice number two sounds right. I like you, Lucy. I'd like you even if you weren't the only person in the world who knows what I'm going through."

She ran her hand across my cheek, along my throat. My body flushed with forgotten heat. "There's no one in your life, Raymond? A cynical, world-weary reporter like you . . . that's a type a lot of women find very attractive."

"Oh, there's always a fair amount of sex lying around, if you're willing to bend down and pick it up. Especially in this town. But as far as anything deeper goes . . . " I reached for her pack of cigarettes. "Can I?"

"Do you?"

"No. But maybe I ought to start."

"We'll get through this, Raymond, without adding any bad habits to your repertoire." She began to follow her caresses with kisses, delicate pecks that left a warm, moist trail.

"Livia had a theory," I said. "I'm incapable of love. Single-mindedly devoted to my career. Control-obsessed. Writing by definition is basically a control-freak's job. Trouble is, she used to say, love likes to take control, too. Those who win at love, let it."

I curled my arms around Lucy, tilting her toward me in a kiss. She pushed up onto her knees, leaned across the emergency brake, glueing herself against me. I felt her breasts beneath our summer clothes, saw them rounded against her buttons, and from that narrow glimpse, I could picture her whole, copper-colored body.

But then she pulled away, smiling and flushed, stray hair pasted wetly to her forehead. "Maybe she's right. Maybe if we weren't in the middle of the weirdest fucking episode of our lives, we could just lose control and see what happens." She checked her watch. "But in the meantime, I have to meet Prosper." She slipped her hand beneath my shirt, drew circles on my skin. "You breathing OK now?"

"Just breathe normally: isn't that what the doctor always says? I don't think I'll ever draw a normal breath again."

She gave me a long, hungry kiss. "Since meeting you, Raymond, I don't think I will either."

———

I couldn't go home. After dropping Lucy off, I prowled the streets, unable to interact with the "real" world just outside my windshield. I couldn't bring myself to do the normal, late-night things I used to do: catch a midnight movie at the Biograph or the last set at Blues Alley. Even a simple transaction like pumping my own gas seemed impossible. Then I realized I was being followed.

I couldn't focus on a specific car or distinguish a telltale pattern of headlights. It was just a cold, stabbing sensation that someone was watching—from behind curtains, from the shadows of alleys and deserted parks, a spooky relay of pursuers.

I drove past the housing project where it all started. The lobby doors had been boarded up again, the steps scrubbed clean. I don't know what I expected: a voice whispering clues to me? A voodoo god to take my hand and lead me to understanding, like a seeing-eye dog? The feeling of being followed was more intense there. Footsteps. Tree branches passing furtive messages. I drove on.

The Haitian embassy gleamed in a halo of outdoor lighting. I parked across the street, wondering if Isidor's presidential guard was in there now, plotting my death over toasts of Barbancourt rum. No, that seemed impossible. It wasn't a sinister building at all. Lights glowed warmly behind lace curtains; it reminded me of an elegant London hotel, the kind of place where you leave your shoes outside your door to be shined overnight. It was quiet. No diplomatic receptions were breaking up. No one came or went. One by one, the office lights winked off. The lulling hiss of traffic on Massachusetts Avenue made me drowsy.

So drowsy, I almost missed it: a V-8 rumble in the alley that flanked the embassy, and the sudden glare of blue headlights!

A huge black car swung out of the alley and headed southeast on Massachusetts Avenue. I slapped my cheeks, forcing myself awake. I kept the car in sight easily; traffic was sparse, and we hit the lights perfectly, like a presidential motorcade. We swept past Union Station, circling the statue of Columbus—the bastard who'd really started it all, by discovering Haiti on his first voyage.

The car turned due south onto Fourth Street, then jogged onto Pennsylvania Avenue, heading southeast again. A shadow on wheels, it seemed to float. The smoked-glass windows made it impossible to see who was driving. To see *what* was driving? I glanced at my car phone. Should I call someone? Lucy? Prosper? Certainly not the police: "I'm Code Three southbound in pursuit of a Haitian werewolf; request backup."

We crossed the Sousa Bridge, keeping to the fast lane. But just as we reached the other side, the car suddenly spurted into the right lane and disappeared down an exit ramp. I braked recklessly and swerved after it.

I raced down the curving exit road, through dark woods. I

zigzagged right, then left, but it had vanished. Then, as I emerged from the trees, it was right in front of me, stopped at a light. I squealed to a stop, nearly nudging it with my bumper.

I held my breath. I could hear the deep rumble of the V-8; I swore I could feel it shaking the pavement, the vibration rippling through the springs and shocks, up the steering column, into my hands. The light turned green, but the loup-garou car didn't move; it waited, like a giant predator crouching patiently in tall grass.

When it shot forward, I was right on it, following it through a checkerboard of deserted streets, no longer caring if it spotted me.

Row houses, quiet and crime-barred, cats curled on front stoops, a candlelit religious shrine in a first-floor window— they all turned an unearthly blue in the loup-garou car's headlights.

Then I knew where we were.

The car slowed as it passed the ruins of the Baptiste house. The rear door opened, and a body flew out as if it had been launched. It landed roughly on the low, brick remains of a wall, legs dangling onto the sidewalk, head and arms thrown back into what was once the living room.

The door slammed shut, the car sped off. I parked and ran over to the body. Jean-Mars Baptiste was a ruin now, too, twisted and splayed like the charred beams of his house, his features fixed in the expressionless permanence of death.

13

His shoes and socks were missing. The sleeves of his blue suit had been rolled up above the elbows, his white shirt ripped open at the neck. The cold, exposed skin was blotchy with bruises, neatly crosshatched with razor-thin cuts. The hair on his ankles and arms was singed black.

The garish insignia of torture. But Baptiste had been dead when I left him. Had he been mutilated postmortem?

It was the dime-size hole and the blossom-shaped bloodstain on the chest that drew me to my knees—the fatal wounds I'd inflicted. I rolled Baptiste onto his stomach. There was a hole the size of a boxing glove in his back. I felt sick—whatever body parts had been in there had been blown out by the impact.

Alone with my victim, I felt the guilt hammering me. Maybe I could make amends by sacrificing myself. Should I use pills? Gas? No, it should be bloody, equally gruesome. But then I turned the old death penalty argument against myself—how would my death bring Jean-Mars Baptiste back? Maybe I could do something about the body: rub away the scars, restore its humanity so that Helene and Etienne Baptiste could have a final, consoling glimpse before burial.

I surveyed the street. No pedestrians. No curious faces in the neighboring windows. I studied my position in relation to the streetlight—even if someone was looking out of their window, they would see me as a shadow at most, maybe assume I was some scavenger picking for goodies among the ruins. I drove to the nearest phone booth. Muffling my voice with my sleeve, I alerted the 911 operator to where they could find the body. A five-second call. No names.

———

"SOMETHING'S wrong," I said. "It was too easy."

"What do you mean?"

"The whole thing: tracing the car to the Haitian embassy, following it tonight. I think I was meant to find the body."

A long pause; I heard Lucy lighting a match. I could picture her at her orderly desk, making notes on a legal pad in her tight script. "Why? Where's the logic behind that?"

"Someone could have seen me. A cop could've driven by, a Guardian Angel with insomnia . . . it was a perfect opportunity to frame me."

"No one needs to frame you, Raymond. You really killed him."

I had driven straight home, but the house that met me was dark. The new circuit-breaker panel had turned out to be the wrong size and the electrician had removed it. I sat in the parlor as a late-night breeze rattled the window sheeting; a dozen candles flickered moodily. They were rose scented and gave off a thick, sleepy fragrance. I felt like a Colonial undertaker keeping an all-night vigil; I could easily imagine a body cleansed and ready for burial in the next room. I followed a curl of smoke up the pine paneling, watched it spread out like a storm cloud against the plaster ceiling medallion. The intricately carved medallion was the house's architectural highlight: cavorting goddesses, reflecting pools, soothing landscapes. But behind the distorting veil of smoke, it seemed to come alive: the Greek gods turned on me with cadaverous stares, tree branches reached down from the ceiling like whips to draw my blood. I shut my eyes, looked away.

"Raymond? Are you there?"

"To have killed a man, to have him literally return to accuse you . . . do you know what that feels like?"

"Not directly, maybe . . ." she said. "But I've known people who've had people killed."

"I appreciate the effort. But if you're going to try and match me villainy against villainy, you're going to lose."

"All I mean to say is, I understand how the conscience can nag. I'm not just another unfeeling lawyer, Raymond."

"They tortured him, Lucy. After he was dead."

"That doesn't shock me. You can't imagine how these people can hate."

"It didn't look like it was done in a frenzy; it was precise, almost staged somehow."

I heard Lucy exhale in exasperation. "Listen, your reporter's mind is starting to run in circles. Why don't you come over?"

"I don't think so. Just keep the line open for a while, OK?" The radio was on in Lucy's apartment, tuned to the all-news channel; she was waiting for the body to be discovered. The wind had died down; it was so quiet now, I could hear Lucy's breath on the line, hear the rustle of her clothing against her skin.

"Lucy, I was stupid to think I could investigate myself! The tried-and-true Ray Falco moves are never going to work. All the sources, the deep background, the off-the-record chats . . . it's bullshit." I pushed out of my chair, slashed open the window coverings, tried to inhale courage from the fresh night air. "I think we need to get radical."

Lucy didn't answer. I heard the volume of the radio increase. "WMET's on it right now," she said. " 'The gunshot-riddled body of missing Haitian activist Jean-Mars Baptiste . . . blah, blah, blah . . . in the ruins of his burned-out southeast Washington apartment . . . police spokesmen are deferring all comment until tomorrow morning.' "

"Nothing about any mysterious stranger fleeing the scene?"

"I think you're OK for now. Listen, the radical treatment Prosper mentioned, even he admits it may not work. He'll need to bring you to a voodoo temple, and they don't usually like to admit blancs into their ceremonies. Let alone blancs who happen to be reporters."

"He's saying he won't do it?"

"No, no, he'll do it. He just wants you to appreciate how difficult it is for him to arrange it."

"How much appreciation are we talking about?"

"Five hundred should be enough," she replied.

"Religion doesn't come cheap anywhere, does it?"

"If it were cheap, would that make it better? Pick me up tomorrow night at ten-thirty. And, Raymond? Everything that's happened up until now, you could theoretically explain away to science or coincidence, even schizophrenia if you were truly determined not to believe. But this you won't be able to explain. So Prosper insists I warn you—don't show up with your mind set in stone, because much of what you see may dash it to pieces."

Throughout the next day I listened to the news updates on my Walkman as the story took on a momentum of its own. Cops were interviewed, ballistics experts speculated on the high-velocity, heavy-load ammunition that had killed Baptiste; the Haitian deputy ambassador issued a public denial of any embassy involvement in the crime; Tony Randolph presided at a raucous State Department Q & A, darkly hinting that nothing could be ruled out when it came to protecting the lives of Americans in Haiti and Haitians legally resident in the United States: "We will not tolerate political terrorism on the streets of America!" he loudly declared. I heard his fist strike the podium. Tony Randolph was a man who had never cried wolf in his life. When he got mad on camera, you knew he had the anger of the United States government backing him up. And indeed, as the secretary of state himself emerged from a closed-door congressional briefing, he called on the government of Rene Isidor to schedule elections within the month or face the "full wrath of an outraged international community."

My phone rang nonstop, but I let it ring, afraid it might be Walter Paisley. Like a vampire, I waited for dark to come out of my lair.

I picked up Lucy at ten. She looked as exotic as I had ever seen her—hair braided into African ringlets, wrists jangling with colorful, Bakelite bracelets. She wore a frothy, loose-fitting dress open at the shoulders, eye-opening red, as brilliant as a Haitian painting. I tried for a serious kiss, but she met me with a businesslike peck. She directed me north into Maryland, beyond the miles of low-slung, high-tech research facilities that crowded toward Washington, and into a well-tended, middle-class suburb: bicycles on front lawns, garages crammed with a do-it-yourselfer's tools, rock gardens and bumper stickers that read, "I'd rather be fishing." The last place in the world I expected to find voodoo.

We stopped in front of a small brick house. Music played softly inside, guests filtered up the cement path carrying trays of food—just another neighborhood potluck party. I didn't see Prosper Telemache's tap-tap.

"You're disappointed," Lucy said. "No snake handlers, no big black pots of boiling witch's brew."

"Really. This has all the pagan excitement of a Welcome Wagon meeting."

The living room was small, crowded with discount furniture sheathed in plastic. Family pictures on the mantle, a leather recliner, sliding glass doors leading to a patio and a small, fenced lawn. Very unexotic, unvoodoo. The guests, all black, mingled, chatted, and snacked. A crowd was gathered in front of the television watching a talk show. The mood was convivial and gossipy . . . until I appeared. Conversation stopped, suspicious faces swung in my direction.

"This is the man Prosper has mentioned. He's a friend of ours," Lucy announced. "He doesn't serve the spirits, but he's paid for the house tonight."

There were grumbles of skepticism. A middle-aged woman confronted Lucy, pointedly ignoring me. "I'm not going to say your friend can't stay," she said, "but just so he know, it's plenty busy tonight." She indicated the crowd behind her. "We got a guy needs help with his mortgage; woman whose daughter was in a bad car accident, she's in intensive care even now; my cousin's going to lose his dry cleaning business to the Jamaican mafia if he don't get some help from the spirits; and I . . ." she lowered her voice, ". . . I got love problems you wouldn't believe." Then, she gave me an acid smile. "It's busy tonight. Just so you know, OK?"

I had no idea what to say. I just nodded, then whispered to Lucy, "What do I have to do, take a number?"

She laughed. She opened her purse, and I saw that she had three mini-recorders and an extra package of batteries. As she began to test them, the door behind us flew open. Prosper Telemache appeared at the top of the basement stairs. He was dressed in a tailored white suit. An unlit pipe dangled from his lips and he wore an incongruous white sweatband around his forehead. His arrival silenced the crowd. We could hear drumming down in the basement. He looked at me without warmth or personal acknowledgment. "She tell you how it's gonna work?"

"Not exactly," I said.

He spun on Lucy, shook her by the shoulders. "Damn it, you get him straight! I don't have time to run no schoolhouse here!"

He stared at her until he felt she was sufficiently chastised. Then he fell to his knees on the top step, made the sign of the cross, and began to pray in French. "He's testy," Lucy mumbled. "Nervous. He's trying something new tonight, and if it doesn't work, it certainly won't add to his reputation."

In tone and rhythm the prayers sounded Catholic; they seemed rote rather than heartfelt. The congregation joined in gradually, drinking and gossiping up to the last minute, when they casually made the transition into a quiet state of observance.

Lucy pulled me aside. "We're about to travel to the center of vodoun—possession. Prosper will call down the spirits, and the lucky ones here, they will be 'ridden' by the loa. They will see the world through that spirit's eyes, comment on the world through that spirit's voice. You'll see people become gods tonight.

"Everyone has a dominant spirit in their life, sort of a guardian angel. For Prosper, it's Legba, the god of roads and paths. Prosper is going to ask his help in retracing Jean-Mars Baptiste's movements on the day he was killed." She handed me one of the tape recorders. "You keep this. I've got Prosper wired, and I'm going to hide the other recorders around the room. We're going to need all the backup we can get; it could get pretty crazy down there."

The Catholic liturgy faded and was replaced by a cascade of African words. Prosper's voice grew louder, chopping violently through the syllables. The emotional temperature of the room rose, and the crowd began to clap along in rhythm. Suddenly, he held a cigarette lighter to the wall, as though he were trying to light it on fire.

Then, he sprayed the wall with a Windex bottle filled with a golden-brown liquid, jumping back as a spectacular jet of flame shot out. The heady aroma of burning rum filled the air. I realized he had ignited candles that circled a tiny shrine to Saint Lazarus recessed in the wall. As Prosper sang to the garishly painted statue, he raised his arms to the roof. *Papa Legba, ouvri bàryè,* " he chanted, over and over.

" 'Papa Legba, open the gates,' " Lucy translated. " 'The gates to the spirit world. Open the gates to we poor Creoles who no longer have Africa.' "

Someone turned out the lights in the living room. Bodies pressed in on me from the darkness. The basement, dimly lit and echoing with drums, tempted the crowd, but at the same time held them at bay. I felt Lucy shiver. She drank from a pocket flask, then handed it to me. I took a deep swig of the rum I had learned to recognize as Haitian.

Prosper stopped his chant. Everyone seemed to be holding their breath.

Lucy gave me a sweet, alcohol-tanged kiss. She brought her lips to my ear. "It's beginning," she whispered.

We filed down to the basement. There, the suburban tract house vanished, replaced by the trappings of another world. White sheets had been stapled to the walls, providing a backdrop for chromolithographs of the Catholic saints, sequined voodoo flags, and even a collection of faded travel posters: "Haiti, it's spellbinding"; "Haiti, for a vacation that's out of this world." The cement floor seemed to move, writhing with intricate vèvès drawn in colored chalk. Linen-draped card tables overflowed with food: exotic Caribbean stews and barbecued meats mingled with bags of American junk food. The guests added their own Saran-wrapped dishes to the buffet, then made a pilgrimage to the centerpiece of the room.

It was an enormous altar that rose to the ceiling, a pyramid of hand-painted statues of the saints, decorated with party streamers, colored scarves, and hibiscus blossoms. Each of the guests left an offering: liquor, pieces of china, money, cigarettes, lingerie, sunglasses, even a handful of shotgun shells. Within seconds, the altar looked like the jumble of a picked-over yard sale.

As they sampled the food and made their devotions, the crowd began to sway to the drumbeat. I realized there were no drums at all, just speaker cabinets and an arsenal of electronics. A stubby man in mirrored sunglasses reacted indignantly, drawing Prosper into a heated argument about the spirituality of synthesized drumming. They jousted back and forth in Creole, until Prosper exploded, splaying himself melodramatically against the speakers. "This is a Korg M1 keyboard, midied with an EPS sixteen-bit sampler and a Linn-Akai MPC sequencer, programmed for self-regulating *rada* and *petro* rhythms. It never gets tired, never misses the beat, and won't ask for a tip at the end of the night. If it goes . . . I go!"

By their relative silence, the crowd signaled that they wanted the ceremony to proceed. The protester retreated to a corner to soothe his wounded pride with a rum and soda; Prosper turned up the volume of the electronic drums. Lucy and I set up the recorders, hiding one in the light fixture that hung from the ceiling. Prosper moved among his guests, listening to their complaints, nodding sagely, whispering advice. Slowly, the rhythm asserted its collective spell, and the people became dancers. They swayed around the room in a counterclockwise formation, their knees bent, their upper bodies rippling like wind-driven blades of grass. Some broke off into solo acts, eyes rolling shut, heads thrown back; others just sat and watched, chatting and snacking.

Suddenly, the beat changed. It became crisper, more distinctive: *rest, two, three; rest, two, three* . . . . There were gasps of excitement as the dancers responded, picking up the tempo. Feet slammed, hands clapped violently, bodies made rough contact.

I didn't even know it had happened. I thought the young woman with the close-cropped hair, and Hawaiian shirt and jeans had fallen, knocked down by the increasing tumult of the dancing. But then the crowd spread out, giving her room. "Celine has a loa!" someone shouted. She lay on her side, coiled in a fetal position, hands knotted, the cords on her neck pulsing, threatening to burst through the skin. She jerked convulsively, her features twisting like melting wax into painful expressions. Then she straightened her legs and shot her arms out in front of her, fingernails clawing at the cement. Her entire body metamorphosed, and she began to slither across the floor, her flicking tongue drawing a moist trail along the chalk-drawn vèvès.

"Damballah, the serpent," Lucy said. "It usually means good luck when he appears first."

People bent over Celine, shouting encouragement, feeding her handfuls of sugar, blotting the sweat off her forehead. She began to tear off the buttons of her shirt, timing her striptease to the beat of the drums, shedding her clothes as a snake sheds its skin. She crawled toward me, and I jumped out of the way. But it wasn't me she was after. She moved between the legs of a tall, young man in a navy blazer, coiling sensuously up his body, thirstily lapping at his denimed thighs. She slowly drew down his zipper. He smiled and sipped his beer, enjoying her attentions, his eyes focused on her brown skin and lacy black bra. Then, she threw her head back and hissed, and clamped down violently on his thigh with her teeth!

He howled in pain, collapsing to his knees. "You goddamn bitch . . . what the fuck are you doing!" He tried to push her head away, but she held on with her fangs, like a stubborn rattlesnake. A group of believers rushed forward and managed to separate the two before blood could be drawn. I looked at the crowd, at the faces struggling to contain their laughter.

"That guy is Celine's husband," Lucy confided to me, joining in the laughter. "A real dictator; she never even raises her voice to him. But sometimes the loa get impatient; they just go ahead and do the things you always wanted to do."

At that moment, the synthesizer accelerated yet again, setting a frenetic tempo that felt like it was spinning into anarchy. The drumming thundered and echoed, like a chain of explosions set off in a mine shaft. Prosper emerged from the swirl of dancers directly in front of me, eyes rolled up into his head, the whites dead, vacant, gone. He was already under.

He came at me with a stoop-shouldered walk, supported by a crutch, dragging one leg, spit coating his lips. Then, as though he had been supernaturally resuscitated, he rose to his full height. He swung the crutch over his head, smashing the ceiling light. The mini-recorder I'd concealed there shattered. When he talked, his voice was cracked and guttural, the voice of a bitter old man. "What's this murderer doing in the middle of the road? I, Legba Grand-Chemin, don't like to see no white killers in the road." He prodded me in the chest with the crutch, driving me toward the wall.

I glanced wildly at Lucy; she fought her way toward me, a second tape recorder held above her head. Prosper whipped around and slashed it out of her hand with his crutch. It flew across the room like a bullet, fell to the floor in the chaos of trampling feet.

"I thought Prosper was on our side," I shouted.

"He's not Prosper anymore," Lucy gasped. She disappeared into the dancers to search for her recorder. Prosper bored the crutch deep into my stomach; I clamped both hands on it, my muscles burning as I tried to force him back. I was linked to the spirit now, and the metal seemed to heat up in my grip. I decided to test him.

"There was someone else there that night!" I screamed. "Didn't you see them?"

Prosper shook his head. "Legba looks in all four directions but don't see no one."

"I guess Legba's not all that observant, is he?" I snapped.

"He becomes a bat, springing into the heavens above the crossroads, but he don't see no one; he becomes a worm burrowing into the dirt beneath the crossroads, and still he don't see no one!"

I was beginning to sense how the loa operated. They were vain, moody, and easily insulted—like the humans they possessed. "You're wasting my time," I said. "You don't know the truth about that night. I should've just gone to a private detective."

Prosper dropped the crutch, then began to circle me, like a wasp preparing to strike. "I'll show you what I know. I'm an old man, I've died and lived a thousand times . . ."

"Older, maybe. But not wiser," I taunted.

"It didn't start at the crossroads. You think I don't know that?"

"So where did it start? Prove it to me, show it to me!"

Prosper's eyelids drooped shut. He staggered away, drifting through the crowd like a sleepwalker. Other people had fallen into trances; the dancers were building to a fevered pitch, dewy with sweat, eyes burning ecstatically. I followed Prosper to a liquor cabinet, where he grabbed bottles at random, mixing himself a deranged cocktail. Between sips, he murmured in rapid-fire Creole. Was this the great revelation from the mouth of the loa? A nearly inaudible ramble, slurred by alcohol? I bent closer to Prosper and cranked up the volume on my mini-recorder.

I felt a gentle mist on the back of my neck, inhaled a thick cloud of cheap perfume. I caught a fleeting glimpse of lace gloves holding a bottle of perfume, then hands were pressed over my eyes. Lips kissed the perfume from my neck, then moved around to my throat.

A tongue probed beneath the collar of my shirt, then the

hands fell away from my eyes and I saw Lucy, her lips painted a brilliant red, like she had been drinking blood. Her cheeks were garishly rouged and she wore false eyelashes, batting them coquettishly, like black palm fronds. "Lucy, what's going on?"

"Don't you recognize your mistress Erzulie?" she asked, in a voice that was suddenly high and girlish. She drew my hand to her hair and slowly guided me through its unbraiding.

"Are you really under?" I hissed. "Or are you just faking?" She didn't answer. She moved to the music, swaying her hips outrageously. Men drifted by; Lucy hooked her little finger around theirs, drew them closer, blowing them flirtatious kisses.

Like a lion waking up from a nap, she shook her unbraided hair in my face, then circled me with her arms. A feeling of lostness flooded into me. I felt weightless, airy, as though a gentle breath could blow me apart. The crowd seemed to disappear—there was only Lucy. She danced me into a dark corner behind the bank of synthesizers. She tore a picture off the wall and held it in front of me: a sad-eyed Virgin Mary, glittering with jewels, a blood-stained knife piercing her heart.

"You see the knife? You threw it, Raymond. My heart's blood . . . bleeding for you."

She took my face in her hands. Her fingers were spiky with costume-jewelry rings. I kissed her vampire-red lips, tasted the rum on her tongue. Sweat dripped onto her cheeks; the makeup ran, thick and streaked like silent-movie tears. It was the clownish makeup that made me want her more: it was proof that she was too real, too desirable to be disguised by artifice. Her body twisted around me, pliant and soft. I pressed her against the wall, matching her hungry kisses with my own. She kicked off her shoes, drew a bare foot up the back of my leg.

"Lucy, can you hear me?" No answer. She began to unbutton my shirt, kissing my chest, warming me with her lips, tantalizing me with her tickling black mane of hair. I slid her dress down over her breasts, felt them press urgently against my skin. I was enveloped, shameless. I would have done anything and taken the consequences later.

Something cold traced a path along my skin, starting at my

neck, sweeping downward, then back up again in a lazy arc. Lucy was drawing on me with lipstick—a bright-red cartoon heart. Then, a series of furious slashes, grinding the lipstick down to its metal container as she sketched the heart-piercing sword. It felt like she was marking me as her property.

I ran my hands down her naked back, loving the feel of her skin, the warm, sharp planes of her shoulder blades. She threw the lipstick away, kissed me roughly. We slid along the wall, a single body, stumbling deliriously over a tangle of cables and plugs.

The drumming stopped.

The dancing roared on full-bore for a few seconds. But without the sustaining rhythm, it trailed off, like dying applause. Those who had been in a trance state staggered drunkenly. Other worshipers helped them to chairs, brought them glasses of water, fanned them with towels.

Lucy shivered in my hands. She blinked, looked at me curiously. She smiled, stretching her body gloriously, as though awakening from a fantastic dream. Then she realized she was naked from the waist up, and quickly covered herself. She stared wide eyed at my lipstick-decorated chest, sniffed at her perfumed wrists, picked up a mirror from the altar, and examined her made-up face.

"Was I . . ."

"You don't remember?"

She shook her head. "They say if you remember, you're lying."

"So it's never happened to you before?"

"I've been to a couple ceremonies back in Port-au-Prince; they even used to stage them for the tourists, but nothing ever happened. How could it—I'm not a believer."

"Don't tell me there's not a single part of your body that remembers. Not even a square inch of skin somewhere?"

She laughed, looked down at the picture of the Virgin, which lay trampled on the floor. She picked it up, smoothed it out. "I know about Erzulie. Goddess of love, of sensuality. The Black Aphrodite." She curled her arms around me. "Sometimes she's just the goddess of basic trashy behavior . . . but deep down, she's a nonstop seeker of love; hundreds of years go by, yet she's never satisfied." She kissed me. There was more fever in that kiss, and more longing, than in a hundred of Erzulie's.

The loa bring our repressed desires to the surface: Lucy's words.

"That's the real you, right? Or is it Memorex?"

"It's me, Raymond. All me."

I wondered if I was falling in love with Lucy? Suddenly, the isolation of my Virginia home seemed terrifying. Its restoration had been the most important part of my life, and now it seemed like a selfish, empty gesture unless I could share it with her.

Annoyed worshipers brushed past us and plugged in the synthesizers that we'd knocked out. But the musical cockpit defeated them; they couldn't get the drums restarted.

"Where the hell's Prosper?" I asked. We searched the basement, but he had vanished. I fought off a surge of panic. "Let's check upstairs." We ran into the darkened living room. A couple of people had fallen asleep on the couch; a man was stretched out on the recliner, randomly channel-changing.

"Tu as vu Prosper?" Lucy asked him. He just shrugged. There was no sign of Prosper in the kitchen, the dining room, or the bathrooms.

"He wouldn't just cut out, would he?" I asked. "Without telling us?"

"Who knows? Check your tape recorder; let's see what we have."

I played back the tape of Prosper's recitation, the frenzied mumble he'd broken into during the deepest throes of possession. I'd developed an ear for Creole by now, but this sounded like another language altogether, made even more impenetrable by the thunder of the drums.

"Shit!" Lucy said. She sped through the tape, but it was all the same. "It's all in *langage:* a ritual, voodoo language. Part Latin, part African, part bastardized Creole. Without Prosper, we won't be able to understand any of this."

I glanced into the backyard, where the full moon had turned the lawn into a ghostly, gray sheet. At first I thought it was an

injured dog dragging itself across the grass toward the patio—
then I realized it was Prosper, crawling on all fours, head drooping lifelessly.

We rushed outside. Prosper looked up at us, his features
painted in fear. We bent down next to him; he gasped through
lips that were flecked with vomit. "Lay me on my back, please.
I want to see the moon."

We gently lowered him onto the grass. I cleaned his mouth
with my handkerchief, then made a cursory head-to-toe inspection—no wounds or bleeding. "My body's doin' OK now,
man," he wheezed. "But I got knocked way out of my spiritual
groove down there. I had to get outside. See the stars, feel the
earth beneath my back."

He stretched out his arms, pressing his palms onto the cool
blades of grass. A concerned crowd gathered on the patio. "I
never felt one like this before," he said. "Usually, when I come
out of a trance, I take a stiff drink, pass the collection plate,
and know I've done somebody some good. But tonight, when
the loa released me, they released me into such pain . . . like
they were angry that I dared to ask these questions about you."
Prosper dug his fingers into my wrist. "Someone was trying
to turn them against me! The spiritual world's all screwed up,
man! Someone ultrapowerful is after you, Ray, he's got the
kind of power it takes a hundred years to develop!"

We helped Prosper to his feet. "Come on, let's get you home.
We'll talk about it there."

He pulled away. "What do you think this guy's been doing
while we've been busy here? You think he's been lying by the
pool? You don't think he knows we've been in conference with
the loa?" Still wobbly, Prosper swept the dirt off his white suit.
The moonlight accented the lines of determination branching
out across his face. "We go after him tonight!"

14

NATURE HAD DONE her best to obliterate the murder. A crape myrtle had shed its showy white blossoms; like a funeral wreath, they covered the blood-stained weeds where Baptiste had fallen. While Lucy and Prosper waited, I got out of the car. I bent down and ran my hands through the soil: this simple patch of road would always be a grave for me.

"From what we can tell from the tape," Lucy said as I slid back behind the wheel, "Jean-Mars Baptiste began his last night at a large house in the woods somewhere. Then he worked his way through the city, making three stops before he met you in Rosslyn."

"This house—could it have been his family's brownstone?"

Prosper played the tape back, shook his head. "It doesn't say, man."

"No address? Not even a neighborhood?" I asked.

"Look, Legba don't work for *Better Homes and Gardens,* OK? I got something about a big house on the edge of the forest. And that's it."

"A freestanding house? Two stories? Georgian, Federal? Does it have a front yard?"

"Maybe. Why the hell not?" he said irritably.

"I'm trying to get a fix on the neighborhood. Different areas of the city have different architectural styles."

"Look, Raymond, this tape is very disjointed," Lucy said. "Full of turns, stops, and starts. Nothing is ever mentioned by name—no buildings, no streets. We're just going to have to work our way backwards from here, keep patient . . ."

"And hope we get lucky," I added.

I drove as Prosper and Lucy played back the tape of the possession, arguing over its English translation. It was the strangest sensation yet: listening to a record of one man's conversation with the gods, using it as a road map to retrace Baptiste's movements the night of the murder. In the beginning, the tape was accurate, guiding me to the offices of *USA Today*, though not following the same roads I had taken that night. I was still skeptical. I had described the murder to Lucy in detail, and she could have shared her knowledge with Prosper. The real test was about to begin: as we crossed the river into Washington, we entered the unknown roads taken by Baptiste on the last night of his life.

Prosper's instructions were muddled and vague. "Turn onto the big street with the light and head north!" he would shout, and it would take me ten wrong turns, doubling back, tripling back, until I found the street that we agreed felt right. He led me against traffic onto one-way streets, down blind alleys, and into cul-de-sacs. "Head due west along the street that has a letter in its name, until you come to the jungle," he said enigmatically.

" 'Jungle'? What the hell's that mean? Is it literal or metaphorical?"

" 'Rain forest,' to be more specific," Prosper said.

I looked at Lucy; she was as perplexed as I was. "Maybe it's a bar," I suggested. "One of those places that serves flaming mai tais in coconut shells."

The lettered streets included half of Washington, and given the city's quadrant geography, the same address could theoretically appear in four different places. I dutifully worked my way along streets *T* through *C,* southwest and southeast, then cut through the Mall on Fourteenth Street, intending to repeat the laborious search in the city's northwest and northeast districts. I turned left onto Constitution Avenue; across the Ellipse stood the White House, always gleaming, always freshly painted.

I winked at Prosper. "Big house, big front yard—you sure that's not it?"

We were not in a neighborhood of bars. This was serious government business—Department of the Interior, the American Red Cross, the Treasury Building. I pounded the steering wheel in frustration. "I can't believe you've got me looking for a jungle in Washington—the whole goddamn city's a jungle!"

I nearly drove right past it. I slammed on the brakes, turned north onto Seventeenth Street, and made an illegal left into the elliptical driveway of a beautiful white building capped with a Spanish tile roof. Polished marble steps glowed in the moonlight, leading up to a trio of arched doorways. "One block that way is a street with the letter in its name: C Street," I said excitedly. "And in there . . . is your rain forest."

"So what is it?" Lucy asked.

We jumped out of the car, and I led them up the steps. "It's the OAS building, the Organization of American States. Of which, probably not coincidentally, Haiti is a member. The central courtyard is this huge garden—palm trees, ferns, tropical flowers." The building was closed and the interior was dark, but we could hear the soothing hiss of a fountain in the patio. I could imagine its cool mist coating the bright green leaves, watering the "jungle." Prosper had appealed to the gods and they had answered.

"I can barely believe it, but you were right," I said.

"Legba was right." Prosper shrugged.

With that simple shrug, Prosper Telemache defined his approach to the religion. To a *vodounist,* the intervention of the spirits was beyond dispute. It was the natural state of things. Like up and down. Yes and no. Why question the unquestionable; indeed, why even be amazed by it?

"He met someone here," Prosper said. "But it didn't start here; they were supposed to meet somewhere else, somewhere private. But Baptiste felt threatened . . ."

"That makes sense," I said. "His house had been bombed, he's scared for his life—he would insist that the meeting be held somewhere he felt safe."

We were attracting the attention of a security guard. I led us back to the car. "OK, listen, what do we have in this neighborhood? White House, Department of the Interior . . . Daughters of the American Revolution. None of them seems like a likely hangout for Baptiste. Come on, Prosper, you're not getting any mental image . . . a room, a face?"

"I'm not a psychic! I can't read minds. When the loa mounts you, your soul is displaced; it goes somewhere else, it has no memory of the possession. I'm telling you, Ray, all I got is this tape."

They looked at me expectantly; it was my turn to lead the investigation. "OK, let's assume this was a backup site. That means they probably walked here from the initial rendezvous. South of us, you got the Mall, the Vietnam vets memorial, Potomac Park—all wide-open spaces. So let's also assume they came from the north; you got office buildings along E Street, F Street . . . all the way up to Mass Ave."

"What about the Haitian embassy? That's close," Lucy said.

I nodded. "It works thematically. But it may be a bit too far. Let's start with the offices on E Street."

"All of them?" Prosper asked.

"I told you we'd have to get lucky."

Prosper took the south side of the street, Lucy and I the north. We slowly patrolled E Street, the only determined-looking people in a nightscape of homeless wanderers and trolling taxis. I watched the minutes tick by on a Chevy Chase savings and loan clock: 2:32, 2:33, 2:34, time dragging itself slowly toward the deepest trough of the night. We stopped at each office building, searching the directories for a familiar name or phrase. We followed E Street as far as Virginia Avenue, then cut up to F Street. By the time we reached the west end of G Street, I was

tired, questioning the whole idea of this tedious search. We re-
fueled on coffee from an all-night doughnut shop. But just next
door, in a drab brick building that seemed to have no potential at all, I found it. White plastic letters tumbling off the black
background of a cracked glass directory: "Zanfan d'Ayiti."

I wasn't surprised. Ever since her mysterious appearance at
the embassy demonstration, I had been waiting for Carmen
Mondesir to reenter my life. She had always been there, circling
just beyond my vision.

Prosper had never heard of Zanfan d'Ayiti; Lucy hadn't either,
until that evening at the art gallery. "But that's not surprising,"
she explained. "Haiti's main source of income is world pity. It
used to feel like every other business in downtown Port-au-
Prince was a charity; you can't know them all."

Peering into the building's central corridor, I read the other
names on the directory. Most of them occupied the rung below
the bottom rung on the ladder of Washington lobbyists: National Association of Stationery Supplies Distributors, Beef
By-products Trade Board, Harmonica Manufacturers Com-
petitiveness Council.

"Wait a minute," Lucy exclaimed. "I *do* know her from
somewhere!"

"Carmen Mondesir," I said. "It's not a name that's easy to
forget."

"Not the name; the name could be false. But the face, I've
definitely seen it before. It didn't hit me that night at the gallery,
when I saw her in that film, but now, as I play it over in my
mind . . ." She shook her head in frustration. "I know there's
a memory there. Damn, if I could just access it!"

"Maybe I can help you." I checked my watch. "Four-thirty,
still plenty of time until sunrise. Listen, you guys go for a walk,
meet me in the alley behind the building. I got to get some
tools out of the car."

"Speaking as your lawyer, I don't like the sound of this."

"I'm already guilty of murder; how much can I damage my
case by throwing in a little burglary?"

I got the car, moved it onto Twenty-second Street, just around the corner from the Zanfan building. I grabbed the toolbox I kept with the spare, and linked up with Prosper and Lucy in the alley. After determining which window belonged to Zanfan, I laid a crisscross of masking tape on the glass, then scored a fist-size pattern on it with a glass-cutter's knife.

"Wait a minute," Lucy asked. "How do you know they don't have a burglar alarm?"

"I don't." I punched the window sharply. The precut piece of glass broke away neatly and fell into my hand. I held my breath: no sirens, no electronic shrieks. "I just went on the assumption that the Harmonica Manufacturers of America don't have anything worth stealing."

But I wasn't done—the window was dead-bolted. I reached through the opening with my Swiss army knife and went to work on the screws that secured the lock mechanism. Two wrist-twisting minutes later, it dropped into my palm. "Write enough crime stories, you can't help but pick up a few tricks of the trade." I slid out the bolt and raised the window. We were in.

The office was a single, cluttered room. Paperwork and files overflowed the metal desks; phone and fax lines coiled beneath our feet; the walls were crowded with maps of Haiti. There was a TV and several VCRs. One shelf was lined with video-tapes, each marked with the name of a different child—the "video letters" that Carmen Mondesir had boasted of in her promotional film.

But it was a giant bulletin board of black-and-white snapshots that drew our attention. The children—their skin peppered with flies, gaunt faces dominated by huge, pleading eyes, all pho-tographed from a strategic high angle designed to turn pity into cash. It worked: I felt guilty for breaking in, wanted to write out a check on the spot.

We hurried through the search but could find no physical evidence linking Zanfan d'Ayiti to vodoun, nothing that con-nected to the killing of Jean-Mars Baptiste.

"Do you really think he was here?" I whispered to Prosper. He shrugged. I could see the doubt in his eyes.

Then, as I leafed through a Rolodex next to the phone, I spotted three phone numbers every Washington journalist knows by heart: the CIA, the Pentagon, and the State Department! I knew by the extension prefixes that they were private lines belonging to high-ranking officials, numbers unavailable to the public. These were heavy-duty contacts, not people Carmen Mondesir could casually corner in an elevator and hit up for donations. I pulled a recent phone bill out of a stack of mail: there were dozens of calls to the same numbers!

Lucy whispered sharply, "Raymond. You have to see this!" She grabbed my arm, guided me to a picture that was the centerpiece of a wall displaying awards and plaques. It was a framed, eight-by-ten color photograph of a garden party. Black-tied men and women in cocktail dresses clinked champagne glasses on a terraced lawn. Among the party-goers, I picked out the Haitian ambassador, and Helene and Jean-Mars Baptiste. Facing the garden was an immaculate, two-story Federal home; behind the house I recognized the dense woodlands of Rock Creek Park. Beneath the photo, a caption read, SUMMER FUND-RAISER HOSTED BY FAUSTIN GABRIEL, PROMINENT ART COLLECTOR AND GALLERY OWNER.

———

DAWN was still an hour away. Branches slapped at us from the darkness, the footing was rough and deceptive, yet I couldn't risk a flashlight. I didn't know how far the grounds of Faustin Gabriel's house penetrated into the woods, and I was afraid he could spot us.

Lights glowed up ahead like tiny half-moons hung among the leaves. As I crept closer, I saw that they were security lights, ringing the backyard. I waved Prosper and Lucy to their knees and took out my binoculars.

"Raymond, listen," Lucy whispered. "I don't know what we're doing here, but one burglary is enough. I'm still a member in good standing of the bar, and I'd like to stay there."

"I'm not talking burglary, I'm talking surveillance."

"The man is a world-recognized authority on Haitian art. He's curated shows in New York and Paris. He helps sponsor up-and-coming painters so they can study in America. What do you think you'll catch him at, forging signatures?"

"The trail of the loa led us here, Lucy. You want to ignore that?"

"I just think that, as your attorney, I should have the opportunity to question him. To lay some legal groundwork to cover ourselves before we resort to the sleazy detective stuff."

"What if he's the goddamn bokor? The guy that started this all? You think he's going stip to that in a deposition? He's going to see those law books of yours, all dusted and alphabetized, and suddenly become so overwhelmed by the majesty of our legal system that he'll forget who he is?"

She sighed and blew the hair out of her eyes.

"I mean, what's really going on here?" I said. "You had no problem with breaking into that office. But now that we're dealing with someone prominent, powerful, it's a different story."

She lit a cigarette. In the flare of the lighter I saw her lip tremble. She looked down at the ground and traced angry patterns in the dirt with her toe.

"Well, am I out of line?"

"I just want to be careful, that's all."

"I can't afford to be careful." I pressed the binoculars to my eyes. I recognized the backyard from the garden party photograph, with its sweeping stone patio and sculpted hedges. Though the windows facing the backyard were dark, the security lights cast a blue-gray glow into the living room. Gabriel possessed a museum-quality collection of antique furniture and tapestries. A silver tea service sparkled on a marble-topped sideboard; a chandelier was suspended above a carved mahogany desk. The far wall, painted in a trompe l'oeil, gave the room the feel of an endless art gallery, lined with paintings framed in heavy, gilded wood.

One picture caught my eye. It was an eighteenth-century

portrait of a slave, perhaps in his early thirties. His features were delicate and boyish, his eyes wide and curious. The tranquil balance of the pose was broken by a grotesque skin disfigurement that ran from the neck, up the length of the left cheek, and curled around the left eye, like a bizarre mask. I felt a deep shudder of recognition, as though I were staring into the face of someone I had once known intimately. I passed the binoculars to Prosper, troubled by my reaction to the portrait. Where and how could I possibly have seen this man before?

Prosper scanned the house and yard; with each pan of the binoculars, Lucy grew more nervous, squinting into the darkness for the first trace of dawn. "Found it!" Prosper said. "Fifty yards back in the woods on the west side of the house." He handed me the binoculars. I followed his directions, but all I saw was a black, nearly impenetrable landscape.

Gradually, the scene took on definition. What I thought was a dense stand of trees was actually a three-walled hut built from lashed-together branches, like a woodsman's lean-to. From the center of the hut, a large post shot up through a roof made of leaves and twigs.

"It's a peristyle, a vodoun sanctuary," Prosper said. "When the loa are invoked, they descend from heaven down that center post."

"Not exactly your typical add-on. I guess Faustin Gabriel's our man."

"He serves the spirits, that's sure. Whether he's the bokor we're looking for, I don't know. We need to get closer."

We circled through the woods and approached the peristyle from behind, so close to the enemy now, I felt a kicking in my stomach.

Inside the temple, I recognized the sequined voodoo flags, the vèvès sketched on the cement floor with colored chalk, the altar with its garage-sale offerings. But beneath the altar was something that didn't fit—a flat, black leather case. I slid it out—it was an oversized folder, the type artists use to carry their work. I looked at Prosper. He just shrugged and nodded at me to open it.

When I lifted the flap, I saw myself.

There were dozens of charcoal sketches, the likenesses rough but clearly recognizable. Gabriel had captured me driving, walking, sitting at my desk, but the details weren't perfect. He hadn't been inside my house, he hadn't been in my car—these had come straight from his imagination. Then I realized they were preliminary drawings; he had been practicing, getting my movements down, my expression, my physique.

At the bottom of the pile was a color painting. Energetic brushstrokes, violent, nearly uncontrollable dribbles of paint. It was a picture of me shooting Jean-Mars Baptiste!

I drew a finger across my own image. This was worse than a photograph or a recording—Gabriel had turned murder into art. Lucy was speechless, she looked shell-shocked. I held up the picture.

"I don't always look this heavy, do I?"

As the joke fell flat, I realized I was wrong: the crime hadn't come first, the picture had.

Prosper whistled, muttered a Creole prayer. "That's how he controls you, man. He don't even need to get near you. It's not like that bullshit voodoo you read about. No pins, no dolls. He don't need a lock of your hair or a piece of your clothing. He just goes into possession and begins to paint. What goes in here," he said, pointing to the canvas, "comes out here." He tapped my forehead. His cockiness had deserted him. Prosper Telemache, ambassador to the gods, voodoo entrepreneur, was afraid.

Brilliant bursts of light swept through the trees. Startled, we ran out of the peristyle to investigate, and stumbled over deep, rutted tire tracks—the middle of an unpaved road. Then, a low mechanical hum to our left—a moving wall . . . a gate! The menacing rumble of a car engine now, skidding toward us from out of the forest, capturing us in the dazzling blue glare of its headlights.

"Lucy!" I screamed. "Get the hell out of here!" She looked stunned, then betrayed. I waved frantically with both hands, as though I could push her away with the force of my gestures.

I knew I was safe, but if they caught Lucy, they would kill her.

"Prosper, get her out of here."

"What about you, man?"

"Just give me a minute. I'll meet you at the car." He looked at me critically. I had heard Prosper talk of *konesans:* spiritual prowess, intuition, the sum total of a houngan's ability to interpret human behavior. Was his strong enough to tell him that I was lying, that I might never even see him again?

"Really, I'll make it. Now get going."

He nodded curtly and bolted across the road, just in front of the oncoming car. It slowed to a crawl, its smoked-glass windows blocking my view. By the time it had passed, Prosper and Lucy were gone.

The car waited for me, idling just inside the gate. I walked toward it, then stopped. I looked up at the sky, which had lightened to a dull gray. I listened—no running footsteps crunching through leaves, no panicked shouts. They were far away by now. Safe.

I stepped into the yard and the gate hummed shut behind me.

15

THE SYMPTOMS WERE less extreme than usual: no fever, no dizziness, no accelerating pulse; just a quiet collapse. Like a junkie, I was becoming immune to the rush of my affliction.

Faustin Gabriel's poise was infuriating as he stepped out of the car and led me across the lawn into the house. He simply accepted that I would follow him, confident in his power, confident in my lack of it.

We settled in the spacious salon I'd seen through the French doors; a Haitian valet brought us a pot of reviving coffee, then retreated, heels clicking across the parquet floor. I quickly drank two cups, black, but Gabriel moved deliberately, stirring in cube after cube of sugar, as though gathering his thoughts from the thick, sweet brew. The last time I had seen him, at the Galerie Creole, he had worn a pure white suit. Tonight he was dressed entirely in black—slacks, shirt, and jacket; even the foulard knotted around his neck was black.

The room was cloaked in the past. There were tapestries from Gobelin and Aubusson, ebony cabinets by Boulle, Louis XIV chairs and lacquered escritoires, shelves crowded with the work of French gold- and silversmiths. A large, velvet-wrapped clay

191

urn was displayed prominently on the mantel, flanked by flickering candles that cast it in a timeless, religious glow. On Gabriel's massive desk, inlaid with copper and tortoiseshell, a fax machine and cellular phone stood out like a technological mirage.

"Would you like to survive this ordeal, Mr. Falco?" Gabriel asked. "Or are you more inclined toward martyrdom, the gallant reporter, *mort pour la patrie?*"

"You're offering me my life? When you already control it?"

"That's the problem. I don't control it. Not all of it, not quite yet." He drank his coffee in a single gulp, leaned against his desk. "No, Mr. Falco, if I had total control, you would not even be here, you would never have connected me to your 'condition.' I probably underestimated your reporter's stubbornness."

I didn't know how to react. I was trapped in some border zone—firmly in Faustin Gabriel's grasp, yet my mind was nimble, spilling over with questions. Maybe vodoun had its limits: they could tell me what to do, but not what to think.

"Get to the point," I said.

"The point is, you are stronger than I had anticipated. You have been able to fight me off, like a drug fights off a virus. But you will eventually run out of that drug, the disease will win. It will be painful and wasting."

"I'll just have to deal with it."

"But why? Why deal with it? Stop fighting us, Mr. Falco. Clean the agony out of your life."

The fax machine hissed. Gabriel read the transmission as it curled onto his desk. His eyes lightened, and he nodded in satisfaction. "Marvelous things, these faxes and satellites and fiber-optic networks. They allow me to keep in contact with my exiled clients, wherever they may be. A certain client in Paris has decided to undergo a course of treatment I suggested weeks ago. After her Western doctors proved useless, of course. In this age of moral uncertainty, of AIDS, the so-called educated classes are turning to vodoun in increasing numbers." He made a note in a morocco-bound ledger, then slipped the fax into his desk. "You see? Surrender. In a way, it's the basis of all the world's religions."

"What makes you think this has to do with religion?" I shouted. "This is mental piracy; you've taken over another human being's life! What's your game plan? Why does it involve me?"

Gabriel coolly averted his eyes. He ran his fingers along the desk's copper inlay, seeming to draw a mystical communication from the contact.

"How far back does your family go, Mr. Falco?"

"I don't know. I never checked. Who cares?"

"We Gabriels have been in Haiti for three hundred and fifty years. We have distinguished ourselves in every era of our nation's history. Confidants to power, the daily intimates of Dessalines, King Christophe, General Soulouque, General Sam; even President Dartiguenave sought our advice during the American occupation, when your marines ran a campaign to suppress vodoun.

"Since 1804, a Gabriel has been near the seat of power; not literally occupying the *fauteuil présidentiel,* of course, but hovering nearby, like a cloud. Ready to rain when necessary, ready to move out of sight and permit the sun to shine when that became necessary.

"No Gabriel had ever been driven from his country before. I was the first, expelled during the anti-vodoun frenzy that swept Haiti after the fall of Baby Doc Duvalier. Knowing that I could not survive in exile without a physical connection to the past, I brought the *objets* you see in this room. My country's first constitution was drafted on this desk. I discovered my love of art at this desk, made my first tentative drawings while seated before it on a stack of books from my father's library."

He moved through the room, extinguishing the oil lamps. "Understand me, Mr. Falco. I fled my country in a spasm of weakness and fear. A moment when measured against history, but it was my moment. And so I must make my atonements."

"By atonement, you mean retaking power in Haiti."

"Not for me, Mr. Falco," he said, a wounded tone in his voice. "For the loa."

"Of course. It's all done in the name of God, isn't it? Is that why you had me kill Jean-Mars Baptiste? God told you to get rid of your political enemies? Did he give you the idea of the loup-garou skin, too? I can just picture you in that perfect white suit, raiding the hospital meat lockers like a goddamn ghoul."

"I certainly didn't steal it myself. I have people who know people . . . and don't be so horrified, or you'll never get through this. Visit the main cemetery in Port-au-Prince, and you will see desecrations far worse."

I heard a car drive up outside. Purposeful footsteps hurried across gravel. I threw open the double doors that led to the rest of the house. Sun glinted through the fan transom at the end of the hall, and as the front door flew open, Carmen Mondesir stepped into the shaft of light. In the orange, low-angled sun, she seemed about to burst into flames.

Behind her I saw the morning: garage doors opening, joggers puffing up a gentle hill; a paper hitting a front porch. Just another day beginning in the real world. Then Carmen Mondesir closed the door, and that comforting reality vanished like a fondly remembered dream.

I backed away from her. Gabriel filled the doorway behind me—I was caught between them.

"Faustin, have you been feeding our subject a steady diet of salt?" she asked sharply.

"That's just peasant lore. A spoonful of salt can no more awaken a *zombi astral* than an alarm clock can."

"But he's here, isn't he? He knows what we are now. He traced us to this house and you told me that was impossible!" Carmen gave me a frank and appreciative appraisal, much as I imagined the slave owners of Saint Domingue had sized up their human purchases. "Maybe I underestimated you, Raymond." She drew her hand across my cheek, her long fingernails scraping against my beard. I noticed they were painted

blue, to match her extraordinary eyes. "Or maybe I overesti-
mated *him*." She spat out the word, like it was an insect that
had flown into her mouth.

Logic and the survival instinct ordered me to get out of there.
But as I tried to slip off down the corridor, a glass wall seemed
to descend in front of me. I couldn't crack it, couldn't push
through it, not even a finger. Was it the power of Faustin Gabriel
that held me there, or my own desperate curiosity? Or was it
both? Vodoun, again tapping into my truest, deepest desire—
to get the story or die trying. The answers to all my questions
were in this house, the creators of my purgatory available for
interview. Even if I could have escaped, I don't think I would
have.

"Carmen, *calme-toi*," Gabriel said. "He's still very control-
lable. Let me offer you some coffee."

Carmen attacked Gabriel in strident Creole, thrusting and
parrying with her finger like it was a fencing foil. "Vodoun!
Moin bouké ac tout bagaye sa you," she shouted. "This vodoun
of yours is exhausting me! How can you guarantee that he'll
do what we need him to do?"

"Which is what?" I demanded. "You run my life; the least
you can do is tell me where it's running."

Carmen ignored me. "You see, Faustin: this stubbornness,
all these questions. He's not tame at all. He's chewing his way
through the leash." She fitted a cigarette into her ivory holder,
then studied me critically. "You want the simple answer, the
headline, Raymond? You're going to help us recapture Haiti."

I laughed. "Don't tell me—you have commandos training
down in the Everglades. A few dozen people with Chinese AK-
47's, rubber life rafts, and a pompous acronym. You plan to
storm the beach, stir up a popular rebellion in the countryside;
twenty-four hours later you're sitting down to dinner in the
presidential palace."

"We will not be stepping onto Haitian soil from rubber boats,
that's sure," Carmen said. "We're a little more sophisticated
than that."

"But at least let me know how I was chosen. *Why* I was chosen."

"The answer will do no harm to your ego—you were chosen because of your reputation. Because you were one of the most respected journalists in the country."

She nodded at Gabriel, who pulled open the top drawer of a filing cabinet. I shivered when I saw what it contained: the life and career of Ray Falco—bank statements, credit histories, news clippings, résumés, a dossier as complete as any intelligence service could compile.

She drew a luxurious breath from her cigarette, her shrewd blue eyes focusing on Gabriel from behind a veil of smoke. "Prove it to me, Faustin. Prove to me that you offer something more than cheap hypnotism, more than catalepsy or drugs. Show me your mastery over our friend Raymond here."

"What kind of a demonstration do you have in mind, Carmen? Something operatic, no doubt," he said caustically. "Do you propose that he walk across hot coals? How would it be if he drank a cocktail of ground glass?"

"Don't be defensive, Faustin. Either you're in control or you're not. Either you're the man for the job . . . or you are not."

I was struck by the openness with which they discussed me. They didn't care that I overheard; to them I was a harmless child who didn't understand the language of the adults.

Gabriel's shoulders sagged. He sat at his desk and sighed, as though he were facing a grueling task. He opened a gold jewel case, took out an assortment of colored felt pens. He cleared the paperwork off his desk to make room for a sketch pad, then ran his hands over the blank pages in a thoughtful caress. I heard Carmen Mondesir's breath catch. Her eyes burned an impossibly bright blue, and when her gaze shifted from Gabriel to me, it turned hungry and probing.

Gabriel closed his eyes and raised his face to the ceiling. Sightless, he began to draw, slowly, precisely. I felt a chill stir through my body, spreading with a speed that matched Gabriel's pen strokes. I edged toward the French doors, my hand reaching for the dead bolt; suddenly, my curiosity and spirit of adventure were gone, replaced by the stark realization that I had to get out of there. If I were ever to reclaim myself, I had to do it now—before they could sink their mental claws into me any deeper. But Gabriel drew a series of rapid, slashing lines, and my body spasmed in response. When he opened his eyes he saw that I was frozen at the door, my hand unable to turn the lock.

He opened another drawer and took out something bright and heavy. Like a shuffleboard player, he skidded a gun across the parquet floor. It slid to a stop at my feet.

"You're crazy!" Carmen shouted at him.

"Go ahead, it's loaded," Gabriel said. "Feel free to shoot your way out."

I picked up the gun, hefted it curiously in my hand, as though it were just a stone I intended to skip across a river. I pointed it at Gabriel, who barely blinked, then panned it toward Carmen. Her lips trembled. I cocked the hammer, my thumb quivering.

"Faustin . . ." Carmen said, her voice cracking.

"Shhhh!" Gabriel scolded. "You asked for this demonstration, now let it unfold naturally."

There was an instant of absolute clarity in which I saw myself pump three bullets into Gabriel, the other three into Carmen, then run down the hall and out the front door to freedom—but the moment vanished, like a drop of rain exploding onto sand. I turned my back on them and fired at the French doors, six explosions, one for each pane of glass.

The aftershock was a muffled silence in which the three of us waited for someone else to make the first move.

Keeping her eyes on me, Carmen spoke to Gabriel with quiet authority. He began to draw again, and Carmen moved sinuously toward me. She licked the sweat off her upper lip, and rolled up her sleeves, revealing arms as smooth and glistening as a grand piano. She stopped just inches in front of me; her skin was maddeningly smooth and desirable; I could feel the heat radiating from her body. She glanced at Gabriel, who nodded.

That nod was like a command to me. I reached into the shattered window frame and pried loose a shard of glass. Carmen seized my hand and drew it to her mouth, first fogging the glass with her breath, then kissing it, marking it with a red smear of lipstick.

Her blue eyes darkened. Still clasping my hand, she reached behind her neck with her other hand and untied her hair—it was a gesture of such calculated sensuality, it was as though she had stripped naked. She shook her head and the hair tumbled past her shoulders, thick and straight, with threads of gray that seemed sewn in for decoration. I had a desire to seize it in tight handfuls and use it to pull her to me. As though reading my thoughts, she brought her face next to mine; her skin was warm and humid, her hair jumping with static electricity. Her breathing was quick and excited, matching my own. Her lips glided across my neck, stopping just below my ear.

"Cut yourself," she whispered. "On your shoulder, right here." She ripped open the top two buttons of my shirt and forced it back, exposing my left shoulder. I nodded, anxious to please her, afraid that if I didn't, she would break contact and I would lose her warmth, her excitement. I held my breath and made the first incision, drawing a trickle of blood. I waited for the needle of pain, but it never came. I wasn't satisfied with a single cut. Carmen watched, aroused now, biting down on her tongue as I sliced the glass across my skin, carving in blood a pattern that leapt from my unconscious. Instead of pain, I felt desire; instead of revulsion, I felt fascination. Carmen lowered her mouth to my shoulder and kissed the blood, sealing the pattern with her lips. My hand went limp, the shard of glass dropped to the floor. When Carmen kissed my lips I could taste my own blood, both sweet and bitter. But it was a taste that didn't linger, replaced by her own distinctive taste of rum and tobacco.

An image of Lucy formed at the misty edge of my vision,

as though she were standing in the doorway, watching in jealousy.

"Lucy?" I called.

"No one's there," Carmen said, quickening the tempo of her kisses. I tried to pull away, to look over her shoulder, but it was impossible—Carmen Mondesir's black intensity would not let me go. Lucy vanished, a ghost returning to my conscience. "She was a mirage in your life, Raymond. You reached for her, thinking she could help you, but it was like reaching for air."

Faustin Gabriel walked toward us. "You don't need a lawyer, Mr. Falco. You can count on us for protection. Please believe me, it does not serve our interests to have you locked away in jail."

"Tell me, Faustin, how would a zombi be as a lover?" Carmen asked. When she smiled, I saw that her teeth were stained with my blood.

"Well, of course I have no direct experience in the matter," Gabriel said. "But I cannot imagine a zombi lover would display much inventiveness. However, he would be wonderful at following orders." He crumpled the drawing, tossed it into the fireplace. "So, have I reassured you Carmen?"

"At the very least, I believe you have a nice sense of *ironie*." With her fingernail, Carmen traced a circle around the pattern I had cut in my shoulder. The blood had gelled, forming a thin, purple-red fleur-de-lis. "You see, Raymond, the slave owners of Saint Domingue often used the fleur-de-lis to brand their property."

Pain was finally invading my shoulder; it throbbed, adding to the layer of dreaminess that was falling on me. "How much longer?" I asked.

"Until what?" said Carmen.

"Until my mission, my assignment, whatever you call it, is over?"

"We're dealing with history here, Mr. Falco," Gabriel said. "Which of course is unpredictable. But let me console you by saying that I am an impatient man, too. Like the journalist, the vodounist believes in deadlines. To a Haitian, martyrdom is not heroism, survival is. We like to see results here on earth."

I once smoked opium while researching a story—there's a little Hunter S. Thompson in all of us—and the way I felt now reminded me of a dizzy, drawn-out opium session: Physically, emotionally exhausted, yet my mind was hyperactive, trying to absorb all the impossibilities it had been fed.

How much longer, how much more? They wouldn't answer.

They asked me if I wanted to lie down. Did I want more coffee, a drink, an aspirin?

Through heavy eyes, I saw them hovering. "As long as you're up, you can get me my freedom," I said.

"Sooner than you think, Mr. Falco," Gabriel said. As I watched him chew on a sugar cube, I realized he had put something in my coffee.

"What was it?" I asked.

"Oh, just a calming agent. Old family recipe, as you might say. To ease the shock. If the mind struggles too hard to reject foreign concepts, it can do irreparable damage to itself. Soon you'll sleep, and when you wake up, none of this will seem quite so bizarre. It will simply be the way it is."

I felt them lifting me, escorting me across the room, my feet seeming to float above the parquet. I stared up at the portrait of the disfigured slave that I had seen earlier. The picture dominated the room, the eyes followed me, full of taunting secrets. If only you could speak, I thought. You're the key somehow; the enigma of my history is painted on your features.

"Who is that?" I asked.

"A relative," Gabriel replied. He opened a door, artfully concealed within the trompe l'oeil, to reveal an outdoor passage leading to the garage.

"I know him," I said.

"Vincent Gabriel died nearly two hundred years ago, Mr. Falco."

They tried to lead me through the door, but I fought them. "I've seen him somewhere, goddamn it. Even talked to him. I can almost hear his voice."

Carmen spoke sharply to Gabriel, who redoubled his efforts

to drag me toward the garage. The urge to write was rising in me now, triggered by this picture. I closed my eyes, fixing the slave's face in my memory. If I could just get to pen and paper, maybe the answers would come rushing out. The past would rescue me. It was an arena Faustin Gabriel and Carmen Mondesir couldn't enter; they couldn't control what had happened to me back then. What if they didn't even know about the diary of Nicholas Townsend, about the dispatches from Saint Domingue that he was sending to his twentieth-century colleague?

I let Gabriel escort me to the car. Keep the diary secret from them, I told myself. Prosper had said they couldn't read minds. Maybe they probably couldn't read memories either.

They drove me home in Gabriel's silver BMW, cloying chamber music on the stereo. A soft summer rain began to fall; rain, mixed with sunlight. "No one will watch you, Raymond," Carmen said, as she idly rubbed in a dab of hand lotion. "There are no rules. When you're needed, you'll know."

"Needed how?" I said archly.

"Don't tease. You know I find you attractive. And maybe someday . . . but not here, not now. When we call you, it will be purely business." She looked out the rain-beaded window, at the wide parking lots and giant, rambling malls. "America's a strange place, isn't it, Faustin? It's good to think about going home."

Gabriel shrugged, his eyes on the road. She gave him a friendly kiss on the cheek. He flinched, wiped away the moisture with an irritated swat. "You see, Raymond? Faustin here wishes he didn't need me. And I wish I didn't need him. But we have reached an *accord,* you know? Each of us views the other as a necessary evil."

They let me out in front of my house; they hadn't needed directions. They were so casual; they knew I wouldn't run, knew I wouldn't call for help. The most ego-destroying role in the world is to be someone else's fait accompli.

One step over the threshold, and I knew that I couldn't stay in the house. I would never be at home there until I was rid of this poison in my blood. I locked the shutters, put away my tools, packed a suitcase. I inhaled deeply, trapping the smell of pine shavings and fresh plaster in my lungs, hoping it would last. Then I made a quick, don't-look-back departure and drove into the rain.

An hour later, I stopped at an intersection that could have been anywhere in America: gas station, fried-chicken franchise, twenty-four-hour coffee shop, motel with pool and free cable TV.

I checked in to the Diplomat Motor Inn. Old newspapers were stacked on the lobby desk, a Ray Falco byline stared up at me. The manager gave me a quiet, back-corner room, apologized for the absence of Cokes in the Coke machine. But there were ten presweetened ice teas and I bought them all.

"And one more thing," I said. "I'll need all the stationery you've got."

I double-locked the door and pulled the curtains. The room seemed out of another lifetime—mine; out of another country—America. The TV, the cheap furniture, the sanitary wrapped glasses were as foreign to me as archaeological artifacts exhumed from an ancient city. I pulled the stationery out of its fake leather ledger, propped a postcard of the motel against the mirror. Maybe I would send it to myself: "Dear Raymond, having a great life, wish you were here."

16

Tragedy soon befell our expedition, as unsparing as the tropical sun. The rainy season was late, the creeks and streams began to dry up, and even the jungle itself seemed to cry out in thirst, the green tongues of the banana trees drooping to the parched earth.

We were a curious and motley corps. Through the force of her will, and the bounty of her purse, Esther LaMartiniere had recruited forty French dragoons from the provincial barracks, mercenaries whose political convictions extended no farther than the tips of their bayonets, but whose loyalty could be assured by a daily ration of brandy and a handful of gold livres. Only their commander, a certain Colonel Vestier, was motivated by other than immediate gain—he was approaching retirement, and had purchased a coffee plantation in Le Mirebalais, where he intended to devote himself to those gentlemanly pursuits he had defended as a soldier. He was refreshingly lacking in superciliousness and other French vices, was a skilled marksman and map reader, and I pinned many of my hopes for our expedition's success on his shoulders. We had also engaged two mulatto scouts, Hilliard and Bienvenue. Their mission was to range ahead of our party and bring their tracking skills to bear on the task of flushing out the elusive black general, Xavier Charlemagne.

And so I marched at the head of the column with my unlikely adjutants: Esther LaMartiniere, the firebrand widow who hoped that the death or capture of General Charlemagne would slow the incipient slave revolt, and thus spare the plantation that was her life's work; and Father Rochefort, who saw the Maroons' African religion as a threat to the laws of God and Christ. We did not expect to engage the Negro general militarily; instead, we planned to assess Charlemagne's tactical strengths and weaknesses, from afar if necessary. But I dared hope for a face-to-face meeting, in which we might confront each other in a civilized mien, as two dignified generals come together to divine the other's intentions on the eve of a battle.

How dreadfully wrong events were to prove me! How ignorant I was of the true nature of man, black and white.

We had followed Charlemagne's band from Au Savanne Rouge into the mountains, and on the evening of the fifth day, Colonel Vestier predicted that we would make contact with Charlemagne's rear guard on the morrow. Consequently, we made camp early, so that we might clean and prepare our weapons, and devote the evening to a study of tactics.

That night a hot, dry wind blew and sleep proved impossible. I slipped out of my tent and executed a brief turn around the silent campsite. The wind blew open the flap of Esther LaMartiniere's tent, and I saw that she had fallen asleep fully clothed, her musket clutched tightly to her breast like a lover. Colonel Vestier lay with his head across his camp table, his maps for a pillow. Our dragoons were sprawled unconscious among the trees, a company of drunks; loose faro cards blew across them like dead leaves.

It seemed I was the only one on the island awake.

The wind stirred the remains of the campfire at my feet. A sudden updraft seized the ashes and lifted them skyward in a spiral. I stood back, like a thrilled spectator at a magic show. The ashes curled cloudlike around the overhanging branches of a mahogany tree, and when they blew away, I had a brief glimpse of a human face! A Negro, his features blighted by a cruel and distorting scar, stared down at me in contemplation from his perch on a limb.

I glanced fearfully around the camp—no one was watching. An appeal for help died on my lips. I reached into the fire and seized a smoldering taper, intent on hurling it at this phantom, but when I looked up, he was gone. There was a rustle of leaves, then a great, dark-hued bird burst forth from the branch the Negro had occupied! It soared straight up, circled above our campsite for a moment, then streaked off toward the distant hills.

I shook my head, unsure of the significance of this fantastic scene. Had this curious Negro been real, or merely a specter lured from my imagination by fear? I retreated to my tent, where I lay sleepless the rest of the night. The wind kept up its assault, bringing with it the awful staccato of drumming—a signal that our enemy was near and was watching.

I managed to find peace with the coming of the dawn, but it was short-lived. I was awakened by a chorus of shouts and the sound of muskets being loaded. Then, Esther LaMartiniere tore back my tent flap, her face blazing with alarm. "Colonel Vestier has been poisoned!"

We rushed to our commander's tent, through a knot of panicked dragoons who were finding it difficult to resist firing at will into the forest. Colonel Vestier was sprawled in the dirt, his table upended; the maps he had been studying were twisted around his legs. His eyes were open, and his tongue protruded from his mouth, black-stained and swollen.

"But we all supped from the same pot last night," Esther said. "How is it possible that the poison claimed him, but left the rest of us unharmed?"

I bent over the shattered remains of the colonel's wash basin, which were scattered across a wide, wet patch of ground. Water was pooled in one of the larger shards; I dipped my fingers into the liquid and held them to my nose.

"The water is contaminated!" I shouted, dashing out of the tent.

Esther paled. "But I drank the water last night myself. As did you, as did we all!"

"Colonel Vestier must have risen early to draw water for his morning ablutions . . . which means our supply was poisoned during the night!"

Even now, other members of our party were gathering at the water wagon, filling their cups and basins. I seized Esther LaMartiniere's musket, poured powder into the firing pan, rammed home a ball, and took careful aim at the broad side of the wagon. "Stand aside!" I shouted, and fired. The report scattered a flight of birds to the heavens, then quickly faded, absorbed by the thickly matted jungle. An awful, penetrating silence then reigned, disturbed only by the rush of water as it streamed out of the hogshead. We stared in awe, unable to tear our gaze away as the life force that was to sustain our expedition vanished into the soil.

It was the first disaster of many.

We wrapped the body of Colonel Vestier in the canvas of his own tent, hoping it would provide protection from worms and such other subterranean disturbers of the dead as might reign on Saint Domingue. We lowered him into a common grave, along with four other dragoons who had died during the night.

As Father Rochefort performed his sad religious duties at the gravesite, Esther LaMartiniere and I grappled with the exigencies of our situation. Without fresh water, neither we nor the horses could continue our manhunt. Return to Au Savanne Rouge was impossible—it was five days' distant and there had been no water along the road. But according to Colonel Vestier's maps, a well belonging to the cavalry of the western province National Guard lay two days to the north, and we elected to proceed in that direction, even though it meant crossing three steep and forested mountain ranges.

I said nothing of the phantom Negro I had seen in the tree-tops. I did not wish to further arouse the anxiety of our troops, nor did I wish to give physical credence to what I believed was an imaginary aberration. The poisoning I blamed on nature, water gone bad in the tropical sun. We scattered freshly picked coffee beans about the grave, in the hope that a tree might sprout and provide Colonel Vestier's final resting spot with a serene and sentimental shade. We then departed that mournful camp-site in all haste.

The march was a slow descent into hell; not a hell of flames and damnation, but a hell of lunacy, of tiny, inexplicable mutinies against reason. It began when Bienvenue and Hilliard, our mulatto guides, went mad.

I had been marking our progress against the track of the sun and become convinced that we were being led in circles. I slashed my way ahead of our party to the edge of a deep ravine, where I encountered our two scouts behaving in an abstracted and curious manner. They were shuffling around a tree in mad circles, chanting to themselves, clapping their hands to a music that only they could hear. When I called out to them, they looked up at me with eyes that had already passed beyond the grave.

"Where are you leading us?" I cried.

"To the well that lies to the north," Hilliard replied. "As you instructed."

"But this ravine faces the south," I corrected.

"No, monsieur, it is the north," Hilliard insisted.

I grabbed the stubborn fellow by the wrist and forced my compass into his hand. "There, judge by the evidence in front of you: this ravine is southern facing!" He stared dumbly at the compass as though he had never encountered it before. "All right, then, which way is east?" I demanded, exasperated.

Bienvenue pointed confidently toward the setting sun.

"And west?"

With equal certitude, Hilliard gestured toward the east. I was stunned—both of our scouts had inexplicably lost their sense of direction!

We were forced to proceed without their expertise. The gifts of speech and balance quickly deserted them as well, and by the following evening they had been reduced to an infantile state, scarcely able to feed themselves.

Several soldiers deserted that same night, taking with them our remaining food stocks. Hilliard and Bienvenue wandered off into the jungle and were never seen again. Having drunk from the same tainted water, our horses finally succumbed; too exhausted to bury them, we trudged on.

Three days' march and still no sign of the well. We sucked on musket balls to battle our thirst; even the water-bearing fruit could not rescue us—to cut into it was to find taunting disappointment in the form of a black and desiccated pit, swarming with insects.

A fever raged among our dragoons, bringing with it a host of bizarre symptoms unlike any I had ever witnessed. One soldier's teeth fell out, another's eyes changed color, then began to fill with a stinking black film. Our lead grenadier lay down in a dusty crossroads at noon, fitted on his spectacles, and gazed into the murderous sun, willingly blinding himself.

Father Rochefort was soon struck down as well. Cuts appeared on his flesh, blood bursting to the surface in tiny geysers, blood that was blacker than it was red. No sooner would Esther and I bandage one cut, then another would appear. For a day and a night, we were kept in constant motion, attending to these hideous eruptions, in the process shredding Father Rochefort's entire wardrobe and a good deal of my own for dressings.

But nothing could stanch the bleeding. Shortly before noon on the second day of his affliction, a beatific smile appeared on Father Rochefort's face, and he drew my ear to his cracked lips. "Do not mourn too heartily for me, Monsieur Townsend," he whispered. "I am dying of the Lord's wounds, here in this pagan, condemned land, and there is satisfaction in that."

He then expired with a shudder, his blood soaking through his bandages to water the parched soil that the tropical rains had ignored. Following a hasty burial during which neither Esther LaMartiniere nor I found the intellectual stamina to utter so much as a single prayer, we and our ten remaining soldiers pushed on.

We scarcely possessed the strength to set one foot in front of the other. My vision swam, impairing my ability to read the compass. In the haze of my derangement, it seemed we had entered a world in which the concept of water did not exist; we were being whipped and prodded on a forced march into the sun.

As the afternoon wore on, and the land slowly gave up its heat, we at last came to the well. But Fate had held her cruelest card in reserve. As I drew the bucket from the well, I spotted something gleaming beneath the water. I plucked it out—it was a gold button from the uniform of a French officer.

I ordered Esther not to drink. With my shaving mirror, I reflected the dwindling rays of the sun into the pit of the well. Floating in the brackish water were the tangled corpses of at least a dozen French soldiers, their decaying flesh a calculated poison that rendered the water unfit to drink!

I felt my last glimmer of hope darken. Cradling Esther LaMartiniere in my arms, I sank to the ground, my back falling against the stonework of the well. I watched the light fade from the sky, waiting impatiently, as I had as a child, for the first star to appear. I swooned into unconsciousness, and of the rest of the night, I recall nothing.

It was the rain that revived me: a life-giving force crashing from the heavens with the fury of a waterfall. Though it was well past dawn, the sky still wore a dark and forbidding aspect as vengeful clouds pressed down on the island. Squinting through the sheets of rain, I realized I was not alone—dozens of vague and wispy figures were moving about me! As I sat up with a fright, Esther LaMartiniere slid from my shoulder where she had slept and sank into the mud. She did not stir— she had died during the night. For this stubborn, seemingly indomitable woman, the rescuing rains had come too late.

I struggled to my feet, mouth wide open, greedily inhaling all that the clouds could offer. The figures closed in, and I realized that their faces were black. I was among the rebels! I cast my gaze about in panic: where were our dragoons? Why were they not engaging the enemy?

The answer lay scattered about the clearing like so many fallen trees. The dragoons had all succumbed, not to thirst or hunger, but to their fellowman: their throats had been cut during the night. With a profound mixture of terror and gratitude to God, I realized I alone of our expedition had survived.

But I was given no time to ponder this miracle. A man's face loomed out of the rain, the same scarred face I had seen in the treetops many nights before. His features were young and delicate, disrupted by the scar, which I now recognized to be a large and hideous burn mark.

"Is this a rescue?" I demanded, trying to sound a challenging note. "Or am I to be dragged off to an execution site somewhere?"

The man did not answer. He peered into my mouth and eyes, inspected my hair, slapped my stomach, ran his hand across my forehead. As we stood there, many more Negroes filtered out from the trees to loot the bodies of the dead. Though clad for the most part in rags, they all wore broad, indigo-colored sashes, a crude uniform of sorts; many carried sabers and flint-locks, others were armed with pikes, lances, and cane knives.

"Do you hear me?" I prodded. "Are you deaf? Or merely ignorant?"

"I am neither," the man replied. He smiled, and ran his fingertips absentmindedly along the length of his scar. "You, however, will be dead unless you put yourself in my care. You are sick, various fevers are at war within you, and your constitution is no match for our tropical climate. You will accompany me to camp."

"What camp? And just who in God's name are you?"

"Vincent Gabriel, chief of staff to General Xavier Charlemagne. Who has ordered that your life be spared. Here, please eat."

I was too weak to resist as Gabriel forced a handful of leaves into my mouth. I began to chew—they tasted of mint and had a slight narcotic effect, which when combined with my depleted state caused me to stumble. Supporting me on his shoulder, Vincent Gabriel led me to a horse-drawn sledge constructed of woven cane and lowered me onto it. I swept my arm limply toward the fallen figure of Esther LaMartiniere.

"We bury her first," I insisted. "Undefiled."

As the rain continued to fall, Gabriel supervised the excavation of a shallow grave, which was little more than a muddy lake by the time Esther LaMartiniere was lowered into it. Having borne witness to so much death in the recent days, it was all I could do to watch as the Negroes filled in the grave by hand, laughing and taking a child's pleasure in their task, throwing handfuls of mud at one another in complete disrespect for the solemnity of the occasion. I alone mourned; I alone did my Christian duty and uttered a prayer.

Gabriel then held a conch shell to his lips and blew upon it a penetrating blast. To my surprise, his men assembled into neat and disciplined military ranks. As he mounted the horse to which my litter was affixed, I summoned the strength for a final question.

"Tell me, if you can: why did your General Charlemagne, to whom cutting throats seems so blithe an exercise, see fit to spare me?"

The rain increased in intensity, forcing Vincent Gabriel to scream out his response: "My general considers himself to be something of a scholar of democracy. He presumes that you, being an American, must be the same. I think he simply wishes for someone to talk to."

Gabriel laughed, then cracked his whip. As my sledge was jarred forward, I chanced to look upon a nearby ridge. Silhouetted against the gray sky was a mounted figure in a military overcoat and tricorn hat, his face obscured behind torrents of rain. He was gazing at me through a telescope!

I lay in a delirium for two days. On the rare occasions when I awoke, I found Vincent Gabriel in attendance, prodding me to drink this vile liquid or swallow that wretched medicament, removing a reeking poultice from one part of my body, attaching leeches to another. On my third day of captivity, I felt the fever receding, and though still bedridden I managed to take stock of my surroundings. I lay in a hut made of mahogany and roofed with banana leaves, at the perimeter of a clearing that had been hacked out of the jungle. The clearing overlooked a vast plain, offering both an ideal observation point and an easily defensible encampment. There seemed to be hundreds, if not thousands of inhabitants: women and children and elderly, in addition to several regiments of Negro soldiers, who passed the day drilling in both infantry and cavalry tactics.

By that evening I was well enough to move about. When he brought my supper, Vincent Gabriel also brought freshly laundered clothes. "You will meet the general tonight," he said, as he helped me dress. "You will look your best; he does not tolerate slovenliness."

"I owe you my life."

"You owe the general your life. I follow his dictates, nothing more. If it were my army to command . . . I might have killed you."

Gabriel held up a mirror so that I could shave myself. I looked him squarely in the eye. "Nothing more? Was it not you I saw our first night out, spying on our camp from the trees?"

"You saw a panther, perhaps."

"Was it not you who toyed with the minds of our dragoons, you who drove them mad? You who somehow conspired to strip our guides of their tracking skills?"

"I'm an aide-de-camp. I attend to details. I carry out the general's more unusual, private commands—such as caring for selected prisoners. I do not have the power to peer into men's minds."

"Yet even before my capture, you had told the general I was an American."

To this, he had no answer. Gabriel brushed my clothes, dabbed lavender water on my wrists, then, satisfied with my appearance, led me off to meet the general. As the only white face, I aroused a sensation as I followed Gabriel through the camp, distracting the women from their cooking fires, the men from their rum and dice, the children from their games. But we soon left the onlookers behind as we followed a footpath into the jungle. We emerged in a second clearing, and I found myself in an alien yet wondrous setting.

Here, in the midst of the forest, were furnishings to rival the reception chambers of Versailles: sofas, chairs, settees, and cabinets were scattered about the clearing in artful arrangement, and great tapestries covered the jungle floor. Uniformed officers bustled portentously back and forth carrying maps and dispatches; liveried valets served coffee and tea from silver pots. It was a palace without walls, bathed in the vivid orange light of a hundred torches.

The man himself cut an unforgettable and threatening figure as he emerged from behind a massive mahogany desk to greet me. He stood well over six feet and I estimated his weight to be at least fifteen stone. His face was a jumble of rough, dark slabs—he looked as if he had been carved with a hatchet, and though he could not yet have attained fifty, his close-cropped hair was nearly white. He wore an officer's uniform that was outrageously resplendent: a red and purple greatcoat ornamented with gold braid covered a waistcoat of blue velvet faced with silver. His broad shoulders supported gold epaulets and his breeches *à la hongrois* were so white and pure they seemed to magically defy the humidity and filth of the tropics. In his right hand, clutched between the longest fingers I had ever seen, was a stout cane made from the trunk of a lemon tree. I could smell its fragrance as he raised it above his head and slammed it ferociously down upon his desk.

It was the signal for his retainers to scatter, and within seconds there were only the general, Vincent Gabriel, and I in that jungle salon.

He stepped closer, inspected me from boots to collar, then averted his gaze and addressed Gabriel.

"His eyes?" he demanded.

"Blue, sir," replied Gabriel.

"Truthful eyes?"

"Not for *me* to judge, sir."

Instinctively, I tried to intercept the general's gaze, but he quickly turned away.

Gabriel laughed at my bewilderment. "General Charlemagne has vowed that he will never look a white man in the eyes until Saint Domingue is liberated. As you are the first white with whom he has had commerce in the last six months, it will be an interesting test of his resolve."

Charlemagne unbuttoned his greatcoat and produced a rolled-up document, which he unfurled and handed to me, his eyes turned heavenward.

"Read this, please. To all of us."

I held the document to the torchlight; to my surprise, it was our own Declaration of Independence. "There is no need for me to read it, General. I long ago committed it to memory."

"Better" was all he answered.

There then followed one of the strangest interludes of my life, as I recited our nation's founding document to the counterpoint of distant drumming, the restless screeching of insects and night birds. Charlemagne kept his back turned and his craggy features pointed toward the skies, which, cleared of storm clouds, provided me with a silent audience of stars.

When I was done, he simply remarked: "Again."

I recited the Declaration a second time, then a third time, my voice sending Vincent Gabriel to sleep, even as General Charlemagne attended my every word: " . . .a decent respect to the opinions of mankind requires that they should declare the causes which impel them to the separation. We hold these truths to be self-evident, that all men are created equal. . . "

"*Halt!*" He bored his cane into the soil. "How do you understand these words?"

"Just as they say: we are all the same in the eyes of God."

"Read further, please."

". . . that they are endowed by their Creator with certain unalienable Rights, that among these are Life, Liberty . . ."

"*Halt!*" he cried again. "Liberty. *Liberté, libertad.* It is the same word in all the languages of this island's conquerors. And how is this meant, in your opinion?"

"Freedom. From oppression, from persecution . . ."

"From slavery?" he demanded.

As I was the prisoner of a bloodthirsty and overpowering regiment of former slaves, I answered in the affirmative. And thereupon began a discussion that lasted throughout the night, the next day, and well into the following evening. Though he was in fact illiterate, General Charlemagne possessed a nimble intellect, and it was clear he had given much thought to the meaning of Jefferson's words.

"So, we must conclude," he said, as the moon rose on the second evening of our colloquy, "that your Mr. Jefferson supports our struggle here on Saint Domingue."

"Well . . . yes," I replied.

"I hear doubt in your voice. Men are either equal, or they are not. Men are either free, or they are not."

"True . . ."

"And being a man of wide-ranging interests, Mr. Jefferson will have read of me, no doubt?"

"Yes, yes, of course!" I said, seizing on his misapprehension. "Your reputation is well known in government circles." Though I had heard no mention of General Charlemagne prior to my arrival in Port-au-Prince, I proceeded along this path of flattery in the hopes that it might lead to my release. "And as a people who have thrown off our own Colonial masters, we Americans have a great interest in your struggle."

The general walked to his desk and produced a bottle of rum. "I wonder if you are being truthful, if the Americans do understand us. I have no illusions about the French. They will never voluntarily permit Saint Domingue to be free, never cut themselves off from the wellspring of their prosperity."

He drank voraciously, draining half the bottle in a single swallow. I pressed my strategy. "As a matter of fact, it is Secretary of State Jefferson himself who has dispatched me here." I handed him my letter of introduction, which he briefly perused, then passed to Vincent Gabriel, who had rejoined us.

"It appears to be authentic, General," Gabriel said.

"And if Mr. Jefferson can be convinced of the justice of your cause," I continued, "he has it within his power to dispatch men and armaments to Saint Domingue, an armada such as this island has never seen."

"And what will convince him?"

I took a deep breath. "My report," I said brazenly.

I remained in a state of suspense as the general sipped his rum and pondered moodily. His head sagged as the alcohol did its work. Finally, just as I thought he would collapse, he weakly waved his lemon cane. "Prove to me you are not lying; show me the depth of your convictions, and I will entertain the notion of not killing you."

Before I could answer, I was dragged away by two lieutenants. They led me to my bed, but now I was securely roped down, restraints placed on my ankles and wrists, my shirt torn off by eager hands.

Of the next two hours I recall only the first minute and the last minute. The first, when the red-hot branding iron appeared, and the last, when Vincent Gabriel swam into my tear-stained vision with a bucket of cold water and soothing, herbal salves. Though I do not call it heroism—my life depended on my lies— Gabriel assured me that I had not retracted my sentiments during the torture and that General Charlemagne was now sufficiently impressed by my sincerity.

"But the general suffers from the hubris of power; he is flattered to be mentioned in the same breath with statesmen such as your Mr. Jefferson. On occasion, it clouds his judgment." Then Gabriel added an ominous footnote. "I, however, can see through the clouds quite easily."

The army broke camp the next day, and I was taken with them. We marched southward, avoiding the highways, always keeping to the jungle. I became a man of two roles: during the day, I was a prisoner, heavily guarded, my wrists bound even at mealtimes, but in the evening I became General Charlemagne's interlocutor, chess partner, and reader. He had a large collection of books, and I read to him from Caesar; Voltaire and Rousseau; the Abbé Raynal's antislavery tract *The Two*

Indies; from tattered copies of Parisian revolutionary papers, and finally, from the *Journal de Saint Domingue,* which I was made to comb for references to the general himself.

He had an incendiary temper. When his adjutants brought him bad news, he put on a fearsome display. I once saw him rip a heavy branch from a tree and hurl it at the offending officer like a spear; I saw him slice off another's thumb with a careless swat of his sword and feed it to his dogs. But it was precisely this cruelty, when combined with a cunning intellect, that made him such a compelling personality. We grappled night after night over difficult questions of race and politics; would the Negro, even when emancipated, ever learn to live side by side with the white man; were persons of mixed blood, so common on the island of Saint Domingue, an improvement in racial development, or a sad dilution? General Charlemagne would discuss such matters with eloquence until dawn, but then, made furious by rum, he might recall a slight that he had suffered from one of his officers. With the suddenness of a tossed coin, another side of the man would surface, and he would rouse the offender from his bed, cut his throat, or perhaps toss the fellow into a ravine. Then, remorse would overcome him and he would demand an herbal sedative from Vincent Gabriel or, like a babe, seek pitiful refuge in the arms of one of his wives.

How did I accommodate myself to captivity? Why did I not succumb to despair? True, both a desire to save myself and a youthful belief in my immortality were at work. But I discovered something else about myself during those days: my thirst for knowledge was so powerful that it outweighed any sense of danger. I learned the lesson of my life in that rebel camp— it is better to die young filled with understanding than live to be a hundred without ever having glimpsed the mysteries that bind the universe.

Some of those mysteries were revealed to me within the week. We had taken up positions across the river from a French garrison, intending to attack at dawn. The mood was tense and secretive. My usual audience with General Charlemagne was cancelled, and I was billeted at some distance from the camp, kept in isolation throughout the night.

The drumming woke me from a restless sleep. It was louder and more frantic than usual. I had become friendly with my youthful guards, and though bound at the wrists and ankles, I prevailed upon them to lead me to the drumming, which issued from the officers' compound.

Charlemagne's generals were all in attendance, crouched around a plot of earth that was blanketed with maps and charts. Behind the officers stood a rank of drummers, naked to the waist and beaded with sweat, their tireless hands producing an unimaginable range of sounds from their primitive instruments. Suddenly, Vincent Gabriel burst onto the scene, completely naked! His gentle features were contorted in rage, his eyes were hot as embers. He raised his head to the forest canopy and began to speak in Creole, a deep growl gradually rising to a frenzied pitch. His body twitched in rhythm to the drums, as though he were suffering a lunatic seizure, and his lips frothed white with foam. He appeared to have taken total leave of his senses!

But the officers' reaction was serious and attentive. They hung on Gabriel's every word, drawing busily on their charts, scribbling facts and figures like dutiful students at a university lecture.

"Ogoun," whispered one of my guards in awe.

I had heard the word before: it was the name the slaves gave to their god of war. It was as Father Rochefort had said—the Africans danced to become God. Vincent Gabriel was possessed by Ogoun and now presided over his supernatural council of war, a direct link between the warrior god and his holy crusaders. Ogoun was not only the rebels' divine inspiration but the architect of their battle plans as well. I felt an explosive thrill: I was certainly the first white man ever to have witnessed this ceremony!

Eventually, Gabriel collapsed in exhaustion and was carried from the scene. The officers folded their maps and returned to their quarters. I detected a hint of lemon in the air, then realized that my guards were gone; in their place stood General Charlemagne himself.

"You were not meant to see this," he said. "Now I shall have trouble with Vincent Gabriel."

"Why?"

"He wants to keep our religion a secret from the blancs. He feels it can be used against us. But I think the specter of a thousand black rebels willing to die for their gods might be an effective weapon."

"You would use your religion to sow fear and terror?"

"Of course. A politician must use whatever means come to hand."

"You have the effrontery to consider yourself a politician?" I scoffed.

He smiled. "While you consider me a monster."

It was true, I had not forgiven him the massacre of the French dragoons at the well, but in the cause of self-preservation I had kept my judgments to myself. He led me to a bluff overlooking the river. On the opposite shore were the campfires of the French troops, protected by picket lines and a battery of eighteen-pounders. On our side, several sentries lay on their backs staring at the sky, engaged in amiable conversation.

"My grandfather was a slave his entire life, my father was a slave his entire life, and I was a slave for forty years of mine. I have witnessed such punishments that even your Christian devil, were he drunk on rum, could not imagine: mothers forced to abort, then cook their own children; men coated with molasses, then staked to the earth so that the jungle ants might feast on them; slaves stuffed with gunpowder, then exploded for the Frenchman's Sunday amusement." The general paused and treated himself to a mouthful of chocolate. "Oh, yes, I hope I am a monster. I pray that I can be monstrous enough."

"But if the French are as dependent on the wealth of Saint Domingue as you say, they will send reinforcements," I pointed out. "And they will keep sending them. All twenty-six million Frenchmen, if necessary."

He gave no answer. He scanned the enemy encampment with his spyglass. "You will have a good view of the battle from here." The laughter of his sentries distracted him. He exchanged a few Creole pleasantries with them, then looked up at the sky. "These men are from a village near the Spanish border, well known for its close connection to the loa. They have talents that may surprise you. Watch."

One of the sentries pointed to a patch of sky on the southern horizon. A minute later, a shooting star appeared there, blazing a silent and beautiful trail.

"They claim they can hear the stars coming," Charlemagne said. "I think they will be able to warn us of a French invasion."

The battle began at dawn, when the miraculous sentries performed an even greater feat of magic.

While Charlemagne's troops assembled in the jungle, the five sentries crept down to the river's edge. I followed their progress as they waded silently into the water, at some distance from a stone bridge patrolled by French pickets. To my surprise, they continued deeper into the water, until they were completely submerged. And there they stayed for well over half an hour, never once emerging to draw a breath!

When next I saw them, they burst to the surface directly below the bridge. They climbed the stonework, and taking the French guards by complete surprise, made short, brutal work of the enemy with their cane knives.

With the bridge thus secured, a charge was blown on the conch shell, and Charlemagne's troops swarmed across the river into the French garrison, their war screams so fearsome and blood-chilling, it was as though the earth had been opened to set free the winds of hell.

I watched as the black troops, greatly outnumbered, fought with a suicidal bravado. They plunged their arms into the French cannons, even after the charges had been set, pulling the eighteen-pound balls out with their bare hands. Occasionally this tactic was successful; often it was not, resulting in the instant and ghastly obliteration of a human being. They loosed baskets of poisonous snakes and scorpions among the French infantry; they deflected musket balls with their swords; they endured endless saber cuts as they fought to drag the French cavalrymen from their horses.

Though his troops sustained heavy losses, the day belonged to Charlemagne. By the time the sun descended, there was not a Frenchman left standing. The night belonged to celebration, to the joyful looting and dismemberment of the French corpses.

I witnessed many such battles in the following weeks. General Charlemagne and Vincent Gabriel proved themselves to be master tacticians. With each victory, Charlemagne's self-regard grew more grandiose. Once, he came to me bearing two drawings of himself, one of each profile.

"Which do you prefer?" he asked.

"The left," I replied, merely to express an opinion.

"I, too. I think it suggests greater dignity."

"To what use are these sketches to be put?"

"Once the conquest of the province is complete, we will issue our own money, divest ourselves once and for all of this infernal French economic exclusive. My blacksmith will strike the premier coin with my image." He thrust out his chin in a regal pose.

They assaulted the plantations, too. I was not permitted to observe these engagements; instead, I was held at camp under heavy guard. But if the wind direction was right, I could smell the burning cane and hear the screams, of women and children as well as men. Often our numbers were swollen by the liberated slaves, who, under the tutelage of Charlemagne's officers, began the evolution from field hand to soldier. But never once did the raiding parties return with a white prisoner.

And always, Charlemagne pestered me with his questions about the armada that I had promised in Thomas Jefferson's name. And always I exaggerated my power within the American government: I would see that the secretary of state delivered whatever the black revolutionaries needed and more. I appealed to logic and the general's sophisticated grasp of international politics: the United States much preferred a free and independent Saint Domingue to the continuance of French power in the Caribbean; nor did we wish to see the British, already well established in the Leeward Islands and Jamaica, expand their influence in the region. Xavier Charlemagne was not a sentimental man. I knew my life depended on an empty promise, and my ability to make him believe I could keep it.

Not a sentimental man, but a literal one. I would lay awake nights, the phrases "all men are created equal" ringing in my ears, and wonder how five simple words could contain within them a world of infinite complexity.

I was never accepted by the rebel army—I was tolerated, the hatred in the eyes of the black soldiers held in check by my sponsor, General Charlemagne. Then, one loose-tongued evening it seemed that my protected status had come to an end . . . and with it, my life.

We were engaged in our usual after-supper discussions, and I had joined the general at his rum. Raised in a house of abstainers and having never been much of a drinker, I was unprepared for the effect the powerful Saint Domingue rum would have on my judgment. I had just explained to the general that though the slave trade was illegal in the United States, the ownership of slaves was not; yet still, there were plantation masters who had moral doubts about keeping human beings as property.

"Then why does he not simply free them?" asked the general. "Free the slaves, free himself of the spiritual burden."

"It's not quite so simple," I said. "Where should these freed persons live? Who would feed and house them? They would be despised wherever they went."

"You paint the slaveholder as a father, concerned for his sons even after they leave his house. *C'est une bêtise,* it's nonsense."

"Not at all!" I spouted, refilling my glass. "You cannot just scatter people to the winds. I myself would not like to see my . . ." Here I paused, realizing the grave error I had made.

"Your . . . *what,* Mr. Townsend?" Though Charlemagne would still not look me in the eye, I felt the scorn of his gaze nonetheless, burning through the back of his head. "Your children? Your property?" he taunted.

"Please, General. Lest you think I have misrepresented myself . . ."

"Misrepresented!" he erupted. "You have proven yourself a shameless liar, like every blanc it has been my misfortune to meet."

"I never claimed I was not a slave owner."

"Sophistry. It is always the guilty who bring such twisted arguments." Charlemagne's hand curled around the hilt of his ceremonial sword, and I feared my throat would be cut on the spot.

"Damn it, I would have sworn to you that I was the emperor of China if it would have saved my own skin!"

Charlemagne grew pensive. "It is the small, harmless lie that the spy tells that clears the way for the bigger, more dangerous lies. Perhaps my advisors are right when they say, 'Let our country's first constitution be written on the parchment of a white man's skin.' "

"I am not a spy, I assure you," I declared.

"How can you assure me?"

"Look me in the eye, you bastard, and see!"

He did not, of course. Instead, he summoned his guards and dispatched me to a temporary prison, which was little more than a pit overlaid with branches. There I languished for five days, sustained only by manioc porridge and the sparest ration of water. I grew sick from fear and heat and I imagined that the general was devising new and elaborate tortures, or that I would be sacrificed to their god of war during some frightful and savage ceremony orchestrated by Vincent Gabriel.

In my swoon I pictured myself back in Virginia, among her soft green landscapes, assuming rightful title to my father's property, married to a beautiful and demure girl with lustrous ringlets of hair and the narrowest of waists, dancing into our future beneath a chandelier singing with light—the life that had been securely marked out for me had I not succumbed to the damnable lure of ambition and adventure.

I was wrenched out of my reverie by rough hands, into a night brilliant with moonglow. I found myself face-to-face with

Vincent Gabriel. I feared my hour of execution was at hand; instead, Gabriel and a squad of regulars led me to a stream where I was allowed to bathe away the prison filth, given my fill to eat and drink, and provided with clean clothes.

"The general—against my advice and counsel—has decided to give you a loyalty test," Gabriel said.

"What? Forgive me if I don't understand, but I'm still quite groggy from my imprisonment."

"To prove that you are not a spy, you must perform a service for us." Gabriel gestured to the far side of the stream. The ground rose to a wide plateau, upon which stood a prosperous sugar plantation, comprised of so many outbuildings it resembled a small village. "The French use this plantation as a clandestine *entrepôt* for gunpowder, which is then distributed to troops throughout the province. The arsenal is heavily fortified with artillery, aimed at the valley where we now stand. To attack it would cost hundreds of lives. However, if the guns were somehow to be pointed in the opposite direction . . ."

"And just how am I to accomplish that?" I asked.

Vincent Gabriel smiled proudly. He then drew me into a lengthy conversation, and a careful ruse was sketched out, a ruse in which I would be sent, alone, into the midst of the French troops.

"You need only gain the soldiers' trust, through whatever means you blancs employ, and spin your story well," Gabriel said. "We will do the rest."

My spirits soared—here at last was my chance to escape! If there were truly gunpowder stocks at the plantation and dragoons to guard them, then I was saved. I would consign myself to their protective custody, then arrange an armed escort back to Port-au-Prince.

Yet I did not want to appear too anxious. "You really think me capable of this deception?" I asked.

"You fooled the general," Vincent Gabriel replied, his voice laced with irony. "You should be able to fool the French."

"If I succeed at this mission . . . you must give me your word that the whites will not be butchered."

"I can make no assurance for the soldiers." Gabriel seemed thoughtful, toying with his earring. "But as for the plantation family, yes, I promise they will be spared."

I was provided with a battered traveler's case and dispatched on my mission. As I waded into the stream, Vincent Gabriel grabbed my arm. "*But* . . . if your true nature surfaces, and you decide to betray us, the deaths of one more colonial family will not be a plague on my conscience."

With that threat, the lives of all the whites on the plantation dropped into my humble hands. If I did not fulfill my assignment, a dreadful massacre would follow, and I would certainly be its final victim.

I started up the hill toward the flickering lights of the outbuildings. Gabriel receded into the darkness, yet I knew he would stay close, watching through his spyglass, General Charlemagne never far from his side, their army massing in the forest.

The plantation was expansive. The fields extended far beyond the range of my sight, and I estimated that the enterprise employed several hundred people, all devoted to the production of a single plant—sugarcane—what a general to Alexander the Great had once called "the miraculous reed which brings forth honey without the help of bees." As I walked closer, the air grew thicker and sweeter. Despite the late hour, the refinery was hard at work. The world's appetite for sweets had become so inexhaustible that the refinery was never allowed to rest. I peered into the great stone structure—the heat was so intense, the Devil would have been comfortably employed there. With incredible strength and dexterity, slaves handled massive wooden ladles known as skimmers, spooning the boiling cane juice back and forth among the giant copper basins, waiting for the moment when it would begin to crystallize. The scalding syrup sputtered and spat, and several of the slaves were disfigured by gruesome burn marks—this, I realized, had once been Vincent Gabriel's task.

I slipped off toward the main house, relieved to be away from the piercing heat. I moved slowly, postponing the moment of decision. How should I proceed? If I warned the residents that the black army was near, were there enough soldiers here to repel an attack? Or would I be condemning us all to death? Should I advise the French to flee, leaving the plantation to be plundered? No, that would only delay our deaths—knowing Charlemagne as I did, I knew he would hunt us down first, then plunder the plantation.

I stood in the yard, inhaling the scent of tamarind. Through the parlor window, I watched the masters of the plantation and their guests at their evening leisure. It was a large and attractive party, the women clothed in silks and lace, the men in velvet. The young wife played the piano, her husband looked on adoringly, his soft hands cupping a cognac glass. A young boy pulled a young girl's hair, a house cat groomed herself contentedly on the cool, marble floor.

It was the life of dreams. It was civilization.

Suddenly, there was something awful about this life built on artifice. An inarticulate loathing seized me: I did not want to present myself to the master of the house, did not wish to cast my lot with him. I backed away from the parlor, from the lilting piano music drifting over the transom.

I looked up at the sky. A giant, ravenlike bird circled above me, a jagged silhouette against the full moon. Vincent Gabriel transformed, or simply my imagination?

I made my way to the rear of the house and crept past the outbuildings. Presently, the ground sloped upward and I found a path that led through the vegetation to a rocky escarpment. There, on the summit, offering a commanding view of the valley, was the arsenal itself, a round, stone building, featureless save for a massive, seemingly unbreachable iron door. Dozens of soldiers stood watch, bayonets gleaming in the moonlight.

Then I saw the guns: there were nine-, eighteen-, and twenty-pound artillery pieces, set in earthen embrasures; I counted at least fifteen naval pivot guns and another twelve field cannon. Ammunition was plentiful, with towering pyramids of round shot stacked everywhere. It was more than sufficient to decimate any force that might attack from the valley floor.

I loosened my collar, mussed my hair, and throwing several handfuls of dirt on myself, I fell into my charade. I staggered up the hill, pleading hoarsely for water and aid, and was instantly surrounded by ten suspicious sentries, their bayonets bristling within a centimeter of my nervously bobbing Adam's apple.

"Please, there is not a moment to waste. They are not far behind!" I gasped in broken French.

"Who is not far behind, and who are you?" demanded a junior officer.

"An American traveler. A salesman. I was taken captive by a Maroon battalion and have only now effected my escape. I overheard them planning an assault on your positions . . ."

Feigning breathlessness, I collapsed to the ground. "Please, show some charity and bring me water. And for God's sake prepare yourselves. There are many hundreds, fearsome fighters, all of them."

A young lancer guided a canteen to my lips, whilst his superiors engaged in frenzied whispers.

"And turn your damn guns around!" I added. "They are not coming from the valley . . . they are coming straight out of the jungle!"

Their commanding officer pushed to the forefront. He was a taut, compact man with a sculpted white mustache and nearly an arsenal unto himself, what with his twin sabers and flintlocks, his steel cuirass and copper-crested helmet.

"I am Marshal Chabron," he trumpeted. "Is it true what you say?"

"I'm only repeating what I heard. Whether it is true I cannot guarantee, of course. As I told you, I'm a simple salesman . . ."

"But why would they attack through the jungle? It is nearly impenetrable, the ground impassable for a modern army."

"They know you expect them from the valley, of course! And they are not a modern army. I'm telling you, they are as at home in the forest as a family of spiders. For all I know, they intend to press their attack via the treetops. I say again, turn your guns around if you hope to survive this encounter!" This last outburst produced intense conversation. "And would anyone have a piece of chicken or pork I might nibble on?"

There was much argument and consulting of maps. Finally, Marshal Chabron bent down and fixed on me a shrewd stare. "Tell me, young man. Did you by chance hear the name of this black battalion's commanding officer?"

"General Charlemagne," I said, eliciting a flurry of alarmed epithets. "A nom de guerre certainly, and a rather presumptuous one at that, but nonetheless . . ."

"And why would this General Charlemagne devote his energies to attacking a simple sugar plantation?"

"For the gunpowder. He says you have enough stored here to blow the French half of the island onto the Spanish half . . . and he means to seize it!"

Thereupon, I collapsed onto my back and gazed into the night sky. The black bird wheeled in front of the moon, then dipped its wings and soared away.

There followed another hour of sober conversation between Marshal Chabron and his officers, but I knew that my ruse had been successful. The proof came shortly before dawn, as with a great groaning of iron upon iron, and muscle upon muscle, the French artillerymen began the laborious process of reaiming their guns. The infantry stood by nervously, their attention turned on the menacing jungle. The sun was well up into the sky before the guns were finally repositioned.

And then the attack came. The assault was preceded by furious wails on the conch shell and a deafening chorus of drums. By the time the defenders realized the attack was not coming from the jungle, but from the valley floor as originally anticipated, it was far too late. Deprived of their artillery, the French were no match for Charlemagne's Negro soldiers, who were fighting in the name of their vodoun gods, secure in the belief that if they fell in battle, they would be transported to Guinée, to the Africa of their ancestors, an Africa before slavery and untransgressed by white men.

As I attempted to remove myself from the furor, Marshal

Chabron caught sight of me. He reached for his sword, intending to run through the traitor who had engineered his destruction . . . and he would have done so had not a lucky musket shot pierced his throat. I scrambled to safety as Charlemagne's men overran the French positions and secured the arsenal. I looked down on the plantation, which was now fully surrounded, and, spying Vincent Gabriel amid the fray, I shouted down to him.

"Gabriel, recall your promise! I have honored mine, and I expect you to honor yours."

I do not believe he heard me above the din of war, but the sight of me was reminder enough. I remained at my perch throughout the waning hours of the battle, and later watched with some gratification as master and mistress of the plantation, their children, and their guests were escorted to a carriage, given fresh horses and water, and dispatched unharmed into the setting sun.

That evening, the etiquette of warfare took its inevitable course, and as I sat in camp among the Negro troops, the sky blazed bright as noon as the plantation was put to the torch.

General Charlemagne appeared, carrying a bottle of wine and two crystal glasses engraved with the crest of the defeated French regiment. "There is a custom which I have often seen practiced among the French and the British. Perhaps you Americans practice it as well," he said.

"Perhaps," I answered morosely, for I was in a highly vexed state of mind. Bloodshed seemed endless, morality a quagmire, my future a path of shadows. I had seen and thought and done too much since leaving Virginia to ever be the same Nicholas Whitney Townsend again.

"I believe it is called a 'toast,' and I would like to drink one to my young American compatriot," the general said. He poured the wine, and I dutifully touched my glass to his.

When I lifted my gaze, he looked me squarely in the eyes.

17

HE'S A YOUNGER me, I realized. Optimistic, ambitious, an innocent abroad. Nicholas Townsend—I was so close to him now, I felt like calling him Nick—had also been a reporter in a way, determined to see as much of the world as possible, before it turned on him.

I had been in that motel room for twenty-four hours. My/ his diary had grown by another sixty pages—I'd had to tip the maid to bring me more Diplomat Motor Inn stationery. The narcotic that Faustin Gabriel had given me had worn off, and like he'd predicted, I now saw the world on his terms. The shock, the denial had faded, replaced with acceptance. This was the situation: I was his tool; did I wait for him to use me again, or did I fight?

I took a long shower, letting everything I'd learned about vodoun percolate. The historical line that led from Nicholas Townsend to me was clearer now: both of our fates had been seized by the Gabriel family, this enduring progression of Creole Rasputins, of advisors to presidents that had begun with Vincent Gabriel, and continued today with his descendant, Faustin.

Yet Faustin Gabriel had admitted that he did not control me entirely. By injecting Nicholas Townsend's personality into mine, Gabriel had gained a foothold, a lever, but the conquest was not complete. Ray Falco, the cocky, prize-winning, and formerly independent journalist was still alive. If I could drive off Nicholas Townsend, manage a personality purge, maybe I could save myself.

The next day, I drove down to Richmond. I had no real game plan, just a vague idea that I should learn more about my supernatural roots. Maybe there was a great-great-great (I wasn't sure how many "great"s would get me from 1792 to the present) grandchild of Nicholas Townsend somewhere who would serve me tea and sit me down with the family album.

"Of course the Townsends were not as prominent a family in early Virginia as the Lees or the Randolphs, but they did have their qualities," explained the archivist at the Virginia Historical Society. She was a young woman, no makeup, headband, white blouse and navy sweater; she was very pretty, though she seemed to be aging too quickly among the antique ledgers and microfilm readers.

"No horse thieves or highwaymen?" I joked.

"Business. Agriculture. No-nonsense sort of people. I suppose you might call them dull."

She flipped through books of Colonial genealogy records, her pale fingers flying over lists of names written in florid, fading script. "Here he is," she said. "Nicholas Whitney Townsend, born in 1769 to Edmund and Martha Townsend in Lancaster County. Their only child."

"When did he die?" I asked.

"Let's see, died . . . that's funny."

"What's funny?" I peered over her shoulder.

"There's no date of death listed. And the Virginia planter class was very heritage conscious, very thorough. They would have recorded it if they knew it." She intently scanned the rest of the book and consulted a half-dozen other ledgers, growing increasingly frustrated. "I don't understand this. As an archivist, you hate to see this kind of detail overlooked."

I nodded sympathetically. "Maybe he didn't die in the U.S. I know that he traveled to the Caribbean from Virginia in 1792. Do you have commercial-shipping records from the period?"

"I'd have to send over to the state library. Can you come back?"

"You won't be able to get rid of me," I said.

I went to lunch. When I returned, I found my archivist wearing surgical gloves, nearly hidden behind two stacks of yellowed documents individually wrapped in protective plastic. She had a triumphant gleam in her eye as she patted the two stacks. "Outbound shipping on the left, inbound shipping on the right." She handed me a passenger manifest from the outbound stack. A merchantman named *Virginia Star* had sailed from Norfolk harbor on August 3, 1792; among the passengers was N. W. Townsend of Lancaster County.

"It docked briefly at Charleston, then sailed directly to the Caribbean, reaching Port-au-Prince, San Domingo, on September second," she read. "It stayed there a week, then continued further south to Saint Christopher and Martinique, returning to Port-au-Prince around mid-December. There, it took on additional passengers and a shipment of molasses. It made it back to the United States on January 17, 1793. There was no N. W. Townsend aboard."

"Maybe he came back on another ship," I said.

"I've been through the first three months of 1793 already," she answered, pointing to the "inbound" stack. "You're welcome to sift through the rest . . . if I could just get you to sign a release?"

"A *what?*"

"It delegates you as an official volunteer. If you damage any of our documents irreparably," she smiled, "we can then hold you liable. Our donors insist on it."

I signed. I was delegated. For the rest of the day, I trudged through captain's logs, bills of lading, and passenger lists. My historian, whose name I never learned, turned to other tasks, dealing with the armies of retired people who passed their long afternoons patiently pruning and grafting their family trees.

Around five-thirty, the building began to empty out. The low sunlight painted the yellowed documents with a deep red glow, like flames burning through the credits on an old Technicolor epic. She leaned over my shoulder, offered me a mint.

"Anything?" she asked.

"By 1796, he still hadn't returned to the States. At least not on a registered ship, not under his own name." I pushed the piles of documents away. My eyes were tired from the marathon of squinting. "Listen, I think his family owned a small tobacco plantation. Could I find the original land records over at the state archives?"

She checked her watch. "They're closing. Anyway, the kind of thing you're after will be stored in the Lancaster County files."

I let out a frazzled sigh, imagining a long, impatient night in a Richmond motel.

"You really want to find out about this guy, don't you? Just sit tight and let me make a call."

I sat down on one of those hard wooden benches that governments install in their offices to make waiting so excruciating that when you're finally served, you're irrationally grateful. My archivist waved encouragement at me from the phone, and occasionally jumped up to consult a wall map of Virginia.

When she hung up half an hour later, she was upbeat. She spread out several maps on the counter. "I got a lot and tract number of the property that belonged to your Edmund Townsend. We did a quick matchup with current street maps of the area and located the plantation . . . here." She pointed at an intersection in southern Lancaster County.

"Which is what?"

"My friend says it's a Kentucky Fried."

I scowled.

"I know. From mysterious gentleman tobacco merchants cruising the Caribbean in clipper ships to the Colonel—it's a long way to slide. Why do you think I'm so into history?"

Nicholas Townsend could have theoretically sailed from Saint Domingue on to South America or Europe; he could have slipped back into the United States under an assumed name, moved thousands of miles from Virginia, and restarted life with a different identity. But that didn't sound like my young idealistic adventurer. I was convinced that the answers to the enigma of Nicholas Whitney Townsend still lay in Haiti.

"Anyway, I really appreciate your help," I said. "You've restored my faith in government employees."

"Actually, I'm a volunteer."

As I turned to go, she tapped me on the shoulder. "Mr. Townsend?" I looked back, reacting instinctively to the name. She smiled. "I thought so. It's usually a relative that gets this emotionally caught up in the search. My friend gave me another address you might be interested in." She handed me a scrap of paper. "It's a little church outside of Lancaster, the county seat? It's where the Townsends are buried."

It was dark by the time I reached the tiny brick Episcopal church, which stood on a gentle rise overlooking the Rappahannock River. Like much of Virginia, it appeared to have been carefully restored and annotated. As I entered the small, adjoining cemetery, my flashlight beam played across the Latin labels that were mounted on every tree and shrub.

The local parishioners had been buried unpretentiously. The gravestones were modest and uniform, classically shaped, almost like Halloween decorations. But still, it was a graveyard, and I was alone in it; the atmosphere began to work on me. The wind rushed straight up from the Rappahannock, stirring the leaves in the elm trees. It's a law that your flashlight gives out in these situations, and mine did. I tapped it—nothing; opened it, reloaded the batteries, then tapped it again on the nearest headstone. It threw out a weak spray of light, and I realized I'd found the Townsend family plot.

I bent down to read the engraving on the double headstone, running my fingers over the deep, water-stained grooves. Edmund Norrington Townsend, born 1741 in Hull, England. Died 1800. Martha Dunmore Townsend, born 1745, died 1809. Nicholas Whitney Townsend, born 1769 . . .

The Townsends must have sensed that their son had come to

a tragic end, because a stonemason had chiseled the word "died" next to his name; but like a hauntingly unfinished poem, there was no date of death. Beneath this was a quote: "May God return you; if not, may God welcome you."

I felt spooked, then slightly reverent. In a way, I was the co-owner of this grave. "He *has* returned," I whispered. "Just not in the way you expected."

I heard a car approaching, saw headlights. Nothing to worry about: the minister, the janitor, teenagers. The car stopped next to mine. Someone got out, leaving the headlights on and the motor running. I switched off my flashlight, crouched behind the headstone. A figure drifted into view, stopped just outside the cemetery gate. The wind stopped; I held my breath.

"Decided to get religion, did you, Ray Falco?"

A match flared in the darkness as Walter Paisley lit his pipe. I got to my feet, walked over to him. His face was furrowed and sober, a silver automatic was tucked showily in his belt. " 'Course, more than a good preacher, what you need about now is a good lawyer."

———

A green metal desk scarred with graffiti and heel marks. Water-stained acoustic ceiling, a window I knew to be a two-way mirror. A savings-and-loan calendar turned to a peaceful country scene. I felt like I had been thrust into the middle of a certain notorious videotape; police interrogation rooms must be the same all over the world, heavy with the hint of torture.

Walter Paisley and/or his men had been following me ever since I'd closed up my house, burning precious District of Columbia dollars while they waited for me to commit an incriminating faux pas. Finally, Paisley's impatience had reached critical mass, and he'd decided to bring me in. I understood; I'd done it myself. Stuck on a story that seems impossible to advance, you try something rash—something with equal potential to be brilliant or stupid. Now Paisley sat across from us, fiddling with a cassette recorder and a file, disturbingly labeled "Falco, R." Lucy was at her most severe: brown business suit, hair pulled back, armed with her own recorder and a fresh six-pack of legal pads, which she unwrapped with angry dexterity. I had phoned her from the car, then ridden back to Washington with a Virginia state trooper while Walter followed in the T-Bird. Lucy and I had no time to discuss our separation outside Faustin Gabriel's house, or what I had learned there that night; I was sure she had even more questions for me than Walter Paisley had.

Walter looked up at me, waiting for an answer to his last question. "Well?"

"Come on, you know I've never carried a gun."

"Never say never, Ray." He flipped through my file. "And never contradict your friendly neighborhood bartender. I have a statement from a bartender at the Deadline on M Street to the effect that he saw you in there with a revolver tucked in your belt, drinking, acting nervous as a cat on its ninth life. A former colleague of yours, individual by the name of Doug Holloway, can back that up."

"Did he give you a signed statement?" Lucy asked.

"Sure did."

"May I see it?"

"You may not. You don't get to just clamp eyes on everything at this stage, ma'am. There's no discovery involved here. Yet."

Walter let the threat dangle for a moment. He assembled his pipe and tobacco; Lucy took this as a cue to fire up a Gitane. "That same night, a half-hour earlier, and just five blocks away, a handgun was boosted from the front window of a pawnshop called the Bargain Barn on Seventh Street. Smith and Wesson .357, model 686 Combat Masterpiece with wood grips, to be specific. Box of ammo disappeared along with it. Not just any ammo, more like artillery shells—hydrashocks, a hundred fifty-eight grain-jacketed hollow points."

"Has the bartender identified the gun he allegedly saw on Mr. Falco as a Smith and Wesson .357?" Lucy asked.

"No."

"So you cannot directly connect Mr. Falco to this specific stolen gun?"

"Well, who knows what a search of his house may turn up?" Before Lucy could ask for it, Walter produced a Xerox of a signed search warrant. "My men are there now. Don't worry; I told them to be careful, that it was a national landmark." He skated a picture of Jean-Mars Baptiste's corpse across the desk. "Let me show you an interesting connection I *can* make. The hydrashock load, it goes in like a BB, comes out like a softball. Jean-Mars Baptiste had a six-inch hole in his back."

I stared at the photograph, pretending I was seeing the body for the first time. Lucy examined it, made notes on her electronic agenda. "Any bullet fragments found in the body?" Lucy asked.

"Copper fragments consistent with the jacketed ammunition in question," Walter said.

"All this forensic minutiae is beside the point!" I blurted. "None of it makes an ounce of sense: why would I kill this guy?"

Walter sighed with genuine regret. "I can't pretend to imagine why, Ray," he said. "For your sake, hell, for my own sake, because I still want to believe that there's basic decency out there, I hope you didn't do it. But we've got a troubling pattern of inconsistencies; . . . I won't even bring up that first night at the housing project. You say Baptiste has disappeared, then phone records show that you two were chattin' like a couple of teenagers. You claim you don't have a gun, it turns out you do; quite possibly stolen, quite possibly the murder weapon. In addition . . ." Walter made us wait while he flipped over the cassette, ". . . eyewitnesses saw a 'real cool-looking old car,' subsequently identified as a 1964 or '65 Thunderbird, cruising Baptiste's neighborhood shortly before the body turned up."

I shot a nervous glance at Lucy. But she was a blank, calmly making notes.

"No one saw anything else?" I asked. "No cars with blue headlights, for instance, the ones Baptiste was terrified of? You've got pictures of them, you know what I'm talking about!"

He pointed to a stack of my news clips. "The cars you mentioned in your articles here? The ones supposedly purchased by the Haitian embassy?"

"What's that mean—'supposedly'?"

"I got photo IDs of every single person employed by the Haitian embassy and showed them to the Pontiac dealer. Zero. He didn't recognize a one."

I felt punchy. Piece by piece, Walter Paisley was building a case against me. I lunged across the desk and grabbed him by his smug, seersucker lapels. "You're so busy being a cop's cop, you've got so much staked on the big collar that you're missing something much bigger."

"Raymond, back off!" Lucy shouted.

"It's OK, ma'am," Walter said. "Let him dig himself in a little deeper."

"Look, Walter, once and for all this is a political murder, OK?" I was reckless now, unconcerned about the consequences of manhandling a homicide detective. I spun him by the shoulders, forcing his face into the photographs of Baptiste's body. "This man was tortured before he was shot. That's how politics is played in Haiti. They don't have lobbyists and sound bites and congressional overrides; make a mistake in a debate and you end up with a burning tire around your neck!"

Walter's huge shoulder muscles flexed in my hands, a subtle warning that he didn't need a gun to take me down. He shook himself free, unruffled.

"But we have no proof of that. No witnesses, no suspects. All the evidence we've got is piled up on your side of the fence. Now, maybe there's some angle here I'm not seeing: you're covering for someone, a source, maybe. Well, it better be the source of a lifetime, the source of two lifetimes, if he's making you take this kind of heat."

My pleas of innocence weren't working; my lies didn't carry any conviction. There was a heavy silence. Walter knocked the dead tobacco out of his pipe, Lucy stubbed out her cigarette. Gestures of finality.

"Do you intend to formally charge my client?" Lucy asked. "With anything?"

"Probably. Unless he's willing to provide us with names, leads, other avenues of investigation. Which is sort of what I'd hoped would come out of this meeting."

"We'll need time to discuss the full range of our options," Lucy said.

"You've got twenty-four hours. I hope you can change my mind. Otherwise I'm going to the district attorney and file for murder."

18

LUCY HAD BIG plans, but she was making me wait. She sat behind the wheel of her car, reviewing the tape of my interrogation on a headset, entering notes on her agenda. We were still in the police garage; I sat in the passenger seat, watching the black-and-whites come and go, listening to the cops tell their war stories.

"OK," she said, putting away her appliances. "Since we're obviously not going to spend the next week searching for an imaginary killer, we have to presume Detective Paisley is going to charge you. Now: an instructive case occurred in Haiti about five years ago. A construction worker in a Baptist mission outside Les Cayes killed his supervisor with a hammer and was charged with murder. His defense lawyer convinced a panel of superior-court judges that the worker had been under the spiritual influence of a notorious local bokor, who was acting for a client who coveted the supervisor's job . . . and the worker was cleared."

"Lucy, listen . . ."

"I've been in touch, via fax, with one of the judges. Smart, articulate, Sorbonne educated. He's willing to fly up here as an

240

expert witness if this goes to trial." She opened her briefcase and scanned her notes. "We can also call on a professor of ethnology in the Antilles Research Program at Yale, the director of Haitian studies at the New York Academy of Sciences, and a professor of psychotherapy from the Université de Port-au-Prince. All of these guys are willing to testify to the extreme psychological stress that a vodoun victim can be subjected to. I think we can mount a very credible scientific/ethnic defense."

"I don't need a lawyer," I said. The words came out quickly, coldly.

"Excuse me?"

"You heard me. I'm not going to allow myself to be arrested. There's not going to be an indictment, there's not going to be a trial; therefore, I don't need a lawyer."

Lucy looked at me incredulously. "You begged me to take this case, and now, just as I'm putting the pieces of your defense together . . ." I opened the door. She grabbed my wrist urgently. "Is this you talking?" she asked. "Or Faustin Gabriel? What happened in that house, Raymond? Tell me!"

"I can't go to jail. And not just for the obvious reasons."

"Be realistic. Even if Paisley does file, a big-name reporter like you? They'll set a low bail . . . it'll be a year before you come to trial."

I tore away from her, jumped out of the car. I marched through the garage, but she came after me. "Stop!" I snapped. "Don't think you can change my mind by being sweet or lawyerly. Or whatever."

"A zombi's gotta do what a zombi's gotta do, huh?"

We spilled out onto the street. "Lucy, if it all turns to shit and I do go to prison, I will never get free. No irony intended. The answers are not here in D.C.; they're certainly not in a goddamn courtroom. They're in Haiti!"

Lucy's eyes widened. "You're not going down there?"

I didn't answer. I walked toward the Metro station at the end of the street. It was happening again: the fever, the dizziness, the dull ache beginning at my neck and flowing down my body, seeming to pass into the ground. It was my self-control bleeding away. I was being propelled toward my next assignment. First orders—cut Lucy Marcelin out of my life.

"I knew this would happen. From the minute you showed up at my apartment that morning," she said.

"Knew what would happen?"

"That I would be dragged back to Haiti. It's not like some small town you can just turn your back on. It's one of those places that never lets you go; I think it even follows you."

"I'm going alone."

She looked more beautiful than ever in the amber glow of the anticrime lights, her face tight with pain. Don't make this more difficult, I told myself. Don't succumb. She cut in front of me; I kept moving, forcing her to walk backward.

"Why are you doing this to me, Raymond?"

"You should be grateful you don't have to go. You can stay here in Washington. Tour the White House, play Miss All-America!"

"How can a prize-winning journalist be so dense? I'll do it for you; I'll go to Haiti for you."

She backed onto the escalator. We rode down into the subway station, facing each other like lovers who couldn't stand to be out of each other's sight. "Look, I don't want to lose you as a client; but I will if it means I can keep you as a . . . as a . . ." The escalator bumped us into the crowded station. Lucy took both of my hands, looped them around her waist. "Shit, Raymond, I might as well just say it. I may be falling in love with you . . ."

I just stared at her, awed and disgusted by my own brutal aloofness.

"And you feel something for me too, I'm sure of it," she said. "I'm supposed to know when people are bluffing and when they're telling the truth. And I don't think you're faking it . . . you're not that good of a liar." She cracked a half-smile. "I mean, I was even worried about that, you know? How is this guy going to do on the stand . . . what if I have to ask him to shade the truth . . . can he pull it off?"

I tried to pull my hands away. She resisted, and we fought each other for a moment.

"Don't let them do this to you!" she screamed. She dropped my hands, then slapped me, once on each cheek.

We were attracting stares—another bittersweet love story, ending on a train platform.

Tears exploded on Lucy's face. She looked at her hands guiltily, then pressed them gently against my ears. "Can't you just shut them out, darling?" she said, her voice choking. "There. You can't hear them now, can you?" She took a scarf out of her purse, held it against my eyes. "What if you can't see them? Is that any better? They're not here, they're nowhere. It's just me, Lucy."

I felt the cool silk against my eyelids, the warmth of her breath against my neck.

"Say something, goddamn you!"

My wordless reply stunned her; I know it hurt her, too, like a hundred tiny emotional cuts. I ripped away the scarf and tossed it into the air. It caught in an updraft from the air-conditioning, sailed up toward the fluorescent ceiling, and stuck, trapped by the crosscurrents. It was my life's most villainous moment: I was throwing away love. Throwing away a person.

I bought a fare card, fed it into the turnstile. Lucy took two steps after me, then stopped. There was that wall of pride that she wouldn't punch through. I could see the decision take shape in her clear, expressive eyes—*there will be no more displays of sorrow in public here.* I ran toward the platform. I had a last glimpse of her in a dirty security mirror. She stood stiffly in the middle of the station, buffeted by commuters: tying her hair back, smoothing out the wrinkles in her blazer, applying fresh lipstick.

———

"LADIES and gentlemen, on behalf of President Isidor, I would like to read the following statement." The Haitian ambassador adjusted his prop bifocals and curled his meaty hands around

the lectern. "To further his long-standing goal of Haitian democracy and national unity, President Isidor and the governing
council hereby announce that elections to choose a president
and a new National Assembly will be held two and a half weeks
from today, on Monday, the twenty-ninth. We are certain that
an atmosphere of respect and dignity will prevail throughout
the campaign and that the elections will be free and open. We
look forward to an era of reform and reconciliation, with all
Haitians working together for a prosperous and secure future."

Dark laughter filled the State Department pressroom at the
phrase "free and open." "A team of American and international
observers will travel to Haiti to monitor the vote, and of course
our government welcomes their participation." The ambassador looked over his shoulder, where Tony Randolph stood in
the middle of a line of white-shirted American officials, briefing
books clenched in their hands. "Mr. Randolph, who I'm sure
you all know, will take any further questions."

The ambassador tried to edge away from the lectern, but the
roomful of skeptical reporters began to fire on him at will. I
sat in the back, fidgeting impatiently like a school kid waiting
for three-thirty. None of my questions would be answered
there—I needed to get Tony alone. I guzzled ice water, mopped
my clammy forehead with a handkerchief. I knew I looked
terrible, maybe even dangerous. I'd seen myself in the men's
room mirror. The Reuters man who'd shared the desk with me
at the top of the briefing had politely decamped for more civilized company.

"Mr. Ambassador, you've just met with the deputy secretary
of state. How much pressure did he put on you to schedule
these elections?" asked an AP reporter.

The ambassador answered with an oily smile. "Fair and democratic elections have always been a goal of the Isidor admin-
istration. The timing is purely coincidental."

ABC, NBC, the *Times,* the *Post*—the questions blended into
each other, trampling the ambassador's feeble replies. "What
about the latest Amnesty and Americas Watch reports? How

do you respond to their allegations of widespread human-rights abuses by your government?"

"Isn't this action really a response to the videotaped torture-murder of an American citizen at the hands of the presidential guard?"

"What about the recent news stories about Haitian-sponsored terrorism in this country? What impact have they had on—?"

The ambassador held up both hands, trying to push back the verbal assault. "Please, please, Haiti is a sovereign, independent nation; as a matter of fact, it is the oldest independent black republic in the world. We do not formulate policy based on the rash speculations of a few misguided American reporters . . ."

His eyes zeroed in on me. I felt a twinge of journalistic pride, an almost-forgotten sensation. Eventually, the ambassador weaseled his way out of so many questions that the room lost interest in him. The rest of the briefing unfolded in drab governmentese, as Tony Randolph explained the mechanics of the election verification process and introduced the first members of the American delegation, none of whom looked thrilled to be there—congressional staffers, a couple of former ambassadors, an Amnesty International executive, and one actual United States senator (not actually present) to lend the group some heft.

As the briefing broke up, I cornered Tony on his way out the door. "Ray? Jeez, you look awful. Where the hell you been?"

"Tony, I gotta talk to you . . . alone."

"I called the house half a dozen times; Livia even drove out there, said the place looked like it hadn't been lived in for weeks."

"Alone . . . OK?" Desperation had crept into my voice. Tony looked at me with a mixture of pity and anger, as though I were a bum at a stoplight, begging to wash his windshield.

He turned to his staff. "I'll catch up with you guys." Tony led me through an unmarked door, into a warren of backstage corridors swarming with civil servants pushing document carts or hand-delivering interoffice mail. "Ah, the glamorous world of international relations." Tony chuckled. He punched me on the shoulder. "Hey, we finally got the Haitians to move off the fucking dime on this election thing. And frankly . . ." He looked up at the ceiling, ran his hand along the wall. "The area does not seem to be bugged, so I guess I can admit it—your stories really helped focus the Secretary's attention."

I nodded absently. I was feeling hot and cramped. My eyes locked on a candy machine.

"What is wrong with you? You hit a grand slam, Ray; you should be celebrating. Instead you look like death on a bad day. Don't you sleep or eat anymore?"

"Barely," I said. "Listen, those NSAM's you were working on—think I could have a look at them?"

"What NSAM's?" he answered.

"Don't bullshit me. The NSAM's on Haiti—you mentioned them the night we had dinner."

I stopped at the candy machine. I had a sudden craving for sugar. I fed in all my change, bought one of everything—Milk Duds, Chuckles, Good & Plenty, Raisinettes—junk food you find only in movie theaters.

"If I did mention them, I was mistaken. And if they did exist . . . you know I can't leak anything from an in-progress memoranda thread . . . God, how can you eat that shit?"

"There's something major in the works on Haiti, isn't there?" I asked.

"You just heard—they're having an election. Which to them is pretty goddamn major."

"Something else. Come on, Tony, you know I have the best antenna in the business. When the State Department gears up a big show like this, it usually means they've got another, even bigger show waiting in the wings."

"You want to cover this election, great. Maybe I can get you a seat on a government plane and a decent hotel room . . . they've got a Holiday Inn down there, I think. But beyond that, I am not in a position to pull strings for you . . . or feed your paranoid fantasies. The American government believes in democracy, Ray—in Russia, in China, even in fucking

Haiti. Sometimes we really are the good guys." Tony watched me eat, his disgust turning to interest. "You know, I probably haven't had a Good & Plenty since . . . let's see, 1963, front row, Varsity Theater, *Jason and the Argonauts*. How were they?"

I nodded, held up the empty box.

He swore, shook his head, and succumbed to sugar lust. As he bent down over the machine to retrieve his candy, his jacket rode up over his password scrambler. I memorized the nonsense word as it cycled across the tiny screen: "scrabtonikovarlou." Tony had said the password was automatically changed every two hours.

Which meant that I had two hours at the most to break into his computer.

———

THE cab got me to Livia Holcomb's Georgetown apartment in fifteen minutes. Of all the artifacts left over from a serious romance, keys are the most telling. Reminders of intimacy: when she lived with you, or you lived with her. Finding them on your key chain months later can make you sad or bitter, even relieved. In my case, add guilt—I was going to use Livia's keys to commit a federal crime.

Not to mention a personal invasion.

I rang the bell several times to make sure she wasn't home, then entered the foyer. The evidence of their togetherness hit me right away: Tony's trench coat hung from the rack, protectively hugging one of Livia's wool jackets.

It was an odd sensation, moving through rooms that I had always associated with Livia and me, to find that I had been so thoroughly replaced. Tony's books shared her shelves now, Tony's baseball memorabilia shared her mantel. Livia and I had seldom taken pictures of each other; our favorite pursuits weren't that photogenic. We were usually at home: in bed, working, or wrapped around each other on the couch, reading. But now, the sideboard beneath the front window held a gallery of pictures of the happy couple at play. Athletic, outdoorsy, flannel-shirted play: fly-fishing, river-rafting.

I went upstairs, found Tony's office. It was an at-home duplication of his State Department office: the same government-issue world maps, the same red leather chairs and Colonial-reproduction brass lamps.

I flipped on the computer, opened a blue vinyl briefing book that held the log-on instructions. The initial access was straightforward, but then I found myself wandering through a menu of networks, unsure which was Tony's. I tried the password at each network prompt. I wasted five minutes bumping into generic "access denied" messages, until "scrabtonikovarlou" finally worked, sending me into the network that served Tony's department. The list of files under the Caribbean section, subheading "Haiti," was voluminous, its titles coded. I didn't have time to read them on-line, so I decided to download as many as I could before the password changed and I was cut off.

I squandered another fifteen minutes learning Tony's communications software and figuring out how to stream the data directly to his printer. At last, I had the system configured; when I pressed the "enter" key with a flourish, it actually worked. The laser printer hummed to life, and the classified wisdom of the United States Department of State began to pile up in front of me. As I sifted through the documents, I glanced down at the street: Livia was climbing the front steps!

What could I do? Turn off the computer and hide? The information was pouring out, and if I logged off now, I might never get into the network again.

Livia inserted her key in the front door, then stopped. Something didn't look right to her—had I forgotten to secure the dead bolt behind me? She squinted into the peephole, then looked up at the second floor. She opened her purse and took out a gun. Since when had she started walking the streets of Washington armed?

She kicked open the door an inch. Waited. Another inch. Finally, she squeezed furtively inside. I padded into the hall, hoping I could monitor her movements downstairs.

"Tony . . . you there?" she called.

My mind was clogged—how should I play this?

"Tony, honey, come on, you're making me nervous . . ."

Please, Livia, now's not the time to turn macho. We went over this that night your neighbor was robbed, remember? If you come home, suspect a break-in, you get the hell out of there. I heard her dial the phone and whisper the word "police."

I had to make a move. I marched loudly to the top of the stairs. "Hey, hey, Livia, relax, it's me."

She jumped. "What the hell . . ."

"I ran into Tony at the two o'clock briefing. He was swamped, and asked me if I could swing by, pick up some paperwork for him."

The fear had drained from her face, but she was still suspicious. The nasal 911 voice prompted her from the telephone. "Well, go on, tell them everything's OK," I said. I watched to make sure she hung up on the police, then ran back into the office. The laser printer was signaling that it was out of paper. I ripped open a fresh box, slipped it into the tray. Livia walked in a moment later.

"God, you scared the shit out of me, Ray. Plus, you almost got yourself ventilated."

"Sorry."

She casually began to sort through a pile of mail. "Well, what the hell. As long as you're here, you wanna screw? I've been slaving over the hot economic indicators all day . . . makes a girl awful horny." She laid a friendly hand on my neck. I tensed violently. "Jeez, honey, it's a joke. Lighten up."

Then, I felt Livia's hand drop away abruptly.

"Action Memorandum number 3795.10? Tony really cleared you for this?"

"Doesn't look like anything special to me." I hedged. "Mostly old news, I think."

Livia ran her finger across the screen. "I know a little bit about how they code stuff . . . this file here, this was compiled four hours ago! There's no way Tony would want you to see this." As she checked the printer, her back stiffened. "My God, Ray, there's over a hundred pages of classified material here! What the fuck is going on?"

I fumbled for an answer. "It's not what it looks like." Understatement of the decade. The computer began to beep, and a garish warning filled the screen: "Session will terminate in two minutes—enter new password now"!

"How did you get into the confidential network?" Livia asked.

"Tony gave me his—"

"Never! He would never give you his password. He locks up the scrambler in a fireproof safe, he's so afraid I'll get up in the middle of the night and use it . . . not that I ever would."

"When did you become such a zealous protector of official secrets? Ms. NPR, Ms. Freedom of the Press gets a promotion, suddenly the government's no longer the big bad wolf."

I turned my back on her, stacked up the documents as they came out of the printer. "I'm not talking politics, Ray, I'm talking relationships. And I would never exploit mine with Tony just to sleaze my way into a story . . . the way you're doing."

Enter new password now!

I pounded the keys randomly, a one in a million chance that I would stumble across the new password. The computer gave off an ugly buzz, then sent me a terse message: "Session terminated." The screen went blank as the State Department disconnected me.

"You're exploiting me too," Livia said. "That's what really hurts."

She reached for the phone.

"Don't do it," I ordered.

"Fuck you, 'don't do it' . . . I'm calling Tony."

She hit the speed dialer, and it seemed to set off an alarm in me. I ripped the phone out of her hands, kicked the jack in the baseboard to pieces. I grabbed the documents, she lunged at me. I pushed her violently aside and she fell against the bookcase. As I slammed toward the door, her hands flew to her face in a gesture of terrified self-protection.

It was a moment that said everything—people I had once

loved were now afraid of me, people who had given me their trust would never trust me again.

"What's happened to you? Did I miss something? You were always angry, a little arrogant, but now you've turned into a real asshole." She pulled the gun out of her purse. "I can't let you take that stuff. Really."

I wanted desperately to warn her, to whisper the truth—*if I damage you, it's not really me, Livia. Forgive me now, for anything I might do in the future.* "Don't believe everything you read about me in the papers," I muttered.

"What?"

I whipped my arm out and twisted her wrist until she gasped in pain, dropping the revolver. I picked it up, burrowed it into the plush red leather of Tony's chair, and fired all six shots. The upholstery muffled the blast somewhat, but a shock wave rocked the room. Dazed, Livia stared at the smoldering hole.

"You're sick; that's it, isn't it?"

"Maybe."

"You looked like hell that night at dinner, and now . . . no one in his right mind shoots a chair, not even that one." Her face softened, she reached out to me. "God, tell me, please, what's wrong with you?"

"Don't do it, Liv, don't come at me with concern and sympathy. I won't be able to accept it; I can't offer you the satisfaction of seeing me cured."

"Cured of what? Come on, I'm not judging you. I just want to see you get some help—"

"Just X him out of your thoughts, OK?"

" 'Him'?"

"The old Ray Falco is gone."

"But I *liked* the old Ray Falco." She stepped toward me gingerly. "Oh, sure, he could be a royal pain, but he had a certain angry integrity; he knew what he was about. Isn't there anything I can do to get him back?"

"No. It would be better all around if you just stopped caring." Then, I noticed how the sun caught her hair, turning it into a frizzy, golden halo. "Don't move," I said. I shut my eyes, composing a mental snapshot of Livia Holcomb as I wanted to remember her—a freckled, sunlit angel.

Eyes still closed, I backed out the door.

———

THERE. I had done it. I'd lost them all: Lucy, Tony, Livia. No one left to hurt. No allies. No support. Exactly how Faustin Gabriel had planned it: rip my life out by its roots, transplant me to a friendless, foreign world. A textbook example of how you make a slave.

I read through the stolen documents in the backseat of the taxi. They bore the lackluster fingerprints of a dozen lawyers and people who have learned to think like lawyers. Scattered throughout the papers were the euphemisms of modern political speech: troops were "force packages," political murder became "unforeseen social repercussions," starvation was called "degradation of human infrastructure." A mind fog of acronyms for Haitian political parties: CAP, HIP, CDH, PAD. Most of the papers were devoted to a discussion of the American role in the upcoming Haitian elections. Though the election had been announced only today, it appeared that the State Department had been studying the possibility for weeks.

Policy analysts had already surveyed the field of potential candidates and found none they liked. Reading around the bureaucratese, it was obvious that they didn't approve of President Rene Isidor and his grade-school socialism either. Plus, the Haitian Army, still filled with unreconstructed Duvalierists, hated President Isidor. They had installed him, but he had gone too far; he was trying to throw off their leash. They were rumbling in their barracks on full idle, oiling their weapons and counting their bullets, just waiting for him to make a mistake.

The election would be it. The violence that always accompanied Haitian politics would be merciless this time. True chaos threatened—order would have to be restored somehow. Though a black-and-white conclusion was not spelled out, the logic was easy to follow: the Haitian Army (they would be called "transitional figures" by the State Department) would rush in to fill any power vacuum. Other memoranda analyzed the strategic ramifications of using United States troops to secure the peace and ensure the safety of the American community in Haiti.

"You sure this is it?" asked the cab driver. I looked up. The shutters were closed on Faustin Gabriel's house. The loup-garou cars were no longer in the driveway. Something was wrong.

"Wait for me, will you?"

The stolen documents secure in my briefcase, I walked warily to the front door. The lawn, the centerpiece of a well-paid gardener's lavish attention, looked a little ragged. I allowed myself a flurry of hope: they had been forced to change their plans, maybe even abandon them. The slow poison of Haitian politics had caught up with them: they were dead; I would be freed.

The front door swung open, revealing a young mulatto man I didn't recognize. Slender and refined, he wore a blue workman's apron over a tailored white shirt ornamented with silver cuff links.

"Ah, Mr. Falco. I'm Richard, assistant manager of the Galerie Creole. I'll take those," he said, his accent more French than Haitian. As he reached for the briefcase, I spotted the two large rings on his right hand: each was engraved with the vèvè of Ogoun, the warrior god.

"Where's Gabriel? Where's Carmen Mondesir?"

"I've been told that they'll contact you."

"Contact me? What kind of cryptic bullshit is that?"

I looked over his shoulder. Cardboard boxes were stacked along the hall; in the living room I saw furniture crates brimming with packing straw, all freshly labeled with the name of a Barbados-flagged freighter and a destination—Port-au-Prince.

"May I have the material, please?" he asked.

I pushed past him, strode down the hall to the living room. He followed, irritated, but not particularly alarmed. Movers were painstakingly boxing Faustin Gabriel's prized antiques. Even his holy mahogany desk was going. It was wrapped in several layers of protective, bubbled Mylar—in the rich glow of the chandelier, it seemed to throw off sparks of history.

My eyes flew to the spot on the wall where the portrait of Vincent Gabriel had hung. It had been taken down. Then I spotted it in the hands of two movers, who were slipping it into a packing case.

"Wait!" I shouted. I ran over to the movers. "One last look . . . ten seconds." I stared into Gabriel's young, hypnotic face. The scar didn't seem gruesome any longer, more like a self-inflicted ornament, a mark of character.

"Miss Mondesir left something for you," Richard said, handing me an envelope bearing the Zanfan d'Ayiti letterhead. Inside was a plane ticket to Port-au-Prince. First class. "You'll find a hotel reservation in there as well. She's booked you into the Oloffson. Not to my taste, really; I would stay at the Moulin sur Mer. But you'll like it. It's old, dripping with local color. American people are quite fond of local color, aren't they?"

I don't remember handing Richard the briefcase, but when I became aware of my hand again, it was gone. My gaze had been drawn back to the painting; the black eyes followed me to the last, as Vincent Gabriel disappeared into the case.

Even he was going back to Haiti.

19

I HAD ALWAYS found it impossible to dream on airplanes. But on the flight from Miami to Port-au-Prince, thirty thousand feet above the Caribbean, dreams somehow wound their way up to me. I soared over the jungles of Saint Domingue, pages of the in-flight magazine scattering behind me like shed feathers; I had a hawk's-eye view of high, green mountain ranges, the Hispaniola that Columbus had described to Queen Isabella by crumpling a piece of paper and throwing it at her feet. I dove into a deep ravine that funneled toward the bright water of the bay; flew through thick mahogany forests teeming with parrots and butterflies.

When I awoke we were flying over a desert. I blinked, confused. Then I remembered my conversation with the UN agronomist I'd met in the Miami departure lounge. A nation of former slaves would never be slaves again; the descendants of slaves would never farm anyone's land but their own. So for two hundred years, the Haitian peasant had been carving up the giant plantations into tiny, private parcels; it was his *héritage*, which he passed on to be divided, then subdivided by succeeding generations. When the soil was exhausted, the trees were cut down for charcoal; when the trees were gone, the people left for the city. That was the Ile de la Gonâve down there, and they were tearing up the thornbushes now. The island no longer sustained life; the population lived off checks sent by relatives in Miami.

As we skimmed over the bay of Port-au-Prince, flight attendants filled out immigration forms for illiterate passengers. No one commented on the irony of an adult able to afford hundreds of dollars for a plane ticket, yet unable to read. Minutes later we landed, filing off the plane in three distinct groups: Haitians, journalists, missionaries. I held Nicholas Whitney Townsend's diary like a shield, and as I walked across the glaring tarmac I recalled his first impressions—he had seen green vistas of sugarcane and densely forested mountains. I saw dry, treeless hills, a dead backdrop ringing the city.

Townsend had been met by the deputy intendant; I was met by taxi hustlers and the international press corps. There were dignitaries on my plane, the first crew of election observers and human-rights monitors. They gave bland statements to the circling print and TV reporters, then headed for the air-conditioned shelter of UN-flagged vans.

"Bloody TV hacks, with their bloody big cameras," growled an English voice behind me. I turned to see a stocky, rumpled photographer snapping pictures of the departing motorcade. He was in his late forties, dressed untropically in corduroy pants and a button-down shirt. "Try to get some local color, and you end up with a shot of a bloody big lens." As he lowered his camera, he also lowered a pair of bifocals from their perch on his forehead in a smooth, practiced motion. "Phil Somerset, AP. Come on, we'll grab a *publique,* beat them back to the bar."

We shook hands. "Ray Falco. I'm—"

"I know who you are, mate. I thank you and my per diem thanks you."

We were joined by a tall, young, exotic-looking woman who spoke with a suitably exotic accent. "Please, Phil, remember who's paying that per diem." She was crisp and clean and Banana Republic. She slipped a tiny video camera into her backpack. "I'm Laura Salameh, TV hack. The BBC sent me here to cover the elections, and as I'd never been to Haiti, I was forced to hire Phil as an area expert."

Somerset wetly nuzzled her neck. "There are still a few areas in which I need to develop further expertise. Say hello to Raymond Falco, dear. He's the primary reason you're vacationing in the land of voodoo and sunshine, and not freezing that trim, Franco-Lebanese ass of yours in Belfast or some bloody place. He broke the torture-tape story." We crammed into a battered Nissan driven by a Haitian teenager, and after a rambunctious round of Creole fare negotiations conducted by Somerset, we bounced out of the parking lot, scattering a herd of goats. "Like I'm always told the generals down here, get some white people killed and the world will beat a path to your door."

We merged onto the airport road and plunged into the country that had possessed me. My first impression was one of relentless, hustling energy. Everyone was selling, making, or repairing something. Everyone was an independent contractor. Vendors hawked pyramids of cigarette cartons, papayas, sugarcane, chewing gum, newspapers, charcoal, soft drinks, counterfeit Chanel No. 5. Men welded engine parts, shined shoes. Blacksmiths repaired bicycle frames, mechanics patched tires. Seamstresses stitched brightly colored dresses by the side of the road, beneath the shade of dusty coconut palms. There were no factories or showcase industrial parks like you find around many Third World airports; this was Haitian industry—one man or woman with a dollar's worth of goods and infinite patience.

Port-au-Prince was a hot, dusty kaleidoscope, a million people crammed into a city that felt like a life-and-death video arcade. Our white skin attracted beggars and hustlers, laughter and dirty looks. *"Hey, blanc, donne-moi cinq dollars,"* shouted the street kids that mobbed our car. *"Hey, journaliste!"* yelled someone else. "I take you to see political killings. No bullshit. Bodies, lots of bodies, just like I show CNN." A one-armed man juggled a bottle of Windex and a dirty rag as he cleaned our windshield; old women with sagging faces held out their hands;

they didn't pretend to be grateful for the dollar bills I guiltily distributed.

It was a city of brilliant colors. Turquoise, red, orange, cobalt blue—a Haitian building was an insistent yank on your sleeve; there was so much sensory input, the architecture had to compete for your attention. Sagging wood town houses were propped up by cement-walled schools, which leaned against tin-roofed shacks, which were supported by cinder-block churches: a city block was like a row of dominoes, and if that woman resting against that corner wall as she cooked plantains over a charcoal fire ever decided to stand up . . .

It was a desperate, collapsing city but it had not given up hope. People were image-conscious. If they could afford it, they dressed flashily; if they couldn't, they still made sure their clothes were clean and creased to kill. There was art for sale on every corner, impromptu galleries blocked the sidewalks; unlike most cities, the street hustlers weren't drug dealers, they were painters and sculptors and commission men.

"It's really not that bad, is it?" said Laura. "Seriously, I've covered much worse. I've been pursued by teenage *sicarios* through the slums of Medellín . . . I mean, one becomes inured, doesn't one? As for the highly touted Haitian political violence—please." She leaned in to me. "I recall sitting on a muddy hillside with the Kurdish People's Army waiting for Saddam to gas us . . ."

"Laura, dear, please bottle it," said Somerset.

"I'm sorry, but it's just not all that threatening."

"Well, it's still daylight, isn't it?" he snapped. We stalled behind a column of tap-taps, the famous hand-painted Haitian jitney buses. They were mobile handicraft exhibits, kitsch-mobiles buffed to a blinding gloss, their names reflecting the dreams, the cultural schizophrenia of their owners: Bébé Dangereux, Insurance du Christ, Magic Johnson Mon Amour. A papier-mâché space shuttle bristled from the roof of one, Sylvester Stallone as Rambo glared cross-eyed from the engine compartment of another. They spewed black clouds of diesel fume as they idled, the only folk art in the world that was carcinogenic. "So, Ray. How long you down for?" Somerset asked. "Just the election, or do you have a longer piece in mind? Spill it out, lad; give us insight into the workings of the American journalistic mind."

I knew that shop talk was expected now. Why else would I be in poor, desperate Haiti if not to cover the election, the street clashes, and the political murders that the reporters secretly prayed for?

"Actually, I came for the snorkeling, Phil."

He winked and nodded. He loved my answer, presuming it meant I was working some hot angle or high-placed mystery source.

Half an hour later, we swung through a heavy iron gate ornamented by a voodoo vèvè, and drew up in front of the Hotel Oloffson. Gabled, turreted, fretted, it looked like a giant, water-stained paper cutout. Once upon a time, Haiti had been the Caribbean Harlem, attracting actors and artists such as Truman Capote, John Gielgud, James Jones, and Lillian Hellman, who had made the Hotel Oloffson their tropical salon. The hotel had been immortalized by Graham Greene in *The Comedians,* a novel that so annoyed Papa Doc Duvalier that the "President for Life" had Greene banned from Haiti for life. Now the hotel lived off misery and crisis. Without the missionaries and foreign-aid workers who spent a few nights on their way to and from the countryside, without the coups that drew journalists and their expense accounts, how would the Oloffson survive? But as I checked in I heard live music—the hotel's Haitian-American manager rehearsing with his voodoo rock band in the Anne Bancroft suite. A cassette and CD were now available.

I fell asleep in my room. When I awoke, it was dark. I heard barking dogs and gunfire. I went down to the veranda, which was one long, white wicker newsroom, buzzing with war stories, the volume notched up by rum punches and Prestige beer. I recognized *The New York Times, Le Monde, Der Spiegel, USA Today, the Toronto Globe & Mail.* All print reporters; I learned that the TV correspondents stayed at another hotel in Pétionville, a wealthy suburb in the hills. It was cooler up there, you could plug in a hair dryer, take five steps outside the bar and do your stand-up in front of a vista of Port-au-Prince.

People knew me by name, they bought me drinks, peppered me with questions about the latest diplomatic moves in Washington. They plugged me into the conversation, assuming I was anxiously following every tortuous wrinkle of Haitian politics.

"Ballots are being printed at some undisclosed location; the election's in two weeks, on a Monday, *USA Today* said. He'd come directly from the cooling hot spots of El Salvador and Nicaragua, and was still living on Latin time—he wore an embroidered guayabera and addressed the waiters in Spanish. "Since the army usually stages its coups on the weekends, by that Thursday we should start to feel something."

"I was down at the Dessalines barracks this morning," added *Der Spiegel*. "I felt a definite, unmistakable sense of . . ." as everyone at the table leaned forward, his mouth curled into a mischievous smile, ". . . confusion."

"The army will never let this election proceed on schedule," said *Le Monde*. She was middle-aged and terminally serious. She drank whiskey and chain-smoked Comme Il Faut, the Haitian cigarettes. "It is simply not in their interest."

"Bullshit. They need this election to get world opinion off their backs," said *The New York Times,* working hard to be the voice of streetwise pragmatism. He was young, ambitious, he'd put in for the Middle East and China, been offered Paris, but turned it down (good food means bad stories). He'd been castaway to the Caribbean, which to his delight included Haiti, a country whose violent inscrutabilities had gripped him with surprising passion. "They stage manage a nice little display of democracy; the UN observers go home, their consciences salved; the army goes back to looting the country. *Plus,* with foreign aid contingent on a fair election, there'll be that much more to loot. Picture it: you're a general sitting in army headquarters, you're right across the street from the presidential palace and you've got all the guns—you think, Democracy, why the hell not?"

The conversation turned into a buzzing blur:

"So who's the army's candidate?"

"Well, they hate President Isidor. They think he's the world's last Communist. . . ."

"My bones say *coup*. They hate world opinion even more."

"Lads," piped in Phil Somerset, as he darted from table to table offering massages to the female reporters, "they hate the fucking Haitian people most of all. That's the thing to remember. Whatever course of action does the most harm to the most people, that's where you place your bets."

"And that is . . . ?"

Before Somerset could answer, a sharp, heavy explosion detonated somewhere in the darkness beyond the hotel walls. I felt it like a kick in the stomach, saw the others react in the same way, like puppets whose strings had been jerked. It takes a big explosion to shut up a patio full of journalists. As we sat there in edgy silence, our waiters ran down the steps into the driveway, sniffed the air, and talked to the drivers/guides who lurked on the hotel grounds, waiting to hustle up clients.

"*C'est rien grave*," shouted a waiter, waving his hands in an all-clear signal. "No problem. A cooking explosion; propane, you know?"

We reacted with nervous laughter. Sure, no problem. Just a cooking fire.

Somerset gripped the bowed balustrade and gazed fondly into the darkness, like a cruise ship passenger marveling at the open sea. "I do bloody love this country, I really do."

Someone ordered another round of drinks. *The New York Times* and *Le Monde* focused earnestly on me. "You've been mysteriously silent, Ray. Don't you have any official Washington wisdom to share with us?"

"Yes, come on. The State Department must have its preferred candidate, but the embassy down here's hopelessly tight-lipped. Who is it? Who gets the official nod from the red-white-and-blue?" Two tables and two continents' worth of reporters waited intently for my pronouncement. *USA Today* ordered me dinner and billed it to his room—I was being set up for an evening-long debriefing. I would be expected to have opinions, preferably provocative, and anecdotes, preferably outrageous. But other plans had been made for me.

I saw him first as a shadow among the trees, a tall, thin figure puffing on a cigarette. The other guides gave him a wide berth as he strolled through the parking lot, casting glances up at the balcony. His eyes seemed to glare, the way an animal's do when they're caught in your headlights—I realized he was waiting for me.

I stood up, tapped my watch. Curious gazes followed me to my feet. "I'd love to chat, but if I don't get this interview tonight, I'll never get it at all." I caught a ripple of intrigued whispers.

"Who gives interviews at this hour?" *Der Spiegel* asked. Five seconds of silence, then everyone exclaimed at once: "The chief of police!"

As I headed for the steps, *The New York Times* snagged my sleeve. "You've been in the country six hours, Ray. How the hell did you get an interview with him?"

I shrugged. "Guess he just likes new blood."

"So to speak," said Somerset.

Jealous catcalls followed me into the dark driveway: "Be sure to ask him about the ten percent stake in the national cement business he got for supporting the last coup; he loves to talk about that."

"And don't worry, Ray, one of us'll be along to identify your body in the morning."

I looked back at the hotel veranda, with its lamplit glow and comforting purr of overhead fans. Let them have their professional envy; it was easier to understand than the truth.

My guide wouldn't talk to me. I had only a brief glimpse of his features—a young man with a long, proud neck and high forehead, his mouth set in a permanent scowl—before he turned and walked out the Oloffson gate.

"Excuse me, don't I even get a name?" I called, following him through the streets. He wouldn't let me catch up: I would close the gap, then he would pull away. "Who the hell are you? Where are you taking me?" Still no answer. I was to follow ignorantly in his wake, like a royal retainer.

His movements were fluid and haughty; he smoothly relit his cigarette without breaking stride. He seemed to own the street. Was it my imagination, or did people retreat into their doorways at the sight of him? Even the dogs stopped their howling as we passed.

He walked into the hills along a major thoroughfare. The massive, four-wheel-drive vans of the elite crawled like tanks over crater-size potholes; tap-taps and *collectifs* clattered toward Port-au-Prince, carrying maids, cooks, and gardeners. Light skin going uphill, dark skin going down. The neighborhoods grew wealthier the higher we climbed, but clinging to the narrow ravines that sloped away from the street were the *bidonvilles,* hillside slums made of scrap wood and surplus bricks. Voices hissed at us; I saw vague, candlelit faces. Pigs grazed and fruit rotted just footsteps away from turquoise swimming pools. The rich in Haiti could not seal themselves off in Beverly Hills–like enclaves—they mingled with poverty face to face, forced every day into fresher and more creative forms of denial.

As we left the main drag and began to poke our way through quiet side streets, the city seemed to respond to some silent alarm. Everybody fled indoors. We were in a neighborhood of high walls, iron gates, videocameras. Fussy, overdesigned houses—Greek Revival, Aspen ski lodge, post-modern bunker.

My guide abruptly stopped. I had learned the etiquette by now, and I stopped too. Twenty feet separated us. Then the streetlights buzzed and went out. The houses went dark, too. It was a power blackout. Both the darkness and the silence were absolute—it felt like we were the only two people in the world. Five minutes passed as we stood there motionlessly; the only betrayal of life was the orange ember of my guide's cigarette. He was listening, waiting.

Then, from the hills around us, invisible dogs began to bark. My guide put out his cigarette, and now there was nothing to mark his presence. I heard a shrill, almost musical bark over-riding the others, and though I couldn't see him, I was certain it had come from my guide!

Seconds later, private generators thundered to life and the houses blazed with light again. My guide was gone. I rushed to the spot where he had been standing. I saw the crushed cigarette in the dirt, but otherwise there was no trace of him. The dogs were quiet again. I shivered like a kid who's just heard a ghost story told around the campfire and now has to walk alone through the woods to his tent. I spun in a circle, scanning the shadows. Was he really gone? From the trees, from behind high walls, from the air itself, I felt I was still being watched.

But my guide had done his job—I knew that the house at the end of the block was Faustin Gabriel's. Unlike the dictator-chic style of its neighbors, it was a beautiful three-story Creole town house. It was a skyline in itself, its gabled roofs, bell towers, and window's walks forming a frantic silhouette.

The mobs had vented their rage on Faustin Gabriel's show-place. I slipped through the gate, which hung by a single bolt. The grounds reminded me of a battlefield after a heavy shelling: trees had been ripped up by their roots, the walkways pillaged for stone. The house had no windows left, the walls were pockmarked by gunfire. Several fires had been set: giant burn marks fanned out across the walls.

I walked around to the backyard and found the remains of a voodoo temple. Large ceremonies had been held here; there were circular stone benches that reminded me of a Roman am-phitheater, but they were scarred with graffiti. The centerpost down which the gods had once descended was charred and teetering.

The yard unfolded toward a filigreed iron fence. Beyond the fence was a series of boxy shapes, painted in bright colors that seemed to glow in the dark—the Gabriel family cemetery. I stepped over a trampled section of fence and was soon sur-rounded by tombs. The Gabriels were buried above ground, in vaults of pink and baby blue, their names carved in white relief. The dead had a spectacular view—spread out below them was all of Port-au-Prince. A few ships glowed in the bay, the airport beacon blinked green and white, but for the most part, the city was blacked out, perhaps darker than it had been in the days of Gabriel's ancestors.

I walked past two hundred years of Gabriels, with their evocative names: Benoit, Innocente, Louisianne, Brilliant, Tonnere. Then I stopped short. Something wasn't right—a smell that you don't associate with dark nights and deserted graveyards. Fresh paint.

Faustin Gabriel was crouched at the foot of the largest vault, a towering, canary-yellow structure trimmed with black tile. With careful brushstrokes, he touched up a black border around the name at the top of the vault—Vincent Gabriel.

"Ah, Mr. Falco. Welcome to Port-au-Prince." Gabriel stood and inspected his work. "I hope you don't mind my summoning you so late, but unlike most Haitians, I prefer to work at night. During the day there are so many distractions; after dark, I find it's easier . . . to get things done."

"Where's Carmen?" I pressed. "If we're going to have a summit conference, I'd just as soon get on with it."

Gabriel capped the paint can, shook the brush out in the weeds. "Every story needs a villain, doesn't it? Even a news story. I brought you here so that I might begin the process of persuading you that I am not the villain of this piece."

"PR?" I exploded. "You brought me here for goddamn PR?"

"Consider where you are, Mr. Falco. Why would the concept of 'public relations' even enter your head?" He pointed at the ruins of his peristyle. "Vincent Gabriel was granted this land by the first independent Haitian government, in recognition of his service to the revolution. Vodoun was conducted on this spot for nearly two hundred years, but look what they have done now."

I realized that several of the vaults had been vandalized, even looted. Coffins had been torn open; I saw bones, tatters of flesh and clothing. I didn't react. I was immune to horror-movie theatrics now, even when they were real.

He reset a toppled headstone in the hard, dry soil. "Haiti has become so desperate that even the loa are deserting her. I must do what I can to bring them back."

It was stifling, as though the tombs were giving off the heat they had collected during the day. I tapped my watch.

"Yes, yes, we're going," Gabriel said. "But what I want you to understand is this: all power seekers are not alike. Some wish only to enrich themselves, others hope to save a country."

"Why do you even care what I think?" I asked.

Gabriel led me out of the cemetery, locking the rusted gate behind him. "Your world-weariness, your professional exhaustion is only skin deep, I think. You are still attracted to a great story; one day you will write this one. And when you do, I hope to see Faustin Gabriel truthfully portrayed."

Gabriel had undercut himself. It's always the villains who are the most image-conscious.

———

We drove in Gabriel's four-wheel-drive jeep to a house higher up in the hills, a fortress the size of a Vegas casino, built by Walt Disney from plans by Albert Speer. A half-dozen guards in jeans and T-shirts patrolled the grounds. They sipped bottles of Teem, swatted mosquitoes, shifted their Uzis nervously on their shoulders. I thought I recognized one of them, but when our eyes met above the barrel of his gun, his blank expression convinced me I was wrong.

The house hummed with tense activity. It had been unoccupied for months and was now being cleaned and repaired by squads of servants. New phone lines were being installed, computers, printers. TVs blared: CNN and the late news from Telenational de Haiti. President Isidor appeared briefly on the screen and was hissed at by a guard, who aimed his gun at the TV.

"Whose house is this?" I asked. There were family pictures above the garish, brass-bordered fireplace—a fireplace in Haiti, where the daytime temperature seldom sank below eight-five. But a massive air conditioner throbbed in the ceiling, giving

the house a bizarre chill; of course a fireplace made sense, what
was I thinking?

"The house belongs to a contributor, a Haitian businessman
who has helped us financially." It was Carmen Mondesir's
voice. She entered through a sliding glass door; it looked like
she was stepping out of a mirror. "He and his family live in
Cannes at the moment, but as you can see, plans are being made
for their return."

"Depending on what happens on election day," I said.

"Many people will return to Haiti. Our best minds. They
will repatriate their money, they will help us rebuild."

Carmen lit a Comme Il Faut and grimaced, walked to the
bar and poured a stiff shot of Barbancourt 5 Star. "We have a
task for you, Raymond. There are polling places being set up
throughout the city. On election day, the American observation
team will pay surprise visits to a select group of these polling
places in order to ensure that the vote is, how do you call it,
lib e onèt, fair and open. We would like their schedule. Mingle
with your colleagues, attach yourself to the American embassy
people, attend their cocktail parties. In brief, do your job. And
when you have the information, you will call us."

"Say I do get this information . . . what then? You release
me, I get my life back?"

Carmen poured another shot of rum, added lime juice and
sugar, and handed it to me. "It will be the end of our association.
If you wish."

"Why wouldn't I wish?"

"Many foreigners, once they have been exposed to Haiti for
a period of time, find it difficult to pull away. It gets into their
blood. Maybe it's the voodoo, maybe it's just the Haitian
women . . ."

Or maybe, I thought, because Haiti is such an unknowable
place, knowing it becomes an obsession. You become Phil
Somerset, a perpetual returnee, jetting in for the annual coups,
addicted to the baroque squalor and violence, spoiled for any
other place.

Gunfire erupted outside. I saw the guards rush across the grounds and pour out the front gate. Tires squealed, an engine revved; more gunfire, then I heard the jackhammer of automatic weapons. I ran into the yard, out to the street, Carmen and Gabriel behind me. Several people were struggling against the wall; fists flew, legs and arms writhed in close combat. Carmen shouted in Creole, but it was like trying to referee a cockfight. A guard—the tall, lanky one I thought I'd recognized—pinned my arms behind me and bored his Uzi into my spine, ensuring that I wouldn't duck out amid the chaos.

It was over in seconds. Carmen's men untangled themselves, yelling, cursing, their attention fixed on the ground. A body lay there, a teenage boy. He was shoeless, wore a Malcolm X T-shirt and greasy jeans. His fingers were curled around a can of spray paint. From the hoarse snatches of Creole, I pieced together what had happened: a pickup truck had driven by, no headlights. It had stopped in front of *this* house, *this* wall; they had known exactly what they were looking for. Two young men had jumped out and begun to paint political slogans on the wall. Carmen's guards killed one, scared the other off. *"Komunis,"* someone spat. They would be taken care of next Monday.

Suddenly, the teenager twitched, as though jolted back to life. One of the guards panicked, let off a burst; bullets chewed through the boy's wrist, severing the guilty hand. I smelled blood, felt nauseated. The street filled with dogs, attracted by the corpse and the commotion. It happened in slow motion, the inevitable conclusion to a violent cartoon—one of the dogs snatched up the severed hand in his teeth and scampered off, the can of spray paint clanging against the pavement.

I heard the Uzi's safety slide off, felt the gun barrel climb up my spine toward my neck like some horrible, poisonous spider. I knew what the guard was thinking: should I have been permitted to see this? Should I be permitted to report on this? Arguing broke out—things were moving too quickly for these young men. Two guards dragged the body into the yard; servants set up a barricade of tires at the gate, scattered nails in the street.

Carmen was shouting orders, trying to reestablish control, but the fear in her eyes was blatant. She flicked on a flashlight. A poster had been plastered to the wall. It was a bad photocopy of an old picture on cheap paper, but it was unmistakably Carmen Mondesir. A slogan was sprayed across it, the letters still dripping: KRIMINEL MAKOUT, ALE!—"Macoute criminals, get out."

Carmen looked at me with her strange blue eyes—she knew that her life and its crimes had suddenly snapped into focus for me. I could picture her as a girl in her poor, dusty village, swooning with admiration for the swaggering Tontons Macoutes in their blue denim uniforms and crisp red bandannas. While her girlfriends chased boys, then husbands, then lovers, Carmen had chased power.

Once a Macoute, always a Macoute—it didn't matter how many orphans she saved.

"So. It's beginning," Faustin Gabriel said, surveying the gruesome scene with detachment. He raised a finger, like a teacher silencing a pupil, and glanced up at the sky. A moment later, a shooting star carved a brilliant path above the blacked-out city. "In another week, Mr. Falco, this will seem like nothing."

20

To wander the streets of Haiti as a zombi is to be at home, like a gray suit on Madison Avenue, a politico on Capitol Hill. You belong. Colorful, alien permutations of life drift past your glazed eyes, but you are not equipped to understand them; injustices and tiny miseries assault you at every corner, but you are powerless to fix them. For the next few days I lived as a zombi/reporter, tagging along with my fellow journalists, taking the pulse, as we say, as the country zigzagged toward its collision with democracy. We were all zombis at the Oloffson, pushed through our paces by our various masters—editors, deadlines, word counts, paychecks—and all of us were helpless when it came to rewriting the tragicomedy of Haiti.

At first, I had no luck pursuing my assignment: the election observers' schedule was a closely held secret. None of the other reporters knew it; the United Nations people, comfortably bivouacked at the Hotel Montana, weren't talking; no one at the American consulate or embassy would be specific; and officials at the hilariously misnamed United States Information Agency claimed no such schedule existed. But finally, alcohol and lobster flan loosened tongues. At a birthday party for the French

270

ambassador, held in the surrealistic surroundings of Haiti's abandoned Club Med, I managed to corner a disgruntled Australian OAS human-rights worker. Years of dealing with tropical bureaucracies had made him surly and addicted to rum punches, and he happily pointed out the flaws in the election observers' schedule.

"They're delivering the ballots by truck—that's a serious no-no, since trucks can be highjacked. And look at this!" he said, waving an official-looking, rum-stained fax. "They're focusing too much manpower on this one polling place just outside Port-au-Prince, when everyone knows that elections are won or lost in the countryside. I smell a major cock-up." My eyes followed the fax as it bobbed drunkenly in the OAS worker's hands; I memorized as much of it as possible, then snuck out to a poolside cabana to phone Carmen Mondesir. She acknowledged my report matter-of-factly; I was just another employee, my loyalty never in doubt.

"So it's over now," I said. "Remember your promise."

"It will be over on election day," she answered, then hung up.

I didn't fight, didn't call back. I had succumbed to the lassitude of slavery. The mutinies I'd plotted back in the States seemed like trivial, childhood escapades. I was easier to control here, the atmosphere of Haiti a better conductor of black magic. I stared into the deep end of the empty swimming pool and wondered what kind of damage I had just done.

———

THERE were six major presidential candidates. "Bloody faceless drones," Phil Somerset called them. The problem was basic: flamboyant, opinionated politicians died. The gulf between the masses of poor and the tiny controlling elite was so wide that any candidate too closely identified with one group would probably be murdered by the other. So Haitian politicians played it safe, recited meaningless economic statistics, promised to invest in infrastructure (a promise that hadn't been kept in decades), and generally tried to avoid giving any hint about what they really believed.

The press corps was waiting eagerly for President Rene Isidor, the one controversial, quotable figure in Haitian politics, to emerge from the palace, where he had been conducting the local equivalent of a Rose Garden strategy, and begin campaigning in earnest. At the very least, he might get shot.

Tension and dread grew on a daily, then an hourly basis. The city was one giant, nervous grapevine. Everyone we talked to— waiters, teachers, tap-tap drivers, priests, human-rights activists, charcoal vendors—had heard a different rumor: radical students from the agronomy college were distributing black-market AK-47's in the slums, prior to launching a mass uprising; Haiti's ten wealthiest families had put a million-dollar price tag on the head of President Isidor; doctors employed by the army were breaking into the homes of political dissidents at night and injecting them with AIDS. Every day more soldiers appeared, running patrols in their Toyoto pickups to keep the population on edge; every night, the streets seemed to empty out earlier. Everyone agreed that something would happen: too much pressure was building up. Like impatient spectators at a voodoo ceremony, the Haitian people were getting tired of all the drumming—they were ready for possession.

At night I lay sleepless on sweat-beaded sheets, the fan aimed at my forehead. I wasn't the only one awake—everyone was afraid of missing something. Reporters stayed up late arguing on the veranda, or shouting over long-distance phone lines. Plainclothes security guards patrolled the hotel corridors until dawn, murky shadows passing back and forth outside my louvered windows. Walking paranoia: were they there to protect me, or to spy on me? I smelled burning rubber every night— the return of Père Lebrun. Named after a Port-au-Prince tire importer, it was the practice of killing your political enemy by "necklacing," or draping a flaming tire around his neck.

In the morning, I would be awakened by the music of a ragged brass band, stagger sleepily to the balcony to see a funeral procession snaking down the Rue Capois, the coffin balanced on the heads of the elegantly dressed mourners. Ten political murders a night in Port-au-Prince—that was the gen-

272

erally accepted figure. There was a body truck, people whispered, that prowled the streets just before dawn to pick up the
corpses and transport them to Titanyen, the dumping ground
outside the city, which cruelly translates into "Little Nothing."
But sometimes a body was left in the street as a warning. Was
this one of the victims? Whatever the cause of death, Haiti
seemed to be having a lot of funerals.

———

FRIDAY night: three days to go until the election. I had spent
the day with Phil Somerset and Laura Salameh, following the
candidates as they stumped for the voodoo vote. Like politics
everywhere, it was about money: in return for a houngan's
endorsement, the candidates promised to unlock the treasury
so that voodoo could be financially competitive with the Baptists, Mormons, and Mennonites who offered food and medicine to peasants who traded in the loa for Christ. It was all
very pragmatic, not the kind of voodoo Laura had in mind.
She wandered restlessly with her videocamera, quietly nudging
Phil: "Can't you get him to sacrifice a chicken or something?
What about that goat? A little blood wouldn't hurt, darling; I
am shooting color, after all."

That evening, a voodoo priest from Léogane cornered us in
the hotel parking lot and offered to stage a ceremony in which
the loa would call the results the day before the election, allowing us to scoop our competitors. When we turned him
down, he drove up to the Hotel Montana to try his luck with
the networks.

A banner was draped over the Oloffson's balcony: TONIGHT—
VOODOO SHOW AND BUFFET. The lobby was shoulder-to-
shoulder, faces glowed with rum-induced good cheer. A dance
troupe re-created a voodoo ceremony, backed up by a five-piece
band. The show had originally been designed for tourists, a
highlight in out-of-print guidebooks to the Caribbean. There
were no tourists now, but there was still an appreciative audience—nuns, priests, foreign-aid workers, volunteer doctors
and nurses. It was their night to cut loose. They spent their

days with the poorest people in the hemisphere, among lepers and AIDS patients, babies dying of malnutrition and dengue fever, and they were entitled to a little fun, goddamn it. They were loud, loosened up: "So a nun's not supposed to drink, so what? Let the pope spend eighty hours a week up to his neck in blood and sewage and see if he isn't dying for a rum punch!"

But I sensed something else, a last-chance-to-party-before-the-Apocalypse atmosphere. The dance floor was a refuge against creeping darkness. There were rumors that a headless corpse had been discovered just outside the Oloffson gate; I noticed that two of the security guards were now armed with pistols.

As I gazed around the lobby, I nearly collapsed with shock—Lucy Marcelin was sitting at the bar! Resisting the urge to rush over and kiss her, I watched her for a moment. She looked beautiful and confident, her gestures theatrical as she talked. She was elegant, poised, sleek as a hood ornament. She wore a low-cut gold dress with purple accents; the overhead fan ruffled the fabric, revealing tantalizing glimpses of smooth, shiny skin. She had on high heels and gold clamshell earrings, a sharp contrast to the earnest drabness favored by the reporters and aid workers. She drew the two bartenders to her without trying; they hovered, each offering a cigarette, each pouring her a drink. She was a relief to them . . . she was a Haitian. She was home.

She glanced casually at me but gave no sign of recognition. Then she asked for the bill, which I knew was a signal. I arched my eyebrows, indicating she should come up to my room, but she responded with a shake of her head. I retreated outside.

I waited for her in the shadowy parking lot. There were no guides trying to hustle up clients; driving after dark had become too dangerous. Before she even reached the bottom step I grabbed her, pulled her behind a UN jeep, frantically kissing every inch of skin I could find, like a man who had been forcibly kept away from women his entire life.

"Where did you come from, Lucy? I mean, thank God you're here, but why?"

I couldn't wait for an answer. I kissed her ferociously, tasting the Oloffson's rum punches on her lips. We writhed in the shadows for a minute, tangled together like vines. She worked my shirt out of my pants; I felt her warm fingertips on my skin. One of her shoes fell off. Then she pulled away, blew her hair out of her eyes. "This place is crawling with secret police. Come on, let's go. I know someplace safer, a little hotel not far from here."

"You still haven't told me what you're doing here."

"In the car," she said, hobbling away, one shoe off, one shoe on.

I followed her to a four-wheel-drive jeep. She roared out of the hotel gate. The streets were quiet, but she drove as though she were at war, pounding the brakes, brutally shifting through the gears.

"Well?" I prompted, after several hair-raising corners.

She appraised me narrowly, a real lawyer's gaze. She lowered the window, letting the breeze pummel her. "When a blanc appears unexpectedly in the life of a poor Haitian peasant—a white missionary has a car accident in front of his house, for example—he thinks of it as an act of Providence. He may have never even seen a blanc before, but he knows they're rich. His life is a relentless struggle for survival, so he thinks, God has caused this missionary to go off the road for a reason . . . to help me. So the peasant and his entire family swarm around the missionary's car, offering to fix it for an outrageous sum, claiming to be tour guides, trying to sell him papayas or sugarcane or 'authentic native art.' It's a once-in-a-lifetime opportunity, and he better not let it get away." Lucy's hand leapt from the gearshift to my thigh. "That's kind of what you've been for me, Raymond. The blanc that dropped into my life without warning, that's given me a chance to . . . shit!"

The tap-tap in front of us slammed to an abrupt stop. Lucy hit the brakes, and we skidded, jolting bumpers. But no one jumped out of the tap-tap to complain. I craned my head out the window and saw that traffic was halted several car lengths ahead; a unit of policemen was working its way down the line, interviewing the drivers. The cops wore blue, they carried Uzis, and they smiled a little too easily.

We were in the middle of Carrefour, a rambling slum/red-light district. Salsa blared through the open doors of Dominican-run brothels, and the *borlettes* were still open, bright, loud little shacks where men gathered to bet, drink, and watch the televised lottery results. At least there's someone around, I thought. But then the music cut out, a couple of the borlettes went dark, doors slammed shut. Were people taking measures to protect themselves . . . or just shutting their eyes in a well-rehearsed game of see-no-evil?

Up ahead, voices rose, tempers seemed to be fraying. "Don't worry," Lucy said. "They don't have the nerve to kill a foreign journalist."

"These guys don't seem to have anything but nerve," I answered. "Look at their eyes." The cops were young, their movements jerky, like speeded-up film, and their eyes burned white-hot, pupils dilated into fat black buttons. "These kids are seriously coked up," I said. "They probably draw their salary in drugs; they don't care who they kill!"

"Calm down. It's routine; let me handle it," Lucy said.

A gum-chewing cop appeared on the driver's side, tapping the door with his gun barrel. Lucy said a few words in Creole. The cop replied in subdued tones, trying to present an officious, in-charge demeanor, but it was a bad act: he was jumpy. The only word I could pick out was *contravention*.

"Traffic violation," Lucy translated, opening her purse with a groan. "The imaginary kind. See, I told you it was routine . . . a routine bribe."

Suddenly, another policeman threw open the door of the tap-tap and yanked the driver out, pushing him to his knees. The passengers were herded out at gunpoint, hands already clasped behind their necks; they knew the drill. They handed over scraps of identification to the cops, who inspected them in the glare of the tap-tap's headlights.

"Bullshit if this is routine," I said. "This is their last hurrah. When the UN monitors hit the streets in force this weekend, these guys'll be out of business. They're looking for someone, and tonight may be their last chance to get him!"

The cop shot a hand into Lucy's purse and yanked out her driver's license. She barked in protest but he was already gone, marching toward a pickup truck that was parked on the sidewalk. The truck's passenger door swung open and a tall plainclothesman wearing slacks and a polo shirt stepped out: haughty, calm, suppressing a yawn, he was obviously the officer in charge. Before he could inspect Lucy's license, a second uniformed cop ran up to him, pointing animatedly toward the tap-tap passengers. The plainclothesman listened, then closed his eyes and exhaled wearily, as though worn out by the sheer drudgery of terror. "This constant, nagging power of life and death that I have over people," he seemed to be saying, "it's such a chore." He gave a curt nod, and climbed back into his truck.

The cops responded quickly, separating three young men from the group of passengers, then prodding the rest back on to the tap-tap. A woman, perhaps one of the men's mother, collapsed in tears. A cop reached into the tap-tap and turned on the radio, producing a screaming merengue from the roof-mounted speakers. The plainclothes officer liked the idea and cranked up the sound system in his truck. The Latin beat pumped into the night in stereo, coiling up the gravel alleys into the hills, masking what was to come.

Engines started up, horns honked. I squinted through clouds of exhaust, and saw the three young passengers being led away.

"What the hell's that?" I asked.

"What's what?" Lucy answered, distracted. "Where's that guy with my papers?"

"That. That's no police station!" I pointed to a low-slung, institutional-looking building set back from the street. It had once been a clinic or a high school, but it was abandoned now: there were no lights on inside its ocher cement walls. Thick walls . . . bulletproof . . . soundproof.

"They're gonna murder those kids right here!" I shouted. I looked around—people faded into the darkness, potential witnesses slinking away. The prisoners were escorted through a gate onto the building grounds; the plainclothes officer sat in his pickup, sipping a beer, head bobbing to the music; the tap-tap pulled away, resigned faces pressed to the glass, garishly painted by red light bulbs that spelled out PRAN KOURAG . . . "Have Courage."

I vaulted out of the car and blindly charged toward the gate. *"Journaliste, je suis journaliste!"* I screamed, reaching into my pockets for a press pass I didn't have.

The guards studied me from the other side of the gate as though I were an insane but ultimately comic figure. They laughed, then caught themselves and began to exchange sharp whispers. That's right, you bastards, I thought, you better take me seriously: I'm *The New York Times* and CNN rolled into one, I've got big bucks and bright lights behind me, I've got the ear of the White House and a hotline to the Pentagon, I snap my fingers and the Eighty-second Airborne turns your face into a drop zone . . .

The guards raised their guns at me, their smiles glinting above the sights. *Perfect. I'm in downtown Haiti, it's late, I've just committed a contravention, I've got three coke-blasted twenty-year-olds with Uzis drawing a bead on me . . . and they're smiling!* The plainclothes officer jumped out of his truck and double-timed toward me, leading another squad of cops. Within seconds I was surrounded. As if on cue, the music changed from frenetic salsa to a mournful bolero.

"The prisoners," I said weakly. "I would like to interview them."

The officer looked at me coldly as he finished his beer. "They are *vagabons*. Not political," he said.

"I'd like to hear their side of it."

"What news organization did you indicate that you represented?" he asked.

Think big, Ray. "CBS," I lied.

"Then you will have a press credential which I may see?"

". . . actually, I'm pretty much freelancing at the moment.

But ask anyone at the American embassy, they'll vouch for me."

"Freelancing, yes, I have heard this phrase." He draped an arm around my shoulder; it felt as heavy as a lead pipe. "It means were you to disappear in Haiti, you would not be missed."

Like a drumroll, the safeties clicked off on a dozen Uzis. What did I think about as I looked down the barrel of death? Family, loved ones, unfulfilled dreams? No. I thought of the coverage: my obituary in the *Post;* my mention in *Newsweek*'s "Transition" column; the proof sheets of my own execution. I imagined the two-page photo spread, my body contorted in the awkward posture of death, the Sygma or Black Star credit running possessively beside it.

Then Lucy appeared in the halo of the streetlight, high heels pirouetting through the garbage with a practiced grace, an urban dance step that a well-dressed Haitian never forgets. The cop who'd snatched her license was behind her, gun drawn, but she ignored him. She planted herself in front of the plain-clothesman, one hand on her hips, the other formed into a hatchet-blade that chopped violently at the air. She tore her papers away from the cop and shoved them in the officer's face.

He refused to let a woman fluster him. He calmly pulled a flashlight from his back pocket and read her papers. He asked a question, she answered. He smiled, she smiled back. Then, to my amazement, he grabbed her by the shoulders and kissed her on both cheeks! They fell away from each other, howling with laughter, setting a conversational speed record with their Creole chatter. Lucy gave him a pouty, spoiled-girl frown and nodded toward the three prisoners. Still shivering with good humor, he wagged his head back and forth pretending to make an awesome decision, like a father debating whether to indulge his daughter's latest, outrageous demand. He finally gave in with a careless gesture, and the guards lowered their weapons. The prisoners froze for a moment, not quite believing their bizarre good luck . . . then fled into the darkness.

"Lucy . . ."

"We're going now, Ray, no questions."

We walked back to the car, Lucy huddling intimately with the plainclothesman. I watched as they brushed cheeks again, shook hands, undoubtedly making promises to call, keep in touch. They were universal gestures, personal and familiar, yet they struck me as stranger than anything else that had happened that night. This was a country of political terrorism and unidentified bodies, wasn't it? I hadn't counted on giggling reunions and sudden displays of mercy.

Lucy slipped behind the wheel, waved, and we drove off. For several minutes we didn't talk, avoiding eye contact. We drove south through the outskirts of Port-au-Prince, on a road that hugged the bay. I concentrated on the sensations of life that were available to me, grabbing all I could: the *ka-chunk* of the tires as we bounced through potholes, the murmur of Radio Métropole, the smell of the ocean.

"Lucy, I'm sorry. I just snapped. It was a moronic gesture, I know. Reporters are supposed to be observers, not heroes. I could've gotten us both killed."

"Don't worry about it."

"No, really. If you hadn't come to the rescue—"

"Please. I can't stand it when men get apologetic. Especially you; you never used to apologize to anyone."

"How do you know what I never used to do?" I flipped on the overhead light so I could read her features. "Lucy, who the hell are you?"

No answer. Her gaze was fixed on the road, on the headlights as they swept past cinder-block shacks and sparked off the glowing eyes of stray dogs. "Tell me!"

"I'll do better than that: I'll show you."

———

WE drove through the tidy, quiet streets of Pétionville, an upscale suburb spread out contentedly in the cool hills above the city. There was plenty to buy: mannequins—white mannequins—preened in boutique show windows, draped in the latest

Italian fashions; gift shops flaunted Swiss watches and crystal knickknacks; gourmet markets displayed piles of pâté and wheels of Camembert; wine shops rented climate-controlled cellar space and held weekly Bordeaux tastings. The stores were artfully lit, their security systems discreet. The only people we saw were clustered in contented post-dinner conversation outside five-star restaurants, waiting for valets to bring their cars around. We could have been in Palm Springs or Beverly Hills, any town that shops diligently by day, then retreats to enjoy the spoils behind high walls after dark.

"This was my neighborhood," Lucy said. "This is where I'd come to ride my bike, shop with my girlfriends, meet boys." We turned a corner, and she pointed out a stone mansion set behind a bougainvillea-draped wall. "Lycée de Pétionville, formerly Duvalier. I went to school there, trained to take my place among the Haitian elite. The female elite, to be precise—it's a girls' school. You learn all kinds of valuable things: menu planning, how to manage a household staff . . ." We wound into a residential neighborhood. Unlike the architectural overkill higher up the hill, these houses were humanly scaled and inviting, landscaped to be enjoyed, not just flaunted.

"And of course we were taught to give thanks to God for the blessings we enjoyed. We were genuinely grateful, especially my father. He's the largest importer and distributor of drugs in Haiti. He has his own container facility down at the port, his own chain of pharmacies. The health of the country is quite literally in his hands."

She nudged the jeep up a steep incline. I rolled down the window. It was quiet and sheltered up here, you heard crickets instead of gunfire. "He made sure that I grew up protected. I never heard of the slums—Cité Soleil, Cité Carton—didn't see them until I was in my twenties, and I'm sure my mother's still never seen them. Vacations? Paris, Miami . . . never Haiti.

"When they sent me off to college in New York, they hoped I'd become cosmopolitan, acquire the skills a bourgeois Haitian woman needs to orchestrate dinner parties. To put it bluntly, they wanted to polish me up into marriage material. Maybe I'd snag a doctor or an industrialist . . . we had industry back then. But, college being what it is . . ."

Lucy lit a Gitane, permitted herself a moment of nostalgia. "When I came back in 1985," she continued, "I had turned all moral, of course, deciding that our money was unconscionable in a country as poor as Haiti, but if we could just get rid of Duvalier, install a democratic government, things would improve. My parents hadn't done anything wrong, after all. Not my mother, this devoted woman who spoiled me, told me stories, filled my head with dreams; not my father, this elegant man who spoke three languages, who played the piano and read poetry that made him cry.

"But my father had changed; there was this angry, resentful core growing inside him. He began to talk politics, something he'd never done; his good manners couldn't conceal his hatreds. He had even hired armed guards, moonlighting soldiers, actually." She looked at me archly. "You . . . met one of them tonight. Once the revolt against Baby Doc began, I realized how many people hated our family for its success. We hid indoors, ashamed, terrified."

Lucy turned off the headlights and parked across the street from a two-story home surrounded by a large, tangled garden. It looked like it had been built in sections, as the fortunes of the Marcelin family rose. The first floor was generic Third World—whitewashed cement walls, louvered windows, while the second floor was all glass and hardwood, framed by a spacious deck.

"The mobs went after anyone with money. One Saturday night, an angry crowd gathered at our front gate. You could smell smoke further down the hill: houses were burning. My father positioned his guards along that balcony, their rifle barrels supported by the railing . . ."

"And they opened fire?"

Lucy smirked. "Every good story has a twist, doesn't it, Ray? They *didn't* open fire." A sliding glass door opened on the second floor of the Marcelin house. We looked up, but the balcony was swathed in shadows. "They couldn't shoot; there was someone in the crowd that my father knew, a neighbor. He was a banker who had often done favors for my father, but he was known to have been well connected with the Duvalier family. The crowd had dragged him from his car, chased him up the street, and he was frantically pounding on the gate, trying to get into our yard. They had his watch, his wallet, he was bleeding. My father made a calculated decision: if he fired, that would stir up the crowd even further and they would come back, maybe torch the house, maybe even kill us. But if he let them have the banker . . .''

Lucy's eyes were moist and her voice quivered as she relived that night. "Have you ever seen ants swarming over a dying spider? Now, imagine you can hear the spider scream.''

I didn't hear any screams, didn't see any blood. All I saw was a beautiful house in a quiet neighborhood; all I heard was ice dropping into a glass as someone stirred a cocktail.

"That night I realized my father would coldly and efficiently, perhaps even gleefully, inflict whatever pain was necessary to keep what he had.''

A light winked on in the house, revealing a comfortable living room furnished with antiques and books; potted palms cast cool shadows across a luminous, white baby grand. Gérard Marcelin, a gray-haired, heavyset man, walked back inside puffing a pipe and sat down at the piano. His wife, slender and agile as a greyhound, brought him a drink. She blew the hair out of her eyes and fanned herself with her hand, laughing about the heat.

"I just couldn't stay in that house, you know? And I couldn't stay in this country. It changed my father, ruined him inside, and I knew that it would finally ruin me.''

Lucy's head drooped against the steering wheel as her father began to play Chopin.

21

WE DROVE FROM Lucy's parents' house to the "little hotel" she knew, on the beach south of the city. Once the country residence of a Haitian president, it was turned into a luxury hotel in the 1950s and became notorious as the most expensive resort in Hispaniola. It was closed now, but the caretaker, Jean-Louis, was a friend of a friend. He gave us a tour of the grounds. The Olympic-size pool was dry, a tap-tap junked in the deep end. Goats grazed on the croquet field, bananas and millet were being cultivated on the nine-hole golf course.

Jean-Louis broke into the wine cellar and sold us an 1898 bottle of Armagnac, and offered to unlock the casino for a night and deal blackjack. Each of the rooms had been designed by a different world-famous architect; Jean-Louis insisted on giving us the most expensive suite in the house. The tariff on the door read three hundred dollars a night; we paid fifty.

In the bathroom was a giant tub, sculpted into a pink porcelain conch shell. I turned on the gold-plated faucet, and it spit out a spray of live spiders. I chuckled, glanced up at the ceiling. Mirrored, of course, and decorated with laminated photographs of celebrity guests in soapy revelry: Mike Wallace,

Mick Jagger, President Mobuto of Zaire, even Baby Doc himself, craftily blowing suds off the breasts of his wife, Michelle, and a second, queasy-looking woman.

Lucy appeared in the doorway with the bottle of Armagnac and two glasses. We toasted, and I kissed her against the flocked red velvet wallpaper. "Listen," she whispered. Then I heard the drumming, pitched slightly above the throb of the air conditioner.

"What timing," I said.

"Timing is everything in life, isn't it, Raymond? If you hadn't shown up at my door that night . . ."

"You'd still be comfy in your little cocoon," I said.

"It was a fake cocoon. This is where I was meant to be; I know that now." She pounded against my collarbone with her fist. "And just as I was starting to feel grateful toward you, you dumped me, you son of a bitch!"

"I told you, there was nothing more I could do in Washington. I knew the answers were here . . . and I was right."

She looked stunned. "Did I miss something? You've cracked the case? Gabriel confessed, you're in the clear?"

"By Monday, it'll all be over," I said. "After the election, I won't be any use to them. I get my life back. If I can just hang on until then . . ."

"In other words, you've given up."

"I thought that was obvious." I poured myself another drink, a big, sloppy shot of self-pity.

"Rather than trying to stop them."

"How?" I demanded. "They call the shots, remember? And stop them from what? We don't even know what the hell they're planning."

I opened the curtains, revealing a postcard patch of white sand beach. A row of palm trees arched over the gentle surf, as though they were posing. Along the shore, boats were under construction, hand-painted mini-arks that would eventually be used to flee the island.

"The guy I saw jump out of my car to save those boys hadn't given up," she said.

"A random outbreak of Hemingwayitis. It won't happen again."

"Too bad. All that indignation, that spontaneous ferocity . . . I loved it." A spider darted across the floor, and Lucy spiked it with her high heel. "I read your old pieces, Raymond. The world used to piss you off so much it was actually scary."

"You want the angry young man back."

"Sure. That's someone I can help, someone I can cope with. Ask any woman if an angry young man's not an improvement over a bitter old fuck!" Lucy stared me down, a pillar of disapproval. "I came back to fight, Raymond. And to get my client cleared of a murder charge. Do you want to be a part of that or not?"

Let's focus here, I thought. Air out the brain. I opened the front door, walked onto the sand. The colors of the night seemed exaggerated, like those of an antique, tinted postcard.

Lucy crept up behind me, circling my waist with her arms. "Why do you think you were chosen to write this story? Out of all the reporters in Washington?"

Voodoo brings our hidden desires to the surface.

"Think about it," she continued. "When Faustin Gabriel went shopping for a journalist, he could've gone after Bob Woodward just as easily. Or Ted Koppel, or Barbara Walters . . . but they didn't need these stories, they didn't need a kick in the ass. The loa guided Gabriel to you."

"Providence?" I smiled.

"Just accept it—you're an investigative reporter, not a country gentleman," she whispered, teasing my neck with her lips. "If anyone can figure out what Gabriel and Carmen are up to, you can. You've got three days till your next deadline. I say get to it."

The drumming grew louder, more intense, and the tempo changed. Somewhere in the shacks behind the abandoned casino, the loa were being called down. I felt Lucy's body press against me, the rhythm of the drums transferring to her thighs. I turned and kissed her hungrily. My hands flew over her dress, the fabric heated by the skin underneath. I lifted the hem inch

286

by inch like a rising curtain, watching in anticipation as the skin was exposed. She led me inside, pulling the dress over her head with arms so long they seemed to reach the ceiling. Silhouetted against the harsh bathroom light, she looked perfectly black and sculpted, like one of those woodcuts of Haitian women I'd seen in nineteenth-century books, an image of pure sex disguised as folk art.

She turned off the air conditioner. "I hate goddamn A/C," she said. Sweat was already beading on her shoulders, on the backs of her thighs. "I want it hot, I want it humid. And leave the window open, I want to hear the music."

Some couples put on Sinatra; we had voodoo drums, the tempo careening crazily, the volume shifting with the breeze. Some people like a fussy little B & B with a four-poster bed and lace curtains; we had glossy, gold-veined wallpaper and a bed with collapsed springs, vast enough to accomodate an emperor and a dozen of his mistresses. But we didn't care; we didn't even bother to pull back the pink satin spread, with its textured pattern of naked satyrs and wood nymphs. As a matter of fact . . .

"I know," Lucy said, pressing me onto my back, her beautiful legs imprisoning my hips. "All this dictator stuff's kind of a turn-on, isn't it?"

"Now we know how Adolf and Eva felt," I said.

"Or Baby Doc and Michelle."

"Ferdinand and Imelda."

"Ferdinand and *Isabella*."

For both of us, that night was more than sex, but different than love. I was trying to extract something from Lucy, a sense of the familiar. Recognizable flesh. The taste of her skin but also the taste of reality; the feel of her lips, but also the feel of life as I used to know it.

She moved on me gently, then sinuously, then roughly. I reached up, desperate to touch her, but she denied me, pinning my arms to the bed, dazzling my skin with her lips, her hair, her breasts. She concentrated fiercely; she didn't lose herself . . . or didn't let on that she did. She was watching me, I realized, studying me, waiting for some sort of recognizable change. She gradually increased the tempo and the warm, swirling pressure, until it felt like she would drive me straight through the bed into the floor. Her lips tightened in anger.

"God, Lucy, what is it?"

She laughed, still moving, twisting on me with her hips. Her hair was plastered to her forehead as though she'd just stepped out of the shower; black, curly tendrils drizzled into her eyes. She tried to blow it free as usual. Suddenly, that simple, uniquely Lucy Marcelin gesture seemed to me the most erotic, arousing movement I'd ever seen—I could have watched her repeat it over and over. She tugged the hair out of her face, drawing it past her forehead with both hands, pitching her elbows out, the muscles defined beneath her arms, her body bent into a perfect, back-leaning arch.

"I'm trying to screw it out of you, Raymond . . . don't you feel it?"

"If anyone can, you can," I gasped, before I nearly went blind.

———

WE become journalists to change the world, or maybe just to see the world. Maybe we think it's about power and prestige, or we're misinformed about the money. But whatever our motives or career goals, all good journalists have a compelling need to witness. We're history's voyeurs, and when it's our own history that's on the line, nothing can make us turn the page or change the channel. Call it the "blaze of glory syndrome." If we're going to flame out, we want to be there to report on it.

Just before dawn, I woke up in a fever of determination. I needed coffee, but there was no phone to call room service, and no room service to call. I opened the minibar, dragged out two dusty bottles of coffee liqueur.

"We know they want power," I said. "Let's start from that premise." Lucy groaned sleepily, still tangled in the naked-nymph bedspread. "How do you get power? Well, you could buy a presidential candidate."

"With what?" Lucy asked. She sat up, checked her watch. I offered her a bottle of the liqueur, but she wisely declined. I grimaced as the thick, sweet liquid went down like brown Pepto-Bismol with an alcohol kick.

"They've got assets. Faustin Gabriel's house in Washington, for example. The art gallery."

"Both rented," Lucy said. To my look of surprise she added: "You left me, Ray, you didn't fire me. I kept researching the case."

"The paintings?" I asked.

"They were Gabriel's. But I went through the Galerie Creole with an art appraiser. Everything in the place adds up to one hundred fifty thousand dollars. You can't buy a president for that, not even in Haiti."

I paced restlessly through the dictator suite, thinking. I stubbed my toe on one of the twin bronze elephants that supported the glass coffee table, and as I hopped there in naked pain, it hit me. "*Zanfan d'Ayiti.* Guilt money! Why the hell does an ex-Macoute set up a charity organization? Because she's suddenly overcome with compassion? That'd be like Kurt Waldheim opening a branch office of B'nai B'rith. You told me yourself—Haiti's biggest import is world pity. Carmen knows those slum kids with their big eyes and swollen bellies are a gold mine. Let's be conservative: say she only skims off twenty percent of every dollar; that's still serious money!"

I marched to the bathroom, doused my face with warm water from the "cold" tap. There were sand crabs in the bathtub, lime-green lizards on the walls. "And the kicker is, unless Haiti magically achieves zero population growth, the money keeps rolling in. They can buy whoever they want! We follow the money, Lucy, trust me; it's at the center of all Carmen Mondesir's secrets."

When I came back into the bedroom, Lucy had gotten up and was stretching luxuriously, her hands clawing the air. I pressed myself against her, absorbing the silk of her skin from toe to fingertip.

"They still own me, you know," I said, kissing her shoulder. "They've planted a time bomb inside of me, and God knows when it's set to go off. Or who it'll hurt."

"If you're asking me not to blame you for what happens . . . I won't."

"I'm just warning you that this won't last. They won't let me play the good little reporter forever; eventually they'll stop our investigation. They've got plans for this country."

She traced a line with her finger from my neck, down my chest, teasing her way to the inside of my thigh. "Fuck them!" she said sharply. "This is my country too."

We dressed quickly, Lucy changing into jeans and a blouse from her overnight bag. She tossed a handful of change onto the night table. "For the maid," she grinned. "If one ever returns."

Outside, the sea was turning from black to gray, reflecting the dawn. People get up early in Haiti: fishermen were already on the water, sails trimmed; charcoal women led overloaded donkeys to market, taking a shortcut across the golf course; uniformed schoolgirls marched in formation through the sand, white blouses pressed and brilliant.

"For one hour a day, it can seem like paradise, can't it?" I said.

———

THE city had changed overnight. It was as if a law had been passed, banning everyday Haitian behavior: no laughing, no bragging, no hustling. Most of the shops were closed, no over-amped music spilled out of open windows, traffic was sparse and the few pedestrians moved anxiously along on private er-rands, eyes straight ahead. Armored personnel carriers blocked the entrance to the Dessalines barracks, sandbags ringed police headquarters, an oil-drum barricade had been erected in front of the National Palace. They had forgotten to run up the flag; the naked pole on the palace roof gleamed in the rising sun, a lightning rod that usually attracted nothing but tragedy. Lucy turned on the car radio. Classical music was playing on every station—a bad sign in a tropical country.

We found a working phone booth in the lobby of the Holiday Inn and called information. Teleco, the national phone company, had a single listing for Zanfan d'Ayiti . . . in Boston. "But not the one you're thinking of," Lucy said grimly. "No Celtics, no baked beans."

We followed the Boulevard Harry Truman north, past the docks, into a wasteland of junked cars and collapsing buildings. Lucy was operating on memory now; there were no more road signs. She turned into a narrow, muddy alley. Just when you think Haiti can't get any weirder or more desperate, it does. Presiding over the entrance to the alley was a billboard promoting condom use, using a hockey game as a metaphor: a goalie dressed as a condom blocked the net, as a wave of hockey pucks drawn as sperm converged on him, trying to score . . . ice hockey as a teaching aide in a country that had never seen snow.

The alley led into Cité Soleil, the worst slum in the poorest country in the western hemisphere. And Boston, Lucy explained, was the worst part of Cité Soleil.

We crawled along a dirt street not meant for cars. The ground was mushy, but it hadn't rained in weeks—where did all the ground water come from? Then I realized it wasn't water, it was sewage leeching up through the soil like sludge from a giant, backed-up sink. Like some grim, diseased Venice, canals crisscrossed Cité Soleil, but these canals were open sewers, too wide to jump across, deep enough to drown in. Rusted car frames served as bridges, kids jumped from axle to bumper with gymnastic ease. Pigs grazed in the sewage; a sweet, nostril-clenching stench rose from it and hung just over your head like a suffocating cloud. Even in the full blaze of sun, there was no color here: everything was gray and black. And overwhelmingly damp. If you had to choose, I decided, dry misery was definitely preferable to wet.

Something was up. Outside their shacks made of cardboard

and tin scraps, people milled in knots, talking, arguing. We passed one of the few businesses in Boston, a pay shower, where for twenty-five gourdes you got five minutes of actual running water. The shower salesman had electricity too, and he'd set up a TV outside so the neighborhood could watch. When Lucy asked what was going on, a hundred people shouted back that President Isidor was about to speak.

"This is where he's from," Lucy said. "These are his supporters." As we inched forward, the entire slum seemed to be on the move, thousands of people scurrying in search of a radio or TV. A dozen tap-taps were drawn in a circle like a wagon train, their radios tuned to the same channel, turned up full blast. "This is the one thing in Haiti the army is afraid of," Lucy said. On the faces, I saw why. They were blank, inert, as if the sheer strain of survival had destroyed their ability to display emotion. These were the true zombis of Port-au-Prince, and I got the feeling that, already dead, they were fearless, willing to die again for the right man or the right cause.

Horn blaring, Lucy tried to build up speed, cutting down blind alleys, pushing deeper into the *cité* until the road grew impassable. We parked on the edge of a smoldering garbage dump, and continued on foot. Children flocked around me, pressing curious fingers into my skin and crying, *"Blanc, blanc, bonjour, blanc!"* Within fifteen minutes, we were lost, hemmed in by suspicious faces who seemed determined to protect the cité's secrets. No one would answer the questions of a mulatto stranger and her white companion.

When President Isidor began to speak, it was as if a giant megaphone hovered over Cité Soleil. Somehow, there were enough radios so that his voice was everywhere, spilling out of dark corners, following us. He sounded frail and he had frequent, exaggerated coughing fits; he seemed to suffer as he spoke, endearing himself to poor Haitians who don't mind pitying their politicians.

". . . consider the bourgeoisie up on the hill," he was saying. "Cool in their air-conditioned houses, comfortable in their ignorance. We will warm them with our love, not with the torch;

we will bring light to the darkness of their ignorance with education, not violence. But they must not avoid the simple truth of their destiny as Haitians—they *will be educated*!"

There were cheers and applause all around us. Heads nodded in approval, fists slapped into palms. I walked faster: "education" could mean many things in Haiti. We came to a flooded clearing that surrounded a gray, stone-walled enclosure. I grew conscious of a dull, droning din coming from inside the compound. Lucy and I followed the sound through a break in the wall, and found ourselves on the edge of an incredible scene— hundreds of people waiting in line for water, buckets balanced on heads and shoulders. Five faucets in all of Cité Soleil, five faucets for a hundred thousand people. The hum of their conversation echoed off the bare walls, turning whispers into shouts, but it was still not loud enough to drown out President Isidor's radio speech. As all eyes swung toward me, the trespassing blanc, Isidor was working up to a climax.

"We will teach the rich and teach the army! We will teach the Americans, too!"

This is the farthest I've ever been from my world, I thought. I'm at the center of theirs now, literally at the life source, a row of leaky, rusting faucets. If the revolution were to start, it could certainly start here. Just one word from Isidor . . .

As if by heavenly cue, the sky began to rumble and a huge shadow passed in front of the sun. I looked up, expecting a thunderhead, and saw an American Airlines 757, gear down, tantalizingly close, eternally out of reach. Out of design or neglect, the slum had grown at the foot of the international airport's runway. Three times a day, American Airlines swooped in low on approach; three times a day the water ritual stopped. Heads tilted back, eyes looked up, but I couldn't read their expressions. Bewilderment? Envy? Anger?

A tiny voice broke into my thoughts. A little schoolgirl in a bright yellow dress was tugging at my sleeve. I handed her some change, but she kept talking. *"Monsieur, monsieur, ece ké ou vlé wé fam blan en?"* Did I want to see the white woman?

Lucy questioned the girl. For ten Haitian dollars, a very good price, she pointed out, she'd take us to see the white woman.

"What white woman?" I asked.

"She won't say," Lucy replied. "But she thinks we've come all this way to see her."

The little girl, who introduced herself as a second-grader named Simone, took us each by the hand and led us back into the alleys of Boston. Now we attracted smiles as we walked, and oddly, with this tiny black hand crushed in mine, I felt protected.

Ten minutes later, Simone stopped. She pointed to a large, windowless cinder-block building surrounded by a wall topped with jagged glass. It was the largest and most secure house I'd seen in Cité Soleil. Sun glared off a new, corrugated tin roof.

Simone held out her hand. When I paid her, she stepped back politely and waited, hoping to observe the reunion of the blancs that she had arranged. I knocked on a padlocked iron gate, but there was no answer. I paced the length of the side wall, which bristled with razor wire. Still no doors or windows. I glanced back at Lucy and shrugged. Simone ran up, bubbling with girlish impatience.

"She says if we want to see the white woman, we should throw a rock on the roof." Then Simone whispered something that made Lucy recoil in alarm. "She says that's what the soldiers always do."

"Get her out of here," I ordered. Lucy cajoled, then scolded Simone, trying to drive her home. We walked to the back of the building. There was another gate, and beyond it, a muddy yard leading to an iron-barred door. To my amazement, the ground was covered with heavy electrical cables, which snaked into the building from a massive generator. Who would need so much power in such a forlorn environment?

We looked at each other. There was really only one move left to us. I picked up a handful of stones and tossed them onto the tin roof. No stirring inside those unmarked walls. We waited five minutes, turned to leave.

Then we heard the sharp crack of dead bolts. The back door

swung open and a woman's face appeared, imprisoned behind thick security bars. A chill rippled through me, driving out the heat of the morning sun. I recognized the deep-set eyes, the dirty brown hair. I had watched this woman die in slow motion a hundred times.

It was the torture-tape victim.

22

SHE RECOGNIZED ME, too. But I was faster, and more desperate. I jumped the gate and before she could recover from her shock, I had wedged my shoulder in the doorway. I forced an ironic smile.

"Good morning, ma'am. I'm a reporter and I wonder if you'd mind answering a few simple questions?" I pushed roughly against the door, ripping it out of her hands. She stumbled backward into the building like an uncoiled spring.

There was too much to take in at once.

The murdered woman, the international cause célèbre, indisputably alive. She looked to be in her mid-forties, wore a conservative, flower-patterned dress and tennis shoes. Bifocals dangled from her neck on a chain. The hair that had been twisted and matted with blood in the videotape was shorter now, a sensible hot-weather cut.

The room: two cheap desks, a filing cabinet, a storage locker, shelves lined with videotapes and a poster of a big-eyed Haitian orphan—this was the Port-au-Prince headquarters of Zanfan d'Ayiti.

My mind caromed, fighting to order a million questions.

Who was this woman? How had she escaped the Haitian police? How had the bruises and scars healed so perfectly? And why hadn't she come forward and announced that she was alive?

"You know, the world thinks you're dead," I said.

"That's their problem," she snapped.

She edged backward toward her desk, her fingers crawling toward a cellular phone. I snatched it away. "It may be your problem, too. Governments have gone on red alert because of you. Don't you feel the slightest obligation to the truth?"

The woman slipped on her glasses and stared at us through heavily magnified eyes. "The truth is, this country is on the brink of death. An entire country, can you imagine? Anything I may have done pales next to that fact."

"What about your family, your friends back in the States?" I asked.

She parried my concern with a disgusted snort. "I vanished from their maps years ago. I'm a nonperson back home. There's no one left to care."

I grabbed her wrists, held them up to the light. "There's not a goddamn scratch on you! What the hell happened, really? Who's been paying you, hiding you all this time? Carmen Mondesir?"

A veil of serenity seemed to descend on the woman's features. She closed her eyes before speaking. "What I did was good, it was right, and you won't convince me otherwise."

"What you did? What do you mean by that?"

I saw a flash of movement in the corner of my eyes. Lucy had pushed open a door behind the filing cabinet and disappeared into an adjoining room. Ten seconds later, she gasped. "Ray, I think you better see this."

I took the woman by the arm, prodded her through the door. My eyes followed the rivulet of blood that ran across the cement floor to a large puddle that had dried beneath a metal chair. Leather straps dangled from the armrests; it was *the* chair. I absorbed the rest in a single glance: the sick yellow walls, the Swiss calendar, the workbench brimming with tools and torture equipment, the dingy overhead lamp, the desk. Against the back wall was a video-editing bench with double monitors. Power cables were neatly coiled next to aluminum camera cases, a light grid hung from the ceiling.

I felt the shock in my stomach first, and then it spread through me in nauseating waves.

"It's a goddamn movie set," I said. I knelt, dragged a finger through the bloodstains. Sugar, food coloring, an aftertaste of tomato—fake blood for a fake atrocity. My mind snapped back to the videotape, to the door inching open—the doorway I was standing in—and the uniformed figure that appeared, nodding for the torturers to go ahead. I could put a face on the figure now: gaunt, hollow eyed, it belonged to one of Carmen Mondesir's guards!

The woman took off her glasses, and for the first time, I sensed faint remorse in her voice. "I did it for these poor, poor people. The people I bleed for and grieve for every day of my life!" She drew a rosary out of her pocket and began to toy with it.

"How does a missionary become an actress?" I asked. "That's what you are, isn't it? And you might as well answer the question that's been on the lips of everyone who's seen the videotape. Who are you?"

"My name is Elizabeth Mosely. And I was with a church, yes. Never mind which one. But I broke with them. Simple-minded dreamers, not up to the task."

"In what way were they dreamers?" Lucy asked.

"They thought if they hung enough crosses and distributed enough Bibles, they could save Haiti. But Christianity alone won't save this country, will it?" She strolled through the torture chamber, gliding her hands over the lights and camera tripods, like a museum curator surveying her treasures. "Only money can do that."

"So how does faking your death on videotape raise money for Haiti?"

Elizabeth Mosely's eyes were luminous with belief. "It discredits the Isidor regime, it brings international pressure to bear on him. Ultimately, we hope it may lead to his removal. With

Isidor gone, we feel the United States and the Europeans will resume foreign aid. When Carmen Mondesir came to me with her plan, of course I recognized it was outlandish, but I also knew it would work. One thing I have learned in this world of do-gooders—God rewards pragmatists."

I felt my anger slowly bending away from Elizabeth Mosely and toward myself. How could I have been victimized by such an outrageous PR scam? Skeptical, seen-it-all Ray Falco, manipulated like a gullible journalism-school graduate. How much else was trickery? How much else had been done for my benefit? The mystery cars prowling the streets of Washington, the loup-garou skin, the firebombing? All of it, I realized.

"Fake, hype: every word I wrote, every headline," I muttered. "Even the murder of Baptiste, that was staged for show, too. Since he was the most visible of the Haitian exiles in D.C., they knew that by killing him they could stir up maximum outrage. And by torturing the body, they had made it look political."

I wilted against the wall. I felt the tropical heat burning through the cinder block, a reminder of time creeping forward.

"Maybe it was more than that," Lucy said.

"What do you mean?"

"Baptiste was going to spill a big story to you the night he died, right? What if this was it?" She waved her hand around the torture set. "What if he'd learned about the whole charade?"

"How?"

"They all knew each other in D.C. Duvalierists, anti-Duvalierists, Macoutes—exile politics is a very small, incestuous stew. He could have overheard a couple words, correctly interpreted a look . . ."

" 'Ghosts are not always ghosts, soldiers are not always soldiers,' " I said, recalling Baptiste's enigmatic phrase. I confronted Elizabeth Mosely. "What do you think that means, Elizabeth?"

She grew stubbornly silent again. She perched on the edge of the torture chair; when she accepted a cigarette from Lucy, she looked like a condemned woman.

"I think you're still trying to fool me," I said. "I don't think that Carmen Mondesir orchestrated this entire deception just to pressure the government into holding an election. Does that sound like the kind of strategy a bigwig in the Tontons Macoutes would hatch?"

She fidgeted. "They want President Isidor out. That is what I know because that is where our interests coincide."

"But what if the bastard wins? Always the downside of this democracy thing, isn't it?" She didn't answer. She stubbed out her cigarette on the artificial bloodstain. "I think they've designed a plan to make sure that doesn't happen. And I wonder if you were going to be part of it."

Elizabeth Mosely's eyes darted guiltily away. As she shifted her rosary from one hand to the other, I caught a glimpse of something gold between her knuckles. A key. I glanced into the office, at the floor-to-ceiling storage locker with its padlock. I forced her fingers apart, snagged the rosary key chain, and marched to the locker. Over my shoulder I heard Elizabeth Mosely jump to her feet.

"I didn't approve of the guns," she protested. "I wouldn't authorize them to store any instruments of violence here, not so much as a single bullet."

I popped the padlock and threw open the locker door. First I saw the cardboard cartons, at least ten of them, all torn open. They were labeled, "Cartridges, small arms. Centerfire, caliber nine millimeter. Remington; Lonoke, Arkansas." Then, in smaller type, a surreal afterthought: "Keep out of reach of children." Inside the cartons were dozens of smaller ammunition boxes. They had each held fifty rounds, but they were empty.

Elizabeth Mosely hovered fretfully behind me. "And my word was law. But the men were growing quite nervous as the election drew nearer; they claimed the . . . supplies weren't safe where they had been keeping them. They moved the guns in here last week."

I shook one of the boxes in her face. "What kind of weapons does this stuff fit?"

Slowly, fussily she fitted her bifocals onto her nose, then peered into the ammo case. "Well, now, let me see . . ."

"Don't stall us, Elizabeth. You know!"

"Well, would it be an Uzi?"

I raised my eyebrows at Lucy. "That's what the presidential guard carries." The rest of the locker was empty, but I could guess what it had contained. Several coat hangers dangled from a center bar; I found tiny strands of gold braid clinging to three of them.

"When did they pick up the guns?" I demanded.

"This morning."

"The uniforms too?"

Elizabeth Mosely sucked in her breath and held it, as though afraid that by exhaling she would be giving up the last of her secrets. "Yes," she sighed. "But don't ask me how they intend to use them; I deliberately held myself at a distance from that kind of thing." Recovering somewhat, she retrieved her rosary key chain from the padlock. "Now, may I presume that your interrogation is complete? While we've been chattering away, three more Haitian babies have been born into poverty."

I looked at her in amazement: she still seemed to believe in the good she was doing. I presumed that at least 75 percent of the money Zanfan d'Ayiti raised in the United States went straight into Carmen Mondesir's Machiavellian pockets, but to Elizabeth Mosely, the tough-minded "pragmatist," that meant 25 percent went to her children.

She read my skeptical frown. "We all put on blinders to survive, Mr. Falco. And when your survival depends on hand-outs," she smiled and cupped her hands around her eyes, "you have to wear bigger blinders than most."

––––––

WE left Elizabeth Mosely to her videotapes and her dreams. I didn't have the heart to bust her to the world. I could expose the deception in headlines, but to what end? The election had gathered momentum; it was two days away, and nothing could stop it now, not even the revelation that at its heart lay a stunning piece of technological chicanery. Let the world keep its blinders on, I thought. As for Elizabeth Mosely herself, no one had stepped forward to mourn her when she was dead; there was no reason to believe that anyone would rejoice to learn that she was alive.

"Shouldn't one of us stay with her?" Lucy asked as we headed back to the jeep.

"Carmen's men won't come back," I said. "They've got their guns, their uniforms; that's all they need. Carmen Mondesir is finished with Zanfan d'Ayiti; its purpose has been served. Elizabeth Mosely can wait there forever, but she'll never see another dollar come in, another kid adopted. In movie terms, it's a wrap."

Out on the Boulevard Harry Truman, the tension had ratcheted up another notch. We passed a column of soldiers, escorted by two of the Haitian army's four armored personnel carriers, heading back toward Cité Soleil. They were going to seal off the slums, caging the primary source of their fear. We drove beneath a political banner that read, VOTEZ VYÉJ MIRAK. "Vote for the Virgin of Miracles." It seemed a very sensible suggestion.

"Soldiers aren't always soldiers," Lucy said. "They're going to assassinate Isidor, aren't they?"

"Looks like it," I said flatly.

"They're going to disguise themselves as the presidential guard so they can get close to him," she continued. "Authentic right down to the damn bullets."

I just nodded, my mind troubled by something else, something that didn't fit into the scenario Lucy was sketching.

"They can afford to pick their moment, waiting until he feels comfortable, protected . . . it's the same way Indira Gandhi was killed. The question is when? Election day?"

When I didn't answer, she grabbed my chin, twisting my face toward her. "Ray, goddam it, are you with me here? We're talking about the murder of the president!

"Stop the car, would you?"

"What?"

"Just stop. I need to get out, walk around."

She slammed to a stop across from a weed-choked park. I got out, darted in front of a hell-bent Red Cross van, stepped over a collapsed wrought-iron fence. A colorful fountain crusted with bas-relief porpoises and mermaids stood in the center of the tall, untamed grass. It was empty, the plaster peeling, a civic reminder of better or at least more flamboyant times.

"Why kill him now?" I asked Lucy when she joined me. "Isidor's given outdoor speeches, he's traveled the countryside in the back of a pickup truck. Six months ago, no one gave a damn about Haiti. That's when they should have gotten rid of him."

Lucy thought for a moment. "They want the publicity? The world press corps is here now. The TV networks. They get maximum exposure."

"But if Isidor's killed while the whole world's watching, doesn't that make him a martyr?"

Lucy lit a cigarette and waved off an old man who tried to sell us a painting. "You're saying they're *not* going to kill him?"

"I don't know," I said. "By killing Isidor, Carmen and Gabriel get rid of the enemy, true. But there's no guarantee that his replacement will be any more to their liking." The artist wandered back, cut his price in half. I stared into the painting's turbulent colors. "I keep thinking about Carmen Mondesir's Rolodex," I blurted.

"What?"

"That night we broke into the Zanfan offices? I didn't tell you at the time, but Carmen had some very interesting phone numbers. Heavy hitters, private lines: CIA, Pentagon. Plus, I ran into her at State one day. She seemed very much at home."

I circled the fountain, trying to work out the kinks in my thoughts. On the other side of the park, enclosed by a massive wall, stood a squat, blindingly clean three-story building. Communications antennae sprouted from its roof like a forest of needles, an oversize Old Glory snapped briskly in the sea breeze. It was the American embassy. I gazed at the marine guards, standing at attention at the front gate in their crisp blue uniforms.

Suddenly, it was like looking through a kaleidoscope and watching the jagged shards at the far end assemble into a clear picture. I knew what Carmen was planning. They weren't going to kill Isidor; they were going to kill the American election observers! By disguising themselves as the presidential guard, they could pin the blame for the massacre on Isidor's government. It was an old Third World trick, with a mass-media twist—with so many film crews in the country, there was a good chance that this massacre would be televised. The torture tape had set the precedent: the Isidor government seemed capable of anything. The murder of Americans, fed via CNN to every living room in the United States—the pressure for military retaliation would be enormous. I thought back on the documents I'd stolen from Tony Randolph's computer. The phrase "to ensure the safety of the American community in Haiti" jumped out from the pages of Pentagon-speak. Carmen knew exactly how the United States would react to the election-day massacre. We'd done it in Grenada and Nicaragua and Panama, we'd even done it in Haiti, in 1915—we'd send in the marines.

I burst out laughing and shook my head in appreciation. I felt like clapping. It was the perfect Haitian hustle, the ultimate Haitian bluff. Not only did Carmen Mondesir want the Isidor regime overthrown, she wanted the United States to do it for her. Those names in her Rolodex would help her grab a position of power in a new, U.S.-approved government.

"Are you implying that Carmen Mondesir works for the CIA?" Lucy asked. "That there's some hidden American agenda at work here?"

I wanted to tell her everything. The words formed at the back of my throat, but I couldn't get them out.

"Ray? Hello in there."

An icy paralysis spread through me. I felt my neck constrict, as though a strangler were tightening his grip. I glanced around the park—was Faustin Gabriel out there somewhere, monitoring the progress of my investigation? I gagged, fighting for breath.

"Ray, what is it? What's wrong?"

This was as far as Carmen and Faustin would let me go. An alarm had gone off, warning them that it was time to rein me in. I could know the truth, but I couldn't pass it on. I began to push from inside my chest, trying to force my thoughts out of their cage, my body out through its skin. To Lucy, I must have looked like some sci-fi creature about to explode.

"Come on," she said. "We're getting you out of here."

"You . . . don't . . . understand," I gasped, every word a separate needle of pain.

"Understand what?" She looked frightened now.

"It's not . . . it's not . . ." The words were clipped, guttural; they barely qualified as human speech.

"It's not what? Not what?"

When I didn't answer, Lucy dragged me toward the car. I felt the fight draining out of my body. This was the lowest, the absolute bottom. They had made me weak at the exact moment when I needed to be strong; they had made me mute when I needed to scream out a warning.

———

I may have slept. Or maybe some mysterious voodoo process had rearranged my internal calendar. Suddenly, it was Sunday and I was somewhere else.

A ghostly face framed by a frizzy black halo hovered above me. "I've warned them, Ray. It's going to be OK."

Was this Lucy? I opened my mouth to speak, but my lips were cracked and dry; they felt like they were about to flake off from my face. I raised my head from a pillow. Where was I?

"Don't try to talk," she cooed. "You've been delirious most of the night, but I've got things under control. I got word to someone on President Isidor's staff. They're doubling his security; they've changed the password required to gain access to his quarters."

That's not it! They're not after Isidor! We're not talking about political assassination, we're talking mass murder! My mind was screaming, but Lucy couldn't hear it. My thoughts were just harmless echoes.

"You're in one of my father's warehouses; I didn't know where else to bring you. At least we won't have to send out for a prescription."

I lay on a cot, cooled by a portable fan. On a table next to me I saw blankets, bandages, bottles of mineral water. But when I tried to peer into the distance, my vision distorted; the walls seemed to curve inward, toward a cathedral ceiling miles above my head.

She pressed a cool washcloth to my burning forehead. "Just hang on; a doctor's on his way."

The doctors aren't going to find anything! They'll diagnose nervous exhaustion, they'll blame it on the water. The frustration writhed inside my head, like a snake trying to escape from a box. There is nothing physically wrong with my vocal chords, I told myself. I reached for a bottle of Culligan, poured the cool liquid down my throat, attempting to soothe it into speech.

"Green freedom in the old bus," I gasped. "Tell 'em baby parachute is here . . . turn off the cranberry sauce . . ." I concentrated ferociously, enunciating each syllable. "If the furniture lapses, history will bend to the root of my shoelaces . . ."

It was just a white noise of nonsense. Faustin Gabriel had taken my professional tools—words—and twisted them into unrecognizable shapes. Lucy evaporated into the shadows. I heard a door slam, retreating footsteps. This is what it feels like to be buried alive, I realized. Unable to connect to the outside world, your fear rattling inside the coffin as the oxygen dwindles and shovelfuls of dirt thump in the darkness above your head.

I struggled to my feet. Speech was impossible, but maybe I could still write! I threw water on my face, trying to stabilize my flailing vision. I staggered through a maze of cartons, hunting for pencil and paper. I found a box of pens, medical giveaways labeled "Johnson & Johnson." But not a scrap of paper.

Don't worry about it. Neatness doesn't count, write on any-thing . . . the walls . . .

How much time did I have? I checked my watch but it was dead. There were no windows in the room, no clocks. Had the sun gone down? Or had the sun already come up on Monday morning, election day?

I started to write, but the words were not in my handwriting. I recognized the flowing script of Nicholas Townsend. Not now, I begged. I have this warning to write, this message in a bottle. I shook my hand furiously, trying to drive him off, but the more I fought, the tighter my fingers clenched the pen. The words poured out like blood from a cut. I worked at a fevered pace, wearing out pen after pen. Speed was the thing. Nicholas Townsend was under time pressure too, a condemned man desperate to finish his story before the sun rose on the last day of his life.

23

LeMirebalais, Saint Domingue
February 1793

"Le Roi est mort. Vive la nation, vive la république!"

On a gray, wintry day in January 1793, Louis XVI, King of France and of Navarre, met the guillotine with distracted stoicism. Following tradition, Charles Sanson, the executioner, held the dripping head aloft so that the masses might appreciate his handiwork. Schoolboys rushed forward to dip their fingers in the blood, and afterward reported that it carried a bitter, salty taste.

All this we discovered in a newspaper found in the library of a plundered plantation. We had attacked at dawn, only to find much of our work had been done for us. The Negroes had already revolted and slaughtered their masters, yet rather than flee to the hills to join the ranks of the Maroons, they stayed to work the plantation. And how they worked it! Blacks still toiled in the fields, overseen by other blacks; indeed, the operation seemed more productive than ever. Within the house itself, the higher-ranking Negroes had donned European clothing and powdered wigs, and mimicked the daily lives of their masters, accustoming themselves to leisure, an idea hitherto unknown to them.

But there was a grimmer aspect to the scene—the decaying corpses of the whites were still in attendance! Like wax figures in a museum, they had been propped up around the plantation house in lifelike poses: at the dinner table, reclining on the sofa, seated at a chessboard, silent observers of the madness around them. The rainy season had brought with it a host of insects, worms, maggots, and they burrowed and nibbled at the human carcasses, making for both a ghastly sight and a loathsome stench.

Indeed, as I sat in the library with General Charlemagne and his voodoo lieutenant, Vincent Gabriel, I was nearly overcome with nausea. I threw open the window, inhaling the freshness of the torrential rains. For hours we had been discussing the political implications of the death of Louis XVI. I knew the king's execution would produce a quickening of revolutionary ardor in France; here in Saint Domingue, General Charlemagne seemed more anxious then ever to launch the epic and intrepid assault to which he had been alluding for months.

"We will carve out the heart of the colonial system," he declared. "The Frenchman's morale, already reduced by yellow fever and the natural frailties of his race, will crumble entirely." He spread a map out on the library desk, the same map once used by the dead plantation master to plot his expanding empire. "Here, just to the north of the bay of Port-au-Prince, is the *embarquement* where many of the slave ships unload their precious cargo. There is a small garrison nearby, but the slave merchants insist that the soldiers keep their distance, fearing their presence will dry up the juices of commerce. We intend to rout this French contingent, then liberate the slave ships themselves! Imagine the spectacle of five hundred Africans fleeing into the brilliant sun, their beings consumed with a hunger for revenge. Now, imagine the reaction of a French planter sipping a glass of Madeira on his balcony as he witnesses the same spectacle!"

It was a bold plan, to be sure, but one whose success I doubted. "You will require first-class intelligence. Someone to enter the town and appraise the troop strength, make a careful study of any tactical obstacles. Someone who will not attract attention . . ."

"Someone white," Charlemagne said.

So he had chosen me as his spy. "But there are five thousand French regulars within an hour's march of Port-au-Prince," I protested. "Not to mention their mulatto confederates within the city itself. They could easily cut off your escape. And if they capture you alive . . ."

"The revolution will have its first hero. And its first martyr," Charlemagne said.

I looked to Vincent Gabriel, to gauge his reaction. At that moment, he was squatting on the floor, breaking up the bones of a dead cock into a deep bowl. He added a libation of rum, then set the mixture ablaze. He shook the bowl, scattering the bones about in various patterns, with hands that seemed impervious to pain. I was oddly moved to witness so pagan a ritual in that decorous and scholarly library. Several minutes later, Gabriel threw the mess disgustedly out the window, where the rain extinguished it with a hiss.

"As I have said so often before, General, the spirits do not look favorably upon this enterprise. No matter what divination I attempt, the result is always the same."

Charlemagne smacked his lemon cane against the library globe, setting it spinning on its axis. "Damn them! Why do they not wish us to succeed?"

"They wish us to succeed. But they fear our motives."

"Our motives?"

"The motives of one general in particular. A general who dreams of seeing his image on the coin of the realm, of hearing his name on the lips of the world's prominent citizens. They wonder: is this still a spiritual revolution, or has it become a quest for personal glory?"

Charlemagne respected his aide-de-camp, but at the same time resented his direct link to the spirit world. He sipped his brandy thoughtfully, his silence as intimidating as his anger.

"Or perhaps they simply fear they are being displaced," offered Gabriel in a more conciliatory voice.

"That may be your fear, Vincent. You are their interpreter. If they are displaced, then so are you."

At that moment, I understood that the slave revolt was more than an armed struggle for emancipation. It was an offering to the gods of Africa, a gift to the loa, who had given the Negro race the strength to endure slavery, and if sufficiently propitiated, would give them the skill and courage to thrive in freedom. How could such an irresistible spiritual force be stopped?

"Bring in the prisoner," Charlemagne ordered. To my surprise, a single white man had survived the assault on the plantation, and he was now led before us. He was a ragged young man with long, chestnut hair and stained, loose-fitting clothes. "Have you your tools with you?" the general inquired. The young man nodded, his fear being too great to permit speech. "Then proceed. And recall, your life depends on your achieving a pleasing result."

As it happened, the young man was an itinerant artist, a portrait painter from Carcassonne who made a handsome living immortalizing the Saint Domingue gentry in oil. And so I watched as Charlemagne and Vincent Gabriel sat for their portraits. The painter's skilled hands soared across the canvas, the threat of death a greater spur to artistic dedication than the vitriol of a thousand critics.

I reflected upon the last several months. With the rainy season driving the French soldiers into their barracks, we had marched southward unimpeded, freeing slaves by the hundreds. I experienced again, on a quotidian basis, the uncompromising horrors of the French plantation system. My moral compass had undergone a series of subtle, then agitated fluctuations, until I, Nicholas Whitney Townsend, Virginia slaveholder, had come to share many of General Charlemagne's goals. I do not say that I had settled in my mind the question of equality among the races, nor do I offer justification for Charlemagne's slaughter of innocent white women and children. But I had concluded that the institution of slavery, this "execrable commerce," as Thomas Jefferson has termed it, stood naked in the firing line of history. If those great commerical enterprises, whose fortunes flowed from the slave trade, elected to stand and fight, the war that followed would be of a scale and fury beyond our imagining. But in the end, when the soil of the Americas could absorb not a single drop of blood more, slavery would fall.

Our company departed the plantation within the week. Charlemagne, as savage as any creature of the jungle, was nonetheless a man of his word, and the young portraitist was allowed to flee to the relative safety of a nearby mission. Our troops advanced into Port-au-Prince province, concealing ourselves in the jungled hills above the city.

On a moonless night in early March, Vincent Gabriel offered a voodoo benediction to the success of a curious and daring mission of espionage. I still had not won Gabriel's trust, and he viewed the teaming of the general and I with stern disapproval. His words that evening were half-hearted, the drumming that accompanied the ceremony lacking in fervor. The loa, it seemed, were reluctant to lend us their support.

Like characters out of a Shakespearean comedy, General Charlemagne and I had reversed roles and donned the appropriate disguises. In order that we might pass unremarked through the slave markets, I was dressed in the clothes of a middling-prosperous landowner—clean breeches, leather gaiters, and a tricorn hat—while Charlemagne had foresworn his uniformed splendor for a slave's tattered loincloth. Completing the picture were the chains that bound the general's wrists and the cowhide whip that I carried at my side.

The most prominent of the Port-au-Prince slave markets was found just to the north of the docks. A ship had unloaded its human cargo within the hour, and the market was alive with activity. As Charlemagne and I plunged into the tumult, we drew detailed mental maps of the area and counted whatever soldiers were on patrol.

The marketplace was a smoothly functioning enterprise. The

fresh arrivals were lined up for inspection, where their teeth were checked, skin and hair inspected, their most private orifices probed. Even their loincloths were shamelessly pulled down by white women, who used their own set of standards to judge the quality of a potential purchase. The Africans were then sold off at auction and immediately branded with hot irons. The final step in this process, which must have been dizzying and incomprehensible to men and women who had spent weeks in dark, cramped confinement aboard ship, came when they were ushered en masse before a local priest. The Code Noir, which regulated matters pertaining to slavery in the French Indies, specified that all slaves be baptized and instructed in the Catholic religion. So here, before the sun had set on their first day in the Americas, the Negroes were baptized in a language they didn't understand into a religion of which they were but dimly aware. Their Christian lives had begun.

Whenever I felt we were becoming the object of suspicion, I brandished my whip, laying into Charlemagne with smart strokes. He groaned and grimaced, lowering his head in obeisance, playing the part reluctantly. But, after the tenth such whipping, he turned on me in rage. "I think you take too great an enjoyment in this charade," he snarled, snatching the whip from my hand.

There came a sudden, suffocating silence around us. I saw shock on a hundred faces, black and white. Who was this insolent slave who dared lay a hand on his master's weapon? Who was this spineless blanc, unable to exercise control over his property?

"You're forgetting yourself," I whispered, retrieving the whip.

"But you have not forgotten yourself, I see," he said. "How easily you revert to your true nature."

"Can't you muzzle that damned pride of yours long enough for us to conclude our mission?"

Without waiting for a reply, I roughly shoved Charlemagne through the crowd. "Move, you damnable nigger!" I shouted for all to hear. "Before I flay that lazy, leprous skin of yours down to the bone." I thereupon delivered a sound, perfectly aimed kick to the general's posterior, a blow which I confess I enjoyed administering.

I drove Charlemagne in the direction of the French *caserne*. I had the sensation that we were being followed, perhaps by someone whose attention had been attracted by Charlemagne's "rebellion"; yet whenever I cast a glance about me, I saw nothing suspicious. We joined the foot traffic flowing past the main gate, and by pretending to repair Charlemagne's wrist irons, we were able to linger long enough to assess the size of the barracks and its corresponding troop strength. I called at a nearby brandy shop, and while taking my refreshment on the second-floor terrace, I had a clear view of the parade ground, its entrances and exits. As I drank, Charlemagne held his peace, chained to the balcony rail; yet by nods and hand signals, he conveyed his opinion that the French garrison could be taken.

There was one final matter to resolve before we returned to camp, a matter of a personal nature. I led us down the warren of dockside streets to the colonial post office. In a scene whose irony will be forever branded in my memory, I held the black general beside me in chains as I posted a letter to Virginia, instructing the overseer to free my slaves.

Immediately suspecting treachery, Charlemagne grabbed my wrist.

"What is this dispatch you are sending?" he demanded. "Read it to me."

"Your shrewdness is failing you. How do you know that I will read you the truth?"

"I will see it in your eyes, and hear it in your voice. Now read it!"

Knowing that trouble awaited me back at camp if I did not accede to his wishes, I led us outside so that we would not be overheard. In a solemn voice befitting the occasion, I read to General Charlemagne my decree of manumission. "Whereas Almighty God has created the mind and body of man free; whereas Christian manners and morals can never thrive in a society that practices the perpetual servitude of human beings,

I do now announce my opposition to slavery, that despotism established in our country by British kings and parliaments. I hereby manumit all bond slaves in my possession, and establish for their benefit a fund to run for five years as of this date. In so doing, I hope to set a course that other Virginians, indeed, other Americans might follow, so that abolition will proceed from the slave masters' consent, rather than their extermination."

Charlemagne fixed me with a haughty gaze. "So, the months you spent with me have been instructive, after all."

Not wishing to further plump up his considerable self-regard, I answered, "Do not credit yourself unnecessarily. I am both a pragmatist and a moralist. This decision simply reflects a reconciliation between my warring halves." So saying, I posted the letter. But I suspected that the slave owners of Saint Domingue would not be moved by pragmatism or morality. In the colonies, as in France herself, terror would soon become the order of the day.

As we emerged from the post office, I was again seized by the impression that we were being observed. Yet a careful perusal of the streets yielded nothing untoward, and I consigned the incident to a severe case of nerves.

Once we were back in camp, the general dispatched our scouts to an observation point above the bay, to watch for the approaching slave ships. As we awaited their report, a fever ran in all our blood; the promise of a history-making battle seemed to catapult the black army to a heightened state of readiness. Three days later, the scouts burst excitedly into camp to report that a ship had been sighted on the horizon and would be docking at Port-au-Prince the next morning.

That night, when the war council convened, Vincent Gabriel made a last effort to dissuade Charlemagne from attacking the slave ship. "Word has come of war in Europe," he announced. "The Spanish and the English have turned against the French."

"To restore the monarchy, that is all. Their fight is not ours," Charlemagne replied.

"But we can make use of them. The Spanish in Santo Domingo have offered to arm us, to send us soldiers. The British are landing to the north, and might be prevailed upon to do the same."

"They want the colony for themselves, damn you! No European power would abolish slavery if they seized Saint Domingue. They have seen the wealth that can be bled out of us. We are trying to remove the Europeans from our waters; why become allies with them? Their time is fading. The American Revolution has shown us the way, and Mr. Jefferson has said he will aid us—*that* is an alliance worth pursuing."

Gabriel abandoned his argument in disgust, retreating into the jungle. But Charlemagne read the concern on the faces of his officers. He vaulted onto his desk, his boot heels planted squarely on the geographic center of the Saint Domingue map. "Lest anyone think that the entanglements of the blanc politicians have led me astray, let me reassure them of my dedication to our cause. Saint Domingue will be a black republic, or it will be no republic at all. Do you remember the war cry that first passed my lips when our struggle began?"

There came a flurry of whispers, which slowly rose to a chant as first the officers, then the troops picked it up.

"Before I am defeated, I will leave only bones and ashes!" Charlemagne roared from his perch.

"Bones and ashes," came the thundering response from a thousand Negro throats. "Bones and ashes, bones and ashes!" Charlemagne picked up a torch and hurled it into the jungle. It threaded a perfect course through the tangled vegetation and landed in an explosion of flames, illuminating the clearing where Vincent Gabriel waited, his naked body illustrated with the swirling insignia of the voodoo loa.

The drumming began, and Ogoun prepared his children for war.

———

THE ship was called *Providence,* and she loomed blackly against the dawn, a nautical torture chamber preparing to disgorge its suffering cargo. A quartet of guards patrolled the dock, a few workers trudged sleepily about, but otherwise the scene was quiet and unsuspecting. The same was true of the French garrison. Through our spyglasses, we saw that it barely stirred. The only soldiers in evidence were those who had collapsed on the parade ground at the end of a night of debauchery, empty wine bottles for pillows. Then it struck me—we were going into battle on a Sunday.

To preserve the element of surprise, no signal was blown on the conch shell. Our troops swept out of the hills in silent waves, their footfalls scarcely seeming to disturb the soil. We moved past the garrison without incident and, establishing a picket line to guard against an attack from the rear, advanced toward the docks.

Perhaps only I saw it; perhaps others saw it but, caught up in the excitement of our assault, they attached no significance to it. Out in the bay, I noticed several hundred pinpoints of light leaping from the water like sparks. As I looked closer, I saw that they were flying fish, their scales glittering in the rising sun. I had never seen them in the bay, or anywhere in such numbers; they were fleeing out to sea, gifted with an intuition warning them of a dire catastrophe. And now I had been chosen to receive the same warning. Had the voodoo gods reached out to me, using nature as their instrument?

I tried to push to the front of the column, but it was impossible; I seized a conch shell and tried to blow the retreat, but it was too late. Charlemagne's army had already fallen into a cunning ambush. Suddenly, the iron casemates on the *Providence* were flung open, revealing the ship's arsenal, primed and loaded. In rapid sequence, the cannons were fired, tearing a bloody swath along our troops. At the same time, soldiers appeared in the rigging, popped up from behind the furled sails, and rushed from below decks and formed firing ranks along the gunwales. A dragoon shot at us from the crow's nest, and even the captain's cabin bristled with muskets; it seemed as though the entire French army had taken up positions on the *Providence*.

The rout was instantaneous, the loss in human life devastating. Counterattack was impossible. Volley after volley cut our soldiers down; the dock ran with their blood. Only I, Charlemagne, Vincent Gabriel, and a few dozen soldiers managed to effect a retreat, and that was achieved only against the strenuous protests of the general, who felt honor demanded that he die with his troops. We carved our individual escape paths through the muddy alleys of Port-au-Prince, knocking our way past sleepy citizens who had been drawn out of their homes by the gunfire.

As I ran, I tried to understand the reason for this surprise attack. Clearly, the slaves had been stealthily disembarked during the night so that the soldiers might take their place, but how had the French commander learned of our strategy? Then I saw the culprit, serenely enjoying his breakfast on a terrace overlooking the bay—the potrait painter, whose life Charlemagne had spared! Surely it had been the presence of this scoundrel I had sensed in the slave market that day. Through his art, he had ensured that Charlemagne would live on for future generations; now, through his treachery, he had nearly brought about the general's doom.

We survivors straggled into camp. The anguish of the women and younger members of the party, when told the tragic news, was fearful to behold. We immediately ran to our concealed observation point, and trained our spyglasses on the scene of the debacle; many soldiers had been taken prisoner, and we were anxious to learn of their plight. The spectacle I witnessed that day was one of profound and affecting tragedy, a dashing of dreams, a slow death march in the tropical sun, with the French masters calling the tune.

Those of our fellows who had survived the massacre were immediately bound in chains, no doubt the same chains that had shackled their brothers on the voyage from Africa. Slaves again, the rebels were whipped and driven onto the *Providence,* which, raising but a single sail, then navigated lazily toward the open sea. At a distance of perhaps half a league from land, the ship swing to. As we watched in horror, the rebels were made to leap into the sea! Bound together in iron chains, their black bodies flashed briefly in the sun as they jumped. Group after group they came, until fully a hundred men had been consigned to that Caribbean tomb.

That night, a mournful silence held dominion over the camp. Fully two thirds of Charlemagne's army had been lost; we were now little more than a tiny battalion of disheartened soldiers, widows, and fatherless children.

Shortly before midnight the general summoned me. It was insufferably hot, yet he was in full military splendor. He resembled an officer primping for a dress ball more than a general who had just suffered his most punishing defeat.

"Un blanc est un blanc," he intoned. "You may dress him in rags, force him to witness the atrocities committed so blithely by his fellows, yet white he remains."

I felt a cold knot of dread in my throat. "General, I know what happened today, I know who was responsible . . ."

"And a slave owner is a slave owner," he continued. "Once he becomes accustomed to other men as property, he can never learn to see them as comrades. You betrayed us, my friend, of that I am certain."

"It was the painter that gave us away!" I shouted. "The very man to whom you showed mercy. He overheard our strategy discussions at the plantation; then, when he recognized us at the slave market, he knew we had come to carry out the plan."

"I didn't see this painter. But I *did* see you post a letter . . . to the French authorities, I must now assume."

"But I read to you the contents of that letter!"

"You read lies to me."

Was Charlemagne stating his own opinion, or was he reacting to the pressures of his surviving officers, who insisted that a white scapegoat be blamed for the massacre? I felt my faith in our common humanity falter; was the chasm between our races so great that even a noble gesture on my part could be so grievously misunderstood?

"And you insisted you could read the truth in my eyes," I reminded him. I brought a torch up to my face. "Read them now!"

He walked around his desk and clasped his hands roughly on my shoulders, his untamed fingernails digging into my back. "I have but one simple question: Is Mr. Thomas Jefferson truly going to send us ships and men?" I couldn't bring myself to lie; too much had transpired since I had created this falsehood to save my own life. Charlemagne answered for me. "There never was an American armada, Mr. Townsend. The American people know little of our struggle, and care even less. But you have not dealt us a death blow. We have other generals, other armies. And every slave the French bring to this island is a potential soldier."

I knew further discussion was useless. My only chance of survival now lay in flight. I looked wildly about me; the jungle stirred, the green wall of lianas and banana leaves parted to reveal the remaining soldiers standing shoulder to shoulder, enclosing me in a human prison.

"I have given much thought to the sentence of death that I now pass upon you. As you can see by my formal dress, it is a task I do not take lightly. What words should I employ? I wondered. Should I adhere to some executioner's protocol? Should I pour out my righteous anger?

"No, I thought. The condemned knows why he is about to die. Why read to him? Let him read to us. Let his last words haunt him, let them fill him with regret and torment; and let his afterlife, if he believes in it, be a restless one." The general then handed me a familiar roll of parchment. "Here. Read it," he commanded.

And so that night passed in the same fashion as the first night I met General Charlemagne, with my reading of the Declaration of Independence. It was still dark when I concluded my last recital: ". . . And for the support of this Declaration, with a firm reliance on the protection of Divine Providence, we mutually pledge to each other our Lives, our Fortunes, and our sacred Honor." I had closed my eyes as I spoke; when I opened them, Vincent Gabriel stood at my side, dressed entirely in white. General Charlemagne was still in attendance, but his back was turned—I knew that he would never look me in the eye again. Had any sort of bond been forged between us, I wondered? Had he ever seen me as anything other than an enemy, a blanc, an emissary from a powerful nation whose resources he wished to exploit? Had he ever seen me as a man?

Gabriel and a squad of armed soldiers led me off. I pleaded with him, I bargained and cajoled, offered my fortune to the rebel cause, but it was all for naught: Gabriel had never trusted me, and Charlemagne's sentence of death served only to validate his judgment. We came upon a vast, open headland that over-looked the sea. A stream chorused merrily over polished stones, but it was a deceptive music. To my horror I saw that a grave had already been dug for me. At that moment, I knew there could be no rescue, no salvation. If I ran, I would be cut down by musket or machete. But if I let events unfold according to my captors' design . . . my sanity threatened to crumble as I imagined the inventive ways in which I could be put to death. Yet I fought to remain composmentis, if only long enough to see my painful narrative to its conclusion.

I was stripped naked and bathed by Gabriel's retainers in a foamy broth of herbs and flowers. I was clothed in simple muslin, and a cross of wet ashes was daubed upon my forehead. But when they attempted to lace my wrists and ankles with leather thongs, I called an angry halt.

"No, that I will not permit!" (How incredibly brave one becomes when all hope is lost.) "If I am not treated with more dignity I will flee, and it will be a bloody, broken corpse that is delivered to your loa."

Vincent Gabriel knelt at my side and produced a beautifully turned ceramic pot, which he reverently wrapped in red velvet. He clipped off a lock of my hair, trimmed my fingernails. He dropped the cuttings into the pot, which he then passed back and forth above my head, chanting softly in the Creole tongue. I suspected that I was being dedicated to some mysterious, higher purpose in the vodoun religion, yet I could summon no comfort from my own religious training. The fine words and prayers of all the Anglican, Episcopalian, and Presbyterian ministers who had dueled for possession of my soul, vanished beyond recall.

The sky grew lighter. I felt that the hour of my execution was at hand. The resigned courage I had summoned thus far vanished. I began to shudder and sweat as my body joined my mind in its revolt against oblivion. My hands clutched the soil, digging frantically into the earth from which I would soon be severed. I felt Vincent Gabriel holding me down, heard him whisper in my ear.

"Only your body is about to die, monsieur," he said. "Take what consolation you can from that."

"Like all priests, you cannot resist offering the dying man religion," I scoffed.

"I offer something much greater, if you would only listen!" he replied forcefully. "A man is many parts: as the physical body, the *corps cadavre,* dissolves into the earth, the soul, the ti bon ange, is released. It lingers above the body for seven days—perhaps it does not understand what has happened, perhaps it is in mourning for itself. During these seven days I will take yours and preserve it in this *canari.*" He brought the velvet-wrapped pot into view. "Your soul will live on, Mr. Townsend. That is what I offer you."

"Live on as what?" I asked.

"Who can say? As a simple ornament, perhaps . . ."

Gabriel was interrupted by a warning hiss from one of his aides. Our eyes flew to a distant hillside, where General Charlemagne appeared on horseback. He sat proud and erect beneath his tricorn, spyglass pressed to his face—the pose of regal aloofness he had assumed when first I laid eyes on him. Then, in a gesture whose interpretation I leave to the reader, he reined his horse in my direction, removed his hat, and held it to his heart.

"But it is more likely that I will employ you as a weapon," Gabriel continued. "Even should we prevail in our revolution, there is a great struggle coming between General Charlemagne and me, between politics and religion, between the loa of Africa and the more modern gods of the Americas. Who knows how valuable the soul of a white man will be?"

An ointment was rubbed onto my throat, a blanket draped across my muslin gown. When I heard the sharpening of cane knives, I knew how I would die.

I do not know if any of my countrymen, or indeed if any man will read this diary; but I would remind those who do that I have told the absolute truth. It is not susceptible to our analysis, it will not yield its secrets to our science. It is not the truth as you have ever seen it, but as I have seen it; not as you have ever imagined it, but as I have *experienced* it.

To my friends and colleagues in Virginia, who I will never see again, I wish long and prosperous lives. To my parents, Edmund and Martha Townsend, I send my unswerving love and devotion: you raised me to be honest, brave, and inquisitive, and I hope I have done justice to that birthright. Do not mourn me inordinately: I know now that I would rather die here than on my front porch at an advanced age, fat and prominent, watching history parade by at a distance. Finally, to Secretary of State Thomas Jefferson, who by dispatching me on this mission gave me such a noble opportunity to serve and who placed in my youthful hands a momentous trust I can never repay, I herewith offer my final report. They are your words, sir, and I beg you forgive my indulgence: "Nothing is more certainly written in the book of fate than that these people are to be free."

Nicholas Whitney Townsend, United States Special Envoy
Port-au-Prince, Saint Domingue
March 12, 1793

24

LUCY FOUND ME on my knees, fingers stained with ink, empty pens scattered across the floor like spent bullets. I was still in a creative fever, exhausted yet exhilarated, as though I had forced out some monumental work of art just under the deadline.

"My God!" Lucy said as she edged into the room. The walls were covered with line after line of my insane scrawl; the dark ink vibrated against the white plaster, making the room seem alive.

"It's over," I said. "This is the last installment of the life of Nicholas Whitney Townsend, as told by Ray Falco."

When she turned from the wall to me, her eyes dilated in shock. "Jesus, Ray. You look like you've lost twenty pounds!"

"The zombi diet," I said. "Works where other diets don't."

Lucy had brought more bottled water and fast food—*cabrit,* "goat in a basket." As I ate and drank, I began to read the wall. For two hundred years, Nicholas Townsend's soul had been unfulfilled; the memoirs that he had struggled heroically to complete had gone unread. He had been handed down by generations of Gabriels, a strange and precious family heirloom, maybe inhabiting other lives and bodies. But it was in me that he found his voice again.

You could never learn all the rules of this damn religion. I wasn't sure where Townsend's conscience ended and mine began, but I believed one thing—with this final blaze of writing, this sprint to the diary's finish, Nicholas Townsend was trying to warn me.

But it was too late. It was Monday morning. The last day of my life was already mapped out. The headline would read, REPORTER KILLED COVERING ELECTION.

Outside, I heard the pop of gunshots, a sound that had become routine, like sirens on a Saturday night. Lucy skimmed my corkscrewing sentences to the end of the diary, reaching out to touch the signature and date. "Vincent Gabriel killed Townsend," she said. "Butchered him, really."

I finished the last bottle of mineral water. I felt drained of most physical sensation; only my wrist tingled from the strain of writing. I threw open the door. The sunshine was soothing to my light-starved eyes. We were on the commercial docks. Across the channel was the city's main port, where cruise ships had once berthed. I could still read the faded WELCOME TO HAITI greeting.

"Ray? I don't like that look in your eye," Lucy said. "Or should I say *absence* of look. Why don't you lie back down, OK?" I could feel the warmth radiating from her body. I wondered if she could sense the chill coming from mine.

I thought she would fight me, so I disarmed her first. I dug into her purse and pulled out a black .25 with a faux-pearl handle.

"What the hell . . ." Her breath caught. "This is it, isn't it? The time bomb you were talking about?"

I checked my watch: eleven. The voting would begin at noon. I backed away from Lucy, onto the pier.

"Where are you going?"

I didn't say anything. I hurled the gun away. It flashed in the sun for a moment, then dropped into the water without a ripple.

"Goddamn it, you can fill walls with writing but you won't talk to me? *Me?*"

Lucy was shouting, but the sound of her voice was fading, her body dissolving into the darkness of the warehouse.

"We were going to fight them together, Raymond! Let me get hold of my father. God knows I don't want to call in a favor, but he has security guards . . . they'll help us."

I ran toward the street. When I glanced over my shoulder I saw her press a cellular phone to her ear. In her desperation, she had reached for a machine instead of reaching for me. I would always remember that gesture, and always wonder.

———

THE line began a mile away. A loud, gossiping column of Haitians, like a ragtag army on the march, led down the gravel road toward the polling place at the Lycée Alexandre Pétion. Vendors wheeled their carts along the lines, selling sticky-sweet *frescos* and attracting flies. I pushed through swarms of beggars, shoeshine boys, soccer-playing teenagers, people attracted by the rare spectacle of one man, one vote. My steps were measured and precise, and I had no control over them. I was walking a path that had been laid far in advance, just for me. I couldn't stop. Couldn't fend off this force dragging me down the condemned man's corridor. Television lights glared up ahead, and I felt a sick tremor of vanity—my death could be a media event.

How would it happen? Would I walk brazenly into a bullet? Would they call out my name so I could see it coming? Or would I be cut down in the chaos, one of those casualties no one notices until the dust settles and the crowd disperses, revealing an anonymous body lying facedown, oozing newsmagazine blood?

The tension was palpable the moment I entered the schoolyard. The impatient crowd jostled and complained as it was routed through a maze built from logs stretched across a line of oil drums, into the two-story, whitewashed schoolhouse. Inside, white-shirted election officials fingerprinted the voters and passed out ballots. Tempers were short, conversations were nervous. Rumors were rampant: they were about to run out of ballots; the army had suspended voting in Cap Haïtien; the airport was closed; Radio Métropole had been firebombed. Photographers and news crews circled the voters like mosquitos, shouting their inane questions: "How do you feel? Who do you think will win? Who are you voting for?"

As if anyone would answer in a country where mentioning the wrong name could get you killed.

"There I was, covering a massacre, when a bloody election broke out!" It was Phil Somerset, diligently rumpled, happy to be wading into political chaos. He was in full battle dress, cameras dangling from his neck, a bandolier of film cans looped over his shoulder. When I looked up, he recoiled. "Christ, mate, what happened to you? You look bloody awful!"

Laura Salameh ran up, videocamera sprouting from her camouflaged, Banana Republic shoulders. She handed out stalks of sugarcane, sucking on hers with a lascivious gusto designed to torment Somerset. "So, when do the fireworks begin? I've got to file by five."

Get the hell out of here! I wanted to scream. Can't you sense it coming? I can't save myself, and I certainly can't save any of you.

"You forget to take your malaria pills?" Somerset asked. He handed me a bottle of Culligan.

I just nodded, drinking gratefully. I looked into his eyes, grasped his wrist in a last attempt to transmit a telepathic warning. But there was nothing.

My thoughts veered around the last corner of sanity, and I found myself addressing Faustin Gabriel directly: this is too much knowledge for one man; why do I have to be burdened with this awful clairvoyance? The pressure's going to kill me, goddamn it! Before your soldiers even fire a shot!

"Uh-oh, here we go," Somerset called. "Lights, camera, bullshit."

They roared through the gate of the *lycée* compound, spewing dust, horns blaring. There were four white vans, pale blue United Nations flags flapping on the fenders, smoked glass concealing the passengers. The TV crews ignited their sun guns and surrounded the vans, pouring out enough heat to peel paint. The UN guards hopped out first, wearing starched khaki and baby-blue berets, and carrying sidearms that had probably never been fired. They ran a snap inspection of the yard, then fell into a perimeter around the schoolhouse. With the area secured, it was deemed safe for the dignitaries to alight.

There were twelve observers, faces ruddy from the tropical heat, their officialdom announced by the laminated credentials that gleamed on their lapels. The women wore skirts and pastel blouses, the men favored bush jackets. I recognized a congressman, the head of the Washington office of Amnesty International, and the chief political officer from the American embassy, a cellular phone pressed to his ear.

It's going to happen now, I thought. They're perfect targets in the high-noon sun. I glanced around wildly, but I didn't see Carmen's soldiers. I tried to rush forward, but I was rooted to the spot.

The election officials marched stiffly out of the schoolhouse and met the observers with handshakes.

Something twinkled on the outside staircase that led to the second floor. I looked closer. A nail? No, something that had caught on a nail. A tiny loop of gold braid! My gaze followed the staircase up to the colonnaded balcony that ran across the front of the building. There were figures there, stirring in the shadows. As they stepped into the brilliant sunlight, I recognized the uniforms of the presidential guard.

I could see the deadly, compact silhouette of their Uzis. Would the first shot be for me? Who would administer the coup de grâce? The soldier I'd recognized? Or would they all unload on me, like a firing squad sharing the blame?

I tried to raise an arm, but it was glued to my side. I felt the heat of the TV lights arc across my eyes as the cameramen panned the crowd; I saw the reporters with their pens and notebooks sweep their gaze slowly past me, unaware I was the key to their survival. *Stop right there!* I tried to shout. I could feel the words writing themselves on the inside of my throat, but I couldn't force them out. *Hold on me . . . zoom in . . . concentrate . . . listen to me!*

The soldiers on the balcony took aim; their victims stood out against the dusty ground, cardboard cutouts about to die.

At that moment, I noticed a stoop-shouldered market woman shuffling into the schoolyard. She wore glasses, a plain cotton dress, her hair tucked into a bandanna, a basket of papayas balanced on her head. A simple *marchande,* like a million others in Haiti.

Suddenly, I was free. Launched forward like a driver thrown from a car wreck.

I charged straight toward the market woman, screaming, pent-up speech spilling out uncontrollably: *"Atensyon, Makout! Se Makout, lie ye!"*

I was speaking Creole.

"Watch out, she's a Macoute!" I shouted, pointing at the surprised woman. "Don't you recognize her? She ran the Gonaïves section, she killed a hundred people in Fort Dimanche herself! It's her, I swear!"

The word "Makout" detonated like a bomb. The voters broke ranks and surged toward us. I saw my hand dart into my back pocket and pull out a folded sheet of paper. I gaped in disbelief as I held it up to the crowd—where had it come from? It was one of the "wanted" posters I'd seen on the wall outside Carmen Mondesir's house.

They didn't need to take off her glasses or bandanna, didn't need to compare the photograph and the flesh-and-blood woman. With a Macoute, they just knew.

In that suspended moment, before the mob descended on her, Carmen Mondesir looked at me through glasses that I saw were fake. Her piercing blue eyes seemed to turn black with fear. Instantly, fear gave way to anger and, finally, to a faint smile of understanding.

Then she disappeared beneath a storm of fists and flashing machetes.

Like ants swarming over a dying spider.

Her soldiers panicked and opened fire, but it was a half-hearted slaughter now that their leader was down. The crowd dropped to the dirt, the observers took cover behind the UN vans. I saw a knot of voters charge up the stairs to the second floor of the schoolhouse, unafraid, dodging the soldiers' bullets. The United Nations guards managed to pop off a few rounds in the general direction of the balcony, but it was the crowd, with their sheer numbers, that forced Carmen's men to surrender. The soldiers didn't go down fighting: to a Haitian, there's no percentage in dying for a lost cause.

Two minutes later, it was over.

Silence hung over the schoolyard. People carefully got to their feet, trading uneasy smiles, not really trusting in their survival. The first sound I became aware of was a scratchy, disembodied voice: "What is it? What the hell happened? What's going on out there?" The questions were coming from the embassy man's cellular phone, which he'd dropped as he dove for cover. Everyone stared at it as though it were alive; then the political officer recovered his composure, snatched up the phone, and moved away from the crowd to conduct a clandestine conversation.

A perfect coda. *What's going on out there?*

Things happened quickly then. The UN guards took charge of Carmen's men, laying them facedown, searching them for weapons. The observers and the election officals huddled, the voters broke up into loud, excited groups. The reporters went into overdrive, interviewing anyone they could, including each other. But it was all just a blur at the edge of the picture—I was hypnotized by Carmen Mondesir.

The crowd edged away from her. She lay on her back, her limbs twisted into cartoonish poses that meant broken bones. Blood seeped from a dozen wounds, already drying in the fierce heat. The papayas that had been the crowning touch to her disguise were scattered around her, spilling their juice into the dust.

"Bloody fucking hell." Phil Somerset crept up behind me. "Who is she?"

"You don't recognize her? An old Haiti hand like you?" I

knelt next to Carmen, removed her glasses, wiped some of the blood off her face. "Carmen Mondesir, former departmental commandant of the Tontons Macoutes, turned international Good Samaritan, turned antigovernment plotter. The soldiers were hers. This entire day was supposed to be hers."

"What's she doing dressed like that?"

"I guess she couldn't stay away, couldn't stand to miss the show she'd spent so long rehearsing."

Somerset pushed his bifocals onto his forehead and examined the corpse. Then he did something out of character; he expressed astonishment. "I don't believe it. You've been holding out on me, mate. How'd you recognize her? And where'd you learn Creole?"

I didn't say anything. I was still working out the answers in my mind.

Somerset whistled. "Look at her eyes. As blue as bloody robins' eggs. Probably gave her a hell of a complex, made her think she was part white. Or made her wish she was *all* white. At the end of the day, that's what they all want anyway."

I stood, glanced around the schoolyard, up at the sky, at the trees. Faustin Gabriel was here somewhere.

A wave of excited shouts in Creole rolled across the yard. A teenage boy darted from behind the schoolhouse, carrying a can of gasoline. He grinned, soaking up the crowd's cheers of encouragement. When he reached Carmen Mondesir's corpse, the cheering stopped, and it was so quiet you could hear the gasoline trickle as he poured it over her skin.

It took several matches, but the fire eventually caught. The smell was sweet and acrid at the same time, forcing people to cover their noses. But nothing could make them cover their eyes; no one could turn away from a burning Macoute. Not even Laura Salameh, who poked her video camera into the scene. She captured ten grisly seconds before Phil Somerset, in a small act of chivalry, blocked the lens with his hand.

The flames weren't as big as Carmen Mondesir would have wanted. We all picture our deaths in a certain way, and I was sure that Carmen imagined dying to more spectacular accompaniment—thunder and lightning, the raging of nature. Not this timid, crackling fire and thin column of smoke rising straight up into the windless air.

———

I became a temporary hero. A defender of democracy. After a five-hour delay, the election officials decided to let the voting continue. Before the TV crews could beam their pictures up to the satellites, the *teledjol,* the Haitian gossip network, had spread the story of Carmen Mondesir's scheme. UN exit-poll-takers detected a sympathy vote for President Isidor building in Port-au-Prince and filtering out to the provinces as news of the aborted attack spread. Any candidate who could be the victim of such a devious conspiracy was surely a man worth voting for.

The political officer drove me to the American embassy, showed me off to his staff, and introduced me to the ambassador as the man who saved the election. In the conference room I ate a steak dinner, drank four Budweisers beneath a picture of the president. In the air-conditioned, windowless room, the morning's *New York Times* on the coffee table and country music on the radio, I nearly forgot I was in Haiti. A secretary cleared my dishes, poured me a cup of watery American coffee, and disappeared. A moment later, a crisp young man in a white shirt and yellow tie entered through a side door and took a seat across the conference table from me: sandy-haired, clean-shaven, perfectly tanned. Yale, weekend sailor, good tennis game. Definitely career foreign service, logging hellhole time while he waited for a cushier posting. He probably walked the streets of Port-au-Prince in loafers. I snuck a glance underneath the table and smiled.

"Mr. Falco, I'm Blaine Connover, deputy ambassador. Do you mind if I ask you a few questions?"

"Can I say what you guys always say: 'No comment'?"

He smiled blandly. "We're not trying to squeeze anything out of you. You're the man of the hour; we want you on our side."

I set down my coffee. "Couldn't get you to squeeze out a drink, could I? Rum, with sugar and lime juice?"

"Haitian style. I must say, you've gone native awfully quickly."

"Oh, I've . . . been here before."

Connover arched an eyebrow. He went to the door and spoke in hushed tones to his secretary. Suddenly, I heard a commotion, arguing voices, then Lucy Marcelin bulldozed into the room.

"I'm sorry, Mr. Connover," said the secretary. "She says she's a friend of Mr. Falco. She has a green card, the guards had to let her into the compound."

Connover glimpsed the briefcase in Lucy's hand, read the businesslike determination in her face. She handed him her card. "Lucy Marcelin, Mr. Falco's attorney."

"Marcelin . . ." Connover mused. "Any relation . . ."

"My father."

"Ah. Well, please come in," Connover said. To his secretary he added, "Better make that three drinks."

The three of us stood there stiffly for a moment, then I cut through the prickly atmosphere of protocol, pulled Lucy into my arms, and kissed her. She caressed my face, as though to reassure herself I was still flesh and blood. "Thank God, thank God" was all she said, over and over, until Connover cleared his throat in embarrassment.

Once we were all seated, Lucy took the offensive. "May I ask the nature of the questions you have for Mr. Falco?"

"Certainly. Although this is not a hearing, Ms. Marcelin. Your . . . client is not being charged with anything. It appears that he managed to penetrate and somehow thwart a rather devilish political conspiracy, one which originated on American soil, so naturally we're interested in whatever background he can give us concerning this conspiracy. It's all in the spirit of patriotism and simple good citizenship. Nothing sinister."

"That sounds like you're asking a reporter to divulge his sources," I said.

"Not at all. We'd just like you to put a little flesh on the bare bones we do have. Starting from your first day on the story back in Washington, preferably."

The secretary brought our drinks. Connover leaned across the burnished conference table and offered a toast. "Let's drink to you, Mr. Falco. An American hero."

I felt the sweet-sour rush of the rum, concentrated on its delightful shiver. Connover sipped, pursing his lips. He fanned out a spread of paperwork with the fluid expertise of a Vegas blackjack dealer. "Shall we begin?"

"You know what, Mr. Connover?" Lucy said. "I think you're getting something for nothing here."

"Oh?"

"Yeah. You want Ray to plug the holes that you should've plugged long ago, fill in gaps that the combined efforts of the diplomatic corps and the American intelligence community overlooked."

Connover's expression soured, and it wasn't just a reaction to the drink.

"Ray saved an election—on your watch. He single-handedly prevented the massacre of dozens of Haitians and Americans— on your watch—*and* he may have even saved the life of a congressman . . ."

Connover shook his head ruefully, and chimed in, "I know, on my watch."

"And for that you're offering what? A plaque? Maybe dinner at the White House?"

"Ms. Marcelin, I'm not authorized to dispense a cash reward, if that's what you're driving at. I should think a true hero would derive his reward from the heartfelt gratitude of the Haitian and the American people." He smiled acidly, then made a point of ignoring the drink and pouring himself a fresh cup of coffee.

"Ambassador Connover," Lucy said, "there are certain charges pending against my client in Washington, D.C. Groundless charges connected to this case that has concluded so dramatically in your favor. If you were to intervene, perhaps through the secretary, and see to it that those charges were reduced, or better yet, dropped, I get the sense that my client would be a lot more talkative."

I snuck an admiring glance at Lucy, reached for her hand under the table.

Connover pushed out of his chair and walked to the American flag that stood in the corner. He ran his fingers along its ceremonial gold fringe, perhaps imagining how it would look in an office in Paris or London. He knew I had saved his career. There was never any doubt as to his answer.

"I'll see what I can do," he said.

"See now," Lucy said.

Channels. To see them work in your favor can be beautiful. The channel that was opened for me led up: from the deputy ambassador to the ambassador, to the assistant secretary of state for Inter-American Affairs, to the secretary of state himself; from there it jumped agencies to a deputy director of the FBI, then started down again, to the assistant police chief of Washington, D.C., to the head of the homicide bureau, all the way down to Walter Paisley, who snatched up his car phone while gridlocked on the Capital Beltway to learn that all charges against me had been dismissed.

So I ordered another drink and told Blaine Connover my story. I began with the discovery of the loup-garou skin, led through the murder of Jean-Mars Baptiste, Carmen Mondesir's dummy charity, the fake-torture tape, the attempt to pin the election-day massacre on the Isidor regime. Of course, I didn't explain the real role vodoun had played; Connover would never have believed it anyway.

"Let me be sure that I'm clear on this," he said when I'd finished. "Carmen Mondesir and her group honestly believed that they could trigger American military intevention?"

"That's right."

"And what did you believe?"

"That it was possible."

"Why?"

"Historical precedent. And . . ."

Connover leaned forward with the smirk of an interrogator who already knew the answer to his question. "And . . ."

"I obtained National Security Action Memoranda that discussed an invasion."

"By *obtained,* you mean 'stole,' don't you?" Connover passed several documents to me. They were duplicates of the files I'd downloaded from Tony Randolph's computer! But there were other memoranda dealing with Haiti as well, dated a week later. "In light of your recent . . . heroism, I suppose we can overlook your theft of government property. Actually, you may have pointed out ways in which we can improve our data security, so maybe a little backhanded gratitude is due. At any rate, the documents you saw were just working papers, rough drafts, if you will, of government policy. The idea of military intervention was considered, but tabled . . . for now."

As I read through the papers, Lucy pulled out her cigarettes. "I'd prefer if you didn't smoke in here," Connover said. He turned a thin, bureaucrat's smile on me. "This is not just another government cover-up, Mr. Falco. Believe me, if we do invade, the whole world will know about it."

"But Carmen Mondesir worked for you," I insisted.

"Once upon a time, of course, we employed all sorts of unsavory characters down here. Beachhead against Castro and all that. We did link arms with a few Macoutes such as Carmen Mondesir, but we severed our connection to her years ago."

"Bullshit!" I said. "I saw the names and numbers in her address book—CIA, Pentagon, State Department. Got a good look at her phone records, too. Dozens of calls, all of them recent."

Connover didn't blink. "And if you'd seen the government's phone records, you would have learned that we never called her back. Frankly, she was a nuisance. She simply wouldn't stay 'severed.'" He collated the documents, returned them to a wall safe. "I'm not an expert in intelligence matters, but it seems to me that most agents tend to overestimate their importance. They begin to imagine themselves at the fulcrum of history. I don't know, maybe we flatter them too much with our attention, we feed their delusions . . ."

"Or maybe we just lie to them," I said. "We tell them we'll always be on their side."

Connover's back was turned as he spun the combination lock on the safe, and for an instant, his shoulder seemed to flinch beneath his Brooks Brothers shirt. When he faced us, his expression was matter-of-fact. "Be realistic. If diplomacy were that static, the world would be an unworkable place. Everyone changes sides."

———

NIGHT had fallen while we were in the embassy. Ra-ra bands roared through the streets, chanting President Isidor's theme song. We didn't need to hear the official election results—music announced the victor. Lucy and I went into a borlette to watch Isidor's acceptance speech.

My mind was still back at the schoolyard. How had Carmen Mondesir hoped to pull off such an outrageous deception? The answer was written on the faces of the Haitian men who sat next to us, watching the lottery results parade across the TV screen. The Haitian always thinks he can cheat the odds. He puts to sea in a leaky refugee boat convinced he can fool the elements; he comes ashore in the United States, and even though he knows that nine out of ten asylum claims are denied, he's sure he'll be the one to fool the authorities.

Carmen Mondesir dreamed grander dreams, more operatic dreams. She thought she could fool the world.

"Lucy . . ."

"Shhh. You don't have to talk. There's plenty of time to tell me everything."

"At least let me buy my lawyer a cup of coffee. You saved me in there, counselor."

"And my bill will reflect that." She smiled, we toasted, but it didn't feel like a celebration. Too many tragedies, too many unanswered questions.

"Say something in Creole," I asked.

She thought for a moment. *"Après bal-la, tanbou lou."*

I concentrated, but couldn't work out a translation. "It's gone," I said. "Why was an entire language given to me for a few minutes, then taken away? And how did I recognize Carmen Mondesir in her disguise? What made me denounce her?"

"You're a hero, Ray. Try not to complicate it."

"But I was supposed to die this afternoon, Lucy!"

The TV picture cut to an office inside the presidential palace. Rene Isidor, the teacher turned president, entered the room, stooped, frail, the glasses that were too big for his head sliding comically down his nose. He wore a pale gray suit; a ceremonial sash of blue and red, the colors of the Haitian flag, was draped over his shoulder. He looked like he'd been crying, like he hadn't eaten or slept in weeks. His TV image was perfect— he'd suffered for victory.

"Today, the Haitian people have spoken with one voice," he began. "They have rejected the lessons of fascism and begun a long and fruitful education in democracy."

"Goddamn!" I hissed. As the camera cut to a wide angle, I nearly punched my fist through the TV screen. "There, against the back wall! What the hell is *he* doing there?" Faustin Gabriel stood among the ranks of Isidor's advisors, joining in the applause. In his sparkling white suit and burgundy foulard, he could not be mistaken for one among many. He drew the light, shimmering with importance.

Dazed, I walked out to the street. The celebration was still raging. Tap-tap drivers rejoiced with their horns, singing teenagers lit bonfires. People were pouring out of the slums, pro-Isidor banners snapping above their heads like battle flags. They brought the sharp smell of clairin with them, the raw, brain-killing rum that is the only liquor the poor can afford.

"What did you say before, when I asked you to speak Creole?" I asked Lucy.

"It's an old Haitian proverb: it means 'After the dance, the drums are heavy.' "

I stared into a burning barricade of tires, watched the dancing, drinking figures distorted by the rising heat. It wasn't over. Somehow, Faustin Gabriel had turned Carmen's defeat into a personal victory. He was a politician now, and one of the most valuable things for a politician to own is a journalist. As long as he had ambition, I would never be free.

"Voodoo has its own internal logic, doesn't it?" I asked.

Lucy nodded. I watched the sparks fly from the fire to join the stars in the sky.

"So, if you can create a zombi, you should be able to uncreate one. If you can take a soul *out* of a body, you should be able to put it back in, right?"

"Maybe. But you'd have to know . . ." She stopped short as she caught my train of thought.

"Where the bodies are buried?" I asked. "It's what we Washington reporters specialize in."

We drove to a heavily fortified, cement-slab house in Pacot. I waited in the car, watched by a trio of suspicious security guards. When Lucy returned, she had a Ruger .357 and a box of ammo. Her expression said, Load the gun, don't ask any questions.

We searched for Faustin Gabriel throughout the night, in the downtown government offices, the voodoo peristyles of Carrefour, the bourgeois haunts of Pétionville, where the elite ate away their electoral sorrows at Chez Gerard and La Cascade.

By seven the next morning, we still hadn't found him. "This is absurd," Lucy said. We sat on the hood of the jeep in the casino parking lot, exhausted. "Trying to chase after a government official in Port-au-Prince. It's just a small town, after all. The grapevine will always be one step ahead of us."

I bought coffee from a sidewalk vendor, paid a teenager five Haitian dollars to shine my tennis shoes. The city had not gone to bed; the carnival bands kept up their furious music. I could glimpse the bay behind a wall of shocking-pink bougainvillea blossoms. That unexpected image of bright water led to another image . . . then suddenly I knew!

"Let's go," I snapped. Lucy stared at me. "Don't ask, just drive. I'll explain."

In the car, I double-checked the gun, dropped an extra handful of bullets into my pocket. "There was a ship down at the docks . . . God, was it only yesterday morning? A freighter being unloaded, the *Fairchild,* from Bridgetown, Barbados. The name bumped around in the back of my mind, but didn't stick . . . turn left here." Lucy veered off Avenue John Brown onto a potholed side street. "I saw the same name on the packing crates in Gabriel's house back in D.C. He lived surrounded by museum pieces, treasures that had been in his family for generations. You want to know how impregnable he feels? He's moving it all back to Haiti, every piece of furniture."

The moving vans were already drawn up in front of Faustin Gabriel's gingerbread palace. The house seemed to glow from within, as though it sensed it was about to be restored to power. Even the bullet holes and burn marks were washed out in the morning sun.

We cruised slowly past the front gate. I didn't see Gabriel among the movers, but I knew he was there; he wouldn't allow a candlestick to be touched without his supervision. "No security guards," I pointed out. "It's like he's rubbing our face in it. He knows the masses have seen him on TV with their hero; he feels protected."

"No one stays protected here for long," Lucy said. We drove to the top of the hill, turned around, and headed back toward the house. The open back of the moving van yawned in front of us like a tunnel. There, deep in the shadows, something white flickered. Lucy saw it too, stopped the car. We idled for thirty seconds while a succession of workmen climbed in and out of the van, painstakingly unloading the contents. Finally, the patch of white moved again, and Gabriel stepped to the edge of the van, into the brilliant sunlight. He held up a crystal goblet, inspecting it for cracks, then spotted us through the perfectly prismed glass.

"Go!" I shouted.

We screeched up to the van. I jumped out, laid my arms across the roof of the car, and leveled the gun at Gabriel. He didn't react with terror or surprise, so it must have been nerves that made his fingers jerk. He lost his grip on the goblet; it spiraled to the ground and shattered.

He didn't say a word for five miles. He sat stiffly in the back of the car like a chauffeured dignitary. Whenever we drove through a crowd, I expected him to execute a discreet, Queen Elizabeth wave. North of the airport, the countryside opened into a flat plain. We passed fields of dying corn, a slaughterhouse, the ominous, walled compound of a mission called The Hands of Love. As we turned off the main road and headed into the brown, eroded hills, concern clouded Gabriel's face.

"May I ask where you are conducting me?"

I turned in my seat, aimed the gun at him through the headrest. "Isn't this the way to *Titanyen*?" I said, referring to the notorious body dump.

He laughed. "You Americans don't have the stomach for that sort of thing," he said smugly. "You're not going to kill me."

"That's true," I answered. "*You're* going to kill *me*. Or at least part of me." I took a pack of cigarettes out of Lucy's purse and offered one to Gabriel. He sniffed it, scowled, crushed it in the ashtray. "In the meantime, you're going to satisfy my curiosity."

He glared at me defiantly. I let fifteen seconds of silence pass, then cocked the hammer on my gun.

"Uh, Ray . . ." Lucy said anxiously.

"Relax. It's a rental car."

"Yeah, on my credit card."

"Don't worry. I'll try to miss the upholstery." I pointed the gun at Gabriel's neck. "I have more stomach than you think . . . want me to prove it?"

He sighed, then waved his hand impatiently, as if he were signaling a waiter to bring the next course.

"What happened at the schoolyard?"

"I let Carmen Mondesir die," he said simply.

"You mean, you manipulated me into killing her."

He shrugged. "If you prefer."

"Why?"

"You have surely read enough Haitian history by now to answer that question yourself."

"Carmen was going to betray you," I said. "Once she was in power, she was going to cut you loose."

"Cut me loose?" he asked ironically.

"Have you killed."

He nodded. "I always presumed that in a year, maybe two years from now, she would try to purge me. By then I would have gathered enough power of my own, enough allies to fight her off. But she was more impatient than I thought."

"Poor gullible Saint Gabriel. Didn't your family's two hundred years in the voodoo business teach you anything?"

Gabriel cracked open the window, letting the breeze ruffle his perfectly combed hair. "She and her soldiers would never have let me put one foot across the presidential threshold. And so . . ."

"You changed sides," I said, thinking of Connover's unintentional flash of wisdom. "And wound up a presidential advisor. How did you worm your way into Isidor's inner circle?"

"I simply told him about the massacre we were planning in his name, and explained that it lay in my power to prevent it."

"You bribed your way into the palace?"

"I negotiated my way in. But more than that, I negotiated a place for vodoun in our country's future, at the center of political power." He leaned foward, ignoring the gun. "There is something you will never understand—Western life is organized like a chest of drawers: this drawer for politics, that drawer for religion, another drawer for society. But in Haiti, all of these concepts must be jumbled up into a single drawer: that is the balance we need to survive."

It sounded like the self-serving statement of a guilty man, but . . .

Carmen Mondesir had never believed . . . had she paid with her life? Maybe it was true: in Haiti, if you didn't feed the spirits, they would make sure that you starved.

I had one final question. "How did Jean-Mars Baptiste find out about your plans?"

Gabriel chuckled. "I made a classic mistake—never invite your political enemies into your home. It was a garden party on a warm summer evening, one of those affairs that keep the Washington society pages in operation. Carmen and I were having a discussion in the living room when, among several other guests, Monsieur Baptiste wandered in. I'm afraid he overheard a few crucial exchanges: he stared at us, we stared back—it was an instant of supreme epiphany for all of us. Then he poured himself a fresh drink from the bar and went back outside."

"He didn't say a word?"

"No one said a word."

"Yet everyone knew what that moment meant."

"*Cą c'est le truc,* that's the whole trick, isn't it? Knowing which are the moments that count."

It was the closest Faustin Gabriel had come to confessing that he'd planned the Baptiste murder. Just a proverb, but it took the premeditation out of my hands. I glanced at my lawyer to make sure she'd heard. She pressed her leg against mine and smiled.

We climbed higher into the hills. A half-hour later, Lucy pulled off the road onto a windswept headland that overlooked the ocean. There was nothing left of the extravagant green forests that Nicholas Townsend had seen; the stream mentioned in his diary was barely a trickle.

But the moment I got out of the car, a wave of dizziness struck me. My body reacted like a divining rod and I skidded down the rocky slope, braking my descent on the thornbushes. I fell to my knees, ran my hands across the ground and felt the electricity coursing through my fingers. I let the dirt, fine as powdered sugar, sift through my hands. I gazed up at the hillside where General Charlemagne had watched Nicholas Townsend for the last time, then saw Lucy and Gabriel working their way toward me.

"This is it," I whispered. "He's here."

I was near tears when they reached me, relief and regret tumbling end over end. I felt like I had come to the end of a grueling search for a missing person, and had found the truth in an unmarked grave.

"Are you ready?" I asked Faustin Gabriel.

He looked puzzled.

"To pull the soul of Nicholas Townsend out of me and unite it with his remains. He's buried here; you've known that all along."

"Would you be referring to a ceremony of *déssunin*?" he asked icily.

"Call it what you like."

"Actually, Mr. Falco, your terms are imprecise," Gabriel needled. "You are asking for a variation of the déssunin. To extract the soul, the blueprint of a human being, that is a very sophisticated procedure."

"You're saying you've never done it?"

"Never successfully."

I blinked in disbelief, felt the air sucked out of my lungs. "You've never pulled it off before? What the fuck are you saying . . . that I'll be like this forever?"

"Do I need to remind you that it was Vincent Gabriel who originated this episode two hundred years ago? Certain details of the rituals that he performed have been lost . . ."

"You're in touch with the loa . . . can't you just pluck the details out of the air? Or has the gene pool gotten a little diluted over the years?"

"He's stalling, Ray," Lucy said.

Gabriel's eyes shifted nervously from me to Lucy, who held the pistol in a shooter's grip.

"You don't really believe this 'lack of confidence' shit?" Lucy said. "An insecure voodoo priest—there's no such creature."

I grabbed Gabriel by his neck. "You've gotten what you wanted out of me. Now cut me loose, goddamn it! I'm sure the finer points of the ritual will come back to you."

"Your case has traveled beyond me, Mr. Falco. It's no longer strictly my decision to 'cut you loose,' as you say."

It dawned on me what he was saying: the Isidor government knew all about me; I was their property now, a valuable weapon they didn't want to lose.

"I'm your ace, aren't I? Your insurance. As long as you control me, you'll never be purged."

Gabriel didn't answer. He tossed a furtive glance at the road, then up at the sky.

"Were we followed?" I demanded. I took the gun from Lucy and bored it into Gabriel's cheek. "Come on, do they know where we are?"

"I don't know . . . maybe . . . they told me they were watching the house."

"How are they coming? By car? By helicopter?"

For the first time, I detected alarm on Faustin Gabriel's delicate, placid features. I could feel his pulse hammering against the gun barrel.

"Maybe both."

"Then we better get started."

"I have none of my materials. No *asson,* no music . . ."

"We'll improvise. Houngans are supposed to be good at that."

He still hesitated, clinging to one last shred of power. "What happens if I kill you?" I hissed. "Am I killing my last chance at freedom? Or am I just adding another number to the Haitian body count? At this point, I don't give a shit—I'll risk it."

In the end, it was simple, human fear that turned him around. He had once told me that to a Haitian, survival was everything. Faustin Gabriel would not martyr himself for politics, or for voodoo. I force-marched him up to the car. Lucy backed it deeper into the brambles, so that it could not be seen from the road. Gabriel took off his coat, laid it neatly across the backseat, then went to work.

Voodoo ceremonies are easy to picture in dark, remote jungles. But to achieve the proper atmosphere by a roadside in the full bore of the midday sun, you need to work a little harder. There was no live music, so Gabriel spun the car radio dial until he found a station that played Haitian *compas,* and zouk music from Guadeloupe. No candles—emergency flares would have to do.

With Lucy holding the gun on him, he made me lie down in the tiny stream. The rocks gouged into my back, the cool water soaked through my shirt. "Water is the source of all life, and it is the element to which all life returns. The body, as it disintegrates into the soil, seeks the ancestral water."

He lit one of the flares, let it burn down, then with the ashes he daubed a cross on my forehead. He lit two more flares and planted them upright in the soil. They hissed and sparked; I could feel their heat singeing the hair on my arms.

He stood above me, one foot on either side of my body. He closed his eyes and began to chant, first in Latin, then Creole, finally in *langage,* the coded, sacred speech that only the loa understand. A cultural purist would have been outraged—it was a ceremony with commercial interruptions. Gabriel would get the rhythm of his chanting in sync with the music, then a DJ would interrupt: "Come visit the Service Station of the Immaculate Conception on Boulevard Dessalines for all your motoring needs—Texaco, *L'Étoile des Routes Haitiennes!*"

He bent lower and whispered furiously in both my ears. Then he lifted me beneath the arms and dropped me three times onto the sharp rocks. I felt the skin break, saw blood dappling the water.

The radio screamed, "Abdalah's Lottery Parlor, where dreams come true and fortunes are made!"

Something was happening. My vision fogged, the sky seemed like it was fading away. Lucy was a ghost, blotted out by the sun; Faustin Gabriel a stretched-out figure, like a reflection in a fun-house mirror. A sudden panic seized me. I snatched his wrist, drew him down to me.

"How do I know this is real?" I asked. "How do I know you're not just putting on a creative show—tourist voodoo?"

He swayed gently back and forth, eyes closed. "You don't," he said quietly. "Vodoun is not a matter of knowing, it is a matter of believing."

Lucy cocked the gun and pressed it against Gabriel's neck. "If you're lying, if you harm Raymond, you can believe this— you will not leave this spot alive."

He increased the tempo of his chanting, turned the flares upside down and extinguished them in the ground. A convulsive shudder ran through my body; it began on the surface of the skin and seemed to travel inward, through nerves, veins, and bones. The radio faded out, replaced by Creole battle cries, the clash of swords, the screams of Charlemagne's captured soldiers as they plunged into the sea: sound bites from the past. My vision went blank, images took over. Lush jungle and Maroon armies, the muddy streets of colonial Port-au-Prince, slave ships tacking into the harbor—historical miniatures painted by the memory of Nicholas Townsend. All running away, shrinking, growing darker.

I had an attack of second thoughts. Was this what I wanted, to lose Townsend forever? Most people never get to lead one life fully, let alone two. The journalist in me was getting greedy: *Hang on, Ray, are you really ready to burn your biggest source?*

Too late to turn back; it was already happening. I sensed it in my shoulder blades, where the two points met the water. I could compare it to a pin popping a balloon: a sharp prick, then a slow, sighing deflation as Townsend's past life drained away.

When I became aware of my surroundings again, it was dark. Lucy held a bottle of Culligan to my lips. I saw Faustin Gabriel leaning against the hood of the car, smoking. The headlights pointed out to sea, the radio was playing a bolero.

———

WHAT would I do, now that I was free to do anything? "After the dance, the drums are heavy."

The world went home, the hotels were empty again. The journalists and TV crews flew off to the next crisis, taking the international spotlight with them. Lucy and I spent a week in Jacmel, a quiet, sunny town on the southern coast. Part honeymoon, part summit conference.

During that week, we realized we weren't in love. There had been lust and affection, heated by crisis into something resembling love. We both fought against the melancholy reality night after night, but our personalities were so damned fact-based that we couldn't fool ourselves. Were we so cold that we couldn't force love into being? Or was it simply—here's that word again, the word voodoo made a permanent part of my vocabulary—fate?

Lucy summed it up best: "I can imagine life without you, Raymond. When you can do that, it's not love, is it?"

She had decided to stay in Haiti and try to open her own law firm. Smart, talented people were the country's last resource; every time a refugee left, he took his hope and ambition with him, and Haiti needed both to survive. Lucy would try to reverse the tide.

And OK, I admit it—I had begun to picture the Ray Falco byline again. I saw it above the fold on a hundred thousand breakfast tables, on front porches, in the hands of commuters. Cynicism had grown as comfortable as old blue jeans, but I couldn't justify it any longer. My stories had led to an election that the UN observers declared fair and credible. Fewer people died than usual. Foreign aid was starting to flow again. I don't mean to portray myself as a hero: I didn't pick up the pen voluntarily, it was forced into my hand. By the loa? By destiny? By accident? It was an impossible question that I finally learned to stop asking.

At sunset on our last day, we sat on the end of the crumbling Jacmel pier with a bottle of Barbancourt. I was feeling generous, and I bought whatever the hustlers had to sell—paintings, carvings, a couple of lobsters, the newspaper. The story was on the front page: CATASTROPHE IN CITÉ SOLEIL! A small plane on government business had lost power on take-off from Port-au-Prince airport and crashed into the slums at the end of the runway. The pilot had escaped with minor injuries; the passenger, identified as F. Gabriel, a highly placed official, had been killed. Planes ordinarily landed over the slums, but a rare and unexplained reversal in wind direction had prompted the tower to change runways just prior to the accident. Sabotage was suspected, but police admitted that the cause of the crash might never be established, since most of the plane had been stripped apart by Cité Soleil residents before investigators arrived on the scene.

Wordlessly, we watched the sun dip into the sea. That's Haiti, I thought—improvisation. A plane falls at your feet, but rather than seeing it as a tragedy, you use the wing to build a roof over your head. I pictured the rich up in the hills, buying bigger and bigger cars to survive roads that were getting worse and worse. They were improvisers, too—eventually they would be driving tanks. I saw the market people in the countryside: when the power cut off they burned kerosene for light; when the kerosene ran out, they turned to candles; when there were no more candles they'd rub sticks together; when there were no more sticks . . .

Lucy stood, kissed me on the back of my neck.

"Come on, it's our last night. Let's make the most of it."

Journalists aren't mystics or shrinks. We hate to psychoanalyze, we get uncomfortable hunting for "deeper meaning." We live for facts, so here they are: Lucy Marcelin saved me and I saved Lucy Marcelin. But vodoun saved us both.

Neither of us slept that night. Around midnight, we got up and went out on our balcony that faced the hills behind the town. We made ourselves comfortable in the brightly painted deck chairs; I poured us each a glass of rum, added lime juice and sugar. We waited like an opening-night audience, gazing into the dense, distant shadows.

Half an hour later, the drumming began.